THE WINDS OF FORTUNE

A novel about 19th Century Fayette, Michigan
by
Janet Flickinger-Bonarski

First Edition

45th Parallel Publishing Co. Gaylord, Michigan

Published by:
45th Parallel Publishing Co.
Gaylord, Michigan

ISBN 0-9716793-1-2
First Printing, 2003

The winds of Fortune

Have beaten me back,

And filled me with despair.

"The Winds of Fortune" is dedicated to my sisters, Lola, Lois, and Virginia. Your encouragement and support have been wonderful. Also a special word of thanks to Ann Blakely whose honest appraisal of my work has helped mold it into a better book.

Jan

Other books by this author:

Insubordinate Bastard, May 2002

> "Insubordinate Bastard is a superbly written military novel that grips the reader from first page to last."
>
>   The Midwest Book Review, April 2002

> "I thoroughly enjoyed the story and found it stayed with me for several days. This would make a really good film."
>
>   Nancy Burke Smith   Plain English

> "The book has a ring of truth to it even if it is presented in the form of fiction rather than non-fiction. It is always interesting to read about someone who triumphs over adversity."   Marquette Mining Journal

Preface

Fayette, Michigan is an actual place, located in the Upper Peninsula of Michigan. The Jackson Iron Company founded Fayette in 1867 for the sole purpose of extracting iron from the ore being mined in Negaunee and other Upper Michigan towns. Fayette's location, on the Garden Peninsula, was chosen for the huge limestone bluff, the small but deep natural harbor, and the immense stands of hardwood on the entire length of the peninsula. Both limestone and charcoal (made from the hardwood in large brick kilns) were necessary ingredients to reduce the raw ore to pig iron.

Railroads carried the ore from the mines to Escanaba where it was loaded on scows and pulled by tugs across Lake Michigan to Fayette. The trip took three hours by boat.

At the height of its productivity, the company owned town had upwards of 500 residents, two furnace stacks, a class-one hotel, an opera-house, and a large general store. During the 24 years (1867-1891) it operated, the Fayette furnace town produced 229,288 tons of iron for shipment down the lakes to Chicago, Detroit, and Cleveland.

In 1891, with the hardwood on the peninsula gone, and soft coal replacing charcoal in the smelting process, it was no longer profitable for the company to run Fayette. The furnaces went cold and the town slowly became deserted.

In 1959 the State of Michigan acquired the property and began restoring buildings. Today the Fayette Historic State Park attracts approximately 76,000 visitors a year. Besides the beauty of the harbor defined by the hundred foot high pure white limestone bluff, there is the attraction of the restored buildings, a campground with swimming at the sand beach, and the square shaped deep harbor that lures many Great Lakes pleasure boaters.

Many of the incidents in this book are based on historical events that took place in and around Fayette, although not necessarily within the 1882-1883 time frame of **The Winds Of Fortune**. None of the characters depicted are based on actual people but are purely created by me to suit the story I tell.

I borrowed the limestone and marble quarry of Mrs. Gouley (see appendix) and gave it to a purely fictional character, Carrie Grey. Any other resemblance between the real and fictional woman is purely coincidence.

Chapter One

L ate in the afternoon of an unseasonably warm day in early May, 1882, the wind started to stir up last Fall's dead leaves at ground level. Higher up it twisted the tops of the white pines behind the house and one large branch crashed into the ground near the kitchen door. The small harbor in front of the house, which she and Albert had named Cedar Harbor for the abundance of thick cedar trees that grew along the shore, began to froth with white caps. Carrie Grey, who had spent the day spring-cleaning, hurried her feather tick into the house and closed all the windows against the rain she knew would begin falling soon. She ran back to gather the quilts and linens from the line and then thought she should pull the dinghy up onto the shore.

Just as she headed down the path to the harbor, pea sized hail began to fall, beating a staccato rhythm against the ground and the roof of the house. The tightly bunched cedars along the path shielded her from the full force of the wind off the lake until she reached the narrow strip of sand and stone beach. She grabbed the hull of her dinghy and heaved it three times until it was as far ashore as it would go.

Carrie was taller than the average woman and strong from the work it took to maintain her homestead on Cedar Harbor all by herself. She thought of herself as not having much daintiness on the outside, although in truth, she was a comely statuesque woman just under five foot eight inches tall.

She tied the boat, fore and aft, to the shore anchor and despite the hail, stood staring at the storm-tossed water the same way she'd stood three years ago watching for the Lady

Grey, her husband's fishing boat to make safe harbor. Albert's boat never came.

The wind whipped a stray strand of chestnut brown hair back and forth across Carrie's face. The hail slackened and a cold pelting rain sent a sudden shiver though her body and snapped her back to the present. She tucked the aggravating hair behind her ear and with a final look at the harbor entrance turned to take shelter in the house. Then she jerked back.

Had she seen something? A boat struggling against the wind? The sky was as dark as night and the rain was now a steady sheet of water sluicing over her. Her clothes were sopping wet; yet she stood, straining her eyes at the lake, sure there was a boat rounding Garden Bluff. Then in a flash of lightning she saw it plainly. Not Albert's fishing boat, but a schooner.

Carrie ran, as fast as she could in her wet heavy skirt, to the boathouse. The tumbled limestone rocks along the shore made running hazardous but Carrie knew the best footfalls by instinct and deftly maneuvered the way. The wind slammed open the boathouse door as soon as she unlatched it. Carrie gasped with the strain it put on her shoulder as it was pulled out of her hands. She let it swing in the wind, opening and closing in a steady rhythm, slamming first against the outer wall, then against the doorframe.

Two lanterns hung on the wall. She grabbed the larger one and fumbled to light it. The second lantern was smaller and she burned her forefinger in a struggle to fix the chimney in place. In another flash of lightening she saw the schooner swinging wide, probably meaning to shelter in the larger Garden Bay. He would be better off in her harbor. Cedar Harbor was small, but deep, and if the skipper came straight in toward her light he would have draft enough not to run aground on the rocks along the western shore line. She had to get the lanterns up.

Her skirt tripped her as she turned back toward the shore.

She didn't have a free hand to hold it safely up so she set the lanterns down, impatiently removed the skirt, and kicked it toward the shed. With just her petticoats on she could move more freely. She ran along the shore with the lanterns. Albert had fixed a post for her to hang the big lantern on, to guide him in the many times he had come home after dark. She fastened the large lantern securely to the post and then turned and ran to the end of the pier where she knew she would be most visible from the schooner. She held the light as high as she could, moving it back and forth so the crew would know it was a signal to guide them in.

The schooner fighting its way to her light was a beauty. She guessed it must be ninety-five feet long and twenty feet wide. She carried three masts, from which most of the sail had been dropped. Carrie's eyes had adjusted to the dim light, or perhaps the sky had lightened as the storm moved in.

The schooner dropped suddenly into a deep trough of water created by a breaking wave and then an immense following wave broke over her; it must have overhauled the deck with a foot of water. Carrie gasped and almost dropped the lantern. She knew the Great Lakes devil was to send its storm waves so sharp and closely spaced that a ship might not recover from one before another struck. *Oh dear God, turn her, Captain, turn her.*

There were three big boulders near the western shore. He needed to approach from deeper into Garden Bay. The schooner moved as if the captain had heard her, swinging wide and then heading straight in. Only the outer jib sail still flew, giving the helmsman just enough pulling power to maneuver with. She didn't recognize the ship, and she knew most of the area schooners that came to haul stone from her quarry.

The water in Cedar Harbor still tossed under the scudding clouds, but Carrie knew the ship was safe now. When the schooner was about thirty feet from the end of the pier she heard the anchor drop with a splash.

Carrie suddenly remembered she'd tossed her skirt aside and that she was standing on the pier in just her waist and petticoats. She turned and dashed up the four long steps from the beach to higher ground where the house stood and ran inside. She had to get a skirt on; she hoped they hadn't already seen her state of undress.

She stopped inside the house, leaned back against the closed door and felt the weakness flow down her legs to her knees. Her hands began to shake and she realized she was gulping in air. She told herself she had no time for this and was instantly calm. Water dripped off her and puddled on the floor. She pulled a towel from the heap of linens that still lay on the floor where she had dumped them. How long ago?

By the time she reached the bedroom she had stripped off all her wet clothes and toweled herself dry. Hurriedly she pulled on a dry waist, petticoat, and skirt and wrapped Albert's old oiled slicker around herself to go back outside. She didn't realize she was barefoot until she stepped into the mud puddle that had formed just off the porch.

The schooner lay anchored thirty feet off the end of the pier. The wind had lessened but it was still raining, although not as hard as it had been. Carrie picked up the lantern and walked to the end of the pier.

"Hello," someone called from the boat.

"Hello," Carrie answered, "Is everyone unhurt?"

"Yes'm and thank you for your help. I've a passenger I'd like to bring ashore, if you don't mind."

The passenger was a woman. Carrie watched as two men helped her into the shore boat. She held an oiled cape over her head. The two men also got into the boat that was then lowered down and rowed to the end of the pier.

"Come up to the house," Carrie said, as she reached out to help the woman onto the pier, "all of you." She didn't wait for the men but put her arm around the woman's shoulders and guided her off the pier and up the path to the house.

Under the roof of the porch, they both removed their wet

slickers and entered the house. It was dark inside, and cold. Carrie set the lantern on the center table and hurried to light others that hung on the wall around the room.

"Please sit," she said to her guest. She scooped the remaining linens from the floor into her arms. "I'll get a fire started."

The door opened and the two men entered. The tall one had to duck to enter. He must have been over six feet tall, taller than Albert had been. He was slim hipped and square chested. He took his knit cap off, revealing wavy hair the color of wet beach sand. His neatly trimmed beard was almost red and his eyes a twinkling blue green. Carrie liked him immediately.

"Andrew McGeary, ma'am," he said. "Drew, for short. This lady is Mrs. Hartson and this is my mate, Zach Milowski."

Carrie nodded to each one and replied, "I'm Carolyn Grey, and I'll build a fire as soon as I can set these linens down."

"I'll start the fire," Drew said. He had a deep bass voice.

Carrie started to protest, but he had already gone into the kitchen and was taking a few sticks of birch kindling from the wood box, filling the firebox of her New Home cook stove. She'd bought that with the first earnings from the stone quarry. She was suddenly glad she'd spent some of her time this morning scouring it clean and reblacking the burner tops.

When Carrie came back into the room, Zach still stood close to the front door, looking uncomfortable, twirling his black knit cap around in his large hands and dripping puddles of water onto the painted wood floor. The kitchen was at the back of the house and he seemed timid about crossing the parlor and dining room to reach the kitchen. Mrs. Hartson had immediately set herself down on the sofa and was surveying the small parlor and its appointments. She kept her gloved hands folded in her lap.

"Don't concern yourself about the floor," Carrie said to the ship's mate. "I'll clean it up later. Perhaps you can light the fire in the parlor stove. It's all laid."

Zach nodded and looked relieved.

"I'll fix us tea," Carrie said to Mrs. Hartson. "Or perhaps you'd like some brandy?" She still had a bottle. Albert had liked to have a nip, as he called it, after supper each night.

Mrs. Hartson spoke for the first time, "Tea, please," but both men said "brandy" at the same time. Carrie retrieved the half bottle of brandy from the pantry and poured a small glass for each of the men. The tea had to wait for the fire, of course, which had taken to blaze right away and soon started to warm the room.

The men stayed in the kitchen and Carrie stood in the doorway. "It's warmer in the kitchen," she said to Mrs. Hartson, hoping to get everyone in the same room. The men were wet and they weren't going to sit in the parlor, but Mrs. Hartson chose to retain her seat.

They talked about the storm, each learning what the others had endured. Captain McGeary repeated his thanks many times until Carrie wished he'd be quiet. Mrs. Hartson didn't say anything. Carrie studied her as she listened to the men. She couldn't decide how old the woman was. In her twenties a woman's face is soft and still pliable, but by her mid-thirties her face is a fairly good mask of her disposition. Mrs. Hartson looked young in some ways, but older in others. Her mouth, overly large for her long narrow face, was surrounded with many small creases, as if she was long in the habit of pursing her mouth in disapproval, the way she did now.

"Is there something I can get for you?" Carrie asked her.

"Isn't the water for tea hot yet?" the woman asked, her voice almost an accusation. Perhaps it was. The fire in the kitchen stove was rarely allowed to go out and a kettle on the warming shelf would have had water simmering at all times, but in her house cleaning fury that morning, the fire had not been tended.

"I blacked the stove this morning," Carrie found herself explaining, "so the fire was out, and I've been so busy all day cleaning..." Her voice trailed off and the pursed lips of the woman sitting on the sofa did not smile.

"I'm sure it's about ready, " Carrie said and fled into the kitchen. She took the bubbling kettle off the stove and filled the teapot. She watched Mrs. Hartson out of the corner of her eye as Zach reached for the brandy bottle and refilled his glass. That's what she disapproved of! Well, what an old prude.

"Please help yourself to another shot of brandy, Captain," she said in her sweetest voice.

"I don't mind if I do, ma'am, but please, just call me Drew. Captain's a title for me crew to use."

Carrie poured a cup of tea and set it on the table next to Mrs. Hartson and then poured one for herself. She sat in the red brocade chair while the men stood uncomfortably near the door.

"Would you like to take supper with me?" she asked.

Drew shook his head. "Me cook will have grub for us, but thank you kindly." He looked down at her and smiled, which deepened the crinkles around his eyes. Carrie picked up a bit of Irish brogue in his voice. He was a man who smiled a lot, she thought. "I expect Mrs. Hartson would prefer to eat with a lady, though. The crew is a little rough for her liking."

Carrie was sure they were. Mrs. Hartson sat on the edge of the sofa, her feet drawn together as if snakes or spiders crawled around her, sipping her tea. She held the china cup with her thumb and first finger, her little finger held straight out. Carrie noticed that her feet were long and narrow and the toes of the black shoes were worn. At least she was wearing shoes; Carrie suddenly realized she was still barefoot and tucked her feet under the chair.

"Then would you keep me company for supper?" Carrie asked Mrs. Hartson, "Please say yes, I so seldom get visitors."

"Yes, thank you," the woman said, sounding friendly for the first time. She set her cup on the saucer beside her and stood. "What can I do to help?"

Drew and Zach moved closer to the door. Suddenly Carrie

didn't want Drew to go. Would she see him again in the morning?

"Perhaps Mrs. Hartson would also prefer to sleep ashore," Carrie blurted. "Surely you intend to keep harbor for the night."

Drew looked to where Mrs. Hartson stood smoothing down her skirt. "That sounds like a dandy idea, Mrs. Grey. I'm sure the lady would like that." He addressed Mrs. Hartson, "I'll have Zach row your bags ashore, ma'am in case there's anything in them you'll need."

He bowed to Carrie, taking her hand as he did so. Carrie almost gasped at the flutter the touch sent racing up her arm.

"I'll send breakfast from the galley in the morning for you," he said. "But early, I'm afeard, at sun-up."

"Oh, that is kind of you, Capt...er, Drew," Carrie said. "I'll be up."

He let go of her hand then, but not before a gentle squeeze of her fingers. "Good evening, ladies."

Carrie stood in the doorway and watched them go. She wondered what she was going to do with Mrs. Hartson all evening. She needn't have worried. Once the men were gone, Mrs. Hartson began to talk and all Carrie had to do was listen and nod in appropriate places or answer pointed questions about Fayette. Her husband was a minister, come to set up a Congregational parish on the Garden Peninsula. That explained the worn shoes. Minister's wives often wore second hand, left for them by wealthier parishioners.

"Reverend Hartson, my husband, comes from a long line of preachers, Sister Carrie," she said. "And my father and grandfather were preachers also."

Obviously this bit of information was intended to impress Carrie. Sister Carrie, indeed! The next time she used it, Carrie interrupted her.

"Mrs. Hartson," she said, hearing the chill in her own voice, "I am not your sister and I do not wish to be called so."

The preacher's wife caught her breath in surprise and pursed her mouth in disapproval. "We are all sisters in Christ," she snapped.

"Just the same, please do not call me sister." What has come over me, Carrie wondered, to take such an instant dislike to someone?

"Would you like more tea," she asked, forcing her voice to be friendly. She stood and filled Mrs. Hartson's half empty cup without waiting for a reply and continued on into the kitchen.

Zach and a skinny man with very wet clothes knocked at the door to deliver Mrs. Hartson's bags. There was a steamer trunk and a carpetbag. Carrie directed them to take the luggage into the small back bedroom.

Carrie took advantage of the interruption to put her shoes on and when Mrs. Hartson emerged from supervising the placing of the steamer trunk, Carrie was in the kitchen preparing supper. Mrs. Hartson joined her and offered to peel the potatoes.

"What was Captain McGeary's boat doing so far north into the bay?" Carrie asked. "Fayette is a ways south of here."

"I wanted to see this Bay de Noquette," she used the full French name, which meant bear paw, instead of the shortened Bay de Noc used by everybody Carrie had ever heard. "Mr. Hartson said it was so lovely, and Captain McGeary consented." She then went on and on about the bluffs and how beautiful it was. The trilliums were in bloom and she'd seen great stands of them, using the Captain's glass.

"Surely you don't live here all alone," Mrs. Hartson said when she tired of talking about the shoreline. It was more of a statement than a question, and her disapproval showed in the pursing of her mouth.

Carrie explained about losing her husband, Albert, three years ago and about the stone quarry she owned. The quarry master had a cottage there with a wife and three children. And it was less than a mile to walk out to the road the stage used. The stage ran between Fayette and Garden daily. Come to that, it wasn't a bad walk into Garden where she had friends to pass the night with if she chose.

"Don't you go to Fayette?" Mrs. Hartson asked. "It's larger, isn't it?"

"Not much," Carrie said. She didn't want to be the one to tell Mrs. Hartson how dirty and noisy Fayette was. The furnaces belched smoke day and night and the continuous clank of the machinery could be deafening. It also smelled bad.

"I have friends there, too. The school teacher, Eleanor Larkin, for one." She knew Eleanor would not like Mrs. Hartson.

They ate their light meal of boiled potatoes and carrots. Carrie opened a small jar of canned blueberries for desert. As soon as it seemed reasonable, she suggested they retire. As she dressed for bed she realized she hadn't even learned the woman's given name. She would ask her right out in the morning, and call her that, not Mrs. Hartson. That ought to set her bonnet sideways. Then, ashamed of herself, she asked atonement in her prayers, climbed into bed and pulled the covers up snug under her chin. They smelled as fresh as she had imagined this morning, when she'd put them out to air.

The day had certainly turned out much different than she could have thought. She wished Drew McGeary had stayed longer. He had a very worthy looking face and she was sure he would have had entertaining tales to tell. His voice had a bit of an Irish lilt, and she remembered the way his smile started at his eyes and made his mouth curve up, rather than the other way around. She wondered if the touch they'd shared had had the same effect on him as it had on her and if that was why he had given the small squeeze to her fingers.

Then she remembered Albert and was suddenly ashamed of the thoughts she'd been having about Drew; a man she had met by chance and didn't know anything about. She had spent the day, as she cleaned, indulging in memories of her dead Albert, and had quickly forgotten him entirely when Captain Andrew McGeary put into Cedar Harbor.

Quit being a silly girl, she scolded herself. She began to deliberately call up memories of Albert. She had met him in Buffalo when his fishing boat was moored at the pier next to that of her father's old friend. She used to go to the docks each evening seeking news of her father, Tom Webster. He had gone west to fish the waters of Lake Huron and Michigan more than a year before, and despite his promise to send word often, he was not heard of again. But Albert Grey had news. The Ida Ruben, her father's boat, had been lost in a spring storm off the Summer Islands in Big Bay de Noc, he said. She had seen those pretty islands off the shore at the end of this peninsula where she now lived alone. Albert's fishing boat had also been lost and for three years now, Carrie had been a fisherman's widow.

Carrie lay in the large bed Albert had made for them out of one of the big white pines he'd cut away to make room for the house. She was aware of the gentle lap of waves against the shore and Jewel, her cat, who lay next to her purring softly. The water was full of memories; the cat was full of life. She had always been aware of the life force in her golden, silky pet. Maybe it was a misplaced maternal instinct, but never had anything made her so aware of the preciousness and the oneness of all life as the cat did. It was the same aliveness that was in her, that had been in Albert. But Albert was like the waves now, constant background, but without the spark of life. Maybe there was no guilt to be found in her attraction to Drew McGeary. She was only twenty-eight years old. Maybe it was time to move on.

When she finally drifted off to sleep it was the sandy-haired Drew McGeary who held her thoughts and showed up in snatches of dreams she could barely remember upon waking the next morning.

Breakfast wasn't the fascinating encounter Carrie had had in her head when she fell asleep the previous evening. She was out of sorts with the stubbornness of her hair to remain in its combs and Drew seemed to have left his tongue aboard the ship. Bertha Hartson, that was her name, Bertha, talked incessantly. Her main audience was Zach who murmured "unhuh" and "no ma'am" every so often.

Carrie picked at her food, stealing glimpses of Drew from time to time only to find him completely absorbed in his scrambled eggs and ham. Only when she brought the coffee to the table did he look at her and grace her with one of his face crinkling smiles. He was more than worthy looking, Carrie decided, he was handsome. His sandy-brown hair was freshly washed this morning. He wore it neatly trimmed above his ears and it lay loosely about his head in undulating waves. His face was perfectly proportioned, his eyes set wide over a just right nose and broad cheeks. The reddish beard was not covering a weak jaw as in some men, but accentuated a strong one. Yes, a handsome man.

After their coffee, Bertha had insisted on conducting a worship service. "Since it is Sunday," she sniffed at Drew when he said they needed to be underway, her husband would be worried. The morning was clear, if a little cool, so they stood outside with her.

Carrie smiled at the way Drew stood stiffly while Bertha read a lengthy piece of scripture from one of Paul's letters about how women should keep their heads covered before men. She wondered that he did not see the irony of it. From the corner of her eye, Carrie caught him looking at her during the long prayer of orders Bertha delivered to God. She flushed, but kept her eyes on the ground until Bertha said, "Amen."

Drew absolutely refused to sing a hymn and declared the worship service was over. He took Carrie's arm and guided her to the pier with him, ahead of Zach and Bertha Hartson.

The bay was just beginning to ripple with the draw of the rising sun. The schooner, named Wave Dancer, had moved closer to the pier and lowered a gang plank across the gap for Bertha. Drew's parting words were only a simple, "Thank you again for your help, Mrs. Grey, " but his eyes and touch seemed to be saying he would see her again. She nodded, hoping he understood she would like that too.

Bertha stood on board and waved to Carrie, her mouth set in a disapproving pucker. Carrie stood on the end of the pier and watched until Wave Dancer rounded the bluff, heading south to Fayette.

Chapter Two

Henry LaTermaine sat atop his gray steed and gazed out over Lake Michigan from atop the headland known locally as the Garden Bluff. This, he decided, is where he would build his house.

The view had the grandeur he deserved. It was on top of everything. Nothing was in front of him but nature, and it was a damn-site better view than the rich lakeshore mansions of Chicago. He knew; he had hired a carriage and driven along Lake Shore Drive last autumn when he was in Chicago to buy goods for the Fayette General Store.

Carrie Grey owned this. Why did she live in that mean little cottage on the bay? The fisherman husband, of course. His life had been the lake and he had lower expectations from life than Henry. Henry had his hand in many enterprises in Fayette, some of them few people knew of. He would be rich and powerful someday, more so than Mr. Jack Sailstad, general manager of the town of Fayette. Jack criticized him for casting his bread on too many waters, but Henry believed in the 'many basket' theory of success.

His thoughts returned to Carrie Grey. She did not know yet that she would soon be wealthy enough to live here, above the rest. But I need to verify it, Henry thought, before I make my next move.

He reined his horse around and let him feel his own way down an almost invisible, steep, and winding path. Emerging from a stand of thick cedar only twenty yards from the edge of the bluff, he heard the ring of sledge on steel. It would be the quarry workers below, driving wedges into the limestone to break it apart. The building quality of the limestone quarried here could not be blasted down with dynamite the way they pulled down the limestone from the bluff at Fayette. He moved the horse to the edge of the bluff and looked down.

Builders from Escanaba ferried more and more of the stone across the lake to feed the building frenzy going on in that growing town. First it was lumber and now that the rail line to the rich inland iron mines was complete, Escanaba was an iron port. The local publisher had even changed the name of his weekly newspaper to The Iron Port. They shipped the raw ore to Fayette for smelting, and Fayette shipped the pig iron down lake to Chicago or Detroit.

Henry had seen the mansion George Niebauer was having built on the bluff overlooking Little Bay de Noc. That's what he wanted. Maybe he would even have his own town here, spread across the plateau of the bluff. A marble quarry to rival iron town. He fingered the envelope in his breast pocket again. Yes, LaTermaine was a good name for a town. Then he would add a flourish to his own name, and become Henry de LaTermaine.

There was also good money to be made from selling the land to those who came to settle his town. He had been surprised when he looked at the plat map and discovered that Carrie owned all of the Garden Bluff, all the way back to the stage road. He didn't want a "company town" the way Jackson Iron owned all of Fayette. Free enterprise was better; let people risk their own capital.

Henry was startled out of his daydream by a shout from below. A short, almost round man, shouted and waved both arms at him. He couldn't make out what the man shouted, so he just waved his hat in acknowledgment and turned the horse back to the trail. That man must be Hugh Brandon, Carrie's quarry master. He had to be careful what he said around him.

Hugh Brandon stood at the bottom of the trail, his feet apart and his fists planted on his broad hips. Henry could see the fellow was upset with him.

"You get down from dat horse and walk him, mister," the man shouted, emphasizing his order by pointing with one finger to the ground. "What you crazy man doing on da bluff?

Da whole ting might crumble, ruining Missus Grey's stone."

As ordered, Henry immediately dismounted and led his horse the rest of the way down and away from the rock face. Once on the beach Hugh confronted him, still scolding.

"You be trespassing. Dis is private property and danger to stupid fools."

Henry doffed his hat at the man and apologized. It would not do to get on the wrong side of the quarry master, but apparently he already had.

"I meant no harm, Mr...?"

"Brandon, " Hugh said sharply. "Harm do be caused by stupid as sure as meaning to. Come, I show you."

Henry left his horse and followed the quarry master. For a man of his bulk, his movements over the uneven surface of broken limestone were agile and quick. Henry stumbled twice trying to keep up with him.

Three men were working along the face of the bluff on a platform suspended from above. The anchors for the scaffold were the cedar trees Henry had been standing in front of. Their narrow work shelf was some twenty feet above the ground. A row of holes, just inches apart, had been drilled perpendicular down the three sections of stone they were working on.

"Now dey feathering. Delicate operation. One slip, rock breaks too soon. Stone ruined, men hurt. Sometimes dead. Maybe dem, maybe you in fall from da top."

Henry felt his knees go weak and his face redden. He had almost caused a disaster. "My God," he swore, "I was being stupid." He mopped his face with a white handkerchief taken from his pants pocket. "How does this quarrying thing work, Mr. Brandon?"

"First we find da natural breaks in da rock, than drill up and down holes to make da side break. One day, drill da holes. Now feathering. Dat means driving two wedges into each hole. Next we drive da plug between da wedges; slow, slow, each hole equal pressure, 'til the stone break and fall."

Henry looked up at the three men swinging on the

scaffold, inserting iron feathers into the holes drilled on the layer of rock they were working to free.

"Won't it hit the men when it breaks loose?"

"Fall straight down," Brandon replied, "if no problem."

"How long before it comes down?" Henry asked, backing away inch by inch as he asked.

"Four hour more," the quarry master said.

Henry gulped and continued to walk away from the rock face. He remembered why he had come and involuntarily felt the paper in his breast pocket.

"How much of the bluff will be brought down?" Maybe a house on the top wasn't such a good idea after all. Carrie's house by the lake was in a pretty spot; it was just a bit small.

"Stone goes in almost one mile," Brandon said.

"And is it all good building stone?"

"Some dimension stone, some good for gravel. Maybe some better."

Ah, here was the opening Henry had hoped for. "Mrs. Grey brought me a sample to send down lake to have polished. Thought she might have found marble. How much of that is there?"

"You be Henry, den, from Fayette?"

Henry acknowledged that he was and extended a hand to the quarry master. Brandon grasped his hand in return with the rough and callused hand of a laborer. "Do it take a polish?"

"Oh, I don't have an answer yet, " Henry told him. "That might take another month or more to get. But I was in the area and thought I'd just see how big the vein might be."

The rotund man led Henry south along the bluff face to where none of the stone had been disturbed. "Up there," he pointed. "When we strip da overburden on top, Missus Grey finds rock different, finer grain. See da sparkle in some places?"

The sun did seem to reflect the light and cause some sparkling. "How far does it go?" For Henry this was the critical question.

Brandon continued to walk along the bluff face. At places the space between the bluff and the water was only a foot or so wide and Henry feared the rotund man wouldn't fit by without slipping, but Brandon walked as if he was on a wide level boardwalk. He walked fifty yards and then stopped. "Here, it stops," he said.

"And does it go all the way to the top?" Henry asked, his head tilted back to see the top of the bluff.

Brandon nodded.

"And how far in do you suppose it runs?"

He looked down in time to see the man shrug. "Who can tell?"

Henry caressed his thin mustache which was meant to thicken an overly thin upper lip. His jaw was strong and determined, but he knew his mouth looked weak without the mustache. He reached across his body and withdrew an ivory bowled pipe from his jacket pocket and tamped it full of fragrant tobacco spilled from a leather bag. He fondled the carved pipe bowl in his hand for a moment and then ran his long slim fingers up and down the stem a couple of times before he lit it with a safety match scraped across the sole of his boot.

"Well, it's like this, as I see it," Henry began. He drew in on the pipe, compressing his cheeks inward. "It would certainly be nice for Mrs. Grey if the assay came back positive. But I've seen marble quarries before and I don't really think that's what she's got here. Just a little bit better grade of limestone than she already has."

Yes, this could be a small fortune, he thought to himself. If Carrie sold limestone for $2.00 a cord, she could get three times that for marble, even the low grade marble the sample assayed at. And there was always the chance it got harder when you got into it. After all, the surface had been exposed to weather for a long time.

"I think it do be marble and marble do take different methods, Mr. LaTermaine," Brandon said. "My boys with drills and feathers can't break marble." He turned and walked back toward the limestone face where his boys were working. "It do take money to get at da stone if it be marble. Missus Grey worried 'bout that."

Henry considered that bit of information. Well, he knew how to get capital if it came to that. Maybe he should just buy the quarry from her. No, marrying her was cheaper and would be pleasant for him in the bargain. He needed sons to pass things along to, to make his name immortal. And Carrie was a handsome woman, and smart besides. He'd escorted her to the opera house once or twice. Always with Eleanor along too, of course, for both women were charming company. It's just that he now found Carrie a little more so than the school teacher.

"Here she is coming now," Brandon said.

Henry turned and watched as Carrie walked along the lake shore towards them. She saw them, Henry was sure, but she didn't hurry her step or wave at them. She had a way of moving that was refined, Henry observed. Like himself, she didn't cringe away from the elements, but kept on, merely holding the fold of her cape against the tug of the ever present wind off the lake. As soon as she was near enough, he removed his bowler hat and bowed slightly to her.

"Good morning, Mrs. Grey. I had no idea your little quarry was such a beehive of activity."

Carrie acknowledged his greeting and turned at once to Hugh Brandon. "I have the pay for last week's cutting for you. Let me just chat a moment with Mr. LaTermaine and then we'll count the new stacks. I put notice in the Iron Port last week, so we should see some buyers soon."

"I'll get my Missus while ya talk to da genterman. We sold some of da cords dis last week," and he hurried off, hat still in his hands, toward the group of three small cottages set in a cedar grove nearby.

"Well, Henry," Carrie said, "Do you have good news for me?"

Henry shifted his weight around and almost touched the

paper in his breast pocket. "Nothing yet," he said.

"I just don't understand that," Carrie said, her voice brisk. "Boats have been moving on the lake for almost a month now."

Henry cleared his throat and tapped the ashes out of his pipe. He fondled the stem while he talked. "I was thinking maybe the sample got lost and we should cut another one. That's why I'm here today."

"Did you ask Mr. Brandon?"

"We hadn't gotten to that yet," Henry told her, hoping that Brandon wouldn't think it strange he only raised the issue now. It had just occurred to Henry that sending another sample was an excellent way to buy time. "He was explaining the quarrying process to me. Most interesting."

"If you'll wait until I've finished my business with Mr. Brandon, I'll walk with you and you can pick up another sample yourself. We cut several pieces last fall when we brought the first piece for you to send."

When Brandon returned, his wife, a tall lean woman was with him. Henry watched as she walked over the quarry debris. Her skirt was short, coming only to mid-calf, and a full inch of flesh was visible before her sturdy boots began. He glanced at Carrie to see if she was scandalized by this, but Carrie appeared not to notice. Perhaps she was accustomed to it. It was sensible, after all, since the woman had to walk among the clutter of broken limestone everyday. Mrs. Brandon had a cloth bag slung across her sunken bosom. When she got near Carrie she removed a ledger book, which she laid on top of a pile of neatly stacked cut stone.

"We sold five cords dis week, Missus," Henry overhead her say. "I got da ten dollar for her here." Carrie took the account book and opened it.

Henry would have liked to look over her shoulder, but instead stood just far enough away to give the illusion of disinterest as he strained to hear what was being said. Carrie studied the book the same way he studied his store ledger and Henry realized she knew how to run this business.

"Why did we need a new sledge?" she questioned Hugh.

"Stephan dropped one and it fell into a crevasse and we couldn't find it."

Carrie nodded. "I'll pay for the rope, but not the sledge. Stephan can buy his own replacement." She handed Mrs. Brandon an envelope which Henry assumed represented wages, and took one from Mrs. Brandon which held sales receipts and the ten dollars.

"Now let's see what you've cut this week." The trio walked among the piles of limestone, each pile measuring four feet high, four feet deep, and eight feet long. Carrie marked the end of each cord with a red mark while Mrs. Brandon marked each one in her book.

"How many cords total do we have now?"

"Eighty-five."

"That's not much," Carrie said. "That could be gone in a week."

"Swen been sick," Mrs. Brandon said. "Cutting goes slower wid only two workin'."

"He's up there now," Carrie said. "What was the matter?"

"Just da spring gripe," Mrs. Brandon answered. "I suppose Stephan and Josef will take down wid it too."

Carrie gave her head a resigned nod and spoke to Hugh. "If you don't have enough when people come, tell them you'll take orders and we'll ship it to them when it's ready."

"It cost money to ship, Missus. Better you tell dem come back, for $1.90 a cord. You and me, we split da dime cost for not havin' nuff."

Henry could see Carrie considered a moment before she replied. "Yes, I like that." She turned back to Mrs. Brandon. "I'll send down some horehound and rose hip tea for you. You make everybody drink some three times a day and maybe the spring gripe won't bother the rest of you."

Mrs. Brandon nodded and then flushed slightly, "Josef married a wife, Miz Grey, maybe ya'd like to meet her?"

When did he marry," Carrie asked in surprise.

"Just when da spring ice go out," Mrs. Brandon said. "One of da Hanson girls from Vans Harbor."

"Well," Carrie said, "then I'll wait until next week to meet her, when I can bring a wedding gift. Now I have to go up on the bluff with Mr. LaTermaine. You send Julie up to the house this afternoon for the medicine tea."

"I'll just send Francine," Mrs. Brandon said. "Julie too near her time to go scampering over da rocks."

Carrie nodded. "Call me when it's time if you need help."

Carrie turned back to Henry who had backed away as he heard the conversation coming to an end. She addressed him with the same authority she had been using with her hired hands.

"Leave your horse, Henry, and come with me."

He was tempted to call her down for talking to him that way, but thought better of it and fell in along side her. She led him back to the area Brandon had shown him earlier, but they went further on. Carrie wore a simple skirt with no petticoats underneath and had no trouble moving along the narrow ledge. It was almost noon and sun was warm enough to make Henry wish he had left his jacket with the horse. The only sound, above the clang of the quarry sledges, was the waves breaking against the rocky shore and the scream of gulls winging over the water looking for fish.

He studied Carrie's back. She was taller than most women and she didn't look frail, or affect to be, as some women did. He would bet she'd never fainted or cried fake tears to twist a man around her finger. Truth is, she did not seem to be trying to get a man at all. She didn't need one; she had a good income and a nice home to live in. That made her all the more attractive to Henry. He did not fancy a clinging vine or a social butterfly. Carrie was sensible and solid, that's what she was.

"Much further?"

"We're here," Carrie said, most of her words drifted away from him with the breeze and were muffled by the breaking waves. She had stopped and was pointing to a steep climb up the face of the bluff.

When he came alongside her she said, "You climb up there and inside the first little cave you'll find where Hugh cut the samples. Pick one out and bring it back down."

Henry looked up doubtfully at the bluff face. How had round Hugh Brandon ever climbed up there? How had Carrie, for that matter, and more important, how was he going to?

"It's not as bad as it looks, Henry," Carrie said. "The path is as wide as it is here, just a little steep. There's a cave just behind those small trees. That's where you'll find the cut samples. You'll find a stout walking stick propped against the bluff where you need it. Take it up with you and leave it there when you come back down. You'd better take your jacket off and leave it with me."

Henry nodded and swallowed the extra saliva that had collected in his mouth. He handed Carrie his hat and his jacket, thinking of the letter in the pocket that really made this exercise unnecessary. She would not snoop through his pockets and find it. She was not that kind. But, he thought as he climbed, he was disturbed for the second time at the way she talked to him. Operating the quarry had made her too assertive, less feminine. That would have to change after they were married.

Behind the cedars the ledge was almost five feet wide, and a small cave, less than four feet deep, made an indentation in the bluff. Hugh had chiseled out a sizeable piece of the marble and knocked several specimens off it. Henry choose an almost square piece, about six by six inches. He could easily carry it down.

He took a minute to look around. The floor of the cave had a black circle where fires had obviously been built. Had some ancient Indians actually lived here? He could not stand upright in the opening but a short adult could have. There were ledges, almost like shelves, cut into the back cave wall; or maybe they were natural. Henry couldn't tell. Yet, it was easy to imagine the Indians at least taking shelter here. Those trees in front hid the cave from view and kept out the wind off the lake. The smoother sidewall had black scratches on it, perhaps drawn by an Indian child with the end of a charred stick. Henry examined them, but couldn't make any sense of them except for one, which was definitely a stick figure of a human. It was cool inside too, almost too cool for Henry without his jacket.

He cradled the rock in his left arm and used the walking stick in his right to ease himself down the steepest part of the path. When the slope became more gradual, he left the stick leaning against the bluff and continued down. Carrie stood below, her fists resting on her hips, looking up at him. He liked the way she wore her rich brown hair, rolled like little pillows above her ears and held there with combs. There were a few stray strands blowing across her oval face as she started forward to meet him. Yes, a man could do worse than to have Carrie Grey for a wife.

"Well," he said, "that wasn't so bad and I got a fine sample. I don't know much about rocks, but it does look like marble to me."

"I'm sure it is," Carrie said. "Next time I'm in town I'll have to be looking at some of your catalogs to find some marble cutting tools."

"I think you should come in Thursday, Carrie, and let me escort you and Eleanor to the opera house. They've got a Spiritualist coming in to put on a show. Eleanor was going to send word out to you."

"Tell her I'll come," Carrie said. "I know how interested Eleanor is in that kind of thing."

Chapter Three

Eleanor Larkin exited her duplex from the front door onto the narrow porch. Steps ran along the sides and front of entire porch, but Eleanor always went down the steps immediately to the right of the door as if that were the only way down. One of the foremen from the sawmill lived in the other side of her duplex and even their three children did not violate the invisible division of the front porch.

It was Thursday, the 13th of May 1882. A cold wind blew down the lake from the northwest. Not a vicious wind, but it swirled her cape up over her shoulder and she had to drop her carpet bag and grab it back around her and fasten it more securely with the large peacock broach.

The house she rented from the Jackson Iron Company for five dollars a month faced northeast. It was on Cedar Lane, away from the harbor and furnace area and it was cushioned a little from the town's noise by the dense growths of cedar. Cedar were about the only trees they had not cut for charcoal, although Eleanor had read in the Iron Port that a man in Garden claimed he could make good coal out of cedar.

She shivered against the cold, or maybe against the idea they would strip even the cedar trees from the peninsula. Lake Michigan was visible just a hundred feet in front of the house, but a wall of the aforementioned cedars had rooted themselves stubbornly into the low limestone wall and kept the slanting rays of the early morning sun from striking her directly in the eyes. It was a pleasant view with glimpses of the white limestone beach and the blue of the lake between the red corduroy trunks of the trees. The sky was a bright shade of blue this morning. At least it wasn't going to rain again.

Tommy, her fifteen-year-old son, had been out ahead of her. He would have built a fire in the schoolhouse stove to take off the chill and brought up a fresh bucket of water. Eleanor had the two water dippers in her carpetbag. She brought them home every night and washed them. She thought there were fewer colds in the school now that she scalded the dippers each night. It had been Dr. Rutherford's idea. He was almost a fanatic about soap and hot water being the best guard against sickness. She used one dipper in the morning and one in the afternoon when Tommy brought up a fresh pail of water.

She was going to miss her boy. Last night while she was correcting grammar tests he had talked to her again about leaving Fayette. First he had insisted on being called Thomas, not Tommy.

"I asked you to call me Thomas now I'm almost sixteen, Mama," he'd said. "When school is out I want to go down to Grandpa's; to Muskegon."

"We already talked about that, Thomas," she had emphasized his name. "I need you here to help me. Mr. LaTermaine said you could clerk in the store. You won't have to work in the furnaces."

"I'm going, Mama." His face had that same determined look she'd seen on her father's face so often. "I'm going to work my way down on a schooner, the A.B. Lincoln. She's a lumber-hooker and if I work all summer on the lake I'll have enough to live with Grandpa and go to high school next year."

Eleanor knew the right thing to do was let him go. He hungered after learning the same way she always had. But she did need him. There was heavy work around the house, not to mention the work of keeping the schoolhouse heated and hauling water up Furnace Hill every morning. If the Company would pay her the fifty dollars a month it paid the men teachers instead of thirty-nine dollars because she was a woman, she could hire some help.

"I've already cut enough wood for the whole of next winter, Mama, and without me to feed you can hire one of the cabin wives to help you here. Matthew Cummins will start the fires and haul water for five cents a week. I talked to him already."

So Eleanor agreed. Maybe she could even get the school board to pay Matthew. She would argue the eleven-dollar wage difference between her and Mr. Standler who taught at the Puffy Creek School.

The school, on top of furnace hill, was a half-mile walk for Eleanor. Although Jack Sailstad was the President of the school board, Jackson Iron Company did not own the school. That was the reason it was outside the town, that and to get away from the noise. She had thought of asking for one of the houses closer to the school, just down from the hotel, but it was noisier and dirtier there. With Tommy gone she might have to board with someone, or take in another boarder herself. They would not allow such a big house to be occupied by a single lady. Boarders were difficult, with her being away all day. Tim, her current boarder, didn't ask much. He ate with them and kept out of the way, you'd almost not know he existed, but two or three more and she'd be nothing but a scullery maid.

The rich black dirt of the road was muddy from yesterday's rain despite the slag they spread occasionally, and she kept to the short wet grass alongside as much as she could. She wasn't young anymore. Thirty-seven next month, and although she called herself Mrs. Larkin, she had never had a husband...only that rascal who was Tommy's father, the one who had left town when she told him she was with child and he needed to marry her. She had been twenty-two, already a spinster. "You're too outspoken," her father always said. "You scare all the beaus off."

When she told him about her condition, he'd sent her off to Chicago to his sister. Her Aunt Louise had raised Tommy until he was old enough for school and then she'd taken him. In Manistee, her first job with him along, she'd conveniently become the Widow Larkin. She'd taught there and in Ludington and Bay City before coming to Fayette. It occurred to her that maybe she should go back to Muskegon with Tommy.

But Eleanor had made a place for herself in Fayette and was reluctant to leave. There was Henry LaTermaine, for one thing. He had stopped by Tuesday evening to invite her to the opera house tonight. They had sat on the low flat rock across the road from the house and talked until darkness fell. Once Eleanor had brushed her arm against his shoulder and he hadn't pulled away. In fact he had kept her hand in his after helping her to her feet and at the foot of the porch stairs that evening he had raised it to his lips and brushed it with a kiss while looking into her eyes.

True, Henry was probably five years younger than herself, but she was educated and they had such interesting conversations about so many things. She was still a good looking woman...she'd kept her shape and used a rinse of black walnut shells to cover the increasing number of gray hairs among the black. It was also true Carrie Grey often accompanied them on evenings out but, of course, that was only for appearances. Carrie wasn't his type at all.

For instance Carrie would be in on the afternoon stage to attend tonight's performance at the Opera house with them. The truth was, Eleanor was expecting Henry to marry her and if that happened she wouldn't have to move. Henry could move out of the room he had in the Shelton House and make them a real family. Maybe Tommy going was a good thing. Maybe having a ready made fifteen year old son put Henry off. And Tommy would be educated. Maybe he could even go to college and become a really educated man, like Dr. Rutherford.

Eleanor admired Dr. Rutherford. Soon after coming to Fayette he'd started the Lyceum Club and immediately after being elected President he had made a motion that the ladies be invited to be honorary members. They could contribute essays on chosen topics, although they could not take part in the debates.

She had her essay ready for tomorrow night's meeting—on the Indian Dilemma. The Apache, Geronimo, had just been recaptured and many thought he should be executed. She had written in support of justice for him, and all of the red-men, using the Indian women who wove the baskets for carrying charcoal for the Jackson Iron Company as her example.

Eleanor was being overtaken by a number of children, all headed for the school. The smallest children all wanted to hold her hand. One of the bigger boys offered to carry her carpet bag and then she was free to hold hands with Missy MacLean and Beatrice Conrad for a short distance. Various women called out a good morning to her as they added their children to the parade.

Cedar Lane came into town behind the hotel. The town was, as usual, a flurry of activity. The morning stage was boarding from in front of the hotel. Supply wagons were coming and going, and black smoke poured out of the tops of the one working furnace stack. The new furnace, built to replace the one that had burned down last fall, was almost ready to open.

Eleanor and the children stayed away from Stewart Drive and Curve Street, walking instead up a footpath that wound among the tiny log cabins where the furnace laborers and their families lived. The forty cabins were set so close together there was barely walking space between them. Most of them were a story and a half tall, with an attic loft where the children slept. Some of the cottages had crude lean-tos attached, which were used variously for a summer kitchen, a storage area, or just an extra sleeping room. Small as they were, Eleanor knew some of the households there took in boarders to supplement their income.

There were children here who should be in school, but their parents kept them away for chores around the house or even sent them to work as helpers in the furnace complex. There was a new state law requiring children to be in school until they were sixteen, but no one was enforcing it.

She was almost at the school when a carriage approached, coming into town on the stage road from Garden. Eleanor stepped off the road to let it pass, but it stopped instead and a lady pulled back the window curtain and called out to her.

"Mrs. Larkin?"

Eleanor stepped closer to the carriage. It looked like one of Dr. Rutherford's buggies from the livery, but the driver was a man she did not recognize.

"I'm Bertha Hartson, Mrs. Larkin. My husband is Reverend Hartson. We've just moved here and I wondered if I might visit your school this morning."

It would have been wrong to have thought this was a question; it had the ring of a command from royalty. Fayette had never had a Protestant preacher before. She had heard there was a protestant service last Sunday but had assumed it was one of the circuit riders who came though occasionally and held services in the music hall or hotel parlor. There was a Catholic Church, St. Peter's, south of town, and they had a resident priest. Most of the laborers were Catholic; the managers who had come here to run the furnace town were not.

Eleanor replied at once, "Of course, Mrs. Hartson, feel free to come in for a few minutes this morning."

"If you don't mind I'll get out and join you now," she said. "It will save me walking back up the hill."

Eleanor waited while the woman got out. A scrawny boy scrambled out behind her. Mrs. Hartson took his hand and pulled him to her side. "This is Aaron, who will be attending your school," she said.

The boy was a homely child, dressed in blue trousers that were a little too large for him.

"Good morning, Aaron. Welcome to Fayette. And how old are you?"

"Seven," the boy said. "But I can do schoolwork with the nine year olds." His voice was self-assured, even defiant. Like mother, like son, Eleanor thought, realizing she had taken an instant dislike to Bertha Hartson.

The other children had run ahead when Eleanor stopped

to talk and were now playing tag in the grass around the schoolhouse. Aaron stood and waited with his mother. Mrs. Hartson struggled to remove a heavy carpetbag from the buggy. Eleanor wondered why the man just sat reining in the horse instead of helping the woman with her heavy bundle. Was he Rev. Hartson? When Mrs. Hartson was finally settled outside the carriage, the man spoke for the first time.

"I'll pick you up in about an hour, then."

The woman nodded. "Help me carry this, Aaron." Between them they began to drag the carpetbag up the hill.

"My goodness," Eleanor said, "What is in there that makes it so heavy?"

"New Testaments," Mrs. Hartson said. "One for every child in the school."

Oh dear, Eleanor thought. The Catholic families would not be happy to have their little ones bring home a Bible. "You wait here," Eleanor told her. "I'll send one of the older boys down to help you."

She turned to Aaron, "Would you like to come with me and meet some of the children your age?"

She saw the eager look of consent in his eyes, but his mother spoke first, "No, he'll wait with me."

The morning was a disaster. The minister's wife took over the classroom and taught a Bible lesson and then passed out the small black books, assisted by Aaron. "Tell your parents we will have Congregational services at nine o'clock in the Shelton House parlor. And Sunday school lessons are at eight. I expect to see all of you there."

When the carriage finally came back up the hill to pick up Mrs. Hartson, Eleanor met Rev. Hartson. He was tall, lean, and quite a pleasant man. His face was long and plain and clean-shaven. She wondered about his sullenness this morning and why he hadn't spoken to her then. After they left she collected the Bibles from all the Catholic children and stored them on a shelf in her book closet.

Eleanor sighed when Carrie Grey dismounted from the stage. She wore a gray polonaise, much worn at the elbow, over a deep red, full skirt that was at least ten years out of fashion. Poor dear. Eleanor loved her greatly but Carrie was, well, not feminine. She was so tall and ... sturdy. She did hope Carrie had no attachment to Henry. They'd never talked about it Eleanor just assumed Carrie wasn't interested. Carrie just wasn't feminine enough to attract a beau, even with her property and little limestone quarry. She wasn't much of a conversationalist either. Eleanor knew that she had strong opinions, but she seldom voiced them.

"Leave your bags, Dear," she said as they embraced. "Tommy..." she caught herself and laughed, "He wants to be called Thomas now, will come and get them."

Carrie wiped her brow with a large white square of linen when Eleanor released her. The day might have started windy and cold, but it was quite warm now. She tucked the cloth into her sleeve.

"You're looking well, Eleanor."

"Oh, I've got so much to tell you," Eleanor said, linking her arm into Carrie's. "I'm very excited about the show tonight. A real live Spiritualist."

"Who is it?" Carrie asked, "Henry didn't know"

For answer Eleanor stopped her on the hotel porch in front of the orange and green poster announcing the performance.

MRS. EMMA HARDING BRITTEN
WELL KNOWN AND RESPECTED LECTURER,
AUTHOR, AND CLAIRVOYANT

"Have you ever heard of her?" Carrie asked.

"No," Eleanor admitted. "But I'm excited about it just the same."

"Elemental spirits," Carrie read, her voice sounded skeptical. "Fairies? Elves? Surely not, Eleanor."

"Oh, Carrie, you're such a skeptic. You need to read the new book I have to understand it."

She could see Carrie's head was still tilted in a questioning way so she added, "Just look at it as great fun, if you prefer. Henry is escorting us and everybody in town will be there. I've invited Henry to have supper with us."

"I brought you some eggs and a fresh killed chicken," Carrie said, patting the large bag she had not left for Tommy to get.

"Then we'll have chicken and dumplings," Eleanor said. "I baked a blueberry pie last night with some of those berries we put up last summer."

"I want to stop at the store first," Carrie said.

"Henry's not there," Eleanor informed her. "He went in to Escanaba on the Lady Washington yesterday and will be back on the Jo Harris this afternoon."

"I don't want to see Henry," Carrie said in a tone of voice that made it clear such a thing had never occurred to her. "Why are you blushing, Eleanor?"

Eleanor ignored her heated face and stood on tiptoe to whisper into Carrie's ear. The benches in front of the Company office were filled with men, probably hoping to be hired to work in the new furnace stack that would be finished soon. They were watching the two women, as well as any others who happened to stroll by, but with the ordinary noise of the town and harbor, nobody was apt to overhear anything they said.

Yet, Eleanor whispered into Carrie's ear. "I think Henry is about to propose marriage to me." She gave a nervous giggle and looked behind them to see if anybody had heard.

"Then perhaps I should be taken with a headache and not go to the opera house with you tonight."

"Oh, no, no," Eleanor protested, setting a brisk pace towards the store. "He won't do it until I've told him Tommy is leaving."

"Where is Tommy going?"

Eleanor finished her word for word recitation of that conversation just as they reached the front door of the store. Carrie stopped to study the window displays. One window was filled with an arrangement of garden tools and packages of Burbank seed, and the other had a drape of flower print cotton and a Singer sewing machine. The machine was black with gold lettering and sat upon a walnut cabinet with three drawers on the side. It had legs of scrolled black metal.

"I wonder how much a sewing machine costs," Carrie said. "Fancy how much time a body could save with one of those."

"More than I can afford," said Eleanor. "I didn't know you had so much sewing to do."

"I need a few new things, everything I have is getting worn."

The sewing machine was thirty-nine dollars, but the young clerk could not show her how it worked. "Mr. LaTermaine can show you. He'll be back tomorrow."

Carrie picked out three bolts of fabric, a rose gray chambray, a yellow flowered calico, and a white dimity. She added several spools of thread and then some white muslin. She told the clerk how much yardage of each to cut and then instructed him to have them wrapped and put on the Garden Stage Saturday morning.

"Yes, ma'am, Mrs. Grey," the boy said as he took her money and counted out change.

"I want Henry to show me that sewing machine tomorrow, Eleanor. I've half a mind to buy it if I think I can make it work."

Eleanor was sure Carrie could. There was very little Carrie could not do if she set her mind to it. Eleanor envied the easy decision Carrie made to spend what to her was a month's wage. Her quarry must be doing very well.

While Eleanor was cutting up the chicken for supper she suddenly remembered Bertha Hartson. "Oh, Carrie," she said, "I met the new preacher's wife today. She said she had met you."

"Did you like her?"

Eleanor wrinkled her nose as if there was a bad smell in the room. "Not at all. She had the effrontery to come into my school and pass out New Testaments to all my students and most of them being Catholic."

Carrie laughed. "I knew you wouldn't like her."

"But how did you meet her?"

Carrie told her about the storm and how Bertha Hartson had spent the night with her. She didn't dwell on Drew McGeary, although she did ask if Eleanor knew him.

"No, never heard of him. I don't pay much attention to harbor traffic, Carrie. There are a dozen schooners a day in and out of here."

"He was a very good-looking man," Carrie said, "and very good company."

Eleanor stopped stirring the soup and turned to look at Carrie. "Interested?" she asked.

Carrie blushed. "Well, I don't even know him, do I? I just observed that he was a fine looking man the same way you once told me Dr. Rutherford was a fine looking man. Where are the Hartsons going to live?"

"I think they're north of town," Eleanor said. "The buggy came along the stage road this morning. They have a seven year old son, Aaron."

Eleanor rolled her eyes at the mention of the boy's name.

"Is he a problem?"

"He's a mama's boy and tries to act years older than he is. She wouldn't let him play outside, said he was delicate and would rather sit and read while the other children ran around outside like wild Indians. Those were her very words, wild Indians. And you should have seen her husband. Now there was a strange man, all sullen and silent sitting up there on the wagon letting his wife lug that heavy bag of books up the hill by herself."

"I take he is not good-looking?"

Eleanor tilted her head sideways and considered. "I'm not sure, Carrie. When he came back to pick her up he was very pleasant. No, no, he's not good-looking, just ordinary."

The chicken was cut up and ready for frying. Carrie mixed up dumpling batter and tasted the soup for flavoring while Eleanor fried the chicken. The smells alone ought to woo Henry, if he liked to eat.

Chapter Four

Supper with Henry that evening was pleasant. By the time they left for the opera house, the air had cooled and both women welcomed a light shawl over their shoulders. They followed Cedar Lane around the back way and came up behind the hotel. The sun was just setting behind the slanting face of Burnt Bluff and Carrie stopped a moment to watch. Henry, walking with his arms akimbo in order to offer an arm to each, hurried her.

"The best seats will be taken if we don't move along," he said. "It looks as if everybody in town is headed there."

"Spiritualism is a fascinating thing," Eleanor replied as Carrie let herself be rushed onward.

The Opera House was upstairs in the tall oddly shaped building that faced the harbor. The meat market, the barbershop, and the shoemaker occupied the lower floors of the building. A man in a black suit, seated at a small table near the open door to the stairs, was selling tickets. Henry left the ladies to visit together and went to stand in line to purchase their tickets.

The level green lawn next to the building was nearly filled with groups of people waiting. The sun was making its last colorful display behind them, but the moon had already risen and was visible over Snail Shell Harbor. The stark whiteness of the limestone bluff rising a hundred feet above the water the full length of the harbor always drew Carrie's attention.

She tried to imagine it with green trees atop it again as it had been the first time she'd seen it with Albert, eight years ago, in 1874. The furnace town had been in existence for seven years already, and just two years ago they had started cutting the trees on the bluff for charcoal. Now they had a railroad down to the end of the peninsula to carry charcoal from the

several kilns down there into town. At some point, they were
going to run out of wood; then what would they do?

"Carrie?" She felt Eleanor's hand on her arm, shaking her
gently. "What daydream are you lost in?"

"Just admiring the bluff, dear," Carrie said. "I never tire of
looking at it."

"I was admiring that dress Grace Sailstad is wearing.
Wouldn't I look stunning in it?"

Carrie turned to see. Jack Sailstad was the Manager of
Fayette, and Grace, his wife, was said to hate living here. She
came from a prominent steel family in Cleveland. Grace stood
next to her husband, holding his arm. Jack Sailstad was an
imposing man, lean and muscular with a Vandyke beard that
gave him a slightly menacing look. The bodice of the much-
admired dress was brocade, a dark green stripe against a paler
green background. It was long and tight fitting. Carrie could
almost feel the pain of the corset stays that must be cutting
into Grace's flesh. The pale green skirt was elaborately draped
at the sides and bustled behind. The front fell straight to the
tops of her kidskin slippers. She wore a tiny hat atop her
coifed honey-colored hair, perched at a rakish tilt. It was
trimmed with feathers and lace.

"You'd be as uncomfortable as she is," Carrie whispered,
"and not look a whit prettier."

Eleanor's dress was yellow chintz, a little too light weight
for May, but becoming on her nonetheless. Carrie looked
around at the other women and thought again of the sewing
machine she wanted to buy from Henry. Her clothes were
hopelessly out of date. She couldn't hope to catch Captain
McGeary's attention in the large hoop skirts that comprised
her wardrobe.

Henry returned to escort them up the narrow stairway. A
chandelier consisting of six brass lanterns with white glass
globes covering each gas flame hung from the ceiling at the
center of the room. This was the first time Carrie had been
inside the new Opera House, which had been completed

during the winter. The room occupied the entire upper floor of the building and featured an angled stage, which accounted for the odd shape of the exterior of the building. It was furnished with benches arranged to face the raised stage. Carrie noticed that the floors were finished in dark oak and polished to a brilliant sheen. When the hall was used for community dances, the benches could be placed along the wall and the floor could easily hold four sets of dancers. On either side of the stage there was a door leading backstage. A small stove to one side furnished heat to the room. The windows were draped in heavy green brocade against a pale green paint.

"It's very nice," Carrie said to Eleanor.

"And the organ," Eleanor said. "It makes a real nice touch, don't you think?"

They found seats on a bench in the fourth row where Eleanor maneuvered the seating so she sat between Carrie and Henry. Carrie watched as Grace was helped to sit down in the front row. The feathers from her hat spiked up into the air creating a slight blockage to Carrie's view of the stage. Dr. and Louella Rutherford came in and sat in the front row next to the Sailstads. Louella turned around and waved to various people behind her, Carrie being one of them. Louella was Carrie's closest friend, next to Eleanor and Melanie DeWinter in Garden.

Shirley LeComte sat at the organ. She was the wife of Frank LeComte, supervisor of the furnace complex. She played the organ at the theatre and at St. Peter's church. Carrie admired the mass of flaxen curls that were arranged so artfully on her head and trailed down her slim straight back. Carrie didn't know her well but Eleanor had warned her never to tell Shirley anything she didn't want the whole town to know.

The green brocade curtain still concealed the stage in the front of the room and the hum of voices rose as the room filled. Some people stood along the side and back of the room; these were mostly the cottage people. Eleanor had spoken truly about Spiritualism being a fascinating thing. It was an unusual show for the Fayette Opera House where the usual fare was trained animal acts and short plays put on by a cast of three or four. Maybe Grace Sailstad had an interest in Spiritualism and had coaxed Jack to stand the extra expense of bringing them here.

The curtains parted and Mrs. Emma Britten swept onto the stage with a flourish from the organ. A back curtain of black muslin accentuated the woman's appearance. She wore a scarlet red dress overlaid with black lace, the leg o' mutton sleeves were black and she wore black gloves. A black lace mantilla hid her face from the audience. When she reached the center of the stage she folded the lace back from her face with a dramatic gesture, causing the audience to gasp at her appearance. Her face was pure white, her lips blood red, and her eyes outlined in black. Her hair was raven black also. Shirley struck a deep discordant chord on the organ.

"She's covered her face with flour," Henry whispered.

"Hush," Eleanor admonished him, tapping his cheek with her fan.

A round table sat just off the center of the stage, covered with a short white cloth. Mrs. Britten approached the table and dumped the contents of her small handbag upon it. There was a clunk as a heavy object hit the table. She picked up a long silver pendulum suspended on a silver chain.

She set the pendulum to swinging and began to walk slowly around the table. She continued to walk around the stage while the large pendulum slowly swung to and fro. As she walked she explained. "I will be able to locate any cold spots on the stage, for the pendulum will stop swinging and commence to spin, indicating a cold spot, where spirits are more apt to be."

Soon she found a place about ten feet from the table and near the back curtain. She called out two stagehands and insisted they move her table and chair to this spot. She seated herself behind the table, facing the audience, and dropped the pendulum back into her beaded bag.

"Now she's close enough to the curtain for someone to hand things to her," Henry whispered. This time Eleanor rapped the back of his hand with her fan.

"I will test this site," Mrs. Britten announced, " by rapping on the table. If any spirits are present, they will rap back to me. If they rap once, they don't like this spot, even though they are present. If they rap twice, the table is correctly placed."

Two faint raps promptly answered her sharp rap. Suddenly a shower of small feathers floated down from the darkness over the stage and a scent of apple blossoms filled the air. Mrs. Britten smiled broadly. "Ah, my favorite fairy, Rosalind, is with us. Feathers are her sign."

Beside her, Carrie could feel Eleanor lean forward with interest. She actually believed this stuff, Carrie realized.

"At this time, I would like my assistant, Lord Joshua Locke, to come out and assist me," Mrs. Britten said loudly.

A man appeared, dressed in a gray tailcoat, a glittering vest, and a tall silk hat. It was the same man who had sold tickets before the show. He bowed deeply to the audience and then to Mrs. Britten. There was a brief burst of applause from the audience, which faltered as if in embarrassment when everyone did not join in. Carrie was sure Eleanor had started it.

"Lord Locke," Mrs. Britten exclaimed, "You forgot to bring the table fittings."

Looking abashed, Locke bowed his way off stage and returned with a black and red tablecloth. He flourished the fabric and let it fall into place over the table, covering it to the floor.

"That's so she can pull things from under there," Henry whispered.

"We've already seen there's nothing there," Eleanor replied before she shushed him.

Lord Locke appeared a second time carrying a candelabra and a crystal bell, which he placed on the table. After lighting the three tapers he left again and returned with a large black leather-bound book. Mrs. Britten rearranged these things on the tabletop several times, apparently at the command of Rosalind who rapped out messages wildly until everything was as she desired.

"Rosalind prefers the bell to knocking," Mrs. Britten said. "Don't you Rosalind?" The bell, without lifting from the table, rang twice.

Lord Locke remained standing. Mrs. Britten looked up at him as if surprised to see him there. "Well, go get the chairs, my lord, and then please do sit down."

The audience laughed as Lord Locke looked offended and once more left the stage. He returned pushing a large overstuffed chair. Two stagehands followed him with three folding chairs.

"What is the meaning of that chair?" Mrs. Britten inquired. It was clear she was losing her patience with Lord Locke.

"I meant to be comfortable while you chatted with Rosalind, my dear," he replied. He flipped up his coattails and sunk into the overstuffed chair. The audience laughed willingly. They were warming to the act.

"If anyone is to be comfortable here, it will be me," Mrs. Britten announced. "Move that chair over here where I can sit in it."

Locke stood and shrugged pointedly at the audience. "And I'm the one with the Title," he said, drawing another laugh.

He pushed the chair behind the table, moving the original straight-backed chair aside. After Mrs. Britten had settled herself in the big chair, the tall back rising over her head, she indicated Lord Locke should sit in the newly vacated chair next to her.

"We are still a chair short," Mrs. Britten observed. "A séance must be conducted by a number of people divisible by three. We need either six people, or three."

"There are no more chairs to be had," Lord Locke spread his hands in despair. "We shall have to conduct the séance with only three people."

"Very well," Mrs. Britten said. She sighed deeply and asked, "Is there someone in the audience who would like to be our third?"

"Oh, do volunteer, Eleanor," Carrie urged. "Stand up."

Several other people also volunteered, raising their hands in the air. Lord Locke had come to the edge of the stage to peer out at the audience and now turned back to Mrs. Britten. "Which one does Rosalind want?"

Mrs. Britten rapped and the bell rang. "Rosalind has chosen someone whose name begins with the letters EL."

Eleanor gasped. "That's me," she said.

Lord Locke came down off the stage and grasped Eleanor's elbow, guiding her onto the stage. He seated her at the table and removed the two extra chairs.

Mrs. Britten now cautioned the audience that they must remain quiet while she communed with Rosalind. "Rosalind is only the intermediary between myself and other spirits waiting to contact their beloved still on this plane."

The three at the table joined hands to form the required circle and the séance began. The bell rang in response when Mrs. Britten intoned a request to "any spirit who wants to speak, speak now." Over the almost constant ringing of the bell, Mrs. Britten began to proclaim "messages." A white filmy scarf probably meant to be a ghost floated overhead.

Carrie heard slight reactions to different messages among the audience and chuckled inwardly at people's gullibility. Then she heard Mrs. Britten say, "Albert says, don't do it." A chill ran down Carrie's spine and she almost gasped as she had heard others do. In another second she dismissed the words and the feelings she had experienced. Her late husband couldn't possibly be contacting her and besides what would it mean, "don't do it?"

Mrs. Britten droned on, "Your mother is so happy for you, L, about your upcoming marriage," and Carrie knew Eleanor would claim that one for herself.

Suddenly the candles on the table sputtered and went out.

Mrs. Britten moaned, "Oh, no. I see a death, oh how terrible."
Again Carrie felt the chill down her spine and the hair on the
back of her neck prickled. Mrs. Britten gasped and then cried
out, "Oh, I can't reveal it, it would be too cruel."

On stage, Mrs. Britten and Lord Locke released Eleanor's
hands at the same time. The table tipped and the candelabra
fell to the floor with a crash. Eleanor jumped up and Lord
Locke immediately escorted her off the stage and left her to
find her own way back to her seat.

Mrs. Britten stood behind the table, lowered the black lace
mantilla down over her face and slowly walked off stage,
leaving Lord Locke to tell the audience thank you and good
night. "Mrs. Britten is too upset to speak," he told them.

After the show Henry took them to the Shelton House for a
glass of sherry.

"There, you see, Eleanor," Henry said as soon as they were
seated. "This Spiritualism stuff is just a hoax. As I see it, she
was an out and out fraud. It was just as plain as could be how
she was manipulating everything. I could see wire moving that
ghost." He laughed loudly.

Eleanor sniffed. "I thought it was very good. I was right
there on the stage, don't forget, and I saw no manipulating.
Just you ask people and see if they didn't get messages from
loved ones. You don't know. Carrie, do you think the Albert
message was meant for you?" She didn't wait for Carrie to
answer. "Well, I did. And I found the ending very upsetting."

Henry laughed again. "I don't want to argue with you,
Eleanor, I always lose. But you must admit people die all the
time. I'll grant you it was a good show. Let's just sip our sherry
and be friends."

"But this was a terrible death," Eleanor lowered her voice,
"I think she meant murder."

Henry laughed loudly at this, his laughter joined with that
of Edward Rutherford who entered the dining room just then
along with a crowd of young managers and their wives, Jack

and Grace Sailstad, and Frank and Shirley LaComte among them. The doctor and Louella stopped at their table to say hello.

"Always a pleasure to see you, Mrs. Grey," he nodded to Eleanor and Henry. "If you'll be in town tomorrow do stop and see my new Irish rooster. I think you'll find him a pretty sight."

"I was hoping to see you," Carrie said, laying her gloved hand on his arm. "I'd like to do some chicken trading with you."

Rutherford laughed again. He had a roar of a laugh and everybody in the lounge turned to look. "I'm more used to horse trading, Mrs. Grey, and you know I always get the better of those bargains. You might want to stay the weekend. I'm going to race Old Tom against the big boss's nag on Sunday."

That started a flurry of wagers being yelled out for one horse or the other.

"Take the bets down, Henry," said Jack Sailstad, who was the 'big boss'. "Anybody wants to bet on the race, see Henry at the general store. Race is at two o'clock sharp on Sunday."

Chapter Five

After Eleanor left for school the next morning, Carrie cleaned the house. It wasn't that Eleanor was a bad housekeeper, Carrie told herself; she just didn't have time. It was an hour short of noon when she finished. The furniture had been dusted, the floor scrubbed, the rug swept, and the dishes done. Now she was ready to venture into town.

Carrie checked herself in the round mirror Eleanor had tacked up over the bureau in her bedroom. Mrs. Collins, back at Lady Jane's Boarding School for Girls in Buffalo, told the girls they should capitalize on their best asset and be proud of it. She patted her hair in approval; her chestnut brown hair was her best asset. The girlhood freckles across her nose had faded and she had ceased to worry about them. Louella Rutherford had once told her she had aristocratic cheekbone structure. She wondered if Captain McGeary had found her pretty.

The house the doctor occupied was larger than any other house in Fayette, with the exception of Sailstad's house next door, known locally as the "white house". The white house, which had been built when the town was first founded had recently undergone an expansion, adding on to the second floor above the kitchen. Along with the new opera house and the expansion of the Shelton House, these improvements were only the latest in Fayette. The general store was slated for expansion next.

Carrie had noticed that the distance between houses defined status in Fayette. There was more space between Rutherford's house and the next one up, for instance, where one of the furnace foremen lived, than there was between the houses on Cedar Lane. Eleanor lived right around the corner in one of a row of duplexes, where there were only three yards between houses, and one privy for every two town houses. The cottages up on Furnace Hill were so close together a person could barely squeeze between dwellings. Three privies served the entire cottage neighborhood. Both the Rutherfords house and the Sailstads had private privies. A white fence enclosed the white house and an expanse of green grass, kept closely cut, surrounded the house. It was rumored that their large private privy was carpeted and wallpapered.

When Carrie entered the outer room of Dr. Rutherford's hospital, it was empty. The Doctor's house was three stories. This, the lowest level, was built of brick. There were a few chairs arranged along the wall and a small desk just inside the door. Carrie stood a moment and then called out,

"Edward, Louella, is anyone here?"

Edward Rutherford's voice came from a room beyond. "Be right there."

A moment later the doctor himself appeared. Edward Rutherford was a big man, tall and solid. His light brown hair had begun to silver at the edges, but his well-trimmed beard was still full-colored. He had kindly brownish eyes that were magnified somewhat by the eyeglasses he wore. This morning his white coverall coat was smeared with blood.

"Mrs. Grey," he greeted her. "You've come on your chicken trading expedition I trust."

"I have," she said. "I heard your rascals waking up the sun this morning. I read in the Iron Port about your new Irish rooster."

"I'll get out of this coat," he said. "I just finished stitching up John Cully's leg. Got a rather nasty gash in it at the sawmill this morning. Seems like I do a lot of stitching up for those men."

"Louella," he called up the stairs, "Carrie's here to trade chickens with me, are you coming along with us?"

Louella appeared at the head of the stairs. She wore a flour-covered apron and presented flour covered hands. "Good morning, Carrie. Sorry, I'm in the middle of kneading bread. You'll be coming to the Lyceum this evening won't you?"

Carrie assured her that Eleanor and she would be there. "Can I help with anything?"

"All under control," Louella said, "you just come along with Eleanor and I'll see you then."

Outside the back door, a path to the right led to Sailstad's, and another path led left to Dr. Rutherford's chicken yard. It was fenced with wire and divided into three sections.

"I'm trying to breed some of the bantams," he told Carrie, "so I need to keep them separated at the back or I'll just have a bunch of barnyard chickens after a while."

The front pen contained his layers and fryers.

"No Leghorns?" asked Carrie, looking around and seeing none of the white chickens like she had in her hen house.

"I won't keep a Leghorn," he said, "they're too skittish. Flap and squawk whenever anything startles them."

"They're good layers though," Carrie replied. "I've nine of them."

"Oh ho, what do you do with all the eggs, my dear?"

"I take about half of them to Hugh Brandon's wife. He's the man who operates the quarry for me. They've got three sons who've got little ones. They need eggs once in a while. And I sell some to DeWinter's meat market in Garden."

Rutherford closed the opening between pens as they passed into the second one. These were his show chickens. He held out his arm and one of the golden brown hens housed there flew up and cocked an eye at him. Rutherford clucked at her and stroked the feathers of her saddle.

"Take the Golden Comet here," he said, "She lays good but she's tamer than the leghorns. Lays brown eggs. Goldie here's about spent, but I can't bear to stew her." He laughed, the roar breaking out of him and startling the chicken. He gentled her again by stroking and cooing at her.

"Louella calls me a sentimental old fool, but Goldie is my

pet. You wouldn't eat your cat or dog now, would you? Besides I keep them because they're beautiful, not for eggs and meat."

Goldie walked her way up the Doctor's arm and perched on his broad shoulder while they continued their tour of the chicken yard.

"You've got some pretties here, Edward. That new Irish rooster is an especial beauty. You don't have any stray red feathers for a lady's hat do you?"

"Louella purloins all those. But I'm sure she'll share one or two with you."

After admiring all the birds, Carrie said, "Now this is what I propose, Edward. I've got a broody hen sitting on a clutch of Black Minorca eggs. If they are what they are supposed to be, I'll trade you two Minorca chicks for six of your Golden Comets."

Rutherford raised his left eyebrow in surprise. "Where did you get them? I've read that they're nearly extinct."

"I took them in payment for some stone," Carrie said.

"Well, well." The doctor put Goldie down and tucked his hands under the back of his jacket. It was his horse-trading stance.

"Well, well," he said again. "A Black Minorca would be a show piece, but six Golden Comets? Why so many?"

"My Leghorns are about spent and ready for the stewpot, and like you said, they are too skittish. A squirrel sets them off. I want to replace them with Goldens."

"But six, Carolyn, I don't have six." That he had used her full name instead of Carrie was another sign of his intense horse-trading position.

Carrie pointed out that he did, and that he had a broody hen sitting on, she lifted the hen and counted, nine eggs. Rutherford paced, his hands hidden under his jacket. Carrie waited five minutes before speaking to him.

"I'm only asking for six Goldens, Edward."

He stopped pacing and looked at her intently. "Black Minorca, you say?"

He picked Goldie up again, placed her on his shoulder and resumed his pace. "Black Minorca, a very showy breed, and hard to come by." He was talking to himself and Carrie did not interrupt. Suddenly he stopped in front of her and placed his arms akimbo.

"You give me three of them, and I'll give you five Goldens."

"Plus a rooster," Carrie said.

"Plus a rooster," Rutherford confirmed.

"Then it's a deal?"

"Indeed," said Dr. Rutherford.

Done with her chicken trading, Carrie headed for the store. She was determined to have that sewing machine. Drew McGeary would be back, she knew he would, and he would not find her in threadbare, outdated, clothing. Not only was she going to make herself a new skirt and two new shirts, she was going to look at the Butterick pattern book and get a pattern for one of those elegant walking suits she'd seen in the Lord & Taylor catalog on her last trip to Escanaba. She'd make it in fine navy blue wool, and get a new hat to go with it.

Carrie walked down the road toward town. The noise increased when she exited the protective barrier of trees. Schooners, tugs, ore scows, and other boats lined the harbor docks. The white limestone bluff across the water gleamed in the sunlight making a good backdrop to the forest of ship masts in the harbor. Carrie scanned each schooner looking for Wave Dancer. She wasn't there. Carrie wove her way though the people on the street, past the grain elevator, the icehouse, and the opera house, until she was in front of the store.

There was a back door on the harbor side with a set of stairs going up and into the store. A wagon was backed up to the big double warehouse doors unloading barrels of something. She wasn't paying attention, she was lost in a daydream of strolling along with her hand resting lightly on Captain McGeary's arm, she in a blue wool walking suit and an elegant hat, carrying one of those little parasols the city ladies carried to protect their skin from the sun. He was wearing a blue Captain's jacket with gold braid on it.

It was because of this she bumped into Bertha Hartson just inside the door.

"Oh excuse me," she said, reaching out to keep the poor woman on her feet. In an instant she recognized her victim.

"Bertha," she exclaimed. "I am sorry. I was lost in thought."

"Is it you, Carolyn Grey?" Bertha said. "What are you doing in town?"

"Oh, I came in yesterday to go to the opera house with Eleanor Larkin, the teacher, you know, and I'll not go home until tomorrow. I've some shopping to do."

The minister's wife clucked her tongue. "That show was a disgrace. Imagine bringing a medium into a Christian town. Rev. Hartson expects to preach his sermon against witchcraft and such this Sunday."

Carrie nodded. Bertha was blocking the stairs and the entrance was not wide enough for her to squeeze past. She was trapped. "It was only in fun," Carrie said, "nobody believes in that stuff." Except Eleanor, she thought.

"Even fun should adhere to the Lord's rules, my dear."

"Yes, I suppose so," Carrie conceded.

"I do wish you'd stay and attend the Sunday service, sister."

"I can't, thank you," Carrie said. "I've chickens and the cow to care for. The Brandon girl was only asked to take care of them through Saturday."

Someone else coming down the stairs forced Bertha to move out the door. While she said hello to the newcomer, Carrie bustled up the stairs and into the store. The store was a mixture of smells, predominated by the odor of dill from the large open crock of dill pickles for sale right at the top of the stairs. Further into the interior, the dry smell of bags of grain tickled her nose. It was better than the heavy stench of the smelter outside.

Henry was behind the dry-goods counter, waiting on Grace Sailstad. Carrie busied herself inspecting the fabrics and looking for the Butterick pattern book. She was sure she'd seen one yesterday. Ah, there it was, next to the spools of thread and lace. She was engrossed in studying it when Henry spoke at her elbow, making her jump.

"Sorry, Carrie," he said in a quiet voice. "I didn't mean to startle you."

He was standing too close and he laid his hand on her upper arm. He smelled of tobacco and shaving lotion and something else Carrie couldn't identify. Whatever it was, she found it unpleasant. She moved away from his touch, but he moved with her. She turned a little and freed herself of his hand.

"What can I help you with?" he asked. "Young Charlie says you were interested in the sewing machine yesterday."

Carrie took advantage of the conversation to move even further away and towards the machine still displayed in the front window. "Is it easy to use?" she asked.

Henry became the merchant. "Anybody could use it, Carrie. One or two easy instruction sessions with me and you'll be sewing like a professional seamstress."

"Thirty-nine dollars is an awful lot of money, Henry. I could buy an entire new wardrobe in Escanaba for that."

"This machine in the best one on the market, Carrie. Singer has made a name for itself with quality and ease of use. Come, I have another one set up in my office. I'll show you how it works."

Carrie followed him up the steps and into the small stifling room Henry called his office. From the full window across the front Henry could see the entire store. A desk was neatly stacked with papers and the sewing machine sat against the wall to the right.

Henry wheeled his desk chair to the machine and showed her how to thread the machine through a complicated path of several catches and holes. "But there's a picture here," he pointed to a small booklet, "so it's really very easy. After a few times, you won't even have to think about it."

The concept of the bobbin holding a second thread coming up from the bottom was a little harder for Carrie to understand.

"You're actually sewing with two threads," Henry said. "They meet in the cloth and interlock, creating a stitch that won't easily rip out."

Henry sewed a few stitches on a small piece of fabric, his feet worked the treadle under the machine to make the needle go up and down. "The hardest part is getting your feet to work with the right rhythm," he said. "Here, you sit down and try it."

Carrie sat. She had to pull her skirt up a little to free her shoes for working the treadle. The fabric jerked forward as Carrie struggled to make her feet go up and down the way Henry's did. She grasped the fabric to slow it down and the needle snapped in two, one piece flying up and hitting her hand.

"It takes a while to get the rhythm right," Henry said.

Carrie sucked at the blood seeping out of the small wound. "Maybe I'd just better stick to hand sewing."

Henry laughed at her. "What giving up already? You?"

Carrie flashed an angry look at him. "Of course not, I'll learn to do this."

Within a quarter of an hour Carrie broke five more needles. But then she managed to complete a long row of stitches without any problem. What a thrill to see the small even stitches the machine made once she learned the rhythm of rocking her feet on the treadle. Oh, she wanted this machine!

"But thirty-nine dollars, Henry?" She turned and looked up at him.

"For you, thirty-five," Henry said hurriedly. "And you won't have to pay it all at once. Five dollars now and five dollars a month until it's paid."

"How would I get it to the house?" she asked. "It might go

on the stage, but then I'd have to carry it the mile back to the house."

Henry smiled broadly, revealing two rotten teeth on the left side of his mouth. "If you want the machine, Carrie, I'll deliver it. I'll drive you home in the morning and set it up for you and give you the second lesson right in your home."

Carrie stood and studied the machine. Henry showed her how it folded inside the wooden cabinet when it wasn't in use. There were three drawers on the side to hold sewing notions. "It's like a fine piece of furniture in your parlor when it's not in use," he said.

Carrie was looking at the machine, but she was seeing herself in her new rose-gray skirt with a white dimity waist, walking along the path in the woods with Drew McGeary. With that machine, she could have the new skirt finished by Sunday night.

"I'll take it," she said. "And I also want to order a pattern from the Butterick book. Does it take long for them to get in?"

"If they have the pattern you want in Escanaba, you can have it next week. If it isn't, then it'll take a little longer. Show me the one you want."

They went back downstairs and Henry wrote down the pattern numbers of her first, second, and third choices. Then she had him measure out the blue wool for the walking suit and some blue chambray for another idea she had in mind.

While she was looking at shoes, she was shocked to look up and see Henry briefly touch himself where the head of his manhood would have been inside his clothing. She quickly averted her eyes to examine the shoes more closely. When she looked up again, his hands were underneath the long white apron he wore. From then on Carrie kept her eyes glued on his face, afraid of what his hands might be doing to himself under that apron.

She settled on a pair of goatskin buskins, laced with only three holes instead of the many of her old shoes. They had a low square heel and a box toe. They cost one dollar.

When Henry added up her bill for the fabrics, machine, and a few groceries, it was a considerable amount. Despite what Henry had said about paying for the machine over a period of time, Carrie wrote him a draft on an Escanaba bank for the entire amount. With the building season just getting started, the money would be quickly replenished with sales of stone from her quarry.

"I can get away tomorrow about mid-morning," Henry said.

"Good," Carrie replied. "I'll be here, ready to go."

Chapter Six

Saturday morning dawned with the promise of a brilliant day. Eleanor and Carrie finished breakfast while they planned a picnic lunch.

"We could just eat at my house," Carrie suggested. "It would be easier."

"But not as romantic as a picnic along the way."

"It would be better, you know, if we saved the picnic for you and Henry on the way back. How romantic can it be to have me standing around?"

Eleanor blushed. "How long does it take to get to your house?"

Carrie drained her coffee cup and pushed the table setting away from her. "It depends. If he's using the store delivery wagon with a team, an hour and a half. If he has a carriage, an hour."

Eleanor stood and started picking up the dishes. Tommy had left to go fishing before either of them was awake. Carrie picked up her own plate of plain white glaze, which the Company furnished with the house, and followed Eleanor into the kitchen. The kettle on the stove was boiling so Eleanor immediately placed the dirty dishes in an enameled dishpan and poured the scalding water over them. She then added several dippers of cold water from one of the two buckets Tommy had filled for her. She scrubbed the dishes with a cloth while they talked.

"I think I like your idea of a light lunch at your house, not enough to fill Henry up, and then he and I can stop about halfway back for a picnic."

"I know the perfect spot," Carrie said, "Along the little stream they call Puffy Creek. It will be flowing now and there's meadow alongside to spread a blanket. What will you pack?"

"I'll look around," Eleanor said as she finished the dish washing. The clean dishes sat stacked on the work surface. She went to the back door and tossed the used water out onto the grass. Then she put the clean dishes back into the pan, arranging the plates vertically around the edge with the cups, silverware, and cooking pans in the center, and poured the rest of the hot water over them.

Carrie was waiting with a linen towel to dry them. "There were three pieces of blueberry pie left."

"If Tommy didn't eat them," Eleanor said. She opened the pie safe. "Two left," she reported.

"Just right," said Carrie.

Eleanor changed the subject as she assembled utensils for the picnic in a large basket. "One of the Indian women down past the sand beach made this for me," she said, which reminded her of the topic of Dr. Rutherford's Lyceum the night before. "I thought the discussion at the Lyceum was interesting last night."

"It was," Carrie said. "Henry surprised me by taking such a harsh position against the red man. It was almost as if he had a personal vendetta against Geronimo."

"Jack Sailstad wasn't much softer, Carrie. Only Dr. Rutherford supported my essay."

"He even quoted from it," Carrie said. "I've always found Edward to be a fair-minded man. But Mr. Sailstad frowned deeply when Edward read the passage where you said you thought the Indian women who wove the baskets for him were treated just barely better than negro slaves and suggested they should be paid more."

Eleanor laughed as she removed her apron and hung it on a hook just inside the pantry. "I would have liked to comment on the uneven pay of the male and female school teachers, too."

"Will you write an essay for next week, On Baseball and the Community?

"No, about the only effect baseball has on this community

is to provide a reason for drinking to excess."

"You could say that."

"I won't. Henry likes baseball and I don't want to upset him by being negative about it. Now, I want you to sit down and read this book while I get dressed." Eleanor led Carrie into the parlor.

The parlor was papered in a pale yellow and blue stripe with a foot high header of twining roses. The window curtains were of white lace, dragging fashionably on the floor. The green paper window shades had been rolled up and the morning sun shown through obliquely.

Eleanor's large pine secretary sat in the corner, the writing surface open. It was the only piece of furniture in the house that belonged to her. Her father had given it to her and she had it moved whenever she moved. A tall glass-door hutch stood atop it, towering to the very ceiling. It held mostly books, but also a delicately painted table setting consisting of a dinner plate, a cup and saucer, and a platter; pale green with red and yellow roses. Eleanor opened the door and took out a dark red leather-bound book and handed it to Carrie.

Carrie settled herself in the rocking chair in front of the window and opened the book. It was titled Isis Unveiled and was by a Russian woman, H.P. Blavatsky. It was sub-titled, *A Master-Key to the Mysteries of Ancient and Modern Science and Theology.* The author was the corresponding secretary of the Theosophical Society.

Eleanor vanished behind the curtained doorway of the bedroom from which she called, "Read page xxix of the introduction. I have it marked, the two paragraphs on Elemental Spirits."

Carrie found the passage and read about the elemental spirits that "will either operate effects as the servile agents of general law, or may be employed by the disembodied spirits and by living adepts of magic and sorcery, to produce desired phenomenal results. Under the general designation of fairies, and fays, these spirits of the elements appear in the myth, fable, tradition, or poetry of all nations, ancient and modern." Turning the page she read further that these were the principle agents of the phenomena demonstrated at seances. She read a bit more and then flipped several pages at once and read where the author declared, "The ancients knew more concerning certain sciences than our modern savants have yet discovered." Pages beyond that, the writer moved between Hindu, Cabalism, and Christian beliefs with no apparent organization of her thoughts. Exhausted with the effort needed to follow the thesis the writer must be building, Carrie lay the book down on the sofa next to her and stood.

"Do you need any help in there?" she asked at the bedroom curtain.

"Oh, please," came the answer. "I can't pull these corset strings tight enough by myself."

"I wish you wouldn't wear one of those things, Eleanor," Carrie said as she pulled back the curtain and stepped into the dim interior of the room.

"Clothes don't look good without them," came the reply, "and I do want to look very fashionable and attractive today."

The dress Eleanor had laid out on the bed was one Carrie had never seen her wear. It was of crème colored lace, looking suspiciously like the lace at the windows in the parlor, with a three-inch band of black grosgrain ribbon at the hem. It was slim fitting down the front and hugely bustled behind. The waist to go with it was ruffled, with a black jabot at the throat and long ruffled cuffs. A black fitted bustle-jacket completed the look.

"I removed the train that dragged behind," Eleanor confided. "It got in the way too much."

"Isn't it rather dressy for a drive and a picnic?" Carrie asked.

"Wait 'til you see how wonderfully young and slim it makes me look." She turned so Carrie could pull the corset laces tight.

"How will you get out of this when you get home?"

"Maybe Henry will help," Eleanor said, blushing so Carrie could see the flush even on the back of her neck.

"Eleanor," Carrie reproached by the tone of her voice, "don't be silly."

"Mrs. Mac, next door, will undo me. We help each other all the time. I just need to knock four times on the wall there, and she'll come over."

"That's a nice arrangement," Carrie said. "I've nobody to help me, so I just don't wear all that stuff. I've learned to value comfort over fashion."

"That's why you'll never find another husband, Carrie. You really should move into town where you could meet a nice man. The school teacher at Mud Lake would be nice for you."

I've met a nice man, Carrie thought, conjuring up a vision of Drew McGeary, seeing mostly his laughing eyes. Maybe I'll do a little corseting for the walking suit, but nothing like this.

Half an hour later, Eleanor had been fitted into the dress. It did indeed make her look regal. Her coal black hair fell in two ringlets over her ears with the rest of it piled under a black wool hat trimmed with russet cock feathers. Eleanor pulled on black gloves and picked up a black parasol. If Henry wasn't impressed to the point of proposing, if he had any thoughts of doing so, which Carrie doubted, today ought to be the day.

Carrie surveyed the mound of baggage they had assembled and decided she would walk up to the store and have Henry drive back to pick up Eleanor and the baggage.

Henry waited for her by the cargo door. The company wagon, loaded with her sewing machine and other purchases, had been hitched to two patient dray horses for almost an hour. When he saw her exit the lane in front of Sailstad's house, he smiled. He had a bottle of sherry packed in ice secured in the wagon, as well as a picnic lunch put up by the cook at the Shelton House. He patted his waistcoat pocket where he had tucked a small diamond ring. Once his mind was made up, he saw no reason to delay. He'd wait until they were at her house, in that little cedar grove near the shore where the bench was, and then propose. He had no doubt she would accept. They would have an August wedding and he'd take her to Chicago for their wedding trip. He had to go then anyway to buy winter supplies for the store. He would tell her the good news about the marble assay in a couple of weeks.

He had decided she should move to town at once, and in the Spring, when he had accumulated enough money from the sale of the marble, they would build a big house east of town. He'd decided he needed to be close to Fayette to keep tabs on his other enterprises, even if he let the Company store go. Hugh Brandon could manage the quarry under his oversight.

Carrie saw him waiting and waved. Henry could see she didn't have her bag and realized he should have offered to pick her up. He climbed to the seat of the wagon and clucked to the team. Carrie stood by the side of the road and waited for him.

"Oh, thank you, Henry," Carrie said as he helped her up. "There was just too much for me to carry."

"I should have known that," Henry said.

Henry had placed a cushion on the seat for her, which Carrie appreciated, but then she began to wonder where Eleanor would sit. There was ample room across the wagon seat, of course, but the cushion was single. Suddenly she knew the plans she and Eleanor had made were a mistake, and at the same time she was grateful they had made them, no matter how difficult it would be for Eleanor.

She commented on the weather as the wagon creaked and jostled along the rutted road. The lake was calm with only light ripples on its surface. "I like days like this, but I suppose the schooner captains prefer a steady blow."

"The steamers can move well in this water, Carrie. I always take steamers when I travel to Chicago. Schooners will all be gone from the lake before too long, I expect."

Carrie didn't reply but searched among the half dozen

schooners in the harbor for Wave Dancer. "Have you ever met a Captain Drew McGeary?" she asked.

Henry glanced at her quickly and then clucked to the team as they began to climb the hill in front of the superintendent's house. This part of the road had been paved with large closely fitted blocks of limestone. While it kept the dust and mud down, it sometimes made slick footing for the horses. Sailstad did not like traffic on this part of the road , it was made to service his house and Dr. Rutherford's. After that it became just dirt packed with slag again.

"How would you know McGeary?" Henry asked.

"I met him at the quarry a week ago," she answered. Something in his tone and quick reply made her wary.

"He's a scoundrel," Henry said.

"He seemed very nice," Carrie defended.

"That's what makes him a scoundrel," Henry replied.

Chapter Seven

They were past Rutherford's house now and in a moment Henry would see Eleanor waiting on the porch for them in that silly lace dress. Henry stopped the team in front of the house and said just what Carrie expected him to.

"What is she doing in that dress?"

"She's coming with us," Carrie replied. "I invited her to ride along."

Henry jumped down from the wagon seat. His lack of an offer to help her down told Carrie he meant for her to stay put, which she did not intend to do.

"Which things are yours, Carrie?"

"Well, all of them," Carrie replied. Despite her intention to get down from the wagon, she hadn't moved.

"Eleanor is going to stay with you for a week with no luggage?"

"What do you mean a week?" Eleanor asked, a slight whine in her voice.

Henry stood up straight with Carrie's carpetbag in his hand and looked at her. "After I deliver Carrie's sewing machine I'm going to Manistique. I'll be gone several days."

He stopped and looked at Eleanor. "You look nice in that completely inappropriate dress, Eleanor."

He turned away from her and placed the carpetbag in the wagon. Carrie saw the anger in his eyes and knew he was lying about Manistique. She stood up.

"Stay there," Henry ordered her. "Are anymore of them yours?

Carrie nodded and sat down. "Yes, the small black bag and," she looked around him to where Eleanor stood, "the one with the feathers in it, Eleanor."

Eleanor's face was blotchy with angry red spots on her

chin and lower jaw. She picked up the bag of feathers Louella Rutherford had given Carrie and threw them at Henry. The poorly sealed bag broke open and feathers drifted through the air. Eleanor put both hands to her hot cheeks and gave a little squeal. Then she tried to bend down to pick up some of the feathers from the porch. As she did so, a ripping sound filled the air. Eleanor was not used to wearing such fashionably confining clothes and had bent from the waist instead of stooping genteelly.

Carrie leapt down from the wagon seat to pick up feathers too. The sound of Eleanor's dress ripping was followed by a sob and Henry's laughter. Carrie came around the horses just as the front door slammed behind Eleanor.

"Henry," Carrie admonished. "Stop laughing. I'm going in to help her out of those clothes. Pick up as many feathers as you can."

Eleanor was in the bedroom. She had flung herself across the bed and was crying into her folded arms. Carrie sat down and patted the heaving shoulders, making soothing sounds to calm Eleanor. The rip in the dress must be under the jacket, Carrie thought, because she couldn't see it. Finally, Eleanor quieted and looked up at Carrie.

"I hate him," she said. "Did you see how cruel his eyes were when he commented on my dress?"

"The thing to do now is get you out of that dress," Carrie said, "so you can mend it. It's a perfectly beautiful outfit and you looked beautiful in it. Neither of us knew he wasn't coming right back, we made a mistake."

Eleanor let Carrie help her remove the clothes and then the tightly laced corset underneath. The back of the tight waist was ripped from just below the collar to the bottom.

"I feel like such a fool."

"Well don't. It was just a plan that didn't work out."

"But I was so obvious, Carrie," she held Carrie's hand tightly. "So obvious."

Carrie didn't reply. She merely squeezed Eleanor's hand

and softly withdrew it. "I need to go now, Eleanor, he's waiting for me."

"Try to explain to him," Eleanor begged. "I mean, make up some excuse so it won't seem that the dress was for him."

"I'm afraid it's rather late for that, my dear. What I will do is scold him for behaving so badly." Carrie moved toward the door. "Thank you for your hospitality, dear. I'll see you next time I'm in town."

Henry was waiting for her on the porch. He was already looking contrite. "Will she be all right?"

"Of course she will, no thanks to you. Now let's get on our way. I'd hoped to be home by now."

Eleanor sat at the table in her dressing gown, sipping tea laced with a touch of blackberry brandy, replaying the disastrous scene in her head and wondering what she should do now. How could she ever face Henry again? Yet he had said she looked nice...there was that. Maybe she should mend the dress at once so it would be ready to wear if an occasion arose. Maybe he would come to apologize and take her to Escanaba on the Lady Washington for dinner at the House of Ludington. She needed to lose weight so the dress fit better. She'd have nothing but water to drink and a single slice of plain bread for a couple of days...until he got back.

At the same time she reached this decision, she popped the last bite of jam-smeared muffin into her mouth and rinsed it down with the rest of the tea. There was a tentative knock at the front door and Eleanor looked up to see the profile of Bertha Hartson though the lace covered window.

Eleanor sighed and went to the door. She opened it only a crack and stood behind it to cover her state of undress.

"Yes?" she said.

Bertha pushed the door open and strode in. Then she looked Eleanor up and down with something like a look of satisfaction on her face.

"Are you unwell, Mrs. Larkin?"

"No."

"Then why are you still in your dressing gown at this time of day?"

Eleanor stammered. "I...I tore my skirt and had to change clothes. I sat down for a cup of tea for a minute." She stopped then. "I am in my own home, Mrs. Hartson, and no one expects callers until afternoon."

"Well put something more suitable on at once, I'll wait."

"What would be suitable?" Eleanor had re-found her initial dislike of the woman. "Are we going to tea or for a walk in the woods?"

"Don't be snippy," replied Mrs. Hartson. "We are going to talk right here in your parlor."

"Then my dressing gown is perfectly suitable," Eleanor said and sat down in the overstuffed chair next to the stove. Bertha could stand or sit where she would. She sat in the rocking chair in front of the window.

"I'll come right to the point, Mrs. Larkin," Bertha snapped. "Aaron tells me that after I left the school you collected most of the Bibles I had passed out and put them in the closet. Is that true?"

Eleanor sighed. "Yes, Mrs. Hartson, it is true. Most of the children from the cabins are Catholic, and the Catholic Church does not allow its parishioners to have Bibles. I did it to protect you, and myself, from the reproach of Father Travally and to keep those parents from removing their children from the school and sending them to work in the furnaces."

"You had no right." Bertha Hartson's face puckered, her lips tightly pursed.

"You had no right to invade my schoolroom and pass those books out in the first place," Eleanor was angry and was not going to be intimidated by this woman.

Bertha stood. "I shall take this matter to Mr. Sailstad."

"Please do," Eleanor said and moved to open the door.

But Bertha had stopped and was looking at something on

the sofa. She stooped over and then picked up the heavy book Carrie had left laying there. Eleanor moved swiftly and took Isis Unveiled from Bertha's hands.

"Give that back to me," Bertha demanded.

"No, it is none of your business," Eleanor said, as she held the book behind her back.

"I saw the title, Mrs. It's a book about witchcraft!" Bertha cried. "What kind of a woman have they got teaching our children in this town?"

"Please go," Eleanor said, pointing to the open door.

Bertha Hartson leaned in close to Eleanor and sniffed. "And what's more you've been drinking. I can smell the liquor on your breath. Mr. Sailstad shall indeed hear about all this."

She sailed out the door and Eleanor slammed the door behind her so hard the glass rattled. She leaned her back against the doorframe and sobbed.

Henry's sour mood deepened as he drove the team over the bluff road. Once they passed the big hay barns where feed for the work horses of the furnace town was stored, he had planned to stop and admire the view back over Fayette and Snail Shell Harbor and beyond to Burnt Bluff with Carrie, in order to begin to set a mood. The water was deep-water-blue with white caps breaking like the ruffled lace cuffs on Eleanor's dress. The day was warming and it would have been a perfect day for the picnic he had packed away, but Eleanor had spoiled it all. And Carrie wasn't speaking to him.

Well, nothing ventured. "The lake is certainly blue this morning," he said.

"It usually is," Carrie replied without looking either at him or the lake.

"But it's so breathtaking after the snow and ice all winter."

"I believe the ice went out more than a month ago, Henry." Her tone was dry and uninterested.

Before the conversation deteriorated to argument, Henry gave in to the silence Carrie seemed to want. He didn't even

call her attention to the spring beauties and yellow adder-
tongues he saw blooming along the road. It was Carrie who
finally broke the silence between them, and it was shortly
before they reached the road that turned off towards Cedar
Harbor.

"You really hurt Eleanor's feelings, Henry. Why did you lie
about being gone for several days?"

"Eleanor is trying to trap me, Carrie. You know that and
you probably helped her lay her trap this morning. She's been
hinting for weeks that I need a wife to take care of me."

"Perhaps you do," Carrie said. "Eleanor would make a
good wife for you, too."

"I intend to marry soon, but not Eleanor Larkin."

"Who then?"

Henry groaned inwardly. Nothing was going right. They
should be under a shady tree, with a glass of sherry to sip and
then he could take the ring out of his pocket, sink to one knee
even, and ask Carrie to marry him. If he didn't speak now, all
would be lost.

He stopped the wagon and turned to her. "You, Carrie. I
want you to marry me."

Carrie looked at him with the most astonished look on her
face that it would have made Henry laugh under any other
circumstance. "Me?"

"Yes." He fumbled in his pocket for the ring and held it out
to her. "Carrie Grey, will you marry me?"

Carrie laughed. Henry reddened.

"Oh, Henry, oh my. Henry, dear friend, I don't know what
to say."

"Say yes?" he reached for her hand in an attempt to slip
the ring on to her finger but just then the horses shied at
something and he had to jerk away to grab the reins. The ring
tumbled from his hands and unto the wagon floor. Carrie
reached down for it, brushing her cheek against his knee as
she reached.

She looked at the small diamond on the gold band, turned

it this way and that to catch the sun and make it sparkle. Henry held his breath and waited, driving the team slowly down the rough lane to Cedar Harbor. He kept her in the corner of his eye as he drove, trying to read her face.

The lane turned, left the open field and entered the deep shade of the stand of cedars, and then suddenly the view opened up again and Lake Michigan in all its blueness lay before them. A tall schooner, white sails gleaming in the sun, lay at anchor in Cedar Harbor. Henry heard Carrie catch her breath, and then she spoke.

"Henry, I am flattered at your proposal, but no, I will not marry you." She leaned over and placed the small ring into his breast pocket and fluttered a light kiss onto his cheek. "I'm sorry."

Before he could react, she was down from the wagon seat and running towards the harbor. Henry looked closely at the schooner moored there and suddenly recognized her; Wave Dancer, owned by Andrew McGeary. Hadn't Carrie asked about him yesterday?

Henry sat for a moment on the wagon seat watching Carrie search for Captain McGeary. The scoundrel was nowhere in sight. Henry switched the lines against the team's rumps and drove the wagon along the lane between the cedar groves and the lakeshore and up to the house.

Carrie came up to the wagon as he started to unload it.

"You certainly seem excited about something," Henry said to her.

She colored and turned away, carrying one of the brown string-tied packages of fabric up to the house. Henry followed her silently with another.

The house was cold from being closed up for three days. The abundance of cedars shading the house kept it cool in summer and protected from the winds and thus warmer in winter. Henry had to admit the house was well placed. The blue water of the lake was visible from the parlor window as well as the accursed schooner, at which Carrie was staring.

"I'll build you a fire," Henry said. "You decide where you want the sewing machine and clear the space for it."

Carrie turned from the window and looked absently around the parlor and then turned back to the window. "I wonder where Drew is," she mumbled to herself as Henry passed her on his way back to the wagon for another package. When he returned, Carrie was lighting the kitchen range and arranging dampers. She looked like she was in charge of her senses again.

"Look here, Carrie," Henry said. "I told you Drew McGeary was a scoundrel and I meant it. He's a pirate and heaven only knows what else. I can see you're starry eyed about him, but, lands end, Carrie, you can't be serious?"

Carrie looked up from the stove. "I think I'd like the sewing machine in the second bedroom, Henry. Put that parcel on the table, I'll take care of it later."

Henry shrugged and dropped the parcel on the table and went back outside. He had just climbed into the wagon to wrestle the sewing machine to the edge where he could lift it down when he heard someone come up behind him.

"Could ye use a bit of help with that, Henry?"

"What are you doing here, McGeary?" Henry growled. "Shouldn't you be out salvaging lumber from some luckless lumber hooker?"

Drew ignored the growling anger in Henry's voice and leapt up onto the wagon bed. He helped Henry carry the machine to the back of the wagon and then jumped down. "Hand 'er down, Henry."

Henry knew Drew could carry the machine without help. He was built like a bull and Henry had watched him in action often enough to know he was as strong as one. As soon as Drew had a grip on the machine from below he positioned it in his arms and started towards the house. Henry rushed ahead and opened the door for him calling in to Carrie.

"Here it is, my dear, where shall we set it?"

"In here," Carrie called from the second bedroom. "I've

cleared a space for it."

When she looked up and saw Drew carrying the machine, she blushed. Henry tried to push his way into the room and jostled against Drew, trapping Drew's hand between the machine and the door jam.

"Hells bells," Drew exploded. "Get out of the way."

Carrie rushed forward to try to free Drew's hand and all three became stuck in the doorway momentarily until Carrie gave Henry a shove on the chest that sent him tumbling backward onto the floor. With space now, Drew set the machine down and shook his hand to relieve the cramping pain in it. From the floor, Henry moaned.

"Oh dear," Carrie said. "Are either of you hurt?"

Henry pushed himself to his feet and brushed off his clothing. Drew looked from Carrie to Henry and started to laugh. "What a bunch of clowns we are," he said. "Of course we aren't hurt. Now exactly where shall I put this thing?"

"There," Carrie said, pointing to the wall opposite the door.

Drew positioned the machine and then catching Carrie by the elbow guided her towards the doorway. "One at a time this time," he said. Henry followed helplessly behind them. He saw the way Carrie looked up at Drew and knew there was no hope for him.

"Henry is supposed to give me a sewing lesson," she told Drew, "but I know very well how to sew and the machine looks easy enough to use just by following the book."

Having been dismissed, Henry began to back towards the door. "Well, I'll be going, then," he said. "If you need any help just stop into the store."

"But don't you want some lunch?" Carrie asked.

"No," Henry said, "I've got a picnic lunch in the wagon. I had the cook at the Shelton House put it up for me." He watched her expression and it was as he had hoped, remorseful, knowing full well he'd packed the picnic lunch for the two of them to celebrate their engagement.

At the end of the driveway, Henry stopped for a moment, uncertain what he wanted to do. He thought of heading back to Fayette and Stoddy's Hole In The Rock Saloon, where he could spend the night with Peony. But unless he had spoken for her in advance she'd be busy. Much as he'd like to keep a woman like Peony all to himself, he did let Stoddy use her for their more discriminating patrons.

So he turned north. He'd get drunk at one of the saloons in Van's Harbor and then take a room in the Garden House for the night. With any luck a bordello schooner would put in and he'd get his woman. He looked back over his shoulder ruefully. No it wasn't likely Drew McGeary would stroll through the saloons in Van's Harbor and Garden with a feather in his cap tonight. He was busy wooing Carrie Grey.

He flicked his whip at the horses and tore off down the rocky road, heedless now of the beautiful spring day and the deep blue of the lake along which the road ran. He needed another way to get at the marble quarry and he'd think of something.

Chapter Eight

D rew stood on the porch leaning against one of the timbers that supported the roof overhang and looked carefully at Carrie. She was taller than he'd remembered from their meeting two weeks ago, and perhaps not as pretty as he'd thought that storm tossed night. But still, she was attractive and well worth some dallying. Besides he admired her spunk.

Carrie finished putting away the contents of the parcels and then felt ready to face Drew. She'd begged for a moment to "put things to rights in the house first" before joining him on the porch. She straightened her hair and finally stepped though the doorway.

"Good," Drew said, standing straight up and stepping away from his leaning post. "Now I've got a man with me from Chicago wants to meet you. He went ahead down to the quarry."

"Chicago?" Carrie was stunned. "To see me? And he's gone to the quarry?" Her hand was over her heart because it had suddenly occurred to her it had to be about the marble. She started at once toward the path that led that way and then stopped when she realized Drew was not behind her.

"Aren't you coming?" she turned and asked him.

"It's quarry business, Ma'am," Drew replied, "and none of my affair. I'll just wait here in the shade and have a pipe or two of tobac."

Carrie was a bit flustered by this, torn between the excitement of a man from Chicago coming about the quarry and wanting to be with Drew. "Well, just make yourself at home then," she said. "I probably won't be long."

As she walked along the path to the bluff end and the quarry Carrie reasoned with herself. The man had just come, like others did, to buy some dressed limestone. So what if he came from Chicago? No one would come in person to report that the sample she'd sent for polishing was indeed marble.

Soon Carrie noticed that she couldn't hear the usual noises that came from the quarry works. There was no pounding on stone, or the sound of mauls tapping the wedges carefully into place. Instead she was aware of the abundance of spring bird song. She identified the two-note whistle of the chick-a-dee, and the trilling call of the robins. It was mating season and the birds were advertising freely for mates.

Suddenly she remembered Henry's proposal. What on earth would she tell Eleanor? Need she tell her at all? As a friend, could she not tell her? After all, Eleanor had really and truly expected Henry to propose to her. She believed the spiritualist, that Mrs. Emma Britten who claimed to be intimate with fairies. What nonsense. But Eleanor believed it and was sure the last message of the evening had been meant for her: 'Your mother is so happy for you, L, about your upcoming marriage.'

Oh, what a mess Henry had made of things by proposing instead to her. Why, she'd never even considered such a thing as marrying him, or anybody else for that matter. She did consider Henry a friend, but there were things about him she didn't like. The picture of him in the store, touching himself when he thought no one was looking, for instance. Disgusting.

Carrie reached the quarry edge. In the distance she could see Hugh Brandon, surrounded by his sons, standing with a short stout man in a striped suit. She hurried her step. Hugh spotted her and waved. Then the boys dispersed back to their work and Hugh and the visitor walked towards her.

Hugh didn't waste any time getting to the point when they met. "Missus Grey, dis is Mr. Bill Jenny, from Chicago. He come ta buy marble from ya."

Carrie nodded her head in acknowledgment and almost extended her hand in greeting, but pulled it back, wondering if it would be proper. Then Mr. Jenny reached his hand towards her, and she did likewise. His hands were rough, like a workman's hands. From the fine cut of his suit she had expected the smooth hands of a gentleman.

"Pleased to meet you, Mrs. Grey," he said. He had a deep resonant voice, small eyes that squinted against the brilliant sun, and a long Roman nose. Carrie put his age at about forty-two.

"I'm sorry I wasn't here when you arrived," Carrie said. "I'd been to Fayette for the weekend."

"I know. I just missed you there, so the good Captain of that schooner said he knew the place and would bring me right here. Your man here," he indicated Hugh, " says you have yet to receive the assay informing you that you have a good grade of marble in this bluff."

"Yes, er, no, we never got a reply. I was about to send another sample."

Mr. Jenny pulled an envelope from the inner pocket of his jacket. "Well, I've got a copy of it. It's dated February, addressed to you at the General Store in Fayette. Here, you can read for yourself."

Carrie took the letter and read it. The sample they had sent had polished quickly and was indeed building quality marble. Carrie hid her elation in a dignified smile and then asked her visitor, "And how did you come by this, Mr. Jenny?"

"Shall we find a place in the shade, Ma'am? The sun is making me a little overheated."

"Of course," Carrie said. "Let's sit on the bench Mr. Brandon has in that cedar grove."

Carrie let him take her elbow and guide her over the rocky surface to the edge of the woods where they sat on the bench. It was cool in the grove, and noticeably quieter.

"I'm an architect," Mr. Jenny began. "I've put up some big buildings in the city of Chicago and I make it a practice to visit the assay office from time to time to locate good building stone. Your marble assay is a matter of public record. I don't generally do these things myself, but I was due for a little vacation, so I boarded a north bound schooner three days ago and had a pleasant sail up Lake Michigan to see how much of this marvelous stone you might have."

"And did Hugh show you?"

"He did, he did. And I want to buy all the marble you produce this season. I'm building a mansion for Mr. John Farwell, he's one of the Farwell brothers of the department store moguls in Chicago, and I want to use your marble. Now Mr. Brandon has told me you don't have the equipment for mining the marble, so here's what I propose."

He went on to lay out a plan whereby he would furnish all the tools needed to quarry the marble, along with a crew to teach Hugh what he needed to know, in exchange for all the marble he needed, for which he would pay her three dollars a cord.

"I know that's two dollars less than I would normally pay, but when this order is complete, the equipment and the knowledge will be yours."

Carrie stood up. She was too excited to continue to sit calmly. She paced in front of the bench while Mr. Jenny sat calmly, twirling his polished walking stick in his hands.

"How many cords of marble do you anticipate, Mr. Jenny?"

"Two thousand, at least."

Carrie almost gasped. Six thousand dollars, in one season. She'd be rich!

"Can we remove and ship that much in one season?"

"You can. In addition to the supervisors who will work with your quarry master, and whom I will pay, I'll send up some experienced laborers for you. You'll have to pay them, of course, and have someplace for them to live, but they can teach others, local men, so you'll have a nice business going forward. And there will be other contracts, with me for sure, and perhaps others. It's almost as good as a gold-mine for you, Mrs. Grey."

Carrie sat down again and then stood. "I want Hugh to listen to this," she said. She could see Hugh standing where they had left him, looking their way. She waved him to join them.

"Mr. Brandon has been with me from the beginning," she explained. "In fact it was him come to me with the idea of mining the limestone a couple of years back. If he thinks your proposal is good, we will find a lawyer in Escanaba to draw up the contract."

Hugh stood while Mr. Jenny told him his plan. He went into more detail about the type of equipment involved, the number of laborers they would need, and the time frame of getting started. While she listened, Carrie ciphered the numbers she was hearing and knew that she would make a tidy profit from the deal and have the equipment to continue removing the marble after the contract was fulfilled. After all questions of both Carrie and Hugh had been answered, Hugh asked Carrie to step away with him for a minute.

They walked a short distance away, out of earshot of Mr. Jenny.

"Dis is a good deal, Missus. And I like da man, Mr. Bill Jenny. I feel he's honest wid ya, and we can do what he sez. My boys can keep cutting limestone like before and da marble be a separate operation."

"Then I'll agree," Carrie said. "And as soon as the marble crew arrives I will give you a salary of five hundred a year in addition to your regular percentage."

"Tanks," Hugh mumbled. "I knew you'd be fair."

"We'll have to build a couple of cottages," Carrie said, "for the laborers he's sending. I'll take care of hiring that done. I'll set them a little apart from your dwellings in case the laborers are rowdy. Perhaps Mrs. Brandon would like to provide board for the men? She could charge them a dollar a week and make a little extra."

Hugh mopped his forehead of sweat and grinned. "Today all our dreams come true, Missus."

On their walk back to Cedar Harbor, Mr. Jenny admired the tall wind-sculpted white pines scattered among the poplars and cedars.

"Michigan white pine," he said. "One of the finest woods in the world. Pine used to be our marble in the era of Greek Revival buildings. Now we use Indiana Limestone and soon your Michigan Marble. It's fire proof, beautiful, and fit to face any building."

"I suppose fire-proof is foremost in people's minds in Chicago now," Carrie said.

"It is indeed," Jenny answered. "That fire, what ten years ago now? That fire made stone the building material of choice. If your stone turns out as pretty as I think it will, I think we can compete with the Athens Marble they're taking out of the Lemont Quarries in Cook County."

"Do you think there's enough of it?" Carrie asked.

"How much property do you own, Mrs. Grey?"

"Just the bluff and the field east of the house."

"I advise you to buy any other significant rock outcroppings along the lake that you can, and as soon as you can."

"Is there also marble at Fayette?" Carrie asked.

"I can't be sure," Jenny replied, "but I saw some very good quality limestone in the buildings at Fayette. Some things, however, should be left alone for their sheer beauty, and the bluff on Snail Shell Harbor at Fayette is one of them. I for one, hope no one ever quarries that bluff."

"But they already have. They blast more limestone out of there every week to feed the furnaces."

"That won't go on forever, Mrs. Grey. Two, three years at most and Fayette will be a ghost town. There are new processes coming in the iron and steel business that will make the town obsolete. Then the harbor will be calm and blue again like God first made it, and the white bluffs will gleam above it in the sun. The forest will grow back and you'll hear birds singing there instead of the clank and roar of machinery and dogs barking all night long."

"Why, Mr. Jenny, you are a poet at heart," Carrie teased.

"I think I am," Mr. Jenny replied, patting Carrie's hand where it lay on his arm.

They had arrived back at the house where they found Drew McGeary, true to his word, waiting on the porch. He may have smoked a pipe or two, but they came upon him taking a nap, snoring softly.

Mr. Jenny cleared his throat, then rapped on the porch railing with his fancy walking stick. That brought McGeary upright immediately. Both Carrie and Mr. Jenny laughed at the startled and sheepish expression on Drew's face.

"See here now, Captain McGeary," Mr. Jenny said. "What will you charge to take the Lady and me to Escanaba this afternoon?"

"I need to go there anyway," Drew replied. "Usual fare is fifty cents."

Jenny dug in his pocket, extracted a leather change purse and handed Drew three fifty cent pieces. "Two to go over, one to come back," he said.

"When will ye want to be underway?" Drew asked.

"Oh, I do think we should have something to eat first," said Carrie. "I'm hungry, at least."

Even as she spoke, Carrie wondered what there was to feed her guests. Anything she had would take time. She'd already arranged for Francine to come up to feed the chickens and milk the cow again today and tomorrow as she anticipated having to stay overnight in Escanaba while the contracts were drawn up.

"Me cook aboard will feed us," Drew answered, "no extra charge."

"Then I'll just pack a bag and be ready in a few minutes," Carrie said.

Inside the house Carrie sorted through her meager closet of clothing, regretting that she hadn't had time to use the new sewing machine. She finally changed into a russet brown wool skirt, a clean white blouse, and put on her new shoes. The old brown hat would have to do. She wondered if she dared take the time to replace some of the worn feathers. Yes, she would. She opened the parcel of feathers Luella Rutherford had given her and found two of the long red feathers plucked from the tail of the Irish rooster that were undamaged after their brief freedom in the dust in front of Eleanor's. She pulled out the worn turkey feathers and replaced them with the reds and then stood back to admire them. Well, she decided, it wasn't the best, but it was a little better.

If only Eleanor were here. She had such a way with clothes. Her only trouble was matching the outfit to the event. Eleanor choose for flattery and prettiness, not for practicality or what might suit the purpose. Perhaps everything would have gone differently this morning if Eleanor had just worn a walking suit instead of a tea dress.

Finally placing some toiletries and fresh linens inside her carpet bag, Carrie was ready. Now that she knew she would have enough money, she decided to visit Lauerman's Department store in the morning and buy a new, ready-made, walking suit and the undergarments it required to look right.

The men sat on the porch talking. When Carrie came out, Drew jumped up to carry her bag and Mr. Jenny offered her his arm.

"I was just telling Captain McGeary that if I could transport your harbor down to Chicago and build a suitable house on it, I could sell it for more than the $400,000 Farwell is paying me to build his mansion on Pearson Street."

Carrie gasped. "Four hundred thousand dollars! How could a house possibly cost that much?"

Jenny laughed. "For one thing, it's very big, and for another, Mr. Farwell is willing to pay that much. He's having it built right next door to his brother's. He wants to outdo Charles and indulge Emma, his wife."

"Well, I'd like to see a house like that," Carrie said.

"And you shall," said Jenny. "If you come to Chicago, you

look me up and I'll show you some of the mansions I've built."

"Chicago," Carrie said, a dreamy quality crept into her voice. "I can't even imagine Chicago."

Jenny guided Carrie up the gangplank and aboard Wave Dancer.

"We'll just go forward to my cabin," Drew said, "and the cook will bring up lunch as soon as we clear Garden Bay."

Chapter Nine

Bertha Hartson maintained her temper towards Eleanor Larkin, all the way from the duplex on Cedar Lane to the big white house on the hill where Jack Sailstad lived, by repeating and embellishing to herself the insults and sins to which Eleanor had subjected her. She paused at the gate to renew her initial indignation about the Bibles being taken from the young Catholics, and then plowed up the steps and rapped sharply at the door. After a brief pause she knocked again. A high-pitched voice from behind her made Bertha turn swiftly on her heel.

"They ain't there. They went hoity-toitying to Escanaba for three days. They took the maid and the children, too."

Bertha squinted into the sun, trying to locate the shrill voice that had spoken.

"I'm over here, ma'am, hanging clothes." The woman's voice rose at the end of the statement, making it almost a question.

Once Bertha spotted the woman she quickly descended the porch steps and crossed the street to the red saltbox house where the speaker stood pegging diapers to the line to dry. Laundry ought not be done on Saturday, Bertha thought, it was Monday work. The woman was obviously lazy. Well, her anger was not to be wasted. Perhaps this woman knew something useful about Eleanor Larkin and her habits.

"You're the new preacher's wife, ain't ya? My husband, Frank, he's French don't ya know, so we go to St. Peter's."

Bertha pursed her lips and regarded the young woman. A dirty-faced boy played in a pile of beach sand next to the open door.

"Is your boy in school, Missus?"

Shirley LeComte looked around at the boy as if she had

not known he was there. "Frankie? Yeah. He's six. He can read McGuffry's first reader already."

"So you know Mrs. Larkin?"

"Course. Everybody knows the school teacher."

Bertha came closer, ducking under the flapping diapers.

"Did you know she has books in her house on witchcraft?"

Shirley dropped a handful of clothespins. "Witchcraft?"

Bertha nodded with satisfaction. The woman had been suitably shocked. Bertha bent and began to help her pick up the clothespins. As they crouched close to the ground, Bertha repeated her embellished version of the visit she had just had with Eleanor Larkin, who was not even properly dressed at this time of the morning.

"I just think Mr. Sailstad, as President of the school board, ought to know what manner of woman is teaching our young people."

"Oh, why I never imagined. Why, Mrs. Larkin has been the teacher here, don't ya know, for almost ten years."

Bertha hadn't realized her foe had been entrenched that long. Who would believe her story if Eleanor hid the book?

"From what I heard she took part in that séance at the opera house on Thursday."

"Oh yeah," Shirley said. "I was there."

At a surprised glance from Bertha, Shirley hastened to add. "I play the organ for the theatre. And at St. Peter's, too, don't ya know. I've a talent for it. And besides, everybody who was anybody was there too."

With all the clothespins in hand the two women stood. "Why don't you sit in the shade there, Ma'am, and I'll get us a cool drink."

"You can call me Bertha. And you are?"

"Shirley LeComte."

"Pleased to meet you, I'm sure, Shirley," Bertha said as she settled herself gratefully onto the narrow wooden bench in the shade of the house. The sun was almost at its zenith, so even that little bit of shade would be gone soon. She could feel moisture coating her body, both from the exertion of her walk and the weight of the brown wool-tweed walking suit she wore.

Shirley handed her a glass of cold water and then sat down on the bench. "Mrs. Larkin has always been out-spoken. Frank don't like her, don't ya know, says she's too uppity for a woman."

"I had the same impression about her," Bertha said. "Does she go to St. Peter's church? I haven't seen her at any of our meetings."

"Oh no. She don't go to St. Peter's. Most of the upper crust in town don't go there. They's mostly protestants."

"Then she's not a Christian," Bertha declared. "She studies heathen religions like Hindu and the Muslims. And witchcraft."

Shirley clicked her tongue against her teeth.

"Let's see if your son has picked up any of her nonsense," Bertha said. "Come here, lad."

Frankie, ankles buried in the sand, did not respond.

"Frankie," his mother called. "Come on over here and talk to the lady."

Frankie hung his head and buried his fingers in the sand.

"Ah, he's shy," Shirley said. She went over and picked Frankie up out of the sand and came back to sit on the bench with him on her lap. He was a small boy for six and he curled into his mother's lap and hid his face against her bosom.

"Come on, Frankie, the lady won't hurt you."

"Bless you, child," Bertha said in a tone she adapted to speak down to children, "Mrs. Hartson wouldn't hurt a pretty boy like you. I just want to ask you about your teacher."

"You like Mrs. Larkin, don't you Frankie?" Shirley prompted.

Frankie nodded his head against her bosom.

"Now see here, Frankie," Bertha said. "You ought to look at me when I'm talking to you."

She reached towards the boy as if to take him from Shirley, at which Shirley cradled him more closely and prevented Bertha from touching him.

"Don't touch him," she said, her voice shriller than it had been before. With one hand she reached for Frankie's chin and turned it up to her. She kissed him on the end of the nose and then turned his face so he was looking at Bertha.

"This is Mrs. Hartson, Frankie. She's a new lady in town and she wants to know about the teacher."

"I have a boy about your age," Bertha said, her tone more softened and cajoling this time. "His name is Aaron. Maybe you saw him in school on Friday when I was there and gave everyone a little book."

Frankie nodded.

"Did you bring the book home, Frankie?"

Frankie shook his head no.

"Why not?"

"Teacher took it."

Bertha gave Shirley a triumphant look. "There, you see, she wouldn't even let the poor child keep the New Testament I gave him."

"A New Testament? Isn't that a Bible?"

"Well of course it is," Bertha replied, "The good news of the Savior."

"Catholics don't read the Bible, Mrs. Hartson, the Priests read it to us. It's much too confusing, don't ya know, for just anyone to make meaning out of it. Of course, Mrs. Larkin took them."

Bertha was upset by this but covered her exasperation and continued to question Frankie.

"Do you know anything about witches, Frankie?"

An affirmative nod of his head.

"Did Mrs. Larkin teach you about witches?"

Another yes.

"Are you afraid of witches?"

Frankie's eyes flashed up at his mother and then to Mrs. Hartson.

"Sometimes," he said softly.

Shirley asked him why he was only afraid of witches sometimes.

"Only the black witches," Frankie said. "The white witches are nice."

Bertha Hartson pounced on that. "How are white witches nice?"

"Because they do good witching. Like for the hundred year lady."

"I think he means Sleeping Beauty," Shirley said. "It's his favorite story."

"Did teacher ever tell you how to do 'good witching'?"

Frankie's eyes got big and he looked up at his mother before he answered.

"You got to get real quiet inside, like we do in m'tation every morning."

"What is m'tation?"

Shirley nodded that it was all right for him to tell.

"Teacher makes us sit quiet and counts backwards while we get all quiet inside. Then we just think about something nice for a while and then we wake up."

"What do you think about, Frankie?" Bertha leaned forward and gripped Frankie's arm. "What do you think about?"

"Ooh," he wailed and shrugged his shoulders away from her. "I don't know," he whined. Shirley placed her arms around him like a shield.

It wasn't much, but Bertha had a starting point. "Well, you go play some more now, lad."

Frankie got down from his mother's lap and vanished around the corner of the house.

"Well, I'll get to the bottom of this. Mark my words," Bertha said. "What business does she have teaching meditation to the children? That's a heathen practice and I don't want my Christian son taught by a heathen."

Shirley stood and smoothed the wrinkles out of her skirt and reached for Bertha's empty glass. Bertha held on to her glass and asked Shirley if there was anything else she'd noticed about Eleanor Larkin that was odd. Shirley paused in her attempt to retrieve the glass from Bertha.

"There was the time she submitted a paper to the lyceum, that's Dr. Rutherford's weekly discussion group, about the Hindu gods. Dr. Rutherford said it made interesting reading, but didn't add anything to the discussion that night."

"What was the discussion about?"

Shirley tapped her long slender finger against her lips. "It had something to do with the constitution and freedom of religion we got here. I can't remember exactly how it was."

"But the teacher was well versed in this Hindu god?"

Shirley shrugged her shoulders and snatched the glass from Bertha. "Yeah, I guess so."

No longer having possession of the water glass, Bertha stood. "Well, I must be going. It was so nice to meet you Mrs. LeComte."

"And you."

Bertha moved off down the hill looking this way and that for an older school child who could tell her more about the 'morning meditations' Mrs. Larkin conducted at school.

By evening, Mrs. Hartson had the town in a general hubbub about Eleanor Larkin. All that remained was for Jack Sailstad to return home and then the witch would be on next boat out of here.

Chapter Ten

It was the Thursday after Carrie had returned from her trip to Escanaba with Drew and Mr. Jenny that Tommy Larkin came. It was well before noon and the horse he was riding had been ridden too hard. He entered the yard at a gallop and dismounted. Carrie had heard the pounding of the horse's hooves and was standing on the lane waiting for whoever it was. She felt herself go rigid when she saw Tommy Larkin. Something must have happened to Eleanor!

Tommy fell against her and she hugged him close, waiting for him to speak. When he finally drew away the look on his face was a mixture of defiance and despair. He opened his mouth to speak, but tears started to his eyes at once.

"Thomas," Carrie said, touching her finger to his lips. "First you must cool that horse down, and then yourself. Walk her halfway up the lane and back. I'll fix us something cool to drink and we'll sit in the cedar arbor. Then you can tell me what's troubling you."

Tommy nodded and swallowed a great gulp of air. It moved past his Adam's apple, swelling it momentarily, and then he picked up the horse's reins and walked with her back up the way he'd come. Carrie went into the house to get two glasses of tea, her mind racing. Clearly something had happened to Eleanor. Carrie ran possibilities through her mind. Injury? Death? But why would Tommy come? Surely Edward would have sent someone else to her if Eleanor were injured and needed Carrie's help? Well, she wasn't going to divine it by herself, she'd have to wait for Tommy to tell her.

Tommy was just returning with the horse as Carrie came out onto the porch.

"Bring her down to the lake and let her drink," she called to Tommy, and she headed for the cedar arbor. The horse drank and then waded into the water and refused to be led out again.

"Leave her," Carrie called. "She likes the coolness. Only keep an eye on her."

The cedar arbor was almost too cool this morning and Carrie found a seat in some filtered sunlight. Tommy sat on one of the stumps and stared at the ground for several moments, the glass cradled in his large hands. He began to speak softly and Carrie moved closer to hear him.

"This morning the new preacher's wife..."

"Mrs. Hartson," Carrie supplied.

"Yeah, Hartson," Carrie could hear the hatred in his voice. "She come to the house and told Mom she had been to the school board about her and that she could just as well start packing up her stuff. She said Mom was lucky she wasn't being tarred and feathered, which is what ought to happen to witches in a righteous town."

"Oh, Tommy," Carrie said. Her hands flew up to cover her face and then she reached out to touch the boy's shoulder. "What did your mother do?"

"She ordered the bitch, oh, excuse me, Mrs. Grey, I didn't mean to say that."

"But you did, and I think that is exactly what Mrs. Hartson is. Now go on."

"Well, she told the woman to leave at once and the bi... woman just sat there and said she would not leave until Mom had given her the book on witchcraft that she had seen there a few days before. Mom told her again to get out. I can still see the look on that b... ah woman's face, like she'd won a great prize and was happy. Not that she'd won, but that someone else had lost. Then she crossed her arms over her chest and just stared at Mom.

"I asked what it was all about and Mrs. Hartson said my mother had been teaching the children at the school witchcraft and she had proof. My mom stood up and again told the woman to leave. She didn't say it nicely, either. She screamed at her to leave and leave at once. Mrs. Hartson stood and went towards Mom's secretary where she kept her books, but before she could open the doors of it, Mom was there in front of it and she hit Mrs. Hartson with a ruler, which had been lying on the desk. Then Mrs. Hartson flew at my mom and got her by the hair and both of them tumbled over the rocking chair and landed on the floor.

"I didn't know what to do, so I threw the glass of tea that was on the table into Mrs. Hartson's face. Then Mom stood up and then the other lady. She was spitting and wiping her face and I grabbed her by the arm and pushed her out the door and slammed it, and locked it. She stood on the porch screaming and pounding on the door for a while and Mom ran into the bedroom and fell on the bed and cried."

Carrie kept patting Tommy's shoulder and when he was finished with the story handed him her own untouched glass of cool tea and he drank the whole glass without stopping.

"And then what?" she asked.

"I finally got Mom to stop crying and she told me to take all of her books out of the secretary and down to the cellar. I told her if anybody came looking for them, that's the first place they'd look. I asked her which book the woman wanted and Mom showed me the new one she'd just got. She saved for three months to buy that book, Mrs. Grey."

"Isis Unveiled," Carrie stated.

Tommy nodded. "Yes, that's the one. Is it about witchcraft, Mrs. Grey?"

"No," Carrie assured him. "It is a book about the Eastern Religions, but to a woman like Mrs. Hartson, with a mind about the size of her small toe, any book but the Bible is considered heretical. What did you do with it?"

Tommy suddenly looked at the horse wading in the lake with an expression of horror on his face. "Oh dash it all! Oh, man alive."

He fairly flew out of the cedar arbor and down to the lake. Heedless of his shoes and clothes he waded towards the horse and grasping her reins he pulled her into shore. From his frantic opening of the saddlebag, Carrie divined where the book was. With a heavy sign of relief, Tommy drew the still-dry red leather-bound book out and hugged it against his chest.

"Now it's time for a proper grooming of that horse, young man," Carrie said. "Get up to the barn where you can take that saddle off and she can be combed, fed, and stabled properly. Take the book with you and secure it someplace out there, but make sure you take the saddlebag back to Fayette with you. Dr. Rutherford's groom will notice if you don't return it.

"How did you pay for the horse, by the way?"

"I used my own money," Tommy said proudly. "I just told the man I wanted to ride out to Garden for the day."

"Well, come up to the house when you've finished," Carrie said, "and you can tell me the rest of it. Are you hungry?"

Tommy didn't answer, but Carrie knew he was. She had known Tommy since he was eight years old, and there was never a time he wasn't hungry. For a moment the thought flashed through her mind that if she hadn't helped Captain McGeary into harbor that night, the wretched preacher's wife might have drowned. But then, she would never have met Drew.

While Tommy ate the plate of stew Carrie put in front of him he explained that his mother wanted Carrie to come in to town, right away if she could, because she feared that her next caller would be Jack Sailstad, who was not only the General Manager of the furnace town, but President of the School Board.

"Isn't there anyone in town showing support for your mother?" Carrie asked.

"I don't know, Ma'am. There haven't been many kids in school all week and Mom thought maybe there was measles or something, but when she went to the kids houses, nobody was home."

"Or not answering the door," Carrie said. "Now you finish up there and then go hook up that fancy horse to my carriage while I put a few things together. I'll meet you on the lane."

Although the school board meeting was held in the Sailstad parlor, it was packed with people. Eleanor did not attend, but Carrie did, along with Luella Rutherford. Edward said it would be a mob and he saw no quarter in attending. Jack already knew that he felt the charges against Eleanor were a lot of rot. Grace Sailstad was conspicuously absent. Mrs. Hartson was loudly there and had to be officially shushed by Jack Sailstad several times. The school board members were Shirley LaComte, John Peterson, Marie Scofield, and Peter Weglarz.

"We have met tonight," Sailstad intoned in his take control tone of voice, "to listen to your concerns about our school teacher, Eleanor Larkin. I will remind you that Mrs. Larkin has taught in our school for many years and, until now, no one has ever found any fault with her. Am I right?"

Less than half of the room nodded or voiced affirmative.

"To make it very clear, Mrs. Hartson, the wife of the new Congregational minister, has charged that Mrs. Larkin is teaching witchcraft at the school."

There was shocked silence. Clearly some of the people who had been urged to attend the meeting had not known what the charge was.

"This is a serious charge and the Board wants to hear what facts," he stressed the word facts, "anyone here can bring forward."

Mrs. Hartson rose immediately and stated she had found the teacher, only a day or so ago, in a state of undress shortly before noon, that she had been drinking, and that she had a book about witchcraft open before her.

Carrie stood up. "If it please the Board, I should like to answer each of those charges on behalf of Mrs. Larkin."

Jack Sailstad nodded and Carrie told about Eleanor putting on a dress and how it had ripped when she stooped to help pick up a package, and therefore Mrs. Larkin would have been in her dressing gown, not a 'state of undress' while she mended the dress. As to the drinking, Eleanor had told her she had poured a small amount of sherry into her tea to calm her nerves after the trying morning. It was no more than most people would do. Carrie did not bring Henry into the picture at all. If he wanted to speak, he would do it. As to the book, Carrie had looked at it the night before and it was a book about Eastern Religions, which the teacher was interested in, not a book about witchcraft.

"The so-called Eastern Religions are all heathen and devil inspired," broke in Bertha Hartson.

"A matter of opinion, not fact," said Jack Sailstad. "When I visited Mrs. Larkin this afternoon, I looked through her books and did not find anything that resembled a book on witchcraft."

"Did you look under her mattress and in the cellar?" sneered Mrs. Hartson. "She's not a fool, whatever else she is; when I failed to bring it away with me, she hid it."

"But she does teach our children something she calls meditation," said Shirley LaComte. "Frankie says they do it every morning. That's not Christian."

The crowd began to murmur among themselves, and the matter of the book was lost. Shirley repeated what Frankie had described as m'tation and they all agreed it was an unusual exercise. Several other parents rose to say their children also had stories of the meditation period.

Mrs. MacLean said her Missy told fantastic stories of things she had "seen" while meditating, and as far as she was concerned, it was surely a form of witchcraft and she, for one, would not be sending her daughter back to school as long as that woman was the teacher.

After listening to the people for more than an hour, Sailstad dismissed them. ""The Board will discuss what is to be done and notify the townspeople tomorrow."

Later in the evening, well after it was dark, there was a small knock on Eleanor's door. "Mrs. Larkin?" inquired the knocker softly from outside the door. It was Jack Sailstad.

He entered, hat in hand. Carrie immediately offered him tea and asked him to sit. Eleanor sat in the far corner, on a dining room chair between the whatnot shelf and the parlor stove. Carrie heard the stairs creak and knew Tommy had crept down and was sitting on the steps to listen.

"Mrs. Larkin," Jack Sailstad began, then cleared his throat and took a swallow of the tea. "I do not for a moment believe the absurd charges of witchcraft that Mrs. Hartson has stirred up."

Carrie watched Eleanor emerge a little from the depths of her chair.

"However, I must, that is, the School Board must, do something to quiet the town down about you. We are prepared to close the school at once for the year...there is only a day or two left in the term, isn't there? You will receive three months salary, in addition to the one you have coming, and we will retain someone else for your position in the fall."

Eleanor drew herself up to a straight backed position and answered him. "Mr. Sailstad, I feel I could no longer be an effective teacher under the present conditions. I do want to say I have never met a meaner woman than that preacher's wife, and if anybody is a disgrace to this community, it is her, not me."

Sailstad nodded, but did not say anything. Carrie felt he clearly agreed with that assessment.

"In consideration of the generous settlement the Board is offering, I would ask you to prepare final report cards and promotion recommendations for the students and deliver them to me so I may give them to the parents. You may live in this company house until the end of the month. I will personally give you a letter of recommendation that you can use at your next position."

Eleanor rose and so did Jack Sailstad and Carrie. Eleanor extended her hand to Sailstad and thanked him for his support. "I will deliver the reports to you within two days, and I will leave town as soon as I can book passage on a schooner."

When the door closed behind the Board of Education President, Eleanor collapsed into Carrie's arms and sobbed. Tommy came into the room and put his arms around both of them.

"Come with me, Mom, back to Muskegon. We'll live with Grandpa and you can teach in a nice school down there."

"Yes," said Eleanor, "I suppose that's what I must do."

Chapter Eleven

Mornings were Carrie's favorite time of day. The lake was almost always calm, sometimes as smooth as glass until the sun rose high enough to exert some influence on it that caused it to begin to jump from it's sandy bed and create ripples, and then waves on the surface. If the wind came up, big breaking waves rolled against the shore and made the view out over the lake cluttered with white foam.

When Carrie slipped quietly out the front door of Eleanor's house on Cedar Lane, she saw that today it was a smooth as glass day. The sleeping household she left behind would also be smooth today; the storm had passed over and for Eleanor and Tommy a new life would begin.

Indeed it had been a storm after Jack Sailstad left. Eleanor had paced and ranted and all of a sudden had demanded to know where her book had gone.

"It's in my bags, Eleanor," Carrie told her. "Tommy brought it to me."

Then the story of Tommy's ride, like the midnight-ride of Paul Revere, was told and the three of them laughed at Carrie's dramatic rendition. Finally Eleanor had cried, deep heaving sobs that shook her slender frame. Tommy cried too and declared he would find passage for them tomorrow, and the town be damned!

It was long past midnight when Carrie had finally gotten Eleanor and Tommy to go to bed. They would sleep for an hour or two yet, Carrie thought as she crossed Cedar Lane and entered the deep shade of the cedar trees. Nothing can grow under cedar trees for their fallen fronds cover the thin soil in burnished bronze, smothering out all other vegetation. Limestone chunks lay scattered about, most of them green with moss because of the dampness and the minute amounts of filtered afternoon sun they received. Carrie carefully climbed down the steep limestone steps and gained the lakeshore. The air was brisk and fresh. Carrie considered a walk around the outer curve of land that formed Snail Shell Harbor, but she knew the rocky shore would be difficult to walk on. She turned instead and walked the short distance to come up behind the sawmill. She continued on through town and then followed the railroad grade. A smell of breakfast cooking, heavy with bacon fat, wafted out of the cottages as she walked past. It wasn't far, following the train tracks coming from Fairport, until she came to a sloping trail that led down to The Sand Beach.

The Sand Beach was free of the clutter of limestone and furnace slag. She and Albert used to walk there and he had told her that off in the woods there was a gin doggery where the laborers from town went to get a drink. Fayette didn't allow the sale of liquor in the town, although it was known that a discreet glass of sherry was available to the right people at the Shelton House.

The sand was hard packed and damp along the lake, but her feet sank into the tan-colored sugar sand beyond the tide line. The water was at low tide; the high water mark was visible on the wet sand as scallops left by lapping waves. Carrie stopped and removed her shoes and then hiked her skirt so she could stride freely in the sand. For a while she followed the ups and downs of the wave marks like a child. It felt so cool on her feet. If Bertha saw her, she'd probably be run out of town as a whore before sundown. Carrie smiled at that and continued, looking at pretty pebbles and shells as she walked.

Suddenly Carrie heard a voice speaking to her. She lifted her head, surprised to encounter another early morning beach stroller. It was a woman, also barefoot with hiked skirts, but with a broad rimmed hat that shadowed her face.

"Good morning," the woman said. Her voice was deep, throaty, with a warmth to it that drew Carrie immediately. She had read stories in the Ladies Home Journal where the heroine was described as having a 'honey-voice'. Now she had met someone who immediately called that description to mind.

"Good morning to you," Carrie said. "I didn't expect to meet anyone."

She didn't recognize the handsome woman in front of her. Her face was tan, like the complexion of a mulatto woman she'd once seen in Buffalo. Her lips were painted red and she had a glow of peach on her cheeks. Her eyes were large and fringed with long lashes. Suddenly Carrie realized she must be one of the women it was rumored were kept at the brothel at the Hole-in-the-Rock hangout.

"The beach is always empty in the early morning," the woman crooned.

Carrie decided to engage her in conversation just to hear her voice more.

"Do you come here often?"

"When I can."

It was then Carrie noticed that the woman was carrying a book. "Do you come to read?"

The woman laughed, like water trickling over rocks. "No, I seldom read. I draw."

She proffered the book to Carrie who turned the pages to see sketches in black and white of Burnt Bluff across the lake, a stand of Indian Paintbrushes in the sand, and the tiny pink Herb Robert blooming against a tumble of limestone.

"These are wonderful," Carrie said. "I don't believe I know you. I'm Carrie Grey."

"Peony," the woman said, extending a slim hand with red-tipped nails. "I'm not the sort of woman you ought to know."

Carrie smiled. "I can't think of any sort of woman I ought not to know. May I watch you work?"

Peony nodded assent and sat down on a large drift log and began to sketch the long reach of sand, calm water, and the two gulls who were skimming the surface looking for breakfast. Carrie stood behind her.

"You go so fast," Carrie said. "I would have thought it took slow carefully strokes to..." she broke off, not sure what to call what the woman did.

The throaty laugh again. "Most things I do have to be done quickly."

Carrie thought she grasped the double meaning in that and felt herself blush.

"Do you ever use colors?"

"I use the sketches as a basis to paint on canvas. I use watercolors. Those I do more slowly. I'd invite you to see them, but my rooms are not..." here Peony paused, and then said quickly, "not my own."

"I understand," Carrie said, "and I truly enjoyed meeting you."

She extended her hand and Peony took it. "And I you," she said.

Just as Carrie turned to go, Peony said, "May I give you this?"

She ripped a page from her book and handed it to Carrie. It was the lakeshore with the hungry gulls which Carrie had watched her sketch. Pleased, Carrie held it to her breast. "Thank you, Peony. Thank you, very much. I do hope we meet again."

Eleanor was up when Carrie returned to the house. The smell of coffee brewing and bread toasting was welcome, as was the heat from the kitchen stove. Carrie laid the sketch on the table and went to hug Eleanor.

"How are you this morning?"

"I'll be all right," Eleanor replied. "It was time for a change, I've been here too long."

They sat and sipped coffee while Carrie told Eleanor about the strange woman she had met on the sand beach.

"I'm sure she was one of the women they say is available at the Hole-In-Rock doggery down there. But she was pretty, and talked as if she had an education. What do you suppose a woman like that is doing working in such a place?"

Eleanor shrugged. "Perhaps it's a profession I'll need to

take up if the likes of Bertha Hartson keep dogging my path."

Carrie laughed at her; glad to see the spunk Eleanor had always had was still present.

After a while Eleanor asked, "Was Henry there last night?"

"He wasn't," Carrie said, "and since you're leaving I'm going to tell you something about Henry."

Eleanor leaned forward, eager to hear.

"The day your dress tore, when Henry drove me home to deliver my sewing machine, he asked me to marry him!"

"Marry him? Henry proposed to you?"

Carrie hoped she hadn't hurt Eleanor with this news.

"I turned him down of course. But later that day I found out why he wanted to marry me. It had nothing to do with him loving me, or not loving you. He wanted my marble quarry. Yes, I'm sure that was the whole thing. He wanted my marble quarry."

Eleanor smiled. "So it is marble. He wanted to propose to you before he told you, didn't he? What a snake. How did you find him out?"

Carrie told her about Drew McGeary and Bill Jenny from Chicago, and the trip to Escanaba aboard Wave Dancer.

"So I sailed on Wave Dancer with him, and Mr. Jenny, to Escanaba. I was so excited, about both the marble and Drew McGeary. He bewitched me from the first moment I laid eyes on him, you know. When I was here before, I couldn't think of anything else.

"Those three days were a whirl. After Mr. Jenny set the lawyers to drawing up contracts, Drew took me shopping. Just like that," she snapped her fingers, "I bought an evening dress, an afternoon dress, and a walking suit, with shoes and hats and corsets, which I swore I'd never wear, and we were off to meet the society set of Escanaba.

"Then Drew sailed me back home and set me on shore with my packages and sailed away again, promising to come back as soon as he could. The next morning, Tommy galloped in begging me to come and help you. Which of course, I did."

"Oh Carrie," Eleanor said, grasping her hands across the table. "You are the only thing I will miss about Fayette. And just when you are falling in love and need someone to confide in."

"Perhaps I'll seek advice from Peony," Carrie said, and they both laughed out loud.

Chapter Twelve

June had almost come and gone. Carrie sat in the cedar grove, her cat, Jewel, purring contentedly in her lap. She could hear the far away sounds from the quarry. Bill Jenny's crew had arrived two weeks ago, and already marble was shipping from her shore down to Chicago to build the $400,000 mansion for John Farwell.

She had purchased additional land along South River Bay where the stone outcropping looked promising. The steamer full of marble that left yesterday carried samples from there for Bill Jenny to have polished.

She was going to be rich. Carrie looked out over the choppy waters of the bay and sighed deeply. Suddenly she was bored by the harbor. The waves rolled in one after the other, hour after hour until she wanted to scream at the unrelenting sameness.

Somehow her life had fallen apart. First there was Drew McGeary. No. First there was poor Eleanor and that terrible busybody Bertha Hartson. Her best friend in the whole world was gone. It was her letter delivered this morning that had precipitated Carrie's deep sadness.

Eleanor wrote that she was fine and had been welcomed into her Father's home in Muskegon. She was making application at one of the elementary schools to teach, would you believe, only third and fourth grade students. She invited Carrie to visit, and certainly to write her often about news from the peninsula. Carrie played with the cat's orange silky ears and blinked back tears. The letter only reminded Carrie of how lonely she was now.

Her friendship with Henry had been ruined by his proposal to her. She had already spent many hours reflecting on that, and in light of what Bill Jenny told her, she felt sure Henry had known about the marble, and had proposed to her only to get his greedy hands on it.

Then there was Drew McGeary. At first, after the trip to Escanaba, Carrie had moved the sewing machine into the parlor so she could watch out the window for his return as she sewed. She made new skirts and waists and the blue walking suit. They were all made to wear over the waist-pinching corset she'd purchased in Escanaba, so were not anything she could wear everyday. She strolled the lakeshore twice a day, watching for Wave Dancer's sails to announce his return. But as the first day of summer came and went, she gave up. Her debut in Escanaba had been fun, but Drew had quickly forgotten her.

The Black Minorca chicks had hatched and proved to be the rare birds she'd been promised. That vein of thought brought resolve to Carrie. She would take the stage into Fayette for the Fourth of July celebration and deliver the chicks, as promised, to Dr. Rutherford. A visit with Louella Rutherford would do her good. She picked up Jewel from her lap and set her on the ground, thinking as she did so that the cat was getting fat, probably with kittens.

Carrie had never been pregnant. Not from lack of trying. She and Albert wanted children; that's why they had built the house with more than one bedroom at the beginning. They had been sure that before the first year was out they would have a baby. But after five years of marriage, and much activity of the sort that begets babies, Carrie became resigned to the fact that she, like Sarah in the Bible, was barren.

Carrie caught the stage into Fayette three days later, the basket of peeping chicks at her feet and Jewel on her lap. Her attachment to the cat had grown immensely in her sudden loneliness at Cedar Harbor, and she could not bear to leave her behind, especially since she was going to have kittens. If she has her kittens while I'm in Fayette, Carrie reasoned I can find a home for them.

Her first stop upon alighting from the stage was to take a

room in the Shelton House. She was given a room in the new west wing. It contained a narrow bed, a chair, and a small bureau. One small window gave her a view of Burnt Bluff, partly blocked by the new two-story privy that served the hotel guests. A covered walkway led from the second floor to that building.

Carrie left Jewel inside the room and made the trip across, feeling the motion of the walkway as she trod along the four foot wide, and maybe twenty foot long, enclosed hall. At the end she found the "Ladies" room on the left and the "Gentlemen's" room on the right. Well, it wasn't carpeted and wallpapered like Grace Sailstad's, but it was nice. Inside the ladies room the walls and floor were painted white and a pretty framed floral print hung from a nail in the wall. There were two stalls with a hook and eye lock on each for privacy. A small window at ceiling height let in fresh air.

When she got back to the room, Carrie realized bringing Jewel had been a mistake. There was no way to keep her in the hotel room and she feared letting her run free. Maybe Louella would let her board the cat with her.

Carrie had left the basket of chicks on the porch under the watchful eye of Missy MacLean. Now she offered the child a nickel to carry the basket to Dr. Rutherford's for her. Missy was a bright eyed eight year old and she chattered all the way.

"I think it was mean that Mrs. Larkin had to leave," was one of her first observations. "If anyone was a witch it's that reverend's wife. That's what my dad says. I liked Mrs. Larkin. A lot."

Then the child began to tell Carrie about Mrs. LeComte and her baby coming to their house late at night, "just soon ago," she said, making Carrie smile at her choice of words, "because there was a big fight at her house and she was pushed out. But in the morning she went back to her own house. She's Frankie's mom."

Carrie changed the subject; she didn't like gossip. "Missy, do you see the little island, way out there?"

Missy stopped and squinted to where Carrie pointed. "No, Ma'am, I don't see it," she said.

"There," Carrie insisted, "right off the end of the bluff. Can't you see all the birds flying around it?"

Snake Island, as it was unaccountably called, was little more than a limestone outcropping upon which enough soil had accumulated over the eons to support the growth of a few evergreens and birches. The cormorants and gulls nested there.

"My mom says I can't see far very well. She's going to take me to Escanaba and get spectacles for me. But I don't want them."

"Surly you'd like to be able to see more things, wouldn't you? Like Snake Island, for instance?"

"Nope. Boys won't like me if I have spectacles."

"How old are you, Missy?"

"Ten," she said. Carrie knew it was a lie, but did not say so.

"Plenty of time for boys later," she said. "Get the spectacles and see what you're missing first."

They had arrived at the Rutherfords house. Carrie welcomed the cool shaded yard. She gave Missy her nickel and proceeded around the back and up the stairs to the kitchen where she knocked on the door and waited for Louella to answer it.

Carrie was welcomed, as she knew she would be. "May I bring the cat in, Louella?"

"Of course, what's its name?"

Carrie set the basket of cheeping chicks on the porch and entered Louella's small kitchen. "Jewel, and I'm afraid she's going to be a mother. I made the mistake of bringing her to town with me and now I don't know what to do with her."

Louella took the orange and white cat from Carrie and stroked it under the chin with her finger. "She's a pretty thing and I think she's going to be a mother fairly soon. Leave her here with me while you run your errands. Did I detect the sound of cheeping from the basket you set on the porch?"

"That's Edward's Black Minorca chicks," Carrie said. "Is he here?"

For answer Louella opened the door to the steps leading down to the hospital and called, "Edward, Carrie Grey is here."

Very soon they heard his heavy tread on the steps. He must look at once at the chicks.

"Carrie, I thought we bargained for three. There are four chicks here."

Carrie sighed. "Only four of the six hatched, Edward, and what would I do with one little black sheep in the chicken yard? None of them are roosters, so you can't breed them, so I brought you all four."

"Well, we shall exchange then. Your four Minorca for six of my Goldens, plus a rooster. How long will you be in town?"

"I wanted to stay a few days," Carrie said, "but I made the mistake of bringing my cat with me and so I'll probably go home in the morning."

"Nonsense," said Louella. "You must stay for the Fourth of July celebration. You and Jewel will stay with us and don't tell me you've paid for a room at the Shelton House."

"I have," Carrie answered.

"Then it's for one night only. Tomorrow morning Edward will pick you and your baggage up and you will stay here. We have an entire upper floor that is not in use."

Carrie did not argue. It was what her heart wanted; to be with someone for a few days and fill the emptiness she felt.

"What do you think about Jewel, Edward? Is she going to have kittens?"

Rutherford picked the cat up in his large hands and examined her gently. "She is going to have kittens very soon, Carrie. Louella, find one of your laundry baskets for me and line it with something old and soft. We'll make a nest for her right here on the landing."

The next morning Carrie arrived at Rutherford's to find Jewel with three kittens mewling in the basket on the landing.

Two were colored like Jewel; the third was pure white.

"I delivered them about two this morning," Edward boasted. "One of the easiest deliveries I've ever attended."

Carrie found herself overwhelmed at the sight of the three newborns nursing and found she had to wipe some tears away. Then she said breezily, "Well, I'm glad I brought her then. If she'd had them at Cedar Harbor some fox would have them by now."

After lunch, Carrie and Louella sat in the parlor and talked. Louella was piecing a Storm At Sea quilt in blues and greens and Carrie helped. She felt calmed by having her hands busy with the piecing. They talked of inconsequential things, but the mere company was all Carrie needed. She hadn't thought about Drew McGeary all day until she thought of not having thought of him. And she quickly dismissed even that thought when Louella suggested they walk up to the butcher shop to see what they might fix for supper.

The butcher shop, which was located in the opera house but on the other side, was up a flight of stairs and next to the barbershop. It was a small affair; three people made it crowded. So while Louella selected three beefsteaks, Carrie stood outside on the landing and scanned the harbor. No Wave-Dancer. She turned away from the harbor with a heavy feeling and made a move toward the butcher shop door when Henry appeared at the head of the stairs. He had been on his way to the barbershop, next door. When he saw Carrie, he stopped, and Carrie felt he would have gone back down the stairs if she hadn't seen him.

"Henry."

"Hello, Carrie. I didn't know you were in town."

"I'm staying with the Rutherfords until after the Fourth of July. Have you been well?"

Henry withdrew his pipe from his pocket and fingered the stem. It was a habit of his when he was nervous.

"Well enough."

Louella came out of the butcher shop then. Henry doffed his hat to her, murmured something and hurried on into the barbershop.

"What was that about?" Louella asked as she and Carrie started down the stairs.

"Oh, nothing. I think he's feeling guilty about not defending Eleanor."

"Then the whole town should duck quickly indoors when you approach. You're the only one who said anything in her defense."

"You were there as my moral support," Carrie said.

"But I said nothing," Louella said. "Edward did not argue when I said I would have nothing to do with the new minister. They've formed a building committee, you know, to try to put up a Protestant church. For now, they meet in the school house."

"How fitting," Carrie said.

They had just finished eating supper when there was a knock at the door. Edward got up to answer it. Henry LaTermaine stood there, asking to see Carrie.

"I have a post for her," he said.

Carrie came into the parlor, with Louella close at her heels.

"Well, come in then," Edward said, standing aside from the open door.

Henry stood framed in the doorway, hat in hand. "I thought maybe you'd like to come for a walk, Carrie."

Carrie started to protest that she must help Louella with the dishes, but Edward waved that aside. "You go walk, Carrie. I'll do my usual duty at the dish pan."

And with that, Carrie found herself walking beside Henry along the lane in front of the house where Eleanor had lived. They walked in silence, neither speaking. Finally, Henry reached into his jacket pocket and handed Carrie a letter, much worn at the edges, dirty and folded. It was from the assay office in Chicago and was dated February 10, 1882. It was the same letter Bill Jenny had shown her in May.

Carrie read the letter and placed it in her sleeve. Then she spoke.

"Why am I just getting this now, Henry?"

"It only came a couple of days ago," Henry said. "It must have gotten lost someplace."

"It has been opened."

"Yes, I noticed that."

"Did you read it? And please don't lie to me, Henry."

Henry looked at her. They were walking along a section of Cedar Lane that was heavily wooded and the evening shadows were deep. Carrie studied him closely.

"Yes."

"Then you know that there is marble in my quarry?"

"Everybody knows it now, Carrie. It is no longer news."

Carrie looked up at him. He looked so innocent. Still she pressed on. "But how long have you known, Henry?"

"Now Carrie," Henry protested, "I think you suspect me of being duplicitous with you. I swear I did not know until Mr. Jenny showed up here looking for you. That letter was in the post bag the Lady Washington brought in this afternoon."

Carrie sighed. She didn't know whether to believe him or not. It didn't really matter anymore.

But Henry still had something to say. "The day I asked you to marry me, Carrie, I meant that." He rushed on before Carrie could say anything. "I've missed you terribly since that day."

Carrie watched his profile as he gulped in air. Then he stopped and turned in front of her, extending his arms to hold her shoulders as he looked intently into her eyes.

"I do love you, Carrie. Please marry me."

Carrie stiffened. But she should have been prepared for this. If Henry was after the marble quarry he wouldn't give up easily.

"If I were to tell you I have sold the quarry to Mr. Jenny

and sent all the money to pay medical bills for my sick sister in Buffalo, would you still want to marry me?"

Henry kept his hands on her shoulders, but his gaze dropped for a minute. "Well, you haven't done that, Carrie," he said, looking at her again. "But yes, even if you had I would press my suit."

Carrie shook her head. "Henry, I don't know what to think right now. My head is in a muddle over so many things."

"Is Drew McGeary one of them?" Henry demanded. "If he is, I've already told you he's a scoundrel. He has a woman in every port up and down both coasts of Lake Michigan from Escanaba to Chicago."

Carrie shook her head in denial while she wondered if it was true. How many times had she seen him? Twice. One, the day his schooner blew into her harbor and two, the day he'd brought Bill Jenny. And then there was that wonderful weekend with him in Escanaba when he had paid lavish attention to her and certainly indicated, if not in words, that he cared for her. And when he'd returned her to Cedar Harbor he had told her he'd be back. Then why hadn't he come?

Henry withdrew his grip on her shoulders and wrapped one arm around them while he walked beside her. She didn't pull away, but let him lead her back towards Rutherford's house. When they neared the house, he released her and started talking again.

"Carrie, think of it a while. We've always been good friends and it would be a good match, for both of us. What I don't want is to see you unhappy."

At the door he addressed her again. "Will you think about it, Carrie?"

Carrie nodded, feeling like a schoolgirl who had been scolded for giving the wrong answer to Grandfather Ruben. "I'll think about it, Henry."

"Well, goodnight then," Henry said.

Chapter Thirteen

The door slammed with a loud bang that made Shirley jump. The baby, Edna, was asleep across her lap and she was engrossed in a new novel Mae MacLean had loaned to her. The title was "That Husband of Mine," and the husband of the heroine in the book was nothing like her husband, Frank.

Shirley hid the book under the baby's blanket and when Frank strode into the room Shirley put her finger to her lips and whispered, "She's been crying all afternoon and I just got her to sleep."

"Where's my supper?" Frank demanded, paying no heed at all to the sleeping babe. He looked around the house at the unswept floor, the piles of unfolded laundry in several places, and Frankie's toys spread all around.

"It doesn't look like you've done a god-damn thing around here all day."

Shirley shrank into the chair, and held Edna across her body as a shield. She'd done it again, after she had promised herself she would never miss Frank's supper again.

"Where's Frankie?"

"I don't know," Shirley whined. "He was here just a little bit ago."

"You've had your nose in a god-damn book all day, haven't you?"

He took the baby away from her and shook the cheap novel out of the blanket. Shirley cringed, but the fist caught her on her inner shoulder anyway and knocked her back into the chair so that it nearly fell over. He never hit her in the face; someone could see that. Her arms and legs however, were always a patchwork of color; newly bruised purple, faded blue or sickly yellow from where he had punched or kicked her. It was her own fault she knew that. She let him down all the time; not fixing his meals, or letting Frankie run wild around town, or not cleaning up the house.

"You are some worthless hunk of meat," he yelled. "Get out there and fix my supper."

Edna began to wail. Frank thrust her at Shirley.

"Another worthless female," he muttered. "Take her up upstairs and put her in the crib before I put her out of her misery."

Shirley took the baby and rushed up the stairs with her, trying to hush her, but when she put Edna in the crib, the outraged infant started to scream again. Shirley put a sugar-tit in its mouth and shut the door, hoping Edna would go back to sleep and not incite Frank to any more anger. Then she hurried into the kitchen. She didn't have anything to fix for supper. She should have gone down to the dock and bought some fish. She opened the pantry door and studied the contents.

She felt Frank behind her. Why was it she could never hear him coming into a room when he was angry with her?

"There isn't any food in there fit for a man," he said. "I'm going down to the hotel. When I get back I expect this place to be cleaned up and to find my son asleep in his bed. Do you understand?"

Shirley nodded.

"Answer me," he screamed. "Do you understand?"

"Yes, Frank, dear, I understand. I have not been a good wife today."

"Nor any other day I can ever remember," Frank said. He thrust his big hand into her blonde curls and twisted hard. "You better be in bed when I get back. There's at least one wifely duty you know how to do."

He released her with a shove backward and Shirley fell against the stove. The hands she put out to break her fall fell upon the hot stove and she recoiled in the other direction, falling over a chair. She lie on the floor face down, holding in the sobs until she heard the door slam behind him.

She stumbled up and plunged her hands into the water bucket on the sinkboard and cried. For ten minutes she stood there with her hands in the cold water, a heavy sob escaping from her now and then, as she listened to her daughter crying herself to sleep upstairs. Well, she had better get used to it; that was what life as a woman was all about.

Shirley picked up the unfolded laundry piles from the parlor, laying them across her arms to protect her burned hands, and carried them upstairs where she used her elbow to stuff them into a small closet in the children's room. Edna was asleep, her mouth working vigorously on her small fist, her blonde curls damp with sweat. Shirley caressed her cheek with the back of her finger and whispered, "I'm sorry, baby." Then she went back downstairs and out of doors to call for Frankie.

Frankie was next door playing with Duke Bertlesman's kids. Shirley fed him a jelly sandwich and then made him pick up his toys and carry in enough wood to fill the kitchen wood box.

"Now sweep the floor," Shirley ordered. She had her hands in the water bucket again.

"Ah, Ma," Frankie protested.

"Don't give me that, young man," Shirley said. "Can't you see I burned my hand on the stove and can't manage the broom? Now please, just this once, sweep the floor for Mama?"

As he began to sweep, Shirley spotted the novel under the edge of the settee. She took her hands out of the water and bent to pick it up. Her shoulder hurt so bad she could scarcely lift it; she used the other hand.

"When you finish that, Frankie, you go to bed. Your Pa was here and was real mad cause you wasn't home. If you're in bed sleeping when he gets back, then probably he won't strop you."

Frankie nodded and Shirley once more climbed the steep stairs. She peeked in the door and found Edna still asleep.

Then she crept into the small attic room over the kitchen

and sank unto a cushion she kept there. She leaned against the wall and sighed. She didn't cry, there were no more tears. Her hands still hurt and her shoulder ached, but she knew what to do about that. She removed one of the wads of newspaper that were stuffed into the spaces between the wall studs and retrieved a small box. From the box she took out a small blue bottle. She counted. There was only three left. How long before she could get to Escanaba and get more? She returned the box to its hiding place and put the book, "That Husband of Mine," on top of it. She replaced the wad of newspaper and crept out of the stifling heat of the attic room.

Frankie was just finishing the sweeping when she came back down stairs. She told him he was a good boy, and warned him again that he'd better be in bed when his Pa came home, which might be very soon now. But she knew better. Frank would eat at the hotel and then go down to the Hole in The Rock, where'd he stay until long after dark. She had time.

The contents of the blue bottle were bitter, but the almost immediate rush of comfort the morphine brought was like sinking into a pillow of comfort. Like being held by someone who really, really, loved you. And her dreams of that lover spun out from there and carried Shirley LeComte across the universe of stars and the cool, cool comfort of clear blue water, to dance in the arms of a lover, handsome and kind beyond compare.

Frank LeComte was relieved to get out of the house. There were some days when he hoped he would catch Shirley like he had tonight. Being foreman of the furnace complex was not easy work and he enjoyed eating at the hotel. It made him feel important to dine while he studied a sheaf of papers he always carried in a pocket of his pants. There wasn't anything important on them; they were just a set of drawings he had made to show the company men how he envisioned changes that should have been incorporated into the new furnace stack that had just came on line. They had accepted some of his ideas and as he studied and re-studied the drawings he was convinced they were idiots for not accepting them all.

When they brought his coffee, Frank put away his drawings and stretched himself out, his long legs reaching into the waiter's path between tables. He sipped the coffee and thought about his wife. He hated to punch her, but, by God, she asked for it.

Shirley was pretty. That's why he'd married her. Those big gray-blue eyes, long blonde curls, and a heart shaped face had beguiled him back in Cleveland. She was pretty, but she wasn't educated, and she didn't take care of the house the way his mother had. Mother had warned him about her evident lack of culture. Frank argued that she played the organ. His mother had said, "True, but she speaks English like a whore."

That's not all she did like a whore and was another reason Frank had married her. But the attractions were beginning to be outweighed by the negatives. Shirley embarrassed him when they were in public. Grace Sailstad obviously snubbed his wife and it was hurting his chances of advancement in the Jackson Iron Company. That's why they had turned down his ideas on the second stack, not because they weren't good.

Frank signed his name to the check the waiter presented. It would be taken out of his pay, like everything else purchased in this company owned town. By the time all the bills were paid, there was precious little left, even for a foreman.

Frank left by the back door and headed down towards the sand beach where Ned Stoddy operated the Hole in The Rock establishment. The doggery was small, but the stock of whiskey and gin was big, and the back door led to the brothel presided over by Madam Peony. There was a dame; but no one ever touched her except LaTermaine— and McGeary, when he was in town.

Frank avoided the ladies tonight. He drank whiskey, played poker for a while and left while he was still ahead. He thought he'd go home and make it up to Shirley.

Shirley was asleep when he got home. He observed the

blisters on her hands and went down to his office in the furnace complex and got some of the honey and petroleum jelly salve he kept there to apply to burns. She was still asleep and didn't wake up when he gently applied the salve to her slim, long-fingered hands. He often wondered how she could sleep so deeply.

The next morning he made love to her before he left for work and left the rest of the salve for her to apply to her hands throughout the day. Tomorrow was the Fourth of July and he promised her they would have a great time together at the celebration.

Chapter Fourteen

Early the next morning, the third of July, Carrie got up with the thought of slipping out for a walk. Louella was already in the kitchen, kneading bread.

"You look dressed to go out."

"I didn't think anyone would be up yet," Carrie said. "But since you are, what can I help with?"

"Nothing," replied Louella. "You take a walk like you'd planned and I'll have breakfast set when you come back. Edward likes to eat at exactly seven."

Carrie tried to protest, but Louella insisted. "You've got an hour." She said. "Now shoo."

As Carrie passed the basket of kittens on the stairway she noticed Jewel was gone and the kittens were all curled in one colorful ball of fur, sleeping. Well, she would need to go out now and then, wouldn't she? With her kittens to care for she wouldn't wander far.

Carrie was surprised at the activity already evident in the town as men hurried quickly to their workstations at the furnaces, the mill, or the quarry. Very shortly, other men would be going home for a breakfast and some sleep. Dogs barking, seemingly from every dwelling, added to the general din of the town. A blast of steam as a huge black locomotive, with the name J.C. Hicks lettered in gold under the window where the engineer leaned out, began chugging south with a string of empty cars to pick up charcoal from the Fairport kilns.

In a building at the water's edge, Carrie detected the steam-driven crusher at work breaking up the limestone before it was used in the furnaces. Carrie had observed this process one day in the company of Jack Sailstad. She hoped to add a crushing mill to her quarry in order to sell crushed flux stone to the mills down-lake. Perhaps now, with the marble bringing in cash, she could afford to develop this aspect of her operation.

Carrie continued her walk down between the hotel and the horse barns and maneuvered her way among the rock and slag on the shore. It was difficult walking until she got past the slag and was able to keep to a number of large flat pieces of limestone. A series of small bluffs, only twenty-five feet high, she judged, continued for a couple of hundred yards until she turned the point, and was out of sight of the town. The railroad to Fairport ran along the tops of those bluffs, she'd walked them before, but that path lay too close to the Hole in The Rock. From the turn she could see the tan color of The Sand Beach ahead. Sand Bay, a gentle inward scoop from Lake Michigan, was larger than Cedar Harbor and around the next headland, which was the imposing Burnt Bluff, lay the village of Sac Bay.

The limestone ended abruptly and Carrie walked on a beach of hard packed sand, damp with moisture and patterned by the swirl of waves. The cedars thinned along the shore and a meadow of tall grasses, thick with buttercups, daisies, and Indian paintbrushes, appeared.

Here, away from the town, the birds were singing. There was a warm wind blowing out of the southwest. The day would be hot.

Carrie was hoping to meet the woman she had met before: Peony. Her playful words to Eleanor that perhaps she'd seek advice from the woman at the brothel had only been half in jest. Peony had seemed intelligent, was certainly talented with her sketch book, and, what's more, she knew more about men than Carrie ever would. Was Henry telling the truth about his reasons for wanting to marry her, and about Drew having a woman in every port?

Even if he was, Carrie still didn't think she wanted to marry Henry. It was only because of the sudden loneliness in her life that she even gave it a second thought.

Just as the town came to life with the sun, so it was

apparent the ships on the lake did the same. Carrie spotted three schooners rounding Burnt Bluff. She stopped and studied them. Surely the middle one was Wave Dancer, and she was headed for Fayette like the rest of them, even though she looked to be on a direct line to Sand Bay.

Carrie turned around and climbed up a faint path from the beach to the railroad grade and began to walk at a fast pace back to town. Her heart gave her the answers she had hoped to get from the genteel prostitute.

Peony sat on the driftwood tree trunk up the beach and watched Carrie. She had spotted her the moment she came around the point from town and figured who she was and suspected that she was Mrs. Grey's destination. The problem of how to handle the situation was solved when the woman suddenly turned around after watching the three schooners for a while.

Peony turned and watched them herself. Wave Dancer continued towards her. The other two swung wide around the rock snags on the northern shore of the entrance to Snail Shell harbor and would be anchored or docked before Mrs. Grey reached the town. Hopefully, she would not wonder what had happened to the third ship, if that's why she had turned around, because the harbor in Fayette would, as usual, be crowded with ships coming and going.

Wave Dancer dropped anchor a hundred yards off shore. Peony stood and waved back when Drew McGeary waved at her. She was wearing an orange morning gown to make it easy for the Captain to spot her from the shore. She was thankful Carrie Grey had not looked up the beach, for she would surely have seen Peony in the orange dress and might have continued on.

A shore boat was lowered. Besides Drew and a crewman to row, there were two other figures in the boat. Good. That's how many Peony had expected. The boat beached nearby and Drew helped the two women out. Each carried a large bag.

Zach helped Drew heave a large sea trunk out, which they carried up and placed on the shore side of the driftwood seat Peony had been occupying.

"Meet me back here," Drew told his mate. "I'll be less than an hour. I'll have Stoddy send a man down to help you with the trunk."

"I'll get my usual bottle of gin?" asked Zach.

"There's no argument about that," stated Drew. Peony thought there was some tension between the two of them, but it was none of her affair.

Drew grabbed her around her slim waist and pulled her up against him. His kiss was demanding and welcome. This was the fourth morning Peony had waited for him, but she didn't ask why he hadn't come earlier. A dozen things could have delayed his arrival, from bad weather to a scavenging opportunity. He released her and patted her buttocks, cupping one with a gentle squeeze and then he introduced the new girls to her.

Peaches was a blonde. She was plump and too dark complexioned for the blonde color to be real. She wasn't pretty, but she was reasonably young. She had an old bruise on her left cheek. Helena was tall and slender with black hair and bad teeth.

"How old are you?" Peony asked Helena.

"Twenty-eight."

Peony laughed. "Thirty-eight, more like. Where'd you come from?"

The woman shrugged, indifferent to the question and observation. "Milwaukee."

"Do you know Peaches?"

"Not until I come aboard."

"What about you," Peony questioned the plump woman. "You come here of your own free will?" The bruise on the woman's cheek prompted the question.

Peaches looked around. "Yeah, one brothel is like another and I figured a change was due."

Drew laughed. "I found her on Clark Street in Chicago. She begged me to get her away from there."

The woman shot Drew an angry look and then replaced it with a smile. "That's right, sweetie, " she said. "He saved me from a pimp who was a little too attached to me and much too violent."

Peony told the girls to follow her; she would show them their rooms. Drew winked at her and asked if Henry was there. "No," Peony told him. "I'll send word to him and you can collect from him in town. Kill fifteen minutes with Stoddy and then knock on my door."

Drew nodded but sat down instead on the log. He didn't like Stoddy, the man Henry had running the Hole-In-The-Rock and attached brothel. The man was like a greasy beaver, the same class as most of his clientele. He looked up and found Zach still there.

"You go up, Zach," he told his mate. "I'll bring the trunk up."

Drew lit a pipe of tobac and relaxed. The trip up-lake had been without incident. Besides the girls, he was carrying a cargo of dry goods for Escanaba. After an interlude with Peony, he'd head there and unload. It crossed his mind to slip into Cedar Harbor and invite Carrie to the 4th of July celebration at Fayette, but if he did that he couldn't anchor off-shore and offer a bit of liquid refreshment and female entertainment to the Fayette boys. They'd be expecting Wave Dancer to provide a floating saloon and a poker table, just as he had done for the past few years. He also had a faro dealer on board who had promised Drew ten per cent of his winnings for the evening in exchange for passage. The two girls he was picking up from Stoddy's were bound for Escanaba where Drew would collect a passage fee for them from the highest bidder in the Thomas Street houses. But that would be after the Fourth of July party and the fifty per cent share he'd get of the money they would earn on their backs in his cabin. Couldn't pass up that kind of money.

He thought about the weekend he and Carrie Grey had spent in Escanaba with Bill Jenny. Jenny was a man who enjoyed the finer things in life, like the theatre, music and dancing, and, if you believed him, a good book. Damn good way to live, Drew thought, and Carrie Grey would be just the sort of woman to live it with. He wondered if he could get her to live with him in Chicago, where all that culture was. He could still run Wave Dancer during the season. Hell, Zach could captain her and he could settle down and be some kind of business man, investing in the commodities Jenny'd told him about. Carrie had that little stone and marble quarry, but she didn't have to be here to run it. She had a competent man doing that already. They could live well.

The more he thought about it, the better it sounded. He could still swing into Cedar Harbor and pick Carrie up. A Fourth of July celebration at Fayette was the perfect courting venue, and unless he had become a poor judge of women, Carrie Grey would be an easy pluck.

Zach could run the off shore saloon. Be good practice for him since he'd agreed to sell Zach a quarter of Wave Dancer for $2000 at the end of the season. Maybe he'd better get those papers drawn up while he was in Escanaba and start Zach in now. He could use that same lawyer Carrie had used, Chester B. Flynt.

His mind made up, he dumped his pipe ashes into the yellow sand and stood up. He was ready, more than ready, for Peony.

Carrie paused outside the house to catch her breath before she climbed the back stairs to the kitchen. Edward was just sitting down at the table when she entered.

"Oh, good," she said, "I'm not too late."

"You've got high color in your cheeks," Edward observed. "I hope you didn't over exert yourself."

"Nonsense, Edward," Carrie replied. "Women are not

delicate creatures who can over exert themselves by a walk on the beach. I only walked too far and had to hurry to get back if I wanted to have breakfast. Louella warned me that you ate promptly at seven."

Louella laughed at this and playfully slapped Carrie's shoulder. "I only said Edward likes to eat at seven, not that you had to."

"I watched three schooners coming in around Burnt Bluff. They were at full sail and I just stood and admired them too long. I do love to see a ship under full sail."

"I think it won't be too many years before such a sight will be rare indeed," Edward said. "Steam is the thing now, more reliable than the wind."

They continued to make small talk while they ate. Carrie was anxious to get down to the harbor to look for Drew, but she also must fulfill her duties as a guest and help Louella clean up. Perhaps she could find a small excuse to go to the general store. The view of the harbor from the back window of the store was the best; looking down on the plethora of ships made it easier to distinguish one from another.

After the morning dishes were washed up and put away, Carrie wandered over to the stairs to look at the kittens. Jewel was back in the box and the small blind babies were nursing.

"I'm going to call that white one Pearl," she told Louella, "and the two orange and white ones will be Topaz and Goldie. I just have to figure out some way to tell them apart."

"Will you leave one for me?" Louella asked. "I think a good mouser around here would be useful."

"Which one do you want?"

"Whichever one you call Goldie."

It was afternoon before Carrie found an errand to run that would take her into town. Louella needed cocoa for the chocolate cake she was making to enter in the cake walk tomorrow.

"Get a tin of Droste's if he has it. It comes in a light blue tin with a red cover. And, oh Carrie, if you don't mind, would you stop at the butcher shop and pick out some chops for our supper?"

"Do you want to write out a list for me?"

Louella bit her lower lip. "Well, there are a few more things."

While Louella wrote out her list, Carrie went upstairs to the room she was using and checked her toilette. She re-rolled her hair and added a black and ivory broach at her throat. The "high color" Edward had remarked at breakfast was back in her cheeks, and it wasn't caused by exertion this time.

The harbor was a forest of masts from the dozen or so schooners anchored there and she could see several more waiting at the harbor mouth for their turn to come in and load or unload. The passenger steamer, Lady Washington was at her berth, but the tug, Jo Harris was absent. Probably on her way back from Escanaba with a line of ore scows behind her. There were more steam-powered boats than schooners. Edward was right about the schooner becoming obsolete. Even many of the schooners had steam engines they used when the wind failed them. She didn't know if Wave Dancer had an engine in it or not. She didn't see Wave Dancer, but with the harbor so crowded, it may well be on the far side.

Carrie climbed the stairs into the store and immediately turned towards the large harbor side window. From there she could see every ship. Henry kept a glass on the windowsill and Carrie picked it up so she could read the names even on the ships outside the harbor.

"Have you found the one you want?" Henry's voice at her elbow startled Carrie, but she didn't stop looking.

"I was just counting them all," Carrie said. "I've counted twenty-three so far."

"And Wave Dancer is not among them."

"I didn't see that name," Carrie said, pretending the very name of Drew's ship didn't make her heart jump. She put the glass down and handed Henry the list Louella had made out.

"Nor will she be." Henry continued. "Captain McGeary was

in port early this morning to leave something for me and then he went on to Escanaba."

Carrie didn't miss the look of triumph in Henry's eyes. "Louella Rutherford wants these items. While you gather them, I have an errand to run at the hotel."

"Shall I have one of the boys deliver them or will you stop back and pick them up?"

"Have them delivered."

Carrie started to walk toward the front of the store and Henry fell in step beside her.

"Will you accompany me to the cake walk tomorrow evening, Carrie?"

Carrie sighed and softened her attitude towards Henry. Dear Henry. He obviously cared more for her than Drew McGeary did. She laid her gloved hand on his forearm and nodded. "Yes, Henry, I will."

Carrie watched his face brighten with genuine eagerness. She softened more and gently squeezed his arm before she said good day and exited the front door of the store.

It was hot. Here in the center of the village where the breeze was interrupted by buildings on every side, the air was warmer than anywhere else. A group of boys ran by, rolling a barrel hoop, trying to keep it upright as long as possible by touching it lightly with the long sticks they carried. The usual line up of men seated on benches in front of the blacksmith and machine shop watched her walk by. She was more conscious of them than she had ever been before she started wearing fashionable clothing. She raised her parasol and held it between her and the men so they couldn't see her face and hurried on to the hotel, where she did not have an errand at all, but had told Henry that so she could get away.

She was in the same position she had been in this morning when she had sought Peony on the beach. If only there was some way she could get in touch with the woman.

Chapter Fifteen

The children were the first ones on the streets. Shirley LeComte let Frankie loose as soon as he finished his breakfast. Now, with Edna in Frankie's wagon, she hurried to join the other women from St. Peter the Fisherman church. The pancake and sausage breakfasts they sold for a nickel a plate were a great hit and hopefully would earn enough money to buy new altar cloths.

By parade time at ten o'clock the town was filled with people from the surrounding countryside. They came most often with wagons, some piled with hay to make a soft bedding for little ones to nap on during the day or to fall asleep on when the older folk swung into their activities after the fireworks.

The Fourth of July in Fayette had been a gala affair from the beginning. The Jackson Iron Company threw two parties a year for its employees; this one and a Christmas party.

Carrie and Louella stood in the yard of the white house, inside the fence with Grace Sailstad, and watched the parade, which was led by the fourteen-piece Fayette Cornet Band and one large bass drum. Dr. Rutherford, with Old Tom wearing a red and gray silk saddle cloth Louella had stitched, sat easy on the small seat of his sulky. He wore the red and gray shirt that identified him on the trotting field. Jack Sailstad, in a similar shirt of blue and white, drove Big Iron, whose harness dripped with blue and white ribbons. Other men in the parade rode atop their horses.

Boys rolled hoops and one lad led a large dog pulling a gaily-decorated wagon. The parade wound along from the sawmill on the point in front of the white house and followed Harbor Street to come up between the general store and the opera house. From there it passed the company office and disbanded at the horse stables along side the Shelton House. The women followed in its wake, falling in with the people who had lined the street watching.

The porch of the hotel was decorated with red, white, and blue bunting. People gathered on the road and lawn surrounding it to hear Edward Rutherford deliver the Fourth of July address. He had a booming voice that carried out over the crowd and perhaps even to the ships in the harbor.

"A year ago at this time," he began, "we had just received news that James Garfield, our 20th President of these United States, had been gravely wounded by an assassin, having held office for only three months. This, following on the heels of the ineffective Presidency of Rutherford B. Hayes, whose elevation to that office was, as we all know, questionable, is almost more than a normal nation could bear.

"But the constitution of these United States has proved stronger than the politicians and the assassins. Ten months ago, Chester A. Arthur ascended from the vice-presidency to become our President, thus proving that men may die, but the fabric of this nation is not rent by these singular events. Our free institutions remain unshaken."

While Rutherford spoke on, Carrie moved away from Louella and Grace, quietly looking through the crowd for a tall man with sand colored hair and a red beard. She had not seen Wave Dancer in the harbor, so there was really no reason to be looking for him, but she searched, nonetheless. Suddenly she saw Peony standing on the edge of the crowd, near the water's edge and at the back of a group of cottage women. Peony must have been watching her, for their eyes met with a look of recognition and Peony nodded at her.

Carrie began to wend her way through the crowd towards her, but when next she looked where Peony had been, she was no longer there. Disappointed, Carrie turned back and slipped in beside Louella and Grace just as Dr. Rutherford finished and began to sing, God Bless America, and the entire crowd joined in.

The Fayette Cornet Band then mounted the hotel steps and began a concert of patriotic songs. While they played, the women began to set food out on the blankets each family had spread on the ground. Carrie and Louella had fried the ten chickens Edward had butchered yesterday afternoon and walked among the cottage families handing each child a piece. Later, from a stand set up in front of the company office, Shirley LeComte and other foreman's wives passed out chunks of cold watermelon to all comers.

While the girls and younger boys took part in bag races and other games, the men began to harness their horses for the afternoon trotting event. Carrie stood in the shade of a tall oak tree near the schoolhouse and watched as the excited men and boys began to crowd near the racetrack. Most members of the Fairbanks and Nahma Trotting Association were there and the afternoon promised a continual succession of races until the final field of four ran against each other.

Henry was in the midst of it, tallying bets and paying off winners. In the heart of all the activity, Carrie was suddenly smitten with loneliness again. She turned around to leave and almost ran into Drew McGeary.

Drew laughed and reached out to steady her.

"How long have you been behind me?" Carrie demanded.

"I've been following you for almost an hour."

"You couldn't have been."

"Aye, but I have, and now that I've been found out, I'm asking you to have a bit of lemonade with me." Carrie took the arm he offered and let him lead her down the hill and into the Shelton House dining room where he ordered two lemonades. They came with chipped ice in them, making them icy cold.

"You'll be hungry," he said. "You and the other woman passed out a lot of fried chicken, but I didn't see you take a bite." He ordered them a dinner of white fish and roasted potatoes.

"Is the marble quarry working?" he asked as they ate.

Carrie found she was anxious to tell him all about it,

which she did. Finally he sat back and looked at her.

"You are a smart and handsome woman, Carrie Grey. I wonder why someone doesn't marry you."

Carrie blushed. "Perhaps I don't want marrying."

Drew caught the attention of the passing waiter and ordered two more cold lemonades. "Put a bit of something in one of them," he told the man and Carrie saw him press a coin into the man's palm.

"Henry LaTermaine doesn't suit you then?" he said, turning back to her.

Carrie put her napkin to her lips to cover the cough necessitated by the bite of fish in her mouth entering the wrong tube. Drew reached over and patted her on the back and then offered her a glass of water.

"I'm not surprised. He has too much of the snake in him for you, doesn't he?"

Carrie simply stared at him. How could he have possibly known Henry had proposed to her?

Drew told her. "He told me, no warned me, to stay away from you. He said that you and he were to be married soon. I told him I didn't believe it. I was right, wasn't I?"

Carrie laughed. "You are the strangest man I ever met, Drew McGeary."

"What I wonder is why he thought he had to warn me to stay away from you?"

Carrie blushed again and sipped water from the glass she still held in her hand. The waiter came with their lemonade and when he left, Carrie changed the subject.

"I saw your schooner yesterday morning, coming around the point by Burnt Bluff. Did you go to Escanaba, then?"

"Escanaba first, Cedar Harbor second. But you weren't there."

"I came into town a couple of days ago to stay with Edward and Louella." She looked at him and then quickly down at the white damask cloth on the table in front of her. Her next words slipped from her mouth without her permission. "I'd waited for you for over a month, and I got lonely. So I came to Fayette to be with friends."

She looked up at him, helpless to stop herself. "It's strange, I've lived alone at Cedar Harbor for the three years since Albert died, and I was never lonely until last week."

Drew touched her knee with his under the table. "I have to work for a living, my dear. If that old schooner doesn't make at least twenty trips a year up and down the lake, I tend to get mighty thin when the ice moves in. Trust me, I came back to you as quick as I could."

Carrie returned the pressure of knee against knee and looked into his blue-green eyes. "I trust you, Drew."

When the sun began to sink, the cooler air revived the older revelers— and the young ones, played out from racing around all day from one excitement to the next, began to fall asleep against their parents. Soon after, they were wrapped in a quilt and carried off to be placed on one of the many wagon loads of hay. Only the older children still watched as the cakewalk began.

Henry LaTermaine walked among the crowd one more time searching for Carrie. He hadn't seen her since before the horse races began. She had been standing under the big oak near the schoolhouse, watching the racers harness the horses and attach the sulkies. What an exciting afternoon of racing it had been. Big Iron had been the ultimate winner, although Doc Rutherford's Old Tom had given Big Iron a close finish. Lots of money had exchanged hands, and Henry had gotten his share for playing the odds-maker. He'd also laid a wager for himself on LeComte's Girlie, a chestnut mare with white feet, and she'd done well enough to beat the odds he'd laid out for her. That meant both he and Frank had made a little money.

Henry liked Frank LeComte; he felt comfortable with him. His wife, Shirley, was helping lay the cakes out on the dance hall floor. She was a pretty one, with her blonde curls swept up and then cascading down her slim back. She was wearing a yellow calico dress with a low cut neckline.

The cakewalk would be starting soon. Where was Carrie? Instinctively Henry was also looking for Drew McGeary. He suspected he might find them together, in which case he fully considered challenging McGeary to a duel. Carrie had promised to accompany him to the cakewalk and he had warned McGeary to stay away from her. McGeary had laughed at him, of course. Told him he reckoned that Mrs. Grey was capable of choosing her own man without any interference from the likes of Henry LaTermaine.

He saw Louella Rutherford as he threaded his way through the crowd. She and Dr. Rutherford stood at the edge of the wooden floor that the workers from the carpenter shop had laid out upon the ground for dancing. Normally a dance would be held in the opera house, but the heat had prompted Jack Sailstad to prevail upon the boys to "throw something together outside". The dance floor occupied the street between the general store and the harbor.

"Have you seen Carrie?" Henry asked as he came up behind the Rutherfords. "She was supposed to meet me here."

"I haven't seen her all afternoon," Louella said.

"Last I saw her, she was walking along the docks with that Andrew McGeary," put in Mrs. MacLean, who was standing close by.

"How long ago?' Henry simmered beneath the calm face he hoped he was presenting to the assembled company.

"Oh, hours ago," Mrs. MacLean said. "While the horses were running."

Henry scanned the harbor. Wave Dancer was not there, but then he wouldn't expect her to be in port. As usual when there was an opportunity for a crowd, McGeary would anchor her off shore and just out of sight so he could ferry men back and forth to the poker tables, sell them watered down bottles of rum, and probably even have three of four women in the afterdeck hold to sell. The worse thing about it was it cut into his business down at The Hole in The Rock.

The cakewalk had begun, with the men strolling along beside the cakes while the Fayette Cornet Band played music. When the music stopped the men had to buy the cake they were standing by and dance the first dance with the lady who had made it. Henry watched the chocolate layer cake Carrie had made, the one he would be trying to be close to when the music stopped if he knew where the hell Carrie was. Ian MacLean claimed the cake, but no lady stepped forward to be his dance partner.

Drew and Carrie sat for a long time in silence watching the sparkle of sun-diamonds on the deep blue surface of the lake. Drew lit his pipe and leaned forward with his elbows on his knees.

"Are you a religious woman, Carrie?"

The question caught her by surprise. "Religious? Well, I believe in God, naturally, don't you?" But I wouldn't call myself religious."

Carrie waited for a response but Drew only glanced at her and drew in on his pipe, compressing his cheeks slightly when he inhaled.

"Are you Catholic?"

"My father was Catholic and I was baptized such, but my mother's parents were Lutheran and when I went to live with them after Mama died—my churching was different then. I..." Carrie faltered. "Why are you asking me this, Drew?"

Drew stood up and knocked the spent tobacco from his pipe by tapping it against the sole of his shoe.

"I'm Irish and therefore Catholic, but never set much store by it. That preacher's wife I brung here—people like her raise my hackles."

Carrie nodded. "I have a friend, a school teacher, who studied Eastern religions. You know, Hindu and Buddhism. She claimed that the modern Christianity has it all wrong about God. We used to discuss it often."

Drew had been standing before her, rocking back and

forth on his heels. Now he sat down beside her again.

"Eleven years ago," he began, some hesitancy in his voice, "I was approaching Chicago with a load of Michigan pine in the hold. From far out we could see the orange glow of the sky and knew there was a big fire. We stood off all night and watched it."

He glanced at her and Carrie nodded to encourage him to go on, curious where this strange conversation was leading.

"Suddenly I was overcome by the oddest feeling. No matter what words I choose to try to tell you about it, they won't come close to the experience. I've tried to tell it to myself a million times, but I can only feel it; I can't tell it."

He stopped and was silent for a long time. Carrie put her hand on his arm, felt the warmth and strength of it and the downy softness of the red-gold hair there. He reached over and covered her small hand with his own large and callused one.

"I suddenly felt like I was in the heart of that fire and that I was part of, the same as, oh hell — like I was there! But on the inside of everybody. I felt their terror and then the great peace as they died. Only I knew they, their souls I mean, didn't die, because suddenly as their bodies went, they — and me, became part of a great big loving wholeness. The loving wholeness was — I can't find the words. It was perfect and utterly empty of everything vile we know. There was no judgement, no envy, no hate, no regret; only this peaceful, loving, total awareness."

He stopped and squeezed her hand. "I went to Mass as soon as I could after that, but it wasn't there. I've never found it again, but I know it's always there. Do you think it was God, Carrie?"

Carrie nodded slowly. "Yes, Drew, I'm sure it was and how I envy you for that experience. There were stories like that in some of Eleanor's books. She called it the "Pearl of great worth" that Christ spoke about. Only, she said, the church tried to put it in a box and reduce it to words, and as you know, you can never do that with the true God."

"I've never told this to anyone, Carrie. But somehow I knew you'd understand. Those stories in her books...did they happen to reprobates like me?"

Carrie shook her head.

"I didn't think so. So why me?"

Again Carrie shook her head.

"I don't know either. So life goes on, but sometimes I think about it and wonder what it all means."

Suddenly they heard scrambling noises behind them and then a fire-cracker exploded. Carrie jumped and then turned to watch the boys run off. The both laughed and stood up.

"Oh my, I'd almost forgotten. I told Henry I'd go to the cakewalk and dance with him."

Drew laughed and hugged her closer to his side. "I'll bet he's running all over town looking for you. Don't worry, he won't find us here."

Carrie slapped at a mosquito on her face. "Maybe not," she said, "but the mosquitoes have found us. Let's go back."

Drew stood and pulled her to her feet. Carrie let him embrace her, stepping completely into his arms, even to feeling him press himself against her with his whole body.

"You know what I want to do?" Drew whispered in her ear.

Carrie was pretty sure she knew, but she didn't know if she was prepared to go that far. She and Drew had spent the entire afternoon together. He'd made her laugh with stories about racing the ball to get through one of the swinging bridges in Chicago, or about Zach and Delbert, his two constant crew members. Carrie had told him a great deal about Albert and her childhood in Buffalo. Drew had told her how his hard-drinking pa had sold him off as a cabin boy on an ocean going schooner out of Ireland when he was only eight, and about the captain's kindly wife who taught him to read and write in between his scrubbing decks and running messages for the captain. And then there was the strange story he'd just finished. He'd shared his soul with her.

Several times during the day, they'd engaged in heavy

sparking, but, like a gentleman, Drew always pulled back. Carrie trusted him now, but she didn't trust herself to deny him again if he caressed and kissed her the way he had earlier.

"What do you want?" she whispered.

"I want to marry you and take you away with me."

His whisper in her ear startled her. This she hadn't expected. She realized that deep down she had believed Henry's story about Drew having a woman in every port. She drew back and looked into his blue green eyes and knew he was serious. She also knew that she loved him, maybe more than she had loved Albert.

"Yes," she said, "yes, yes, yes."

He kissed her, really kissed her, and then once again drew away. His voice was husky when he spoke.

"Here's what we have to do milady. I will take you back to Henry and you will attend the cakewalk and dance with him as if nothing was going on. I will board Wave Dancer, take her to Escanaba first thing in the morning and obtain a cargo. You will go home to Cedar Harbor tomorrow and pack. I will be there for you the day after tomorrow and we will sail away to Chicago together."

"And not tell anyone?" Carrie wasn't sure about that.

"No, no. You can send a message to your friends, the Rutherfords, by post, telling them what we've done. After I drop my cargo, we'll spend a week in Chicago. I'll take you to the theatre, shopping at Marshall Field's, and then we'll come back and settle you into Cedar Harbor as Mrs. Andrew McGeary. At the end of shipping season, I'll dry dock Wave Dancer there and we'll be snug as two bugs all winter."

"Carrie McGeary," Carrie laughed as she said it. "It has a queer sort of off-rhyme to it, doesn't it?"

When they neared Fayette and could hear the music playing and all the revelry, Carrie paused. "I don't think I can pretend I'm not the happiest woman alive."

"Let Henry think it's him you're happy with," Drew suggested. He kissed her cheek and released her hand. "It's best I go my separate way now. You can tell them you felt tired and went back to the house for a nap. Just get away early tomorrow so you can put things in order at the quarry before we leave."

Carrie watched Drew walk down the street and jump down onto the dock at the harbor. He must have had a shore boat tied there, for he got in and began to row. He had told her he left Wave Dancer outside the harbor, in fact she had seen it riding at anchor on the gentle swell of waves when they walked the beach. There had been quite a lot of people on board. When she remarked on it, he said Zach was taking a few passengers for a pleasure cruise to the Summer Islands. "Just a way to make a few more dollars."

Carrie stood and watched the dancers. Sam Howinski was calling the dance and there were four squares of dancers on the makeshift dance floor. Henry sat on a spread quilt with Louella and Edward. His was scowling as he repeatedly fingered the bowl of his pipe.

She looked away and pretended to be searching the crowd for him and found herself watching in fascination as a tall well-muscled man staggered out of the dark holding a cudgel of cedar over his head like a weapon. The man pushed into the crowd at the edge of the lantern lit dance floor, and holding the cudgel with both hands cracked it down on the dance floor with such force, the plank cracked. The music and the dancers stopped and turned, as one, toward the drunken man.

Shirley LeComte, standing on the dance floor next to Delbert Julliard, dropped his hand and rushed forward. Delbert was one of Drew's crewmen, the one Drew had just been telling her, loved, above all things, to dance. Shirley put her arms around the shoulders of the man with the club and began to plead with him.

"Frank, don't. I was only dancing with him because he bought my cake. You weren't here, you know, and I couldn't hardly take my cake out of the cake walk."

Then Carrie recognized the big man as the blonde

woman's husband. He was one of the foremen, the one who lived right across the street from Sailstads.

"He only buys one dance," Frank growled, "not all night."

When Delbert determined that he was the cause of the brouhaha, he looked confused. He took a step towards the arguing couple, and then turned around and ran down toward the harbor. Unfortunately, Drew had just left with the shore boat he was looking for to take him to the safety of Wave Dancer.

Frank LeComte pushed his wife away and brandishing the cedar cudgel gave chase. He had taken just a few steps when he fell, or tripped over something, and landed heavily on his face, which was saved from hitting the dirt by Carrie's chocolate layer cake. Jack Sailstad and Edward Rutherford were upon the man at the same time.

"Here now, Frank," Sailstad said. "You're drunk."

Shirley rushed over and knelt beside her husband, a linen towel in her hands. She tried to clean his face, but he grabbed the towel from her hands and pushed her away. Carrie saw her cringe away from him when he raised his hand, but Rutherford stopped the blow by wrenching Frank's arm down and twisting it behind him.

"You strike that woman in my presence and you're a dead man," Edward said.

Louella helped Shirley to her feet and Edward released his twisted grip on Frank's arm. Then Edward and Sailstad pulled the man to his feet and guided him up the hill to the water pump where they cleaned the frosting from his face and almost drown him with the quantity of cold water they pumped over him.

"And where have you been?" Carrie heard Henry ask.

After watching what one controlling man had threatened against his wife, Carrie didn't have the patience to deal with one herself.

"I had a headache and I've been at the Rutherfords taking a nap." She knew her voice sounded snappish. "I'm sorry if it spoils your evening, Henry, but I'm going back there."

She was three steps ahead of his offer to escort her and with no encouragement, he soon gave it up.

Chapter Sixteen

As she climbed the stairs from Dr. Rutherford's office to the main floor, Carrie suddenly realized how exhausted she was. When she reached the landing where the kittens were, she stopped and lowered the small lantern she held to look at them. Jewel was gone again and the kittens were mewling and crawling around the nest searching for their mother's warmth and teats. Carrie sat down and picked them up one by one until all three were in her lap. She put the tip of her little finger into the blind open mouth of Pearl and felt the tiny pull of the baby sucking.

"How long has your mama been gone?" she asked. "You act absolutely starved." She withdrew her finger from the white kitten's mouth and it immediately began to mew again. She gave her finger to Topaz and then Goldie; both sucked hungrily at it. Carrie put the kittens back in their basket, first holding each to her cheek and relishing the warmth and smell of them. They smelled so new.

Carrie walked back downstairs and stood outside the door calling, "here kitty, kitty. Here Jewel," but the mother cat did not appear. Carrie walked around the house. No Jewel. She climbed the back stairs into the kitchen. She found some milk in Louella's icebox and heated it by adding some hot water to it from the stove reservoir. Then she sat down again next to the basket and fed the babies by dipping her little finger in the milk and letting them suck.

By this method it took a long time for them to finish. While Carrie fed them she reflected on the afternoon she had spent with Drew. The girlish excitement that had rushed through her and made her gush, "yes, yes, yes," to Drew's proposal returned. He loved her! She held Topaz against her cheek and nuzzled the living ball of orange and white fur. "He loves me," she told it. "He loves me. And the day after tomorrow, I'm going away with him."

The cat mewed and dug its tiny claws into her dress. The small conveyance of fear by the kitten changed Carrie's emotions immediately. "Oh, what will I do with you kittens? And what of the chicks Edward has for me?"

She loosed the kitten's claws and put it back into the basket. Its hunger must have been satiated, for it curled against its nestlings and slept.

Carrie continued to talk aloud, ostensibly to the kittens. "Where has Jewel gone? She shouldn't be gone so long. And if I leave, then you'll be deserted a second time. Oh dear, I should never have acted so impulsively. Love has made a silly goose out of me." She continued to stroke the sleeping kittens with a finger as she tried to work out a way to be sensible and still go away with Drew the day after tomorrow. She would have to confide in Louella, that's all there was to it. Louella would let her leave the kittens here, and the chicks. It just couldn't be a secret the way Drew wanted it to be.

Carrie started to go over it all again in her mind. The next thing she knew, Louella was gently shaking her shoulder and urging her to wake up. She looked up at her hosts, uncomprehending for a moment, and then attempted to rise. Edward offered his hand.

"How long have you been sleeping there?" Louella scolded in a kind voice. The kittens were mewling again and a hasty glance told Carrie that Jewel was still gone.

"I came back right after that drunken man chased Delbert with the club. And Jewel was gone, so I fed the kittens. And Jewel is still gone." Carrie felt she was close to tears. She breathed in deeply and willed her throat to relax.

Edward put his arm around her waist and walked her up the four steps to the kitchen.

"I'm afraid I have bad news about that, Carrie." He patted her hand with his. "We found Jewel, just now, on our walk home. I'm afraid someone has been monstrous cruel where

Jewel is concerned. We found her little body in the road, between Sailstad's and LeComte's. It appeared someone had kicked her several times."

"No," Carrie cried, the former defeated tears now starting immediately down her cheeks. "No one could be so cruel."

"Cruelty in this world is abundant, my dear, but one is always shocked to find it in his back yard."

He seated Carrie at the table and Louella placed a cup of steaming tea before her. Carrie sniffed a few times, blew her nose and turned to look down at the three orphan kittens crawling around the basket looking for their mother.

"What will become of them?" she asked.

"Beth Underwood keeps a cat," Louella said. "Her kittens have just begun to run around and play. Sometimes a mother cat will adopt orphans. Tonight Edward and I will feed them with a medicine dropper and tomorrow we'll visit Beth."

"But I'll feed them," Carrie protested, "I'm not tired now."

Edward patted her shoulder as he filled a cup with milk and hot water. "You will be, my dear. I slipped a drop of laudanum into your tea. Take her up to bed, Louella. I'll feed these tiny rascals."

The next morning Carrie awoke with a real headache. Laudanum always left her with a dull throb for half a day. She wished Edward hadn't assumed she needed a sedative to sleep. She packed her bag, made up the bed, and went downstairs as soon as she heard Louella in the kitchen. She'd hoped to be able to talk to Louella alone, but Edward was up too, sitting on the landing feeding the kittens again.

It reminded Carrie that she had been an orphan. Only three when her mother died, and fourteen when her father's fishing boat failed to return, she'd been raised by her grandparents. It wasn't until she was almost seventeen that she had learned from Albert that her father's boat had been lost in a spring storm off Big Summer Island in Lake Michigan. Almost the same place Albert's upturned boat had been found three years ago.

So first an orphan and then a widow. She reflected that she had been alone more than half her life and this new happiness she had found with Drew was all she wanted now. To belong with someone, someone she loved and who loved her. And dare she dream even of a child? She and Albert had never conceived it was true, but maybe now? She was only twenty-eight. That wasn't too old.

Half way through breakfast, a patient came into Dr. Rutherford's office, and she and Louella were left alone at the table. Now was her chance.

"Can we see Beth about the kittens soon?" Carrie asked. "I'm supposed to catch the stage at nine."

"Why don't you stay another day, Carrie?"

"Thank you, Louella, but I really can't. And if that mother cat won't let my kittens nurse, well, then, I'll just have to ask Edward to take care of them."

"Well, of course we will," Louella said.

"No, I didn't mean that," Carrie stammered. "I meant to have him put them, well, you know, painless, and..." she began to weep.

"Beth's cat will nurse them," Louella said. "Don't you fret about it."

"Louella," Carrie put her hand out and Louella grasped it. "There's something else I need to talk to you about."

Louella listened quietly to Carrie's plans as they carried the basket of orphaned kittens and walked slowly on the shaded lane up Stewart Avenue. Beth ran the boarding house, where they found her dusting and cleaning the common room. Five kittens were scattered outside the door, wrestling and chasing grasshoppers. The mother, a brown and black calico, lounged on the porch in the sun. When Beth put the first hungry kitten to her teat, she looked down at it surprised, but them merely licked its tiny head as it greedily sucked. She greeted kitten two and three the same.

"But after they're weaned, you'll have to collect them," Beth said. "One or two good mousers are all I really need. This town is already overrun with dogs; it doesn't need a surplus supply of cats too. God only knows what I'll do with those five." She pointed her broom towards the cavorting kittens on the lawn.

Both Louella and Carrie assured her they would take the kittens as soon as they could survive without nursing.

On their way home, Louella finally commented on Carrie's news.

"Carrie, how well do you know your gentleman?"

Carrie related how they had met and the weekend she'd spent in Escanaba with him and Mr. Jenny. "I feel like I've known him forever, Louella. Imagine a man you can talk to, who listens and converses with you."

Louella nodded. Carrie knew Edward was such a husband, but she also knew such a one was rare.

"Why is it necessary for you to run off to Chicago with him?"

"He needs to keep Wave Dancer moving, Louella, to make money, you know. And what an adventure, to take a wedding trip to Chicago. Tell me if there is anything you want from Marshall Field's and I shall get it for you. I shall get you something at any rate."

"So you want Edward to keep the chicks for you until you return and you don't want me to tell him until the day after tomorrow?"

"Oh, as to Edward," Carrie felt her cheeks flush, "you can tell him right away. Just don't have it about town until I'm gone. Especially I don't want Henry to know. He's apt to come riding out with a shotgun to try to prevent it."

Louella laughed. "Henry?"

"I hadn't told you he asked me to marry him too. But all he wants is my quarry. And he told me Drew was a scoundrel and he even warned Drew, yesterday, to stay away from me."

Louella hugged Carrie shoulder to shoulder as they

continued to walk. "I've also heard that Captain McGeary is something of a scoundrel. But I can see the stars in your eyes and nothing I can say will dissuade you. Instead I wish you great happiness and remind you that you always have friends in Edward and myself."

Once she got home Carrie stayed up almost all night to finish sewing yet another walking suit for herself. She'd sent Louella into the general store to get a rust colored linen for it, along with a pair of matching brown shoes, and then daydreamed about Drew and Chicago on the stage trip home. She packed her trunk carefully, wishing she had more fashionable clothes. She would have to get Drew to take her to Marshall Field's first so she could have something suitable to wear when she met Mr. Jenny's wife. Mr. Jenny had told her that when she came to Chicago he and his wife would take her to the theatre.

The next morning she bathed in the large tub she set in the kitchen. She hummed happily as she scrubbed. Finally she stood and poured a pitcher of warm water over her body to rinse off the suds and stepped out. As she did so she looked at her body as she hadn't in a long time. What would Drew think of her? She ran her hands from under her breasts along the slight curve of her waist and along her hips. She felt the firmness of her hipbone and stopped at the triangle of brown curled hair where her legs met. Her skin was still tight and young looking. Her breasts although ample stood up proudly and she noticed the pink nipples had hardened and she blushed at the pleasure she felt.

She dried her skin vigorously, until it glowed pink, sloughing off more dead skin as she rubbed the rough towel against her. She would be married today, married to the man who had occupied her thoughts almost constantly since she had first met him two months ago. She put on her robe and dressed her hair carefully, remembering that it was her best feature. As she put on one of her new skirts she thought longingly of the beautiful white lace dress Eleanor had worn the day Henry had first proposed. It would never have fit of course, Carrie was fleshier than Eleanor, but still, it would have been more suitable than a plain blue skirt and blouse. Carrie supposed they would be married on board Wave Dancer. What else could Drew have had in mind?

The weather was fair, with a good wind, so Carrie expected Drew to arrive around ten o'clock. That gave her an hour to talk with Hugh Brandon about the quarry business and make arrangements for Francine Brandon to continue to mind the animals for her. She and Brandon were still going over the accounts by early afternoon, but Wave Dancer had still not entered the harbor.

Finally Carrie closed the books, satisfied that they were producing even more cut limestone and marble than she had thought possible. She told Brandon she would be gone for two weeks and instructed him to pay wages and run the entire operation with the cash on hand and what he would collect. She took two gold double eagles and six ten-dollar eagle coins with her. She planned to hide half of it in her trunk and put one double eagle in her corset. The other thirty dollars she carried in a black beaded handbag along with her handkerchief and comb.

By nightfall, Drew McGeary still hadn't appeared. Carrie fell asleep, fully clothed, on the parlor couch.

Chapter Seventeen

Louella waited almost a week before she calmly announced at breakfast one morning that Carrie ought to be in Chicago by now and married to Captain Andrew McGeary.

Edward nearly choked on the egg in his mouth and started up from the table. "My God, woman, I thought I heard you say Carrie Grey was married to Andrew McGeary."

"That's what I did say," Louella said. She reached over with an end of her apron and picked up the mouthful of eggs Edward had spat out and added them to the slop pail. "Is there something the matter with that?"

"Matter? Matter?" Edward was near to shouting. "My God, woman, don't you know what manner of man he is?"

Louella shook her head. "I know only what Carrie told me, with stars in her eyes, I might add. She said he was a kind man, one very like you, who really listened to her when she talked and that she was in love with him. She turned down a proposal from Henry LaTermaine you know."

Edward Rutherford began to pace the length of the house, from the front door to the rear, his hands clasped behind his back. Every now and then he stopped and asked Louella another question.

"When did she leave?"

"The sixth of July."

On his next turn through the kitchen he asked. "Were they traveling on his schooner?"

"Of course."

And finally, "why didn't you tell me at once?"

"Carrie asked me not too. She said Drew didn't want her to tell even me, but she did."

Edward exploded. "Of course the bastard didn't want her to tell anyone. Anyone in this town would have stopped her."

Louella still sat at the breakfast table. "Your language, Edward. Do sit down and tell me what it so awful about Carrie marrying a man she is in love with."

And so Edward told her. It was the first Louella had heard that the doggery near the sand beach had a brothel attached to it and that Drew McGeary supplied the girls. It was the first she had heard about him running other ships aground and "salvaging" their cargo. It was the first she had heard that no decent citizen, here or in Escanaba, would do business with the man most called the Great Lakes Pirate.

"But he's in town often. Somebody here must be doing business with him."

"Only the brothels and the doggeries that buy liquor from him. He anchors his boat outside the harbor and has a shore boat to row his customers out where he has gambling, rum, and girls of his own aboard. It's rumored that his main cargo between Escanaba and Chicago is women."

"Oh my," Louella stood up and sat down again abruptly. "Oh, poor dear Carrie. Oh Edward, you don't suppose...?"

"No, he's not taken her to a whore house. But he's taken her for her marble quarry, you can be sure of that. There is nothing we can do now except stand ready to help her when she returns."

"Should we not tell anyone else?" Louella asked. But she had already told Grace Sailstad, yesterday.

Edward threw his hands up in the air, shook his head, and headed down the stairs to his surgery. With any luck a patient would present soon and take his mind off Carrie Grey. The former Carrie Grey.

On the third day of waiting, Wave Dancer finally sailed into Garden Bay. Carrie had unpacked her trunk each evening when she remembered what Mrs. Britten had said, "Albert says don't do it." But then in the light of day such things seemed silly to her and so she repacked each afternoon, sure that Drew would come. She avoided going to the quarry and didn't remember to eat until the second afternoon when the pangs of an empty stomach could not be ignored. She cried herself to sleep each night.

The sight of the tall white sails of the schooner gliding before the wind late that morning caused a rush of joy within her and she ran to repack the trunk. If she'd been a girl she'd have skipped up the path. She almost did. As she carefully folded her two walking suits and her other new clothes in the trunk she suddenly grew angry with Drew that he was so late. Then she rationalized for him, as she had done the two previous days while she repacked the trunk. He may have had trouble finding a cargo. He told her the competition between lumber hookers was keen. He wasn't to blame if he had to spend days finding a cargo bound for Chicago.

Carrie changed her clothes, cinching herself into the hated corset and putting on the simple rose colored skirt and blouse and then almost ran to the end of the pier to wait. Wave Dancer was already so close she could see Drew at the helm. He waved at her. When the schooner came close to the end of the pier Drew leapt to the dock and grabbed Carrie around the waist and swung her off her feet in an exuberant embrace. Then he kissed her mouth, searching it with his tongue, feeling hers in return and finally held her away from him and looked her up and down.

"You look wonderful," he said. "Are you ready to go?"

Carrie could not resist a small reproach. "I've been ready for three days."

"Oh, Lass, I'm sorry about that. Took me a day and a half to find a cargo and another to get it loaded. But we're off now, aren't we?"

"I shall have to get used to you never being here when you say, I suppose?"

"That would be about right, Mrs. McGeary. But you can be sure I'll always come."

Carrie blushed at him calling her Mrs. McGeary. She'd been trying it out herself, and of course, she wasn't yet; but she liked the sound of it.

Two men came down the gangplank and stood a little aside, waiting. "You show these men where your trunk is. Can you be ready to leave in half an hour?"

"Less than that," Carrie said. "I only have to close up the house. I've got a bundle for your cook, no sense leaving good eggs and butter behind."

Carrie was surprised to see that the cook was a woman. She was short and stout, with red cheeks and short wiry hair and she wore trousers instead of skirts. The galley was cramped. A wood-fired cook stove with a rail around the top, which Carrie supposed was to keep pots from sliding to the floor with the roll of the vessel, had the heat beyond bearable. The woman's name was Bobbie and she welcomed Carrie aboard with a warm smile and kind words for the Captain. "Don't you believe any of the stories people will be telling you about your new husband, Ma'am. He's a popper, but he's got a heart o' gold."

Carrie laughed and wondered what the woman meant.

The cook and the galley were established in the aft portion of the deckhouse. Drew led Carrie though the kitchen and the cook's sleeping quarters into the room beyond reserved for himself and the First Mate, who was Zach. The room held two beds, a desk filled with charts and a rack of pipes, a table with two chairs, and a chest of drawers. Carrie's trunk sat next to the chest. All three sides of the cabin had porthole windows with curtains that could be pulled shut for privacy. Another door opened forward right behind the helm. Carrie felt the motion as Wave Dancer began to move away from the pier. Drew kissed her lightly and told her to make herself at home while he went above to "steer 'er out of the harbor."

Alone in the cabin, Carrie wandered around looking at the various objects hanging from the walls. There was a clock and a pair of crossed swords as well as a rifle and a set of ivory handled pistols. The rifle was fitted into a maple rack, but the pistols were nestled in a padding of dusty blue fabric. Carrie blew the dust away and watched as the motes resettled. The pistols looked old, like antique display items. Two books lay on the chest near the bed. She picked one of them up. It was Walt Whitman's "Leaves of Grass" and the other was "Billy Budd" by Herman Melville. Interesting reading.

Carrie peered out one of the small round windows and discovered she could watch Drew behind the big maple wheel. He was a fine specimen of a man, tall and well muscled. The wind blew through his sandy brown hair and wafted the smell of his tobacco towards her, which mingled with the pervasive odor of the tar used to caulk seams and the smells from the galley.

Only after they had passed though the Door Island channel and out into Lake Michigan proper late in the afternoon did he turn the helm over Zach for the second watch.

"Come out and watch the sunset with me," he invited, "while Bobbie sets our dinner out."

Carrie ducked her head and went out onto the deck with him. There was lumber piled on every inch of deck and Drew told her the hold was full besides. Wave Dancer was bigger than Carrie had first thought. She was 127 feet long with a twenty-seven foot beam and eight foot deep hold. The crew consisted of Bobbie, Zach, Delbert, a youngster about Tommy's age, and two other men who were just then asleep in the forecastle.

"That's Peter." Drew called her attention to the boy climbing the mast. "This is his first year on the Lake. He wants mothering, gets a bit wild in port. Maybe you can take him in hand like my old Captain's wife did for me."

"You were only a lad," Carrie replied. "Peter looks beyond steering to moderation."

Drew shook his head in the negative. "You'd be surprised how supple lads, even grown men, remain to a woman's influence. Just give him a nod and a word or two before we reach Chicago. Chicago is a rough place along the river."

The wind was light, perfect for sailing Drew said, and they'd be in Chicago day after tomorrow if the wind held. When Carrie began to shiver from the evening coolness, he pointed her towards the cabin. Bobbie had laid a supper of ham and sweet potatoes with apple cobbler for dessert. Drew poured her a glass of wine and toasted her.

"To my beautiful new wife, may she smile like that forever."

Carrie was smiling and she toasted him back. "To my handsome husband, may he always have a fair wind to bring him home to me."

After several glasses of wine Drew led Carrie to the bed and began to unbutton the front of her blouse.

Carrie drew back. "Drew, we're not married yet."

Drew threw back his head and laughed. "I'm forgetting myself, am I?"

He reached into his pocket and pulled out a red velvet box. He extracted a gold ring from it and grasping her left hand, slipped it onto the third finger. It was a perfect fit.

"We're married, Carrie. And as soon as we reach port in Chicago we'll have the preacher bless us with legalities. But surely this is our wedding night?"

He pulled her to him and nuzzled her neck while he again unbuttoned the blouse. This time Carrie didn't protest.

In the morning Carrie awoke to sunshine streaming in one of the little round windows. Drew was gone, but the smell of him lingered on the coverlet of the bed. He smoked a tobacco that had a hint of apple in it. Carrie pulled the cover under her chin and breathed deeply of it, then she stretched like a cat just awakened and wondered what, if anything, was expected of her on board. She'd never gone on Albert's fishing boat except for that first trip from Buffalo to Mackinac City. Albert had been anxious to be making a living for her, catching fish, and so she had waited at Mackinac City for their furniture, which was coming overland, and then for the schooner Albert had booked passage on to take her and the furniture to Fayette. It seemed so very long ago, a lifetime ago.

It was, for Carrie, another life now. She had a new husband. She leapt from the bed and quickly wrapped her morning robe around her naked body. She had never before in her life slept naked, but Drew had insisted upon it. She knelt before her trunk and selected the blue wool skirt and blouse. She brushed and braided her long brown hair and wrapped it atop her head to secure it against the lake wind, and then picked out a short jacket of crème boiled wool.

Just as she finished dressing there was a light tap on the door between Drew's room and the galley.

"Come in," she called.

"Please, Ma'am, if you could open the door?" It was Bobbie, the cook. Carrie opened the door to find her standing there with a cloth-covered basket from which delicious smells emanated.

"The Captain is comin' directly," she said. "I'll just get the table laid for the two of ya." She winked at Carrie and set the heavy basket on the floor next to the table.

Bobbie spread an almost white tablecloth on the table and then two blue tin ware plates and cups. A large platter contained sliced ham and scrambled eggs.

"The very eggs you brought me," Bobbie confided to her. "The butter is your very own too."

Carrie picked up one of the warm biscuits and tasted it.

"Excellent, Bobbie."

There was another tap at the door and Zach entered carrying a large coffee pot that matched the blue tin ware plates. Bobbie set out a jar of sugar and some milk and, finally, a vase of yellow brown-eyed-susans.

"I picked them for ya," she said, her voice continuing to have a confidential tone to it. "You have a nice breakfast, now. Nobody'll be disturbing ya again until the afternoon."

As the cook left, Drew entered. He looked her up and down with approval and kissed her neck where a few stray strands lay that had not been swept up into her braids.

"You look lovely, Carrie." He held her chair for her and then sat across from her.

"I feel lovely, Drew. What a delicious night it was." It was true; Carrie had not known how much she missed the physical aspects of having a husband. "Would you like me to pour your coffee?"

"I like to take my coffee after I've eaten," he said.

Carrie liked to have hers with her meal, but she deferred. Coffee with or after a meal was not important. From now on she would have her coffee when he did.

"I won't tell you you're the first woman to be in this cabin for breakfast, Carrie," he began. "You'll find out soon enough what manner of man I've been. But I will say you are the first woman I've had in this cabin that I've been in love with, and there will be no others now."

Carrie felt herself blush. "A woman in every port is what they told me."

Drew laughed and did not deny it. "I like women, and it makes me damn mad to see them treated badly. You'll hear stories about the ones I've rescued from the streets in Chicago and taken north. Pay 'em no mind, most of 'em are lies."

Carrie raised her eyebrows, but he said nothing more about it. Instead he reported that they had a good sail and would be in Chicago tomorrow. In the meantime, it would be best if she stayed in the cabin. Bobbie would take care of her needs.

"Well, most of 'em," Drew said, the smile Carrie loved so moving from his blue-green eyes to his mouth. "It's too bad you put all those clothes on before breakfast."

They made love quickly, as if from some desperate need in both of them and then Drew got up and dressed. "You can sit outside by the wheel, if you want. I'll bring one of the chairs out for you."

Carrie dressed again and spent the rest of the morning on the deck. At noon Bobbie served bread with slabs of roast beef and slices of cheese along with a bowl of fresh peaches. All hands ate on deck and finished up with cups of steaming coffee. After lunch Carrie went inside to take a nap and get out of the hot sun.

That evening Carrie and Drew danced in the small area of the cabin. Drew had one of those new phonographs that played music from a cylindrical black disc with grooves in it. He said the music was hidden in the grooves and when the needle of the phonograph passed over the grooves, the music was released again. There was a handle that had to be wound before each disc was played, and Drew only had two. One was Viennese waltzes and the other one Irish music. Carrie watched while Drew danced a jig for her and they both fell over onto the bed, laughing when he tried to teach her to do it.

Then they snuggled together in the bed for another delicious night of lovemaking while the schooner continued to dance over the waves, southbound.

Chapter Eighteen

Henry paced from one end of his office to the other with his pipe in his hand, his fingers running up and down the stem. He stopped in front of the window and gazed across at the Shelton House, not really seeing it until a woman came out of the door and stood on the porch. His heart jumped, because for a moment she looked like Carrie. He even turned from the window and headed for the stairs to intercept her, but stumbled on the waste bin and cracked his shin. He ruefully rubbed the barked shin as he turned back to the window and watched a tall man join her. It wasn't Carrie, of course; the woman was too short.

If what Shirley LeComte had just told him was true, Carrie Grey was in Chicago by now. Shirley said Carrie had run off to Chicago with Drew McGeary and that she was going to marry him! He should have been more explicit in telling Carrie what manner of man Drew McGeary was. All he could remember telling her was that he was a scoundrel. Well, he was certainly that, and more.

Henry's first impulse had been to saddle his horse and ride out to Cedar Harbor. Instead he went up to Rutherford's to see if what Shirley LeComte had told him was true.

He had to wait while doc stitched up the leg of some sawmill worker. The man screamed twice and then Henry heard some whimpering. Shortly thereafter the man came hobbling out of the surgery with a bandage wrapped around his leg from just below his knee to his ankle. Dr. Rutherford came behind him, warning him to "keep it clean, and don't let Gloria be dumping any of her remedies into the wound. Come back tomorrow so I can look at it. If you don't come, I'll have your foreman trundle you in."

Henry could appreciate the man's position. He knew the man was already in hock to the Company for several months' pay and couldn't afford to miss work to visit the doctor if his leg felt all right. Chances were that without the threat to have "your foreman trundle you in" the man would rely on his wife, Gloria, to continue the treatment. Henry knew Dr. Rutherford subscribed to the new antiseptic methods of medical practice, believing in small-unseen "germs" as the cause of infection and disease. To that end, soap and water were his most prescribed treatments. Henry knew; he sold more soap in the Fayette General Store than most stores did.

"Well, Henry, are you ill?" Rutherford asked, once the stitch up patient was gone. "You certainly look pale."

"Is it true that Carrie ran off with Drew McGeary?"

Edward polished his glasses on the sleeve of his coat. "That's what Louella says. Carrie told her she was leaving with him on the Sixth of July and asked her not to tell anyone. If she'd told me at once I'd have tried to stop it, but there's nothing can be done now. As it is, she told me this morning, and from what I gather I was the last to know, since she told Grace Sailstad yesterday."

Henry balled his right fist and pounded it into his left palm again and again. "Damn him," he muttered. "Damn, damn, damn."

"Precisely, Henry," Rutherford said. "Carrie Grey was one of my favorite people."

Henry left the Doctor's house and went to the stables to saddle his horse. Then he rode up furnace hill and along the road to The Hole in the Rock. He wondered if Peony knew about it, and if she did, what she intended to do about it.

Ned Stoddy counted out the receipts from last night's business, putting more than a dozen coins into his pockets before he wrote the remaining amount down in Henry's goddamn account book. He was tired of doing all the work while LaTermaine took ten percent off the top and insisted he pay the girls five percent of what they brought in. And McGeary changed girls too often, charging him twenty dollars passage for each new girl he brought up from Chicago and never giving him credit for the girls he took away. Not that he ever dealt face to face with McGeary. Henry paid McGeary and then charged him, with a hefty mark-up, no doubt.

Only Peony was permanent, and she belonged to Henry, not Stoddy. Booze was another issue. Henry bought the stuff from McGeary and resold it to him. If Stoddy didn't water each bottle by half and add a little pepper to spice it up, he'd have been broke before daylight.

Well, any day now, things would change. The new house was almost ready and the girls he put there would be his and his alone. The two bits a trick they brought in would all be his too. The hell with paying the girls five percent. His new place, which he called The Stockade, because that's what it was, a stockade to keep the girls in, would be open for business soon. He had one girl already. She was a sorry little thing who had answered his advertisement in the Milwaukee newspaper for a companion for his wife. Luckily she'd come though Fayette with no one paying much mind to her and so far she was happy with her new quarters. Stoddy told her his wife, who was non-existent, was "taking the waters" at the Big Springs near Manistique, and she could just settle into her room and wait. He was expecting a second girl from the advertisement any day now. As soon as she came, he could open up. The first week he was going to charge four bits, since the girls were virgins. He figured on maybe a hundred dollars take for first week alone.

When Henry walked in the door, Stoddy felt his bowels loosen. He must have had four dollars in unreported cash in his pockets and he knew from past experience that Henry didn't trust him. More than once Henry had searched him for stray silver after looking at the account books. That's why he hid his money in a jar buried in a cave only he knew about.

So Stoddy acted pleased to see Henry, which each man knew was a lie. Lucky for Stoddy, Henry seemed to have something else on his mind.

"Peony here?"

"Guess so. 'Less she's out on the beach with that stupid book of hers, drawing posies."

Henry nodded and passed through the dingy, smelly barroom to knock on Peony's door. Stoddy caught a glimpse of the dusky woman's orange robe when she opened the door to admit Henry. Miss Highfalutin' herself, as if she wasn't a common whore like the rest of them. Stoddy swiped at the glass with his dirty rag and put it on the shelf with the rest of 'em.

Peony was unprepared for the news Henry brought, but she wasn't surprised. And she challenged Henry directly.

"And are you any better of a man for the lady to marry? Bah, your hands are as dirty as his."

Henry protested that he was only a businessman.

"So much the worse, Mr. LaTermaine. Drew has rescued most of the girls he brings here from conditions in Chicago you can't even imagine. He simply makes you pay for their passage rather than collecting from the ladies. Not a one of them will speak ill of him, to you, or anyone."

"So you don't expect anything to change?"

Peony thought about that a minute. "I can't be sure. Perhaps if Drew really loved a woman he'd be faithful. At least for six months."

She laughed. Henry forced a smile.

"Still, I can't see how marriage will affect our business. He will still have to work for a living."

"Don't be too sure about that," Henry said. He began to pace on the richly carpeted floor of Peony's suite of rooms. He stopped before the painting in progress she had on an easel in front of the window. It was a woman, walking on the beach with her skirt hiked up and her shoes in her hand. He turned abruptly to look at Peony who sat on a brown velvet chair watching him.

"Where did you meet her?"

"Her? The woman in the picture? On the beach, just as you see her. I thought she had a certain beauty. It's Carrie Grey isn't it?"

Henry nodded. "She knows about you?"

Peony laughed again, a short wry laugh. "Everyone knows there is a brothel here, Henry. All Carrie Grey knows is that I am one of the women who work here. I saw her one morning when she was out for a walk along the lake."

Peony saw no reason to tell him of the second time Carrie had come looking for her, nor of the exchange of glances between them at the Fourth of July celebration. When Peony saw Carrie, she knew she shouldn't have chanced coming into town and had quickly walked back to the brothel along the railroad tracks. If things were different she knew she and Carrie would be friends. It didn't surprise her that Drew liked the woman. He liked to talk about what he called 'deep' matters, things that men like him were not expected to think about, and she imagined he had found that in Carrie. Even in their very brief exchange on the beach, Peony had known that Carrie was an exceptional woman. She had been trying to capture that in the painting, but felt she had not.

Henry continued to study the picture. "You don't have her eyes right. They are smaller than that, and the expression you have makes her look like one of those angels in a classical painting. It looks a little silly on her. Too girlish."

Peony came up and stood beside Henry. "I wanted to capture her innocence, mingled with knowing and non-judgement. Don't you see those qualities in her?"

"No." His voice had an angry edge; "She has a business sense as astute as Drew's. She owns a little stone and marble quarry, you know. She's as wealthy as anyone on the peninsula, or will be."

Peony looked up at him. "And you think Drew married her to get her money? Because that's what you wanted to do, wasn't it? Don't deny it, Henry, I can see it in your face."

Henry shrugged, picked up his hat and left. After the door

closed, Peony went to stand in front of the painting again. She picked up her book with the sketches she'd made of Carrie Grey. The first one had been hasty, right after Carrie left that first day. The other two had been made on the 4th of July as Carrie watched the parade, scanning the crowd as if searching for someone. When she'd seen Peony, her face had lit up, and that was the expression Peony was trying to capture. Henry was right; she hadn't gotten it. She picked up her palette and a rag and washing out the face, she started again.

Chapter Nineteen

Carrie and Drew sat on the roof of the deck cabin and watched the port of Chicago loom up in front of them. The ship traffic on the Lake had been heavy since they had sailed past Milwaukee at dawn. About every third ship was, like Wave Dancer, a schooner, but there were more steam-powered freighters.

"Most of the schooners have a steam engine below that they'll use if the wind fails 'em," Drew said.

"Do you?"

"No, I know how to coax a full sail out of a couple of sailors breathing heavy."

Carrie laughed. Drew was confident in his own daring do, no matter what the subject was. She had observed that right away and admired him for it.

"So what happens now?" Carrie asked. She wrinkled her nose as a breeze from the shore blew by them. "Phew. Chicago smells as bad as Fayette."

"That's the stock yards, my dear. Chicago brings in beef on the hoof, slaughters the cattle, ices the beef down with Lake Michigan ice and ships it East. Everything the West grows they ship into Chicago on trains and we take it East on the Lakes."

"What types of cargo do you carry when you go back up Lake?" Carrie asked.

"Whatever I can get. Henry usually has an order of dry goods for me to pick up. Being a schooner Captain is like being a gambler. I buy most of my cargo and bet that I can sell it at a profit in Escanaba, Green Bay, or somewhere along the way. The easy trip is down Lake with timber. There's always a market for timber in Chicago."

"But you have to buy that too?"

"Yes, and the haggling over the price is what takes so long.

The timber owners read the Chicago market prices and think we should pay them almost as much as we'll get when we sell it. Trouble is, the price could drop before we get the timber down there, and we have to pay a crew and provision the ship. Last trip down I sat in port for a week waiting for the prices to go up so I could break even."

"Then why don't you sell your own timber?" Carrie asked.

Drew laughed. "Sure, I've got a sawmill and acres of timber."

"But I've got timber lands, Drew. Timber I haven't sold to the Jackson Iron Company like most everyone else has. Why don't you put your crew to work this winter cutting timber? We can build a mill on the harbor, you know, towards the old boat house, and next year you can haul our lumber."

Drew looked at her with surprise in his eyes and then they crinkled at the corners with a smile and then a laugh. He picked Carrie up and swung her off the deckhouse roof and made her dance the jig with him in the small deck space available. Carrie was aware of the crew pausing to watch them, but she didn't care.

"Carrie, my wife, I love you. I didn't know I was marrying a business woman."

Breathless they both stood and watched the growing forest of ships masts as they approached the mouth of the Chicago River. "Just you wait, my lady," Drew said. "Together we'll make the greatest team you've ever seen."

"But what happens next, Drew?" Carrie said again. "When will we be married?"

Drew looked down at her and then around at the other ships lining up to enter the river. "Right now," he said. "There's the Mary B. I'll send Zach over with the boat to bring back Captain Alphonse and he'll marry us. Boat captains can do that, you know."

"On the ocean," Carrie said, "but on the Lakes too?"

"Of course," Drew said. "It's an old tradition, even if seldom used. You go inside and put on whatever fancy dress you want to be married in. I'll send Bobbie in to help you."

Carrie kissed the tip of his nose and giggled. "All right, Captain. I'll be ready when you are."

Captain Alphonse was an old man with a well-trimmed white beard and brilliant blue eyes. He wore a blue jacket with gold trim and pulled a well-worn Bible from his pocket as he stood in front of Drew and Carrie. Bobbie stood to Carrie's right, a clean apron covering her overalls and Zach stood up next to Drew. Captain Alphonse read from the Bible where God commanded a man to leave his father and mother and cleave to his wife. Then he read the part where St. Paul tells the women to obey their husbands and the husbands to love their wives. Finally he asked Drew if he took Carrie Grey to be his wedded wife. He did. Then he asked if Carrie took Drew to be her wedded husband. She did and he said Drew could kiss the bride. Alphonse accepted a bottle of whiskey from Drew in payment for his services and Zach rowed him back to his boat.

As Drew and Carrie stood on the deck to watch the boat pull away, Drew held her close with his arm around her shoulder and said, "There you are, Carrie. Now you are really and truly Carrie McGeary."

"And the happiest woman alive," she replied.

"And now, Mrs. McGeary, I suggest you go inside and pack up your trunk. As soon as I engage a tug to pull us into the river I lose control of the ship. When we come to the Clark Street Bridge, the crew will be furloughed and you along with them."

Carrie looked up at Drew in alarm. "I'm to be put ashore without you?"

"I'll need to stay with Zach. This will be his first experience at the lumber market and it will be better for you to be without me than him. The wolves in the lumber exchange are worse than those in the panel houses."

"Where will I go?" Carrie asked. She began to be frightened and although she wasn't a woman given to tears she felt the gathering of them behind her quickly fluttering lids.

"Don't worry, Lovely. Delbert will take you to a boarding house where I'll join you in a day or two. You'll be fine, just don't venture out onto the streets until I come. I've given over the Captaincy of Wave Dancer to Zach for the trip home so we can have our week of shopping and theatre." He kissed her mouth and then the tip of her nose and pushed her towards the cabin. Carrie turned at the doorway to watch Drew converse with a man aboard a small tugboat with black smoke trailing out of its stack. The crew was busy taking in the last of the sail and raising the anchor. Zach was leading the chantey song the men worked to.

Carrie carefully removed her light blue walking suit in which she'd just been married and laid it in the trunk. Then she thought perhaps she should have left it on. She had no idea how the ladies on the streets of Chicago dressed. Finally she decided to put on the rust colored linen walking-suit, which was darker in color and therefore more conservative. By the time she had everything in readiness she could feel the steady rhythm of the tug engine reverberating though the schooner. She went outside to watch.

The open lake with its fresh breezes had vanished. There were vessels of every description crowding the narrow river; there were schooners under tow by the tugs, grimy rowboats with two to six people in them, and great scows piled high with black coal, not to mention the noisy steam powered cargo ships pouring smoke into the already hot atmosphere. The air was palpable with dust and Carrie could feel the grime in the damp air settling on her skin and clothes. She was glad she had taken off her wedding suit. The dark color would conceal the dirt. The July heat was smothering and Carrie wondered if the black beads of sweat she observed on the brows of the crew were duplicated upon her own.

The shoreline was crowded with ugly buildings, the most prominent being a series of tall, red, grain elevators. Smoke poured from tall chimneys along the shore adding to the smell and general haze, all of which became Carrie's first impression of Chicago. They were approaching a bridge and Carrie was amazed to see it swing open from the cement base in the middle of the river to let them through. There was barely room between the shore and the bridge support in the river for them to pass. They came so close to a schooner moored to a dock that Carrie was afraid they would scrape.

Then Carrie became aware of the incredible number of people on the street waiting for the bridge to swing closed again so they could continue. She watched as one young man, dressed in a business suit and carrying a leather case, leapt from the shore to the almost closed bridge and began to dash across the still moving road to the other side. She observed many well-dressed women among the crowd, as well as young women in the simple garb of servant girls. Almost without exception, the young men were suited and wore bowler hats.

She heard Drew shout and turned to see the cause. He was shaking his fist and shouting a stream of language the likes of which Carrie had never heard. It was easy to tell he was upset with the tugboat captain about something.

"He won't stop at the Clark Street Bridge to let us off unless Drew pays him an extra twenty dollars," Bobbie explained. Carrie turned, surprised and glad, to see the cook standing by her elbow.

"Why?"

"Because the bridge is open and he'll loose too much time to let us off. We'll have to stay aboard until we have to stop for a closed bridge. Then he'll inch us close enough to shore so we can jump off."

Carrie was appalled at this news. How was she to make such a leap? And how then was her trunk to be off-loaded? She made her way to Drew's side.

"If they want extra to make a proper docking for us I'll pay it," she said. "I fear I'll..."

Drew turned towards her, his face in a countenance she had never seen before. "I will take care of my wife, thank you.

No one has asked you to pay your own way. Now get back to the cabin until we dock. You won't be having to endanger yourself."

He turned and glared at Bobbie. She glared back at him, but she didn't meet Carrie's eyes when Carrie passed her on her way into the cabin. Carrie sat on her trunk and listened to the unnatural noises of the passage, noises to which she could attach no action. It seemed like forever until the cabin door opened and Drew entered and stood in front of her. He still looked angry.

"We'll be docking at the Wells Street Bridge. Delbert has gone ahead to secure a hack to meet you and carry you and your trunk to Daisy's place. You've got five minutes."

"Drew?"

"What?" He snarled, and then his voice softened. "Carrie you need to understand this is a delicate business, passing through the Chicago River. It takes all my attention."

He strode to his desk and removed a small tin box that he handed her. "There is enough money in here to pay for your meals and any little thing you might need until I join you. Daisy will take care of you. Don't leave the building."

He put great stress on the last four words.

"How long will you be?" Carrie asked, forcing the hesitancy she felt out of her voice.

He turned and kissed her quickly on the cheek, a dry peck that contained no warmth. "I don't know. As soon as I can. You just wait."

Just then Peter and another man entered the cabin and picked up her trunk.

"Stick close to me," Drew said to her. "We need to get you off the ship quickly."

Carrie followed on their heels. The schooner bumped heavily against a dock and Drew screamed more obscenities at the tug captain as Carrie fell against the mast to keep from sprawling on the deck.

"He bumped us hard a purpose," Drew said, as he righted

her and held her elbow tightly. "Hurry now."

Drew stood at the side and helped her climb from the schooner deck up a three rung ladder to the dock. Peter and the other man heaved the trunk up alongside her and then Peter jumped up beside her. Before she could comprehend what was happening, Wave Dancer was swinging back out into the river. She watched as the large metal bridge in front of them started to swing open. She feared the bridge would take out the forward mast of Wave Dancer as the tug surged forward to be into the channel in the first possible moment of opening.

Young Peter stood beside her, obviously anxious to be on the move. "Del is supposed to meet us here," he said, "with a taxi to take you to the hotel. Don't be scared, I'll wait with you. I just hope he isn't too long."

Chapter Twenty

Strangers weren't unusual in Fayette. The Shelton House, especially since the large addition had been finished in the spring, attracted visitors. The Lady Washington brought most of its lodgers across Lake Michigan from Escanaba. Company officials, along with their wives, visited regularly. The new wing had a VIP suite in the north corner known as the Fayette Brown Suite. Besides the sitting room there were two bedrooms (where the beds had the new innerspring mattress) and a dressing room. The rooms were wallpapered in a red flocked floral and the large new windows let in a lot of natural light. The best part was the view of the beautiful white bluff and the blue waters of Snail Shell Harbor. The chairs were mostly man-sized and upholstered in red leather. The ladies chairs were done in red velvet. Gaslights along the wall and others on marble topped tables lit the room after the sun had gone down. Another slightly smaller and less ornate suite with only one bedroom was just across the hall. Their view was of the town, looking up Cedar Lane, but the furnishings were as rich as they were in the Fayette Brown Suite.

Occasionally a lodger would arrive via the stage from Manistique. A woman, a young woman, travelling alone, however, was sure to start the gossips in town speculating. Shirley LeComte saw the stage arrive and the young woman alight. She was "barely a girl," Shirley told Bertha Hartson later that afternoon.

Bertha had acquired the habit of stopping in to visit Shirley every Thursday afternoon. Although Shirley was Catholic and played the organ at St. Peter's, Bertha would practice the Sunday hymn selections for the Protestant services with Shirley before thumping them out on the opera house organ for the small congregation Reverend Hartson gathered there each Sunday. In addition to the organ lessons, which occupied very little time, really, the two women traded the latest news about any and everybody in town.

The girl, who had arrived on the Manistique stage "couldn't have been more than thirteen or fourteen years old," Shirley said. "And she was dressed in rather cheap clothing. She went into the Shelton House first, she only had one small bag, don't ya know, and then she went over to the General Store. I seen her in there, talking to Mr. LaTermaine over by the window. When I came close to them, Mr. LaTermaine turned the girl around to keep me from seeing her face and talked, loud enough for me to hear, about the unique nature of our harbor. I'll just bet she was interested in that."

Bertha nodded in agreement and leaned across the table where they were having a cup of tea and asked, "Is she still here?"

Shirley shrugged. "I ain't seen her again. She was probably a bride for one of the cottage workers, don't ya know. She seemed to be of that class."

Bertha sipped her tea. "I'll visit a few of the huts on my way home. Not all the newcomers to that area are Catholic, you know. Has there been any news about our Mrs. Grey?"

Shirley tossed her blonde curls and laughed. "Mrs. McGeary, you mean. You met the Captain, ain't you?"

"A vulgar fellow, I'm sure," Bertha replied. "I merely took passage on his schooner from Escanaba to Fayette and we got caught in that terrible storm. That's when he and Mrs. Grey met. I dare say he must have visited that isolated little harbor of hers frequently after that for them to run off together less than three months after they met."

"But you must admit he is a handsome rogue," Shirley said.

"Handsome is as handsome does," snapped Bertha. "From the first Carrie struck me as a woman who had little sense. Living out there alone, so far from town. But I understand the Rutherfords set great store on her, and the Sailstads too. I just thought she may have written one of them and you'd heard what she had to say."

Shirley shook her head, "I'm sure I wouldn't know. Although Frank is almost second in command in Fayette, they shun us. We ain't been invited to the big house except when all the managers are." Her pique at this was obvious and Bertha smiled secretly as she lifted her teacup to her mouth.

After Bertha left, Shirley started preparations for Frank's supper. While she peeled potatoes she thought about Delbert, the young man who had bought her cake at the Fourth of July cakewalk. He was a member of Captain McGeary's crew. He was handsome too, although he lacked the self-confidence of the Captain. She had danced several dances with Delbert after the first she was obligated to because he had bought her cake, and then they had walked down to the harbor to cool off. He was so shy she'd had to place his hands on her breasts as she felt for his manhood in the dark. But he squeezed them all right once she'd whispered that she'd like him to squeeze hard enough to hurt her. She almost swooned with the excitement he'd given her when he pinched her hardened nipple tightly and twisted. She gripped his hardened cock and pressed herself against him.

Shirley looked down at the potato she was peeling. There was practically nothing left of it and she felt again the weakness his pinch had left between her legs. If only Frank hadn't chosen that moment to come looking for her. He could have stayed all night at the Hole in The Rock for all she cared. Luckily she'd heard him coming. He sang when he was drunk, a loud version of Camp Town Races, and when she heard him she broke away from Delbert.

"It's my husband," she told him. "You wait a while before you come back to the dance floor. But watch me, and when he passes out, like he always does, I'll leave the dance. If you follow me, I'll wait for you behind the ice house."

Delbert hadn't waited long enough and somehow Frank

knew. He must have stopped in the dark away from the dance floor and watched as she and Delbert danced yet another set. Then he came crashing into the party with that club. Oh, he was terrible when he drank. Shirley watched the harbor everyday looking for Wave Dancer. She thought she'd still like to meet Delbert behind the icehouse.

The pot was finally full of peeled potatoes and Shirley put it on the stove to cook. Then she salted the beefsteak and cut it into three pieces, two small ones for herself and Frankie and the large piece for Frank. She had raspberries and cream for dessert. Bertha had informed her that one of the cottage ladies had fresh picked raspberries for sale and she'd sent Frankie running to buy a quart. Frank loved raspberries and cream. Tonight might be a good night.

Chapter Twenty-One

At least twenty minutes passed while Carrie and Peter waited for Delbert to appear with the taxi. Carrie watched the curious assortment of people who passed by them. There was everything from young men in business suits to old ladies creeping along with a stick for support and heavy shawls thrown about them despite the clinging moist heat of the July day. The wind blew constantly off the lake, making Carrie glad she had put on the bonnet that tied under her chin, else she'd have been chasing it down the street as she'd seen a young man chase his hat just a moment ago.

The street was likewise filled with traffic. Horse drawn Omi-buses, private carriages, and men on horseback. Everything came to a periodic halt when the Wells Street bridge swung open to let a tug or two pulling a ship through.

"Don't you think perhaps we might hire some boy to watch the trunk and we could walk to this hotel?" Carrie finally asked.

"Oh, no, ma'am," Peter replied, removing his hat, "Boys in these parts are not to be trusted for such as that. No sooner did you turn your back and they'd be sawing off the locks to get inside and sell whatever you have in there."

Carrie was aghast at this news. She looked down at the heavy trunk she'd brought, plus two carpetbags, and sighed. "Oh well, then we shall continue to wait."

She sat down on the trunk and stretched her feet out in front of her. It was then that she saw the elegant white carriage drawn by a team of four coal-black horses coming down the street. It had gold-rimmed wheels and the driver upon the box was dressed in dark green livery with gold braids looping at each shoulder.

"Look there, Peter," she said, "one of the rich businessmen

in town, no doubt."

Peter looked up and laughed. "Not on your life, Mrs. McGeary. That's Daisy Brighton, the proprietress of The Palace on Custom House Place."

"The Palace? Isn't that the hotel Drew said we were to go to?"

Peter's grin was wide. "Yes, ma'am. I wouldn't be sending any bride of mine there, but Miss Brighton is a friend of Captain McGeary."

Before Carrie had time to question his curious remark the white carriage had stopped in front of them and Delbert stepped out. A footman from the rear of the carriage jumped down, and between them he and Delbert hefted her trunk onto the back. The footman, in the same green regalia the driver wore, placed a small stool in front of the carriage door and helped Carrie in.

Delbert handed in her carpet bags and then scrambled up and sat beside her while Peter stood on the dock, hat in hand, and waved good-bye to her.

"Delbert how did you... I mean where is the taxi?"

"I met Miss Daisy in the lobby and when I told her I was looking for a taxi to fetch Captain McGeary's new wife to her place to stay until he himself, should come, she said, I'll send my own carriage to pick her up." He drew in a deep breath after so many words and settled into the cushions.

The inside of the carriage was as glittering as the outside. The seats were covered in plush green velvet. The window curtains were of the same material and the roof had a glass pane in it to let in the natural daylight. The ride over what must be rough roads was as smooth as sitting on the sofa in her parlor.

"It is far to The Palace?" Carrie rather hoped it was because she wanted to ride in the elegant carriage as long as possible. She moved the edge of the window curtain and looked out the window. She had been raised in Buffalo, a town of not inconsiderable size even ten years ago, but never had she seen so many buildings and so many people.

"It's a ways," Delbert replied. He was a man of few words and Carrie knew that he would offer no more than a concise answer to any question, so she was free to gaze at the passing scenery.

The buildings were almost all of stone and brick. She could see why Mr. Jenny was so sure there was a big market for her marble in Chicago. The buildings were all right up against each other with only an occasional alley between them, and these seemed to be full of women just lounging against the wall or waving at the passing men. She turned to ask Delbert about them, but his eyes were closed and his head was back on the cushions, so she supposed he had fallen asleep.

All at once Carrie gasped and dropped the curtain. Almost immediately she peeked out again. She had not been mistaken; in the open windows of the building they were passing sat young women in their underwear! Some sat with their legs pulled up so Carrie was sure the passersby on the street could see more about the women than anyone should want to merely by looking up.

Her gasp had apparently roused Delbert from his nap. He reached over and took the curtain edge from her and let it drop back in place. "We're in Little Cheyenne right now, ma'am. It's not a fit or safe place for a lady like you. Don't worry, we're just passing though."

Carrie felt her face flush. Prostitutes, fallen women, strumpets; she must have seen twenty or more of them sitting in the open windows and walking the street in dresses with low cut necklines revealing almost everything.

"There's no way to get off the docks without passing though one low place or another," Delbert said.

Carrie was surprised when he continued to talk. "Even The Palace has ladies for hire. But Miss Daisy runs a high class house and you'll never see them displayed like the fare in Little Cheyenne."

"Ladies for hire?" Carrie repeated.

"Don't you worry none," Delbert said. "The floor you'll be on is separate from the house, and you won't see them at all. But," he paused. "Captain told me to make sure you understood this. You are not to go outside. You are to stay inside the room and wait for him."

Carrie had visions of the eight by ten foot room she'd passed the night in at the Shelton House. She would go off her head if she had to stay in such a place for long.

"How long will it be before Drew comes?"

"At least two days, maybe three," Delbert said. "It takes a long time to sell a cargo at the Board of Trade, and then they's another long wait to get unloaded."

"How shall I eat if I'm not to go out," Carrie heard herself whine and immediately regretted it.

"Oh, there's a dining room at the hotel. You can go there, you're just not to go out of doors. And the Captain said you're not to worry about money. He'll pay for everything you need later. I got it all set up with Miss Daisy."

Carrie sighed and sat back into the soft velvet cushions. Her excitement about the city was gone and she began to wonder if Louella had been right, that it was a reckless thing she had done to run away with Drew McGeary.

At length the white carriage stopped at in front of a grand looking building. The six marble columns in front rose two stories high and supported a roof that covered a paved mezzanine. Two men stood at the brass-decorated doors dressed in the green livery she was now familiar with. She was helped from the carriage and met immediately by a handsome woman who wore a pale yellow afternoon dress of the latest fashion. Her hair was elaborately dressed, piled high on her head with an abundance of ebony curls falling almost to the middle of her back.

"Please follow me, Mrs. McGeary," she said with a very decided French accent. "I will show you to your rooms."

The suite of rooms Carrie was lodged in was bigger than her whole house! She had a sitting room, complete with a piano, a bedroom with a canopy of pale blue dotted Swiss, and a room with a marble bathtub and two sinks. The woman showed her how to get hot or cold water by turning the white knobs above a spigot, and now to replace soiled water in the commode with fresh by pulling the rope that hung from a white tank near the ceiling.

"And here is your dining area," the girl said, throwing open a door to reveal a small polished table and two side chairs. "Madam has only to pull this," she indicated a green braided cord, "and the steward will come to the door to take your order.

"My name is Vivette. If you ask the steward, he will send for me and I can bring anything you desire."

"Thank you Vivette, I can't imagine there is anything I'd desire except perhaps a little to eat."

"At once, Madam. The steward will bring your luggage soon."

Alone in the room, Carrie went at once to the window and looked out. Although lace curtains covered a wide swath of the wall, the window itself was long and narrow and the view restricted to the building across the street; a red brick two story with gold lettering in the window proclaiming that D. Blackmum, Dentist, had offices there. Carrie noticed with delight that the lamps in the room were electric. She had read that most of Chicago was lit by the new electric lights instead of gas, but hadn't expected to actually be in a room with such advancements.

The wallpaper in the room was a striped brocade of three shades of green bordered by a wide display of roses. It reminded her of Grace Sailstad's dress. The sitting room, obviously a ladies room, had a writing desk where Carrie found several sheets of pale ivory writing paper of good quality and a quill. A search of the several small drawers revealed a bottle of ink. There were also two books in a compartment of the desk. Both were novels, one *The Coquette* by Hannah Webster Foster, the other *Charlotte Temple* by Susanna Rowson. Carrie had read them both at Lady Jane's Boarding School for young ladies back in Buffalo.

Grandfather would have been horrified that she had read either of the books, as he would have been at the papers she read published by Elizabeth Cady Stanton, the esteemed Women's Rights leader.

Carrie remembered the day Mrs. Cady-Stanton spoke to an assembly of the young ladies at Lady Jane's school. How Carrie had exploded inside with excitement upon hearing Mrs. Cady-Stanton speak with such authority and feeling about the rights of women to be educated and live a life of their own choosing.

It's what Carrie had done after loosing Albert, why she hadn't moved into town as everybody thought she should. It's why she had the nerve to develop the limestone quarry, now a marble quarry from which she would be well off.

And what would happen now? How well did she know Drew McGeary? She'd been overtaken by her infatuation of him and chosen to ignore the rumors and outright warning of Louella and Henry about the man. Was he, like Henry, really after her marble quarry? She'd thrown over every lesson Lady Jane and Elizabeth Cady-Stanton had taught and the lesson from the novel *Charlotte Temple* that she now held in her hand.

So here she was, at the Palace Hotel on Custom House Place in Chicago—alone. Alone in a place Delbert said was a brothel and warned her not to set foot outside her room. What kind of a man would send his new wife to such a place?

Carrie, book still in hand, wandered over to the window to look again from the narrow window at the dentist's office across the street. The street looked like an ordinary business street. Besides the dentist across the street she had seen a milliner's shop and an apothecary. A large church stood on the corner, not two doors from The Palace.

Perhaps Delbert was wrong about The Palace. She had seen no sign that it was other than a fine hotel. There had not been scantily or scandalously clad women in the lobby. She had, in fact, seen only two people, obviously gentlemen who were dressed in expensive and fashionable suits, sitting in the green damask chairs in front of the window reading newspapers.

Somebody came out of the dentist's office, his hand cupping an obviously sore jaw. Carrie watched as he walked swiftly up the sidewalk and out of her view. With a sigh she sat down in one of the plush lady's chairs and opened *Charlotte Temple.*

Carrie read only the first few pages of the novel (in which the two men, villains really, who star in the novel were introduced; Montraville, a Lieutenant in the British Army, and his fellow officer Belcour, as they contrive to meet the beautiful young maiden they spotted coming out of church) before she nodded off. She waked with a start when someone tapped on the chamber door.

Her trunk was delivered by one of the liveried men she'd seen at the front door on her way in. Behind her came Vivette with a tray holding a bowl of chicken noodle soup, two biscuits wrapped in a linen towel set inside a pretty basket, and a teapot.

"Miss Daisy says travelers should always have chicken soup for their first meal at The Palace, it soothes any upset stomach." Carrie quite agreed with that.

After Vivette arranged the table for her and Carrie had seated herself to eat, Vivette said, "Miss Daisy invites you to dine with her at seven. She is most anxious to meet the new wife of Captain McGeary."

Carrie consented to dining with the owner of the elegant white carriage who was obviously a friend of her husband. Left alone, Carrie ate her soup, which was very good, and ate both of the warm buttered biscuits. The tea had a brisk but pleasing flavor. When finished she placed her dishes on the tray and set it outside the door as Vivette had instructed. She heard voices from the room across the hall, but saw no one.

Immediately she turned her attention to unpacking her

trunk. If she was going to be here for two or three days she may as well hang everything and let the wrinkles fall out. The roomy closet in her bedroom had plenty of wooden hangers.

Carrie's whole attention was on what she should wear to dinner. In the end, of course, she only had one evening dress, the one she'd bought in Escanaba that weekend with Drew and Mr. Jenny. Then again, maybe the violet afternoon dress was more suitable. Finally Carrie pulled the green-braided cord she'd been told summoned the Steward and when he appeared she asked for Vivette.

The evening dress was red, Carrie's favorite color. The front was inset with lace at the hem and about the throat, and the back was bustled a little. Eleanor would have told her red was not her color, that she should wear pastel shades, but tosh on Eleanor she'd thought when she picked it out. Drew liked it.

Vivette tapped on the door and entered. "Madam requires something?"

"Oh, Vivette," Carrie said, " which dress shall I wear to dinner? I have no idea what women in Chicago wear."

Vivette examined the two dresses plus what Carrie had in the closet. "The red one," she finally said and Carrie knew that none of what Vivette had seen was suitable.

"Oh dear," Carrie sighed. "Perhaps I should decline Miss... is it Miss or Mrs. Brighton?"

"It's Miss Brighton, but she'll ask you to call her Daisy. And you'll not decline. The red dress is exactly right. I only liked the violet one also."

At that moment Carrie liked Vivette very much. She was obviously well bred, what was she doing here?

"If madam wishes a bath," Vivette suggested, "I will draw it for you."

A bath! Of course, in that beautiful long white tub in the bathroom. Vivette picked up an ornate bottle and poured a quantity of the yellow contents under the water that gushed out of the golden spigot over the tub. Soon the tub was full of warm water and bubbles.

Vivette ushered her into the room and helped her undress. "Madam can soak for a while and then I return to scrub your back and wash and rinse your hair."

Without waiting for Carrie's consent to the arrangement, the girl was gone.

"So that's what it feels like to have a ladies maid," Carrie said out loud. "How deliciously spoiled I could become here."

Vivette returned, announcing her arrival with a loud knock on the outer door and a call, "Madam, I am come back."

She whisked into the bathroom with a basket full of bottles and brushes. As promised she scrubbed Carrie's back and then washed her long chestnut hair and poured several pitchers of clear warm water over Carrie's head to rinse out the suds.

Finally she held a large white towel of fluffy cloth and commanded Carrie out of the water where she was immediately wrapped in the towel and gently rubbed dry. While Carrie sat before the mirror at an ornate dressing table Vivette rubbed her hair dry with another towel and began to comb it.

"Madam has beautiful hair," she said. "I will dress it for you. While I do so you can have a mudpack for your face."

"A what?"

"A mudpack," Vivette replied. "It will tighten and soften your skin and clean deeply."

"How can mud clean my face?"

"Just you watch, Madam."

Vivette wrapped a towel around Carrie's hair and piled it atop her head. Then she rubbed a cream that smelled of almonds into the skin of Carrie's face and neck. She opened another jar that did indeed look like mud and slathered it all over Carrie's face so when Carrie looked in the mirror all she saw besides the brown mud, were her two eyes.

"No, Madam," Vivette said, "do not laugh. Do not even smile or talk for the mud must dry and harden, and if you move it will break and..." she threw her hands into the air, "and all will be a waste of time."

So Carrie turned away from the mirror so she wouldn't see herself and laugh. She thought of Eleanor, with whom she'd like to share all this, and of Bertha Hartson, who she knew would disapprove of this and everything Carrie had done since she'd met Drew McGeary.

Vivette removed the towel and began to fuss with Carrie's hair. Carrie could feel the mud on her face drying, pulling at her skin. Finally Vivette said, "Now give me your hands."

Carrie obeyed and Vivette turned them over to look at both palm and back and sighed with regret over them. "What do you do, Madam? Your hands look like you've been a washer woman."

Startled Carrie pulled her hands away. She couldn't answer because of the mudpack, but she knew she was blushing with shame.

Vivette reached once more for Carrie's hands. "No matter, Madam, I can fix them. Please, I am sorry for what I said."

Carrie nodded. Vivette brought a basin of sudsy water and commanded Carrie to place her hands in it. After a few moments Vivette lifted one out and began to work it over with a pumice stone followed by a heavy coating of the almond cream.

"Put on this glove," she said, handing a white cotton glove to Carrie. While Carrie was wondering how she was to do that with one hand still in the water, Vivette slipped it on for her and immediately went to work on the second hand.

Finally it came time to remove the mudpack. It almost peeled off and after Vivette had rinsed her face with clear water Carrie felt as if she were fifteen again. Vivette fussed more with Carrie's hair until long ringlets fell over Carrie's shoulders from a high crown. When Carrie looked in the mirror she wondered who it was looking back at her.

"Now I will finish your manicure, Madam," Vivette said. "Take off the gloves. You must rub your hands with the almond cream every night and then wear the gloves to bed. Then your hands will feel like the hands of a baby all the time."

Carrie put her hand to her cheek; both cheek and hand were so soft and silky feeling she couldn't resist caressing them. Vivette watched her and smiled. "Neither can the Captain resist to touch you."

"Oh, Vivette, you will completely spoil me. I've never been so pampered."

"It is a wedding gift for you from Miss Daisy. Put your hand here, on the pillow."

Carrie complied and Vivette shaped Carrie's fingernails with a file and then painted them red! The paint made the ends of Carrie's fingers feel unnaturally heavy. "Do not move, Madam. The paint must dry, once, twice, three coats of paint."

Finally Carrie felt she must be done. Vivette pulled Carrie's corset tight and then slipped the red evening dress over her head.

Carrie watched herself in the mirror on the bedroom door, a mirror that covered the entire door and revealed all of her as she had never seen herself before.

"If I met myself on the street I wouldn't know me," she whispered. Then aloud, "You have transformed me, Vivette."

"But I am not yet finished, Madam. Sit so I can do your face."

"What else can you do to it?"

"A little rouge, a little powder, a little kohl around your eyes to make them look bigger. You are a handsome woman, Madam, I don't wonder our Captain married you."

Carrie watched in wonder as Vivette "did" her face and she wondered about the girl's choice of words, "our captain." By the time Vivette announced her finished, it was time to go to dinner. Vivette led her down the hallway and up a wide flight of carpeted stairs, down another hallway and then into a large room where a long table was set for dinner. Carrie had expected to dine privately with Miss Brighton; instead there must have been twenty people in the room.

Vivette whispered something to a man in livery at the door and he in turn offered Carrie his arm, moving her into the room while he announced in a loud voice, "Mrs. Andrew McGeary."

Everyone turned to look at her. Carrie immediately felt like a small dull sparrow put into a cage with brilliant bluebirds and canaries. The women all wore beautiful dresses with low cut bodices from which the tops of their white bosoms could be seen. Every last one of them wore necklaces of pearl or colored gems. Carrie wondered if they were all whores and immediately scolded herself for such a conclusion.

A tall thin woman dressed in a pale green dress dripping with pearls stepped forward. Everybody else returned to his or her former conversations.

"My dear Mrs. McGeary," she gushed picking up Carrie's gloved hand and pulling her into an embrace. "I am Daisy Brighton and am so pleased to have you as a guest. Drew has kept you a secret, that naughty boy."

She threw back her head and laughed in a most unlady like way. She still had Carrie by the hand and led her to the table where she placed her to the right of the head of the table. She nodded, apparently to one of the servants who rang a bell to get the attention of the other guests. The room was immediately quiet.

"Dinner is served," announced Daisy and she sat down in the head chair, held for her by a tall black man in the now familiar green livery. Carrie saw with surprise that his seeming twin held a chair for her. Around the table gentlemen seated their ladies and then themselves. As if on signal all the ladies removed their gloves so Carrie did the same, laying them over the arm of her chair. The buzz of conversation immediately resumed.

Daisy leaned towards Carrie and laid her hand on Carrie's arm in a confidential manner. "You don't need to worry,

Carrie...may I call you Carrie? No business takes place on the third floor."

Carrie nodded as if she knew what Daisy meant. "You can call me Daisy, everybody does. We're not very formal here."

They may not act formal thought Carrie, but they certainly looked it. She had never seen so many jewels. Daisy wore a choker of pearls around her slender neck with a pendant of emerald hanging from it. Her earrings were emeralds, surrounded by tiny sparkling diamonds and she wore a gigantic emerald ring on her finger. The other women also wore gems everywhere; rubies, opals, diamonds, and stones with which Carrie was not familiar.

A plate of greens was set before her and Carrie waited until Daisy had picked up her fork before she picked up her own. Between mouthfuls of the cool crisp greens Daisy asked, "Did you enjoy the beauty treatment by Vivette?"

"Oh, very much," Carrie said. "I felt like a princess with all that attention. Thank you."

"Our Captain won't be able to afford to pamper you that way, you know. But he's a kind man...a very kind man."

Carrie had finished her salad and waited while the staff set a plate of roast beef and small red potatoes in front of each diner. Under the cover of the noise of forks and knives she asked, "Why does everyone, I mean you and Vivette, call him "our" captain?"

Daisy laughed loudly and several people turned to look at them. Daisy's glare turned them back to their plates and previous conversations.

"I first met your," she put emphasis on your, "Captain one night several years ago when he pounded on my door demanding to be let into my private rooms. It was early in the morning and of course, I was still asleep. Even Rufus," she indicated the black man, who stood behind her chair, "couldn't keep him downstairs. He had a bedraggled looking young girl with him. Said he'd found her on Clark Street and that she was hiding from Mary Hastings. He demanded I hide the girl for him for two days. Offered me a sawbuck."

She stopped and drained her glass of wine. It was immediately refilled by one of the servants. "Such audacity took me so off base I agreed and took the poor trembling thing into my room and put her to bed. Drink your wine dear." She lowered her voice to a whisper and confided, "Mary Hastings is that fat woman in the red dress at the other end of the table. She has absolutely no class and runs one of the worst establishments in the city. I knew she sometimes procured girls from slavers, but this little lady's story was unbelievable."

Carrie choked on her mouthful of potatoes and Daisy reached over and slapped her hard between the shoulder blades.

"Are you telling me," Carrie began, but then she realized that she had been right. They were all proprietresses of brothels, so she stopped speaking and reached for her wine glass.

Daisy chuckled. "Yes, we are. But not all, or even most of us stoop so low. My ladies petition to work at The Palace and I treat them well. We entertain only the carriage trade. Mary Hastings is the lowest of the low. Anyone can use her girls."

Carrie could not believe she was having this conversation.

Anyway," Daisy continued, "our, I mean your, Captain comes back in two days to collect the girl, gives me another sawbuck and says he's taking her to Michigan where at least she'll be treated decent. I tried to get him to leave her with me...she was such a pretty thing, that dusky skin, almond shaped eyes and deep throaty voice that men like..."

Carrie dropped her fork. Peony? The fork clattered on the plate and tumbled onto the floor. A servant immediately set a clean one beside her plate.

Daisy continued talking with no notice of Carrie's reaction. "I liked the Captain. He's got balls, honey. Hairy balls."

Carrie's face, she knew had turned bright red.

"And what's more, he has a heart. If he'd had any money I'd have snapped him up right off as my solid man. But he's got Lake water in his veins, he doesn't like dry land; especially Chicago."

Dessert was a dish of fresh peaches in cream. When the meal was over and Daisy stood up, everyone turned to look at her.

"You're all wondering about my guest. She's a lady, mind you; I want no one to offend her. She is staying with me until her new husband, Captain Drew McGeary, whom you all know, gets his cargo unloaded. Ladies and gentlemen, Carrie McGeary from Michigan."

A round of applause welcomed Carrie and afterward as people mingled in the drawing room across the hall most of them stopped to greet her. Mary Hastings did not. Perhaps she knew who had rescued Peony from her.

At last Vivette appeared to take Carrie back to her room. She helped Carrie out of her dress and into her nightclothes. The electric lights in the room glowed softly. From the street Carrie could hear the constant clatter of carriages and people calling to each other. Vivette brushed Carrie's hair out and braided it for the night and then turned down the covers on the elegant bed.

"Goodnight, Madam. Don't forget the cream and your gloves before you go to bed. Lock the door behind me and do not open it unless you hear me," and with that ominous warning she went out.

Carrie rose immediately and slid the heavy brass bolt across the doorframe. She didn't know whether to laugh or cry. She had just dined with ten whorehouse keepers, been treated like a princess in the most luxurious room she had ever been in, and learned that her new husband was...what? What was he?

She sat down at the writing desk with a sheet of writing paper and began a letter to Eleanor.

Dearest Friend,
        You will never believe where I am.

Chapter Twenty-Two

The second day at the Palace, Carrie was content enough to pass a pleasant day in her luxurious suite of rooms working with her needle and floss at a cross stitch she intended as a small gift at Christmas for the quarry master's wife, Mrs. Brandon.

Her thoughts were often on the quarry and how she missed walking down, at least once a day, to watch the men at work. She often dealt with the stone buyers herself when they arrived at the pier to load dressed limestone, and now marble.

She felt a little pride over the discovery of the marble and the business arrangement she had made with Mr. Jenny, of this very town. She and Drew must call on him as soon as they quit the Palace and took up rooms at the Palmer House, close to Marshall Field's grand store where she meant to buy something wonderful for Louella.

Oh, were Jewel's kittens thriving? She surely hoped so and she shuddered again to think of what Edward Rutherford had told her of the manner of the end of the poor little mother's life. Carrie had immediately formed the opinion that the drunken husband of the gossipy organ player was the culprit. The way he had banged that cudgel down on the dance floor and made his wife jump. Carrie had seen the cringing fear in the woman's eyes. What was her name? Shirley...yes Shirley. Carrie could bet her burly, often drunken, husband had slapped her down more than once.

Vivette brought in a light lunch and invited Carrie to walk abroad with her. Carrie considered a moment what Delbert had said about her not going out on the street.

"Is it quite safe for a lady on the street?"

Vivette laughed. "You wouldn't want to be by yourself, not

knowing where you're to go, but I thought you might like a little fresh air. I'm but going to the market in the next block to buy flowers."

Carrie responded she was anxious to go out, and Vivette said she would return for her in an hour. Carrie finished her bowl of beef vegetable soup and plate of fresh sliced peaches and quickly changed from her simple skirt into her rust colored walking suit.

The day was hot and although Vivette had used the term "fresh air," the odors of the city street smelled anything but fresh. The smell of rotting fruit and meat, mingled with the horse droppings in the street and the stench of human waste along side...these accosted Carrie's nostrils so strongly she drew her linen handkerchief from her sleeve and pressed it to her nose.

"Does Madam find the air displeasing?" asked Vivette.

Carrie nodded and spoke through the linen. "Apparently you have never smelled real fresh air or been where the breezes brought the pleasant scent of pine and warm sand to your attention. There is a perfume in the summer pine woods that cannot be described. To think I've always taken it for granted."

"The flower stall will please you then," Vivette said as she pushed through a flock of small boys who obstructed the entire sidewalk with a circle where they shot marbles. The action occasioned calls from the boys of such words as Carrie didn't understand, but knew from their tone they were not polite words. Then Carrie felt a sting in the middle of her back and surmised that one of the brats had thrown a marble at her.

"Do not stop, Madam," said Vivette taking her by the arm and pulling her along. "If you scold them they will throw worse than a small pebble at you."

They came to the corner and there was indeed a church there as Carrie had thought the day before. It was built of red stone, and from the statues of Saints in the alcoves above the door, she concluded it was a Roman Catholic Church. Set back from the street some distance was a matching red stone house where the priest must live. Carried marked it as a place of refuge if a person on the street should be in need of such but then noticed that the gate in the high iron fence was chained shut with a heavy lock.

She glanced side long at Vivette and then recalled Delbert's words. His words of warning seemed to have more wisdom in them than Vivette's careless dismissal of danger. But then, she lived here; she had to be content with what was.

On the next block was an open area of small stalls where almost anything seemed to be for sale. Vivette guided her past the outer merchants calling at her to buy a lovely locket or a straw hat. They stopped at last before a neat tented stall where jar of water held a great variety of cut flowers. There were roses, asters, and white ox-eye daises (which Vivette ordered a great quantity of) and yellow brown-eyed Susans, and a tall purple spike of blooms Carrie couldn't name.

Vivette picked out armloads of blooms and ordered them delivered to the Palace by five o'clock.

"Miss Daisy is giving another dinner party tonight," Vivette explained. "You are invited, of course."

Carrie almost whined, do I have to, but checked herself and said instead, "I have nothing to wear, Vivette. I can't wear the same dress again."

"Do not worry," Vivette said, handing her a nosegay of roses and carnations. Carrie buried her grateful nose in it at once. "I will borrow a dress for you. One of the girls is about your size and won't mind. It's a yellow one and I think you'd look smashing in yellow."

One of the girls? She was expected to wear the dress of a prostitute?

"No," Carrie said firmly. "Tell her I cannot come."

"You cannot refuse, Madam." Vivette had paid for the purchases, including the nosegay for Carrie and was pulling her to another stand where she bought peaches, a round fruit she called a melon, and a quantity of red cherries. These she placed in a basket she carried.

"Miss Daisy wishes to show you off again. This time the guests will be the ladies of St. James aid society and sewing circle. Miss Daisy entertains them once a year and they all come because she makes a generous gift to their society."

Carrie was relieved to hear this. She would like to meet the respectable women of the neighborhood. She hadn't realized until then that in the back of her mind she had been looking for an escape route from the Palace. She needed to think about her reasons later, when she was alone.

"I will wear my afternoon dress then," Carrie said, her tone breaching no argument from Vivette. Then feeling perhaps she had been a trifle too adamant, she laid her hand on Vivette's arm and added, "but thank you for the offer of the yellow dress."

Back in her room, Carrie had several hours before dinner. She picked up the cross-stitch but soon grew bored with it. She dropped it and picked up the novel, *Charlotte Temple*. She read several chapters and found herself expressing scorn for the author's ideal woman. Perhaps it was a suitable novel for a fifteen year old to serve as a warning against silver-tongued devils, but as a grown woman and a widow, she felt its lectures were naïve.

By the standards of the book, first published in 1791, she, by mere association with Daisy Brighton, had tarnished her reputation. Thank goodness Elizabeth Cady Stanton had taught her better. She was a modern woman who made her own choices.

Carrie returned to her thought on the street. Why was she planning an escape route from The Palace? Did she, deep down, wonder if Drew McGeary would really come for her? She had chosen Drew, but again and again she questioned the wisdom of that choice. Perhaps, after all, she was gullible and more like Charlotte Temple than she thought.

And again today she had caught herself ready to whine...a most unbecoming habit that she must shrug off at once. She glanced at the large clock face set in what looked like marble Grecian style columns and determined it was time to dress for dinner. She had expected Vivette to appear to help her.

"Spoiled already," she said aloud to herself as she entered the bedchamber and began to remove her walking suit. "As if I can't dress myself and roll my own hair the way I usually wear it."

The dinner party that evening was very much less formal and glittering than that of the evening before. She did not feel at all out of place in her light lavender afternoon dress. There were ten ladies from the parish and she soon ascertained that with the exception of Mrs. Paddy McGuire, they were wives of men who worked at various middle-level clerking positions.

She was delighted to learn that the husband of Mrs. Timothy Callahan, beside her, worked at the Board of Trade. Mrs. Callahan was a young matron and confessed to being relieved to leave her two small sons in the care of her husband for the evening so she could have some time away.

"A handful they are," she said. "Jake, he's five, is bound to run the streets with the ruffians, and the baby, Patrick, well, he's just beginning to walk and into everything."

"And you don't have any help with them?"

"Ach, no. What with Tim just starting to move up at the Board of Trade, there isn't enough money for help, even if I wanted it. That's a luxury for those above us."

For some reason Carrie felt herself compelled to offer advice to Mrs. Callahan. "Doesn't the parish, St. James, offer a place where, perhaps once a week, you could leave your children for a few hours? If you banded together with the other women, you could take turns at minding the brood, who are always easier to manage with play-fellows around."

Mrs. Callahan clapped her hands together in delight and

immediately clanked her fork against a water goblet to the attention of the other ladies.

"Just listen to what Mrs. McGeary has suggested."

Surprised, Carrie repeated what she had said, elaborating a little on the details as she saw the need. She could see heads nodding along the table and at the head Daisy too, listened intently.

When she had finished, a general discussion followed until the ten resolved to make it a project of the sewing circle to establish a child-care co-operative at St. James.

Daisy cleared her throat in a meaningful way and all turned their heads toward her.

"Ladies, in addition to the $200 I usually donate to your charity, I will put up another $200 to furnish a room in the church halls for your child-care co-operative."

The ladies all spoke their thank yous at once.

"I have one stipulation however," the brothel keeper added. "I want it known as the Daisy Room."

The congregation present readily consented. Daisy continued, "And as a special recognition to Mrs. McGeary for making such a worthy suggestion, a plaque is to be placed on the window ledge to remind all to pray for the continued good health of the lady."

Carrie was flattered. "Why thank you. I never imagined that a mere bit of conversation would merit one prayers for one's health forever."

After the conversation at the table had resumed, Carrie deemed to ask Mrs. Callahan something she had wanted to at once.

"I walked by the church yard yesterday and couldn't help but notice that the rectory gate was locked. How does one reach the Priest if one needs him?"

Mrs. Callahan nodded gravely. "The neighborhood is not what it used to be before the fire. The bad element keeps moving in on us and if the lock were not there...well," she rolled her eyes meaningfully toward the woman at the head of the table and lowered her voice, "ladies would be using the front porch for their assignations."

"No!"

"Indeed," Mrs. Callahan imparted eagerly; "Father Mitchell found a couple there one evening, and another time a drunk curled into a corner. So the fence, gate, and lock went up." She sounded triumphant.

Suddenly she looked Carrie right in the eyes and lowered her voice, "If you have a need, there's a pull rope to the side what rings a bell inside and a man will come out to let you in."

"Oh, I see," Carrie said. She found comfort in that news, but at the same time she recoiled from Mrs. Callahan, sure the woman had suddenly seen her as one of Miss Daisy's girls! Just like Charlotte Temple, she, by mere association with Daisy Brighton, had tarnished, or at least called into question, her reputation. What had Drew gotten her into?

Since the meal was at an end, Carrie stood, and excusing herself to Mrs. Callahan, she left the room and returned to her own.

It took Carrie a long time to fall asleep that night. She listened to the noises inside and outside the building. Long after she usually fell asleep she heard voices in the hall outside her door, and the sound of people moving through the corridor. Once there was a bump against her door and Carrie, alarmed, sat bolt upright in her bed to listen. She heard a woman giggle and a man laugh and then footsteps running and a man shouting, "Vive, stop."

"Shush," came a loud whisper, "you'll wake the Mrs. there." Then it was quiet and Carrie finally fell asleep.

Immediately after breakfast in the morning, Carrie decided to take a bath. She had awoken with absolute certainty that Drew would be coming for her before noon, and she wanted to use that luxurious tub with instant warm water and bubbles one last time.

A glance out her narrow window revealed a cloudy day, and just as Carrie was drying herself off a peal of thunder sounded. She put on her dressing gown and peeked out the window. It was raining and the street was full of black umbrella heads weaving down the sidewalk. How strange it looked from above.

A sudden jagged show of lightening was followed almost instantly by a loud crack of thunder. The electric lamps in the room went out and Carrie was left in a dim darkness as the storm moved in. Rain pelted the window and she could hear the wind whistle as it rushed down the narrow canyon of a street created by the buildings on either side.

"Dear merciful heaven," Carrie murmured, "I'm glad I'm not on the lake."

After the front of the storm passed, the rain settled into a steady drizzle. Carrie had found and lit the oil lantern and set it next to her so she could work on her cross-stitch. She worked three re-threadings of her needle before she grew restless and let the needlework lay on her lap. The sky was lightening and the rain lessened. She glanced at the face of the large clock on the table. It was eleven o'clock. The electric lights blinked twice, and then remained on. Carrie set her needlework aside, she was feeling tired and felt if she didn't get up and move around she would fall asleep in the chair.

Besides, now that the lights were on she really needed to get dressed. Drew might appear any moment. A wanton thought occurred to her, that perhaps she should remain in her dressing gown until he came. She immediately dismissed that idea and went to the closet to pick a costume. Since they would undoubtedly be leaving The Palace, she choose her blue walking suit. As soon as she and Drew were settled in at the Palmer House she intended to go shopping and buy one or two dresses suitable for the theatre.

They could wait until tomorrow to contact Mr. Jenny, Carrie decided. She had his business address, on North Dearborn. While Carrie sat in front of the mirror at the walnut dressing table brushing her hair she stopped to count the days since she'd left home on the seventh of July, a Friday. They had arrived in Chicago on Tuesday morning, so today was Thursday. Almost a whole week and they had been married on July 11, 1882.

Carrie stopped in the middle of a stroke with her hairbrush. Had that boat captain, Alphonse, left a certificate of the marriage? She didn't remember there being any papers for her and Drew to sign. She had been so caught up in the excitement of everything it had never occurred to her until now.

With a yank Carrie drew the brush through her hair and hastily rolled it into place and pinned it. As she worked she grew angrier and angrier as she realized that she probably wasn't even married. And she had been ready to play the harlot for him again!

Suddenly Carrie felt the need to hurry. She packed as much as she could into her largest carpetbag. She carefully tucked the jar of almond hand cream Vivette had given her between clothing to keep the jar from breaking. She looked around for the cotton night gloves and found them on the table next to the bed. Then she packed everything else into the trunk. She didn't know how she would get it out of The Palace. Perhaps she would have to just abandon it. She retrieved her money from the several places she had placed it and was about to put in all into her wrist bag when she thought better of it. In a place like this there were likely footpads lurking to steal a bag with a quick grab, it swinging from her arm. She placed all but two dollars of her money under her ample breasts where it was secure in the tight corset. She left the box of money Drew had given her on the table, picked up her bag and turned out the lights in the room. It was almost one o'clock. The rain had stopped and the air was hot and heavy.

Carrie listened at the door before she opened it, but the hallway was quiet. She was a little surprised Vivette hadn't appeared with lunch for her. She undid the bolt and opened the door, put just her head out and looked up and down the hallway. She saw a figure disappearing around a corner to her right.

She and Vivette had come and gone out the side door yesterday. It was only a few steps from her room to the door of the staircase they'd taken. Just as she reached for the doorknob, the stairway door burst open and two men in the Palace uniform almost ran her down.

"Pardon," one of them said. He looked at the heavy bag she was carrying and asked, "can we help you with something?"

Carrie was tempted to direct them to go get her trunk, but then where would she ask them to put it? Then it occurred to her that they might think she was sneaking out without paying her bill and prevent her from using the stairs.

"Excuse me," she said, "I must have the wrong door. Vivette asked me to meet her at the side door. She said she would escort me to the tailor shop to have my dress mended," she held up the carpetbag, which she intimated held the offending garment.

One of the men laughed. "Vivette...no ma'am, this is the door. Down these steps and then you'll find the door to the outside on your left. You best hurry, Vivette is out of favor with Miss Daisy just now and she probably won't wait long if you don't meet her on time."

He held the door for her and she nodded her thanks. Well, that statement about Vivette being out of favor with Miss Daisy would explain why Carrie hadn't seen her since their shopping trip.

Carrie reached the door breathless. She could hardly wait to get outside before she encountered anyone else inside The Palace. Drew had said he would pay all her expenses when he arrived, IF he arrived. Oh, he would come all right, and expect to find her waiting eagerly for him, the anxious little wife. The gullible backwoods woman who was not his wife!

The rank smell of the alley upon which the side door

exited was even worse after the rain. The moist heavy air seemed to have soaked up the filth like a sponge. Carrie almost gagged with the stench as she hurried down the narrow alley to the street. The sidewalks were crowded with people and carriages, which moved in both directions on the street. She looked to see if the boys from yesterday were playing marbles again and was relieved to see they were not.

Carrie hurried toward the corner and when she reached the gate to St. James rectory, she found the rope and rang the bell without hesitation.

Chapter Twenty-Three

The dim light in the room made it easy for Peony to remain unseen. From the beach she'd seen Henry had a young girl with him and it appeared that he pushed her into the back door of the Hole-in-The-Rock, the entrance to Stoddy's dingy office.

He called it an office, but it was his one room living space. It was furnished with a table for his paperwork, a large over-stuffed chair with the stuffing poking out of several rips in the once green covering, two wooden chairs by the table, and a bed. The bed could be partitioned off from the rest of the room by drawing a curtain hung from a pole next to the ceiling, but Stoddy never bothered. He never bothered making up the bed either and it usually looked like a gathering place for filthy rags.

Peony had her own private outside entrance to her rooms and when she saw Henry she had picked up her sketching supplies and gone immediately into her room. There she took off her light yellow robe and put on a dark colored skirt and blouse before quietly opening the door between her rooms and the saloon. She could hear Henry and Stoddy talking. Arguing, Henry and Stoddy never just talked, they yelled at each other.

She approached Stoddy's door, which he hadn't closed, and stood close to the wall, listening.

"I know what you're up to," Henry shouted. "Do you think I'm stupid?"

"Yeah, I think yer stupid," Stoddy shouted back. "And a greedy son-of-a-bitch besides. What I do on my own is none of your business."

Henry didn't yell back but lowered his voice to a normal pitch. Still his words held an ominous, warning tone.

"Listen, you worthless worm. I'm trying to tell you I don't

care. You can have your Stockade if you want, but not more than two girls. I know you got one already and I'm giving you the second one."

Peony heard a yelp that could only have come from the girl. She pictured Henry hurting the girl in some way. He probably had his hand in her hair and twisted or yanked it. Peony chanced moving closer so she could look through the hinge crack of the partially open door.

The girl had long red hair that hung from her bonnet to the middle of her back like a horse's tail; she was tall and slender as a reed. Henry had her by the arm. He must have squeezed that small arm hard enough to make her yelp and leave bruises.

"Yeah, how much?" Stoddy growled.

"Nothing."

"Nothing?" Stoddy clearly didn't believe that. "Cut the shit, what do you want for her?"

"Three percent of your take."

"You bastard!" Peony jumped as Stoddy hit the table in front of him with his fist. A metal box that was close to the edge of the makeshift desk clattered to the floor and coins rolled and scattered unto the dirty floor.

Henry loosed his hold on the girl and looked at the pile of gold and silver coins that had tumbled out of the box. The girl immediately started for the door. Peony jumped back out of sight. From the squeal, she knew Henry had recaptured the girl so she returned to looking through the crack.

Henry now had her by her hair, his hand twisted into the long strands. He pulled her around and slapped her hard across the face. Peony cringed as if she'd also been hit.

"You try that again and I'll bust your arm," Henry shouted, and he hit her again.

The girl started to whimper in fear. Henry pushed her into Stoddy's dirty overstuffed chair and kicked her in the stomach so that she doubled over. "Now stay there."

He turned to Stoddy. "Three percent or I tell McGeary. You

know what he'll do."

Stoddy cursed Henry with about every word he knew, uttering a long list of things Henry could do with himself.

"Three percent, and I break her," Henry repeated. "You got beds in that stockade yet?"

Stoddy shrugged. "Suit yourself."

"And where in hell did you get all this money?" Henry asked, kicking at a pile of coins.

"It's my share. I don't spend much you know. I don't wear fancy suits and buy fancy horses."

Suddenly Stoddy had a pistol in his hand. "You touch a cent of it and I'll kill you."

Henry looked up from his bending position and saw the gun.

"What the hell? Put that away. I don't want your damn money. Show me where I can take the girl."

Peony backed away from the door and moved quickly back to her own room so the two men coming out of the room wouldn't see her. Henry was carrying the girl who had passed out when he kicked her.

So that's what the big fence Stoddy had had built on the other side of the tracks was all about. He was adding on. He already had one girl? Why would Henry give him this girl and only ask three percent to not tell Drew? Peony sat down on the chair next to the window and stared at the lake, letting the whitecaps rolling into the sandy beach lull her.

She remembered when she had been taken and "broken". God...she'd been fifteen years old, walking down a well worn path from the butcher shop to her parents house just about dusk that June evening. She had had a string bag with some onions and a piece of salt pork that her mother had sent her to the market for. Two men, she never saw them, threw a smelly blanket over her head and then knocked her over the head. When she woke up with a headache she was on a schooner rolling through a choppy sea. There were three other girls in the dark dingy hole with her.

She had never seen Cleveland again. They threw food into them twice a day, but they never cleaned anything out. When they arrived in Chicago, the four girls were taken out, had their wrists tied together, and were linked together with little more than a foot of rope between them. It was dark, although she could see the street lamps of the city just off the pier. Two men threw bucket after bucket of water pulled out of the filthy harbor over them until they had the surface filth at least cleaned off of them. Even though it was June, a cool night breeze blew in from the lake and girls shivered in their wet clothes.

They'd been loaded into a wagon and driven a long way to a large stone house on a street filled with men and women strolling about. Some of the couples were kissing and more, right in the open street. The two men pushed the girls into a narrow alley and then though a back door of the house. A few minutes later a woman appeared. She was well-dressed and for a moment the girls hoped they had been saved. Alas, that was not the case.

"I brung ya four young mares," said the bigger of the two men. "Hundret dollars a piece."

The woman walked up to the girls and inspected each one. She felt their breasts and looked at their teeth. Then she turned to the men. "A hundred for these three, twenty-five for the ugly one."

She was referring to the short girl who had protruding teeth and a very round face. Peony remembered her name was Kathryn.

The woman produced a purse, paid the men, and then turned her attention to the girls again.

"I'm Mary Hastings," she said, "and you belong to me now. You are going to work in my house. If you behave you'll be paid and treated well. You'll have a room and three meals a day. But if you don't learn what I'm going to teach you, if you try to run away or resist me, I'll kill you."

She grabbed Kathryn by the hair and yanked, eliciting the

same sort of yelp the girl in Stoddy's office had uttered. She slapped the other three across the face and said, "follow me."

Like four prisoners on a chain gang, the roped girls followed her up two narrow flights of stairs to a room where there were five beds and a few chairs. Gas lights on the walls lit the room. Elizabeth noted one small window high in the wall, just below the ceiling.

"I'll send up food and water for washing. Take off your clothes."

The girls looked at her and each other. "Of course," Mary Hastings said, "You'll have to be untied. I'll send Freddie up with a knife."

She left the room, closing and locking the door behind her. All four girls had been weeping, but now they began to lament loudly. Peony, her name had been Elizabeth then, Elizabeth Allen, tried to quiet them down.

"They're going to make whores out of us," cried the one known as Mary. "I'd sooner she did kill us."

"Speak for yourself," Elizabeth said. "I mean to escape."

Kathryn soiled herself, standing there at the end of the roped girls. She threw herself on the floor and all the rest of them were jerked down on top of her. They were just getting themselves upright, a difficult task with their hands bound, when they heard footsteps outside the door. There was a key in the lock and a big man, coal black, stood there with a twelve inch long knife in his hands.

Kathryn fainted, the other three screamed in fright. The man entered and cut the rope holding Kathryn to the rest of them. He looked at the others, and cut Mary off, leaving Elizabeth and Alicia still bound together. He slit the rope holding Mary's hands together and ordered her to undress.

"Undress?" the girl stammered. The big man stepped up to her, grabbed her garment in two hands and ripped it apart.

"Undress," He repeated.

She hastily removed the rest of her clothing, keeping her gaze on the floor. When she stood there completely naked, the man grabbed her crotch. When Mary shrank away from him he grabbed her hand and pulled her from the room. Another man came in, this one a tall white man with dirty hair falling to his shoulders. He led Alicia away, leaving Kathryn and Elizabeth standing there, their hands still bound although no longer tied to each other.

Kathryn was hysterical. Elizabeth began to look for a way out. The window was too high to be reached, although she was sure she could reach it if she stood on one of the chairs. Just as she began to move the chair, the key turned in the lock again. Kathryn collapsed on the floor in uncontrolled sobs.

When the door opened this time two girls entered. One carried a tray of dishes and the other a beaker of water.

"Now, now, don't take on so Miss," the one with the water said to Kathryn. "Sit up and let me clean you up. You'll feel better then."

The other girl set the dishes down and came to Elizabeth and began to untie her hands. "I know you're scared," she said, "but facts is facts and if you don't fight them it'll go easier for you. I'm Dolly and you're Peony."

Elizabeth started to protest, but Dolly shushed her. "No, forget all that, you are Peony now and you're a right pretty thing. With your dark coloring you'll look so pretty in orange. Maybe I should have named you Poppy, but I like Peony better, don't you?"

The other girl turned to Peony and offered her a warm wet cloth. "Wash your face and hands and we'll feed you. I'm Sally."

She nodded towards Kathryn who was still sobbing. "That one we'll call Baby. Don't ever use any other names. Mrs. Hastings doesn't like it."

Both girls nodded. Baby's sobs turned to sniffing and after she'd blown her nose several times and had her face washed again she had calmed down enough to eat the soup and bread the two girls had brought them.

"The boys'll be back for you tomorrow," Dolly said. "I

suggest you try to get some sleep. There's no way out of here, so forget about trying to escape. Even if you did, Hastings would catch you, or have you caught." She drew her fingers across Peony's throat in a meaningful gesture.

Dolly and Sally stood on either side of the door, leaning back with their arms folded across their chests. Both girls were brawny and smiled at Peony whenever she looked up at them. As Dolly cleared the dishes away, she grew talkative.

"Being a whore isn't all bad you know. We get fed three times a day, have a warm roof over our heads, and we get paid a nickel a trick. Hastings will give you one dress, you want any more you have to save your money and buy it yourself. After a while you'll be able to go outside, come and go as you please as long as you're here for work every night.

"Don't think of running...the last girl did that was found with her throat cut in the alley in the next block. Your families don't want you back neither, once they," she nodded at the door, "finish with you."

Kathryn, Baby, began to cry again and she soon threw up all the food she had eaten. Sally handed her a rag and an empty bowl and ordered her to clean it up. When Baby didn't comply, Sally kicked her in the butt. "Clean it up."

"And take off those stinking clothes," Dolly added, all the friendliness gone out of her voice now. "I'm going to leave the basin. You wash up and then go to bed."

When Baby had cleaned up the mess she'd made on the floor, Sally stood and watched until Baby had taken off her dress. "Now you," she said turning to Peony. "Give up the clothes."

Both girls were in bed and under the covers when Dolly and Sally left, taking the clothes and dishes with them. As soon as their footsteps faded Elizabeth got up and, with a blanket wrapped around her, moved one of the wobbly chairs beneath the window and climbed up on it. The window was small and there was no way to open it, but Elizabeth thought that if she broke it and removed all the glass she could wiggle her way out. She looked down. It was a long way; they were on the third and top floor of the house. The window looked out on an alley and another large house behind.

Elizabeth had just gotten down from the chair to find something to break the window with when she heard footsteps outside the door. She hurriedly moved the chair away from the window and sat down on it, still wrapped in her blanket, but the footsteps went past the door. Elizabeth hastily gathered up all the blankets from the other three beds in the room and started knotting them together.

"What are you doing?" Baby asked.

"I'm going to escape."

"But you heard what they said."

"I'll take my chances. Do you want to be ravished by those two men? And then be a whore for the rest of your life?"

Baby began to whine. "But there's no way out."

Elizabeth looked at Baby and then up at the window. "You're right," she said cruelly, "you're too fat to fit out the window."

At that the girl turned her face away and pulled the covers over herself. Elizabeth could hear her sobbing.

She worked as fast as she could; knotting the blankets together until she had a length she thought would reach the ground. She needed something to tie it to. There was a gas light built into the wall about a foot away from the window. Peony tugged on it and found it secure. She tied one end of her blanket rope to it and climbed up on the chair. It was still dark outside, but dawn would be coming soon. She had to hurry.

She wrapped a blanket around her fist and slammed it into the window. It shattered and she heard pieces of glass fall on the floor. She held her breath for a moment, afraid someone might come, and then, in case they did, she hurried faster to clear the jagged edges of glass away. She dropped her rope out...it was not as close to the ground as she had hoped, but close enough. She tied a thin sheet around her bare body as best she could and then holding the knotted blanket rope she squeezed out the window, gasping when a piece of glass cut her shoulder open. Hand over hand, she went down the rope and finally dropped the last ten feet onto the mud in the alley. It must have rained recently, or she'd landed in a spot where they threw wastewater, because her landing was softened by mud.

Elizabeth looked around her. The sheeting she'd wrapped around her body was coming off and she re-wrapped it to cover as much of her naked self as possible and began to run down the alley. Just before she reached the street, somebody grabbed her.

"Well, well," said a male voice, "what did I catch? A ghost?"

The man turned her around, still firmly held in an arm lock. "A pretty one, running away from Hastings House, I'll wager."

Despite herself, for the first time since they'd arrived in Chicago, Elizabeth began to cry.

"Oh please," she begged. "Let me go. Take me back to Cleveland and my father will pay you. Please."

But the man only laughed. "No, 'e won't. Once you've been taken 'e won't want ya back. They never do. Come on now, I know a nice place where we can have a little fun."

Besides rum the man's breath stunk like a barnyard as he pulled her head back and kissed her, forcing his dirty tongue into her mouth. "We got to get a ways from this place," he said pulling her along beside him. "We get caught it's curtains for the both of us."

He must have pulled her a block or two up the street. Except for a few drunks laying on the sidewalk, the streets were deserted. By this time of night even the brothels in Little Cheyenne were closed and the ladies sleeping.

Finally they came to a house with three wide steps leading up to the ornate front door. The man pushed her down on the top step and before she knew what was happening he'd forced himself between her legs. She screamed and fought, wrapping her hands in his long dirty hair and pulling while he pumped to a climax inside her. Then he stood up, buttoned his britches up and threw her a coin.

"You better hide, missy, if The Hastings catches you..." he crossed his neck the way Dolly had done.

When the man was gone, Elizabeth lay on the stairs and cried. She was about to crawl into a corner and sleep when she heard someone behind her. She jumped and tripped over the sheeting.

"You look hurt, miss," a tall man said. "Look here, there's blood all over. Zach, help me out."

A second man appeared out of the darkness. Although the man's voice sounded kind, Elizabeth didn't trust that. She tried to run, but he picked her up and held her tightly against him.

"Where did you come from?" he asked.

"Cleveland," she told him, "and you'd better let me go."

"Kidnapped weren't you?" he asked.

She nodded, rubbing her face against his rough clothing.

"Mary Hastings?" he asked.

She nodded again. "Dirty rotten whore," the man said. "Did she break you yet?"

Elizabeth guessed what the man meant and shook her head no.

"Zach, give me your coat." The second man complied and the tall one helped her put it on. She was at least covered down to her knees now.

"What you gonna do with her?"

"I'm gonna take her to The Palace."

Drew had taken her to Daisy Brighton who had cleaned her up, bound up her cut shoulder, and dressed her. The next day the two men came back and took her away. Drew explained that there was no place in Chicago where'd she be safe, even in The Palace as one of Daisy's girls. If Mary Hastings found her, she'd be dead.

So he put her on his schooner and took her to Escanaba

and then to Fayette where he put her in charge of the small brothel he and some other men ran. She was still a whore, but she was well treated and she lived like a queen in the rooms Drew gave her. She had her own money and could have left, but she stayed because she had fallen in love with Drew. And she really couldn't go back to Cleveland. When she finally accepted that she told Drew to call her Peony from then on.

Chapter Twenty-Four

The priest's carriage was black and plain, but the seats were comfortable. The windows had shades over the windows and Carrie was surprised that she could see through them. She leaned over to examine them closely. They were like the net of a ladies hat, only denser. When she got up close she couldn't see through the shades at all.

She sat back to watch as the carriage, drawn by two horses, passed through the streets on her way to William Jenny's uptown office. As interested as she was in the many buildings, they soon all began to look alike and her mind began to review what Father Mitchell had said.

Oh, she hoped she was doing the right thing! What if Drew was honorable? Father Mitchell said he didn't know anything about the legality or procedures a Lake captain could or must follow in performing a marriage. He told her about the fake wedding chapels that could be found in almost every block of...he'd named several vice districts; Little Cheyenne, Hell's Half Acre, and the Bad Lands were all she could remember. The very names were disgusting. She certainly had not envisioned Chicago in this way. This area, Custom House Place, he said, was slowly being taken over by the bordello's and so-called resorts.

"You are perfectly safe at The Palace," he told her. "Especially if Miss Daisy herself has undertaken to watch over you. And as to your husband," he lifted his voice to indicate they both knew that Drew's status was in question, "if he is honorable, then he will consent to bringing you to me to repeat your wedding vows. In which case you can be assured that you are legally married."

Carrie had wept. She couldn't help it, she felt so torn apart by everything. Finally Father Mitchell had suggested that she seek out Mr. Jenny and have him secure her a room at the Palmer House, if only to save her from having to attend anymore of Miss Daisy's dinner parties.

"Aye, that will be expensive, Carrie," he warned. "I trust you have some money?"

Carrie assured him she had, and that as she did business with Mr. Jenny he could advance her whatever she needed.

She had written a note to Drew, which Father Mitchell said he would deliver to Miss Daisy himself. He would also arrange for the rest of her baggage to be sent to the Palmer House. The note simply said that Carrie had decided to transfer her lodging to the Palmer House, and that Drew should join her there.

Now she wondered...would he be angry? Had she acted hastily?

"Dear me," she said aloud, "I haven't acted with a shred of sense since I met the man."

What was it he'd told her, and she had agreed. That he might not ever be on time, but that he would always arrive. Tears filled her eyes again and she started to remember the good things about him. The way he listened to her, the way his smile moved from his sparkling eyes to his lips and then often burst out of him in a loud guffaw. The tender way he had explored her body and made love to her on board Wave Dancer. The story he had told her about the Chicago fire..."

And everybody here spoke well of him. Bobbie, the cook had told her not to believe most of what was said of him. And Miss Daisy certainly considered him to be an upright man. But then, how much would it take for such a woman to judge a man upright?

Miss Daisy. She remembered what Father Mitchell had said of her. That she came from a good family in Boston and had arrived in Chicago at the age of eighteen and how, after observing how little the girls who worked in the stores as clerks and file drawer keepers were paid, she decided to become a prostitute. She had apprenticed herself to the

Madam of one of the best houses in town and five years later, when the old Madam died, had inherited The Palace.

"Vivette," Father Mitchell said, "is Miss Daisy's current apprentice and assistant. It is rumored that she will buy shares in The Palace before the year is out."

Carrie thought about that. It was probably true that a proper lady could not make a living in the world. Very few women had the luck to have discovered marble on their property, nor had someone like Hugh Brandon to assist them. Without the quarry, Carrie would be penniless. She would have had to remarry almost at once to keep from starving.

Would Henry have been such a bad match? Would Henry have been interested in her without the finding of marble? She doubted it. Despite the way Drew talked, Carrie never thought of herself as an attractive woman. She was just ordinary, a little fleshy, and, Eleanor would have said, not concerned enough about her appearance.

That made her think of the pampering she'd received at The Palace. Vivette had made her almost pretty! For that alone, she should have stayed.

Carrie was jolted out of her reveries when the carriage stopped in front of a grand building. The Palmer House was huge and occupied half of the block on State Street and half of the block on Monroe. It was all stone and windows and the corner was topped with a round cupola. A green awning stretched from the entrance down to the street so someone disembarking from a carriage in the rain would not get the least bit wet.

The driver helped her down and then handed her her bag. A man in green and gold livery rushed forward to take it for her.

"Thank you," she said to the priest's driver and stood and watched as he pulled expertly back into the flow of carriage traffic on State Street.

Then she followed the door man into the Palmer House.

The lobby had a high ceiling from which hung three crystal chandeliers. These were reflected back in the long mirrors that lined the hall, broken only by the many entrance and exit hallways. The mirrors were draped like windows in green velvet held back with golden braided cords as thick as her arm.

"Are you alone, Madam?" asked the doorman, interrupting her obviously awed gazing around the room. His voice surprised her and when she turned she was startled by the hostility she read in his eyes, which were level with her own.

"For the moment," Carrie replied coldly, "I'd like to register for a room, please."

The doorman nodded and escorted her to a long counter where eight men stood ready to serve. She stood in line behind a man and woman and two small children. When it was her turn, she was embarrassed to be told that the hotel did not offer rooms to unescorted women. She inquired the price and was astounded when he told her forty-five dollars a day. It was twice what she had expected. She thanked the clerk and turned to the doorman holding her bag. He had a small "I told you so" smirk on his face that Carrie disregarded.

"Will you please place my bag in a safe place until I return? And when the rest of my luggage comes, please receive it also." She handed him her calling card with the name Carolyn Grey on it and a coin from her wrist bag. "Can you obtain a carriage to take me to 130 North Dearborn Street?"

It was only after she was in the hackney that she remembered that her luggage would arrive under the name of Mrs. Drew McGeary.

The hired carriage drew up in front of a three-story red stone building. She paid the requested fare to the driver and he helped her down. A signboard just inside the door listed William B. Jenny, Architect, on the second floor.

William Jenny was surprised to find Carrie sitting in his office lobby. Despite her attempt to appear business like and composed she was nervous and she saw immediately that her presence there unescorted made him uncomfortable also. He invited her into his office, a large room with windows on both sides. A large walnut desk sat in the corner where its occupant could look out the windows in either direction. Mr. Jenny seated her in a brown leather armchair in front of the desk and then sat down in the chair behind the desk.

"What a pleasure to see you again, Mrs. Grey," he said. "What brings you to Chicago?"

"Shopping," she replied and then she told him she had attempted to take a room at the Palmer House but had been refused because she was unescorted.

Mr. Jenny laughed. "They don't want to become an assignation house for high priced street walkers."

Carrie blushed and Jenny hurried to explain that she didn't in the least resemble one of those women, but all of the respectable hotels in town had similar rules.

"It is quite expensive," Carrie said. "A street girl would have to be very high priced to afford such a room."

"Some of them are," Jenny said. "Would you like me to arrange the room for you Carrie?"

"I'm not sure I can afford it."

"How long will you be here?"

"I'm not sure. If the Chicago-Northwestern leaves tomorrow, I will be on it."

Jenny raised an eyebrow at that and Carrie knew that he was wondering how she got there.

"I came by lake schooner, Mr. Jenny, and thought it would be easy enough to make arrangement for the return trip once I was ready."

"The train will not run again until Monday," he said. "I will send my clerk to the Palmer House immediately to make arrangements for you."

Jenny steepled his fingers and tilted back in his leather chair and looked intently at her.

"Are you alone, then, Carrie Grey?" he asked.

She nodded, feeling a sudden weakness in her jaw that

wanted to tremble. She willed it under her control, which made the muscles in the side of her neck cramp painfully. She wondered if her eyes were still red from the weeping Father Mitchell had drawn from her in that interview.

Perhaps, no surely, he saw, because he quickly turned his chair so its back was to her and began to search though a stack of papers on a credenza behind him. In that time Carrie softly blew her nose in the linen handkerchief she carried in her sleeve and was composed when he turned back to her.

Mr. Jenny held a piece of paper in his hand. He studied it a moment and then handed it to her.

"This is the amount due you so far," he said. "Will you need more than The Palmer House expenses?"

Carrie studied the statement. It was much more than she had imagined it could be. She need have no concern about money.

"No, I have money enough, at least I think I do. I want to visit Marshall Field tomorrow."

"If you need more, you can talk to the concierge at the hotel and they will add it to your hotel bill. My clerk will arrange it."

He rang a bell and a man appeared at the open doorway. He explained what he wanted the man to do and then he looked at the gold watch that hung from his vest and said, "It is time for lunch. Let me escort you and we can visit some more."

With Carrie on his arm, Jenny walked her a block down to State Street and then a block north to a dining establishment called Johnny's Fine Dining. The large room was filled with tables. White clad waiters carried large silver trays of food to the tables, occupied mostly by gentlemen, but here and there a lady sat with a gentlemen. Jenny spoke to the headwaiter and they were soon seated at table towards the back of the room, sheltered from view by three large ferns in brass pots.

After they had ordered, Jenny sat forward and looked earnestly at Carrie.

"Something is bothering you, Mrs. Grey. It hardly seems likely to me that you arrived alone with no arrangements for yourself."

The tears Carrie had held in for so long escaped and streamed down her face. The tension was just too much to contain them any longer. Jenny waited until she had composed herself again. When she looked up at him he was sitting back in his chair looking at her expectantly.

"I did something very foolish, Mr. Jenny, and I am trying to recover myself. Pray, don't press me for details. I must leave Chicago as soon as I can, and since I can't leave until Monday, I will shop at Marshall Field's as I've always wanted to do."

"Very well," he said, seeming relieved that her tears were few. "If you are to be in town anyway, then you must let me keep my promise to take you to the theatre. Mrs. Jenny and I will take you to the Grand Opera House on Saturday. Do you like opera?"

"I don't know. Do you?"

Jenny smiled broadly at her. "Your honesty is charming, dear lady. But it doesn't matter; The Grand Opera House seldom presents an opera. I don't know who the performers are tomorrow. Mrs. Jenny would know, but I enjoy going whoever might be doing the entertainment for us."

"We call our town hall in Fayette an opera house too," Carrie said, "but I doubt if anyone in town even knows what an opera is. With the exception of Grace Sailstad, and maybe even our Dr. Rutherford. He is a man of unknown depths."

So they agreed to attend the theatre and arranged a time to meet in the main dining room of The Palmer House for dinner before going to the theatre. For the rest of the meal, Mr. Jenny entertained her with stories of how the building of the Farwell mansion was proceeding. The Farwell brother's owned Farwell Mercantile, a large dry goods store. They were very competitive, both with men in general and between themselves. Charles already had a mansion on Pearson Street that had just been completed, and John was having his built right next door.

"Let me order my carriage and I'll take you for a tour along Michigan Avenue," he said, "and then return you to The Palmer House."

Carrie said she'd love to and she soon found herself in a dark plum colored phaeton with the top folded back. The day was warm but a pleasant breeze blew. She felt better than she had since she had been hurried off Wave Dancer three days ago.

Everywhere Carrie looked she saw new buildings in progress. "Are any of these your buildings?" Carrie asked.

Mr. Jenny pointed out one, built of terra cotta. "That one," he said, "and I'm trying out something entirely new on a building for the New Home Insurance Company. It will be taller than any building in the city...in the world, nine stories. I expect that one to be done early next spring. But right now I'm concentrating on John Farwell's place."

"The water tower there," Mr. Jenny said, "and the pumping station across the street are the only things that survived the fire. It's constructed with big limestone blocks."

"It looks like a castle tower," Carrie said, "with all those small towers about the main one."

"It's called gothic style," Jenny responded. "The tower surrounds a steel stand pipe so the stone surrounding the steel makes a very strong structure. It's this model, a steel structure surrounded by stone, that I'm using in my nine-story building."

They turned east onto Pearson Street and stopped before a Queen Anne style house. Beyond that another, even larger, house was being built.

"This, dear lady, is your very own Chicago landmark."

Carrie was overwhelmed not just by the size of the homes, but to see marble from her quarry actually in use. "Oh, it is gorgeous!"

Like the house beside it, John Farwell's home would be three stories high, but built in a completely different style.

Charles Farwell's Queen Anne, with its distinctive flared chimney tops and rounded window frames, looked softer than the square windows and pointed gables of John's house. A turret was taking shape on the east corner.

"It will have a steam-heating system that heats the entire house with a boiler in the basement and pipes into each room conducting the steam warmed air everywhere in the house." Carrie could tell he was excited about the house. "There will be only two chimneys. The fireplace in the parlor will be for decorative use, not for heat, and the other one is a flue for the boiler."

They alit from the carriage and walked around the construction site. Mr. Jenny introduced her to the mason and his crew who were handling the marble. The head mason complimented the marble. "It dresses like a lady in a ball gown," he told her. "This house will shine in the sun."

"Just like the tall white bluffs along the lake where the stone comes from," Carrie offered.

Next Jenny took her to Central Park. "Even more than buildings," he said, "I like to design parks. This was known as Central Park until last year. When our President died, the city renamed it Garfield Park in his honor."

He parked the phaeton and they got out. The park was designed for strolling and this they did. There were boaters on the large, tree-lined lagoon. Swans swam back and forth along the shore and children threw them bread crusts trying to entice them closer. Mr. Jenny told her the lagoon was not natural but he had designed and engineered it to drain the parkland, which had been quite marshy. A building within the park was low and graceful, suitable to its setting. Carrie commented on the natural way it fit into the park without calling attention to itself.

Finally they re-crossed the river and drove south on Michigan Avenue to an immense building. It had three cupolas, and from the center one flew a large American flag.

Mr. Jenny pulled over to the curb and stopped. "This is

the Inter-State Exposition Hall. Boyington built it in 1873; he's one of my chief competitors. The fire completely cleared this area you know and this was one of several big buildings to be completed at about the same time. The mayor wanted to prove to the world that Chicago was not beaten. As soon as it was done, it hosted an Inter-State Exposition, which ran from September through November."

Carrie thought it was an ugly building. With its rounded ends it appeared to be just a huge barn with some fancy Greek revival facades. "What is an exposition?" she queried.

He laughed, "It is a place where sellers and buyers meet. The seller builds a display of his wares and the buyers see them and invest. My firm was awarded several jobs as a result of the Exposition. There are several such shows a year now, but on a smaller scale. The circus performed under the central dome just last month."

It was late afternoon by the time Mr. Jenny returned her to the Palmer House. While Mr. Jenny checked on her arrangements, Carrie sat in one the plush chairs next to a tree that grew in a brass urn. The urn itself was five feet tall and as wide and she had to touch the tree to assure herself it was a real tree, for she had never seen anything like it except in a magazine picture once. The trunk grew straight and only at the very top did huge green branches extend from the top and fall gracefully downward. A placard on the urn identified it as a palm tree.

Mr. Jenny brought her her room key and escorted her to the second floor where he opened the door to the room with a flourish and after a good-bye until tomorrow, he was gone. Her room was almost as spacious as the one at The Palace had been and Carrie was pleased to see it had a white porcelain bathtub in it. She wondered if there was some way her house could have what Mr. Jenny had called "modern plumbing."

Her carpetbag sat on a low table and she quickly unpacked it. She wondered if it would be possible to get her trunk, if it had arrived. She freshened her face and hair and wandered to the lobby where she asked one of the liveried porters where she could find the concierge.

He sat behind a polished mahogany desk. He listened politely while she explained that her trunk and other baggage had been sent, but under the name of Mrs. Andrew McGeary. He checked his records and coldly informed her that nothing had arrived under that name. He took her room number and asked her what her assumed name was.

"It is not an assumed name," she replied indignity, "it is my real name. Mrs. McGeary is my mother, who at the last minute could not accompany me."

The man nodded, clearly not believing her, and said that if the luggage arrived it would be delivered to her room. Carrie went back to her room and picked up her needlework. She was not used to the ways of the world and she thought she didn't want to be. Life was too complicated here.

Marshall Fields, Carson Pirie Scott, Farwell Mercantile, and the Grand Opera House theatre where she heard Lynn Crownwell sing; it all whirled though Carrie's mind as the Chicago and Northwestern Railroad carried her north through Wisconsin to Escanaba. Neither her trunk nor Drew had followed her to the Palmer House. She was exhausted from the trip, too tired to know if she was relieved or disappointed that he hadn't shown up demanding an explanation for her removal from The Palace.

Or perhaps Father Mitchell had told him her fears and he'd been ashamed to follow her. Whatever it was, she had no tears left. She'd cried herself to sleep all three nights at the Palmer House and awakened Monday morning resolved to put the whole experience behind her.

It wasn't until she reached Escanaba Tuesday morning that she began to think about what she had to face in Fayette. Bertha Hartson must surely have whipped her small-minded faction in town into a self-righteous fury against her. But she wanted the solace she knew Louella and Edward would offer her and suddenly she thought of her kittens and yearned for one of them to hug. Animals were so much easier to love than humans, so undemanding and non-judging. For a moment she thought about taking a room at the House of Ludington and sending for Louella to come to her, but then decided that was cowardly.

The Lady Washington docked at Fayette at half past six. There were a few passengers on board that she recognized, but did not really know, and none of them paid any attention to her. The town was in an uproar over something, that much was clear at once when not one person was on the dock to meet the incoming steamer. Carrie could see a large crowd gathered in front of the Shelton House and she took advantage of this to slip unnoticed up the hill to Rutherford's.

Chapter Twenty-Five

The coal train from Fairport usually rolled into Fayette just about supper time and people didn't pay much attention to it. This afternoon, the engineer Lawrence Trunsky, was at the controls of the newest of the Jackson Iron Companies two locomotives, the J.C. Hicks. He began blowing the train whistle as soon as he saw the hotel and he didn't cease blowing it until he rolled to a stop under the big birch tree just in back of the Company Office.

His alarm had the desired effect, for a crowd had gathered along the tracks and he could see more people running from the Hotel, the Jackson Iron Company office, the General Store; from the boarding house, and especially from the cottages on Furnace Hill.

Lawrence leaned out the window and asked someone to fetch Doc Rutherford.

"Who's hurt?"

"How bad is it?"

Everyone in the crowd had a question and they all talked at once. A twelve-year-old lad named Billy took off at a run down Harbor Street followed closely by half a dozen others.

Jack Sailstad came out of the company office and pushed his way through the crowd. He pulled himself up into the cab, afraid of what Trunsky might have for the doc. A year ago, the train had gone run-away on the downgrade and one of the men had been hurt badly when he jumped out of the out-of-control train.

What Jack saw was a girl, huddled in the corner. She was near naked and had black and blue welts across her legs. What he could see of her face through the tangle of wild red hair was puffy; whether from crying or from beating, Jack couldn't tell. He pulled his jacket off and threw it around her shoulders. She was very dirty and Jack almost recoiled at the smell of her. She didn't look at him, but remained unmoving, curled as tightly as she could into a protective ball with her head resting on her knees.

"Don't worry," he said. "You're safe now." What he needed for her was a woman." Do you see Mrs. Underwood?" he asked Lawrence, "or the preacher's wife?"

Lawrence scanned the crowd. "Both of 'em," he said.

Jack leaned out of the engine and instructed one of the men to bring Beth and Mrs. Hartson to him. He turned back to the engineer.

"You stand down and keep everybody else away. Have someone bring a closed carriage right up here next to the cab, we'll want to transfer her without exposing her to the people if possible."

Lawrence climbed down and helped the two women up. He spotted Frank, the furnace complex foreman. "Frank, boss says bring a closed carriage, pronto."

He heard the gallop of a horse and looked up. "Doc's here," he announced to Jack.

Inside the engine, Beth Underwood knelt next to the girl but when she tried to touch her, the poor thing shrank away. Bertha stared in disbelief. "Merciful Jesus," she said. "Where did he find her?"

Dr. Rutherford entered the car and suddenly it was too crowded for everybody.

"I'll wait outside," Jack said.

"That's the girl Shirley saw come into town on the stage last week, she mentioned the red hair," Bertha said. "Last she saw of her she was talking to Mr. LaTermaine at the store. I asked around, at the cottages, thinking she had come to visit one of them, but nobody had seen her."

Beth was talking quietly to the girl. Although the girl raised her head she just stared at them all, her eyes wide and looking right through them. When the doctor tried to touch her she grabbed for Beth and gripped her arm so tightly Beth wondered if anybody could pry her loose.

"Now, now," Dr. Rutherford said in a gentle voice, "I'm the doctor, I'm not going to hurt you."

"It's all right," Beth cooed, "whatever it is, you're safe now."

Bertha continued to stand next to the door, praying out loud for the poor creature. Her prayer tapered off when she realized that Lawrence was telling Jack Sailstad how he'd found the girl.

"We picked her up along side the tracks where Stoddy built that new Stockade of his. I think she was one of his girls. I heard he had two of three or 'em. From what some of the guys were saying, they were all virgins on opening night. He said you never heard such crying and carrying on from a whore in all your days."

Bertha turned and looked at the girl. "Is that true, girl? Were you kept at that...that, place, against your will?"

Bertha's sharp voice broke the girl's trance-like stare where the soft talk of Beth and Dr. Rutherford had had no effect. At Bertha's question, the girl began to cry and shake violently, and letting loose of Beth's arm she slapped at the doctor and raked her nails across his face. But her fingernails had been torn or bitten back to almost below the quick and inflicted no damage. Rutherford grabbed her by the wrists and Beth got behind her and pulled her back against her bosom where she stroked the girl's dirty hair while she began to sing a lullaby. At that the girl crumbled against her and began to sob.

Bertha scrambled down from the train and went around to the other side. "You listen to me, everybody," she called. Her voice carried to the furthest edges of the crowd and they all turned to listen.

"They've got a girl in there. Not more than fourteen years old. She escaped from that evil establishment down on the Sand Beach. She's been assaulted and used by the men from this very town. She's been beaten, but somehow escaped and the train picked her up where she was wandering on the tracks."

The crowd hushed and then began to murmur among themselves.

Bertha seized the moment. "I say it's time to rid the town of those dens of iniquity. "

She grabbed a pickaxe that lay against a coal crate. "Who is with me?"

Others looked around and started to grab shovels, coal rakes, or whatever they could find and, led by Bertha Hartson, they began to walk back up the tracks.

Jack had heard the talk and started to stop them, but then thought better of it and let them go. The officers of the Jackson Iron Company had discussed the Hole In The Rock and it's side business many times, but since it was outside the town, there was nothing they could do about it. A mob of angry women might be just the thing.

By the time she had reached the top of Furnace Hill, Bertha had almost the entire town behind her. They descended on the low building at the edge of the Sand Beach. Stoddy and a couple customers came out and watched the crowd approach. Then Stoddy dashed back inside and barred the door, leaving his two customers to be the first to face the angry mob. That hapless duo ran south, into the woods.

Inside, Stoddy grabbed his cash box and moved towards the back door, but a dozen men barged through the door and into the dimly lit doggery at the same time four more busted into the back door of his office. When they grabbed him he lost control of his box. He tried to get away from them and retrieve his money. He dove for the floor and almost got his hands on it but someone grabbed him by the ankles and dragged him outside.

"Where does he keep the girls?" Bertha shouted, and one of the men pointed down the hallway.

She came first to Peony's suite and pounded on the door. Peony had been standing inside wondering what was happening but afraid to look. She opened her door as soon as Bertha rapped on it. "What's happening?" she asked.

"We're closing this place up," Bertha told her. "Get the other girls and get out. We're going to burn this disgraceful place down."

"Can I take my things?" Peony asked, thinking of her sketch books and the painting of Carrie she was working on. Bertha nodded and looked into Peony's room, curious about the rather nice room she saw before her. She did a double take at the portrait in progress that must surly be Carrie Grey.

"There's another place," Peony said over her shoulder as she stuffed clothes, paints, and sketch books into a carpetbag. "Across the tracks and back in the woods. I think he has some girls there too."

Shirley LeComte had come up behind Bertha. She had the four women from the back rooms with her, all with their arms full of clothing. "I think this is all of them," she said.

Bertha turned and looked at the women. They were all older women and she dismissed them with a wave of her hand. "Take them into town, Shirley, to the Shelton House. We can put them on the boat to Escanaba in the morning."

Peony showed Shirley and the four women out her private door and onto the beach. "Take my things, Peaches," she said as she shoved the carpetbag into the arms of the short plump blonde. I'll meet you later."

"I'm going with you to the stockade," Peony said to Bertha. "There's one girl there, at least, and she's going to be scared out of her wits."

"We already have that one," Bertha said. "It was her coming into town half naked and beat up that started all this."

"A red-head?" Peony asked gripping Bertha's arm. Bertha pulled herself free and wiped her sleeve where the adventuress had touched her.

"Yes," Bertha said. "Are there more?"

"I don't know," Peony said, "but I'm sure there must have been. Stoddy has been acting like the top dog around here for the last week. Did you find his cash box?"

From the bar came the sound of tables being smashed with axes, hammers, and anything heavy people could find. "Hurry," Bertha said as she headed for the door Shirley had gone out of.

"Wait a minute," Peony said and ran down to the hall to Stoddy's office with Bertha close behind. She found the cash box under the edge of the shabby green chair and grabbed it.

"Come on," she screamed, as she grabbed Bertha again and pulled. "They've set the building on fire." This time Bertha did not wipe the offending touch away but followed Peony out the back door. When they reached the end of the beach and began to climb up the railroad grade, they heard the crackling of the flames eating up the dry wood of The Hole in The Rock. They turned to watch. Near the water's edge, by the log Peony liked to sit on, she saw a body left laying as the people who had been kicking it turned and ran closer to watch the building burn. She felt no sorrow for the brothel keeper.

Some of the men had already reached the Stockade and set it on fire and when she saw it, Peony started to run.

"There are girls in there," Peony screamed as she ran. "Did you get the girls out?" She ran towards the open door of the building but just before she ran inside someone grabbed her.

"Ain't nobody left in there," he said. "The women took her already."

Peony backed away from the building and sank down on the ground, hugging Stoddy's cash box to her heaving chest. Bertha stopped and stood beside her panting. "You all right?"

Peony looked up at her and nodded. "He said they already took her away."

Bertha nodded and offered her hand to pull Peony up. They walked, together with several other women, up the tracks. When they reached the edge of the town Peony stopped. "Thank you..."

"Bertha. I'm the minister's wife."

"Thank you Bertha. My name is Elizabeth." She handed

Stoddy's cash box to Bertha.

"I think you'll find a lot of money in there. Give it to the minister. He'll know what to do with it."

One of the women said, "I think that money ought to be given to the women. Give them something to get a new start in life."

"That's right," added another one. "Otherwise what are they going to do? Just go someplace else and be used?"

Bertha agreed. "I'll leave the box with Mr. Sailstad. He can pass it out in the morning after everyone has gotten a good nights sleep."

From the second story window of the General Store, Henry LaTermaine watched the train and the crowd. He saw Rutherford and Sailstad put the girl and Beth Underwood into the carriage. It moved up the street headed to Doc's hospital. As soon as the center of town was all but deserted, he grabbed up his valise, emptied the safe of his papers and money and walked to the stables. He saddled his horse and headed towards Garden. It would be better if he were out of town for a few days.

Chapter Twenty-Six

Carrie found Louella standing under the maple tree in front of the house. When Louella recognized her she came running to embrace her.

"What's going on?" Carrie asked, nodding towards town.

"I don't know," Louella said. "Some boys came and got Edward. Someone's been hurt, I guess."

"The whole town must be gathered in front of the hotel."

Louella had linked her arm though Carrie's as they walked back and sat down on one of the benches under the maple. "But what are you doing here, Carrie?"

Carrie felt herself wanting to bury her face in Louella's motherly bosom and cry, but she bit the inside of her lower lip and said, "Oh, Louella, it's been such..." she paused, looking for the right word, "an adventure."

"Did you marry him?"

"I don't know," Carrie replied, tilting her head to one side. "I'm don't really know."

"Well, where is he?"

"I don't know. Someplace in Chicago, I suppose. I haven't seen him since he put me ashore a week ago."

"He what?" Louella demanded. "He put you ashore?"

"Oh, not like that," Carrie said. "He had to unload his cargo and he sent me to a...hotel to wait for him."

"But you didn't wait?"

Carrie nodded yes and then no. "For a few days. Then I looked up Mr. Jenny, he's the man who is buying the marble from me, and then I came home on the train."

Louella was about to ask another question when they heard the carriage coming.

"May I go inside?" Carrie asked. "I don't want to face

anyone else right now."

Louella patted her arm. "Of course, dear. Go upstairs to the room you were in before. I'll come up and visit you as soon as I can."

"I left my luggage on the dock," Carrie said. "The Captain said he'd deliver it."

Louella nodded and gave her a push inside the hospital door just as the carriage drew up. Carrie stopped half way up the stairs to the living quarters above the hospital and listened.

Beth Underwood, the woman from the boarding house who had taken Jewel's kittens was there, and the doctor, and the patient.

"What she needs most, I think, is a bath," she heard Edward Rutherford say. "If you'll fill my tub, Louella, and find the lass some clean clothes while I just check her over. Mrs. Underwood, I think you should stay here with her."

Carrie heard Louella approaching the stairs so she hurried on up ahead of her and waited in the kitchen. "Can I help?" she offered. "Who is she?"

"I don't know," Louella replied, answering both questions. "She's just a girl. I've never seen her before. She's been beaten and she has very little clothing on. Did you hear Edward say she needs some clothes?"

Carrie nodded. "How big is she?"

Louella shrugged. "She's tall. She's only about fourteen, I'd guess. Do you know how to fill the bath tub?" Carrie nodded. That was one thing she'd learned in Chicago.

"Good. Why don't you do that while I find some clothes?"

Probably the Rutherfords were the only ones in Fayette outside of the Sailstads, to have a bathtub with warm water always ready. Carrie put the large rubber stopper in the drain hole and opened the tap, first for the hot water, and then gradually adding the cold until the water was just the right temperature. She wished she had her bags from the dock with her for she had brought Louella a tall cut glass decanter full of bath bubbles like the kind Vivette had put in her bath at The Palace.

Just as Carrie reached over to close the water taps, Beth Underwood led a tall, skinny, girl into the room. The girl had her head down, looking only at her feet. Beth looked at Carrie with mild surprise, but said nothing other than hello to her. Carrie nodded at them and quickly left the room only to bump into Edward Rutherford in the hallway.

He gripped her by the shoulders. "Carrie Grey? Or should I say Mrs. McGeary?"

Carrie was not sure if his voice was angry or not.

"Not now, Edward," Louella said from behind him. "We can hear that story after we get the girl taken care of. I take it she is not badly hurt?"

Rutherford released Carrie and turned to his wife. "I think all the hurt is on the inside, mother. It's best to leave her in Mrs. Underwood's hands right now. Do you have enough of your chicken soup to feed five?"

Edward stood in the doorway and told them what he knew of the girl while Louella rolled bisquits and Carrie set the table and stirred the large pot of chicken soup that simmered on the stove. When he told of Bertha Hartson leading a mob down to the Hole in The Rock to deliver the other women and alleged girls held there, Carrie thought immediately of Peony and everything she'd learned in Chicago. She wondered if Peony, like Daisy Brighton, had chosen her profession because it paid enough for her to live well, or if like the girl, she had been forced into it.

Her thoughts were interrupted by the appearance of Beth and the girl at the door. Carrie took one look at the girl and sat down very quickly on the nearest chair. It was like looking at Andrew McGeary! The red hair, the green eyes, the set of her mouth. Hadn't the others noticed?

"This is Lainey," Beth introduced her. "And Lainey, this is Dr. Rutherford, whom you've already met, and Mrs. Rutherford, and," she raised an eyebrow at Carrie and then said, "this is Mrs. Grey."

Carrie sighed with relief that Beth had not named her Mrs. McGeary. She wondered if anyone else saw the resemblance; certainly no one remarked on it.

"I'll bet you're hungry, Lainey" Louella said, holding a chair for the girl.

They had just finished eating when they heard someone enter the hospital room downstairs. Edward stood at once and excused himself. Bertha Hartson's voice drifted up the stairs.

"Oh no," Carrie said, "I'm not ready for this."

"Go upstairs then," Louella said. "Would you like to go with her Lainey?"

Lainey looked at Beth. "Let's all three go up," Beth said, and she held her hand out to Lainey.

Carrie let Beth and Lainey precede her up the staircase and paused on the steps to listen. Bertha was inquiring about the girl.

"She's fine physically, Mrs. Hartson," she heard Edward say. "She's taken to Mrs. Underwood and I think it best if she remains with her a day or two."

The voices grew louder and it was evident that Bertha was continuing into the living quarters despite Edward's attempt to contain her. Carrie retreated to the top of the stairs.

"I won't stay but a moment," Bertha said. "I just want to let her know that we rescued the other girl also."

"I'll tell her," Edward said. "She's resting now, sound asleep I'm sure since I gave her a dose of laudanum."

Louella's voice now. "Mrs. Hartson, won't you sit and have a cup of tea, you and your friend?"

Carrie had been about to continue up the stairs but stopped when she heard that.

"This is Elizabeth. She was one of the five women we found in addition to the other girl, poor little thing. They're all at the hotel. I find it impossible to believe how respectable men in this town let those establishments exist for so long. Anyway, she insisted that she be allowed to talk to the girl."

"I'm pleased to meet you Elizabeth," Louella said. "Please sit down."

"Why do you want to see the girl?" Edward asked. "Did you know her?"

"No," replied the woman, "but I think I might be able to help her, having gone though the same treatment myself at about her age. I understand how she feels."

Peony! Carrie was sure of it. That husky voice could not be mistaken. So she had been right, Peony was the girl Drew had rescued from Mary Hastings ten or so years ago. Carrie was torn between facing Bertha Hartson and wanting to talk to Peony, who now called herself Elizabeth.

Edward diverted the conversation again, asking Bertha what had happened when they rescued the girls.

"We burned both of those evil places to the ground," Bertha declared. "Somebody found the man's cash box and we, all the women, think we should divide it between the slaves he kept there. They've all assured me that with the money they will be able, and intend to, leave the life of adventuring. Elizabeth has agreed to escort the young ones back to their families."

"That's all very well," Edward said, "but do you think their families will accept them?"

"But who will know if they are returned discreetly?" Peony asked. "Why blame the girls for their plight? If I hadn't been told it was impossible to go home, I would surely have gone back. I know now that my mother would have sheltered me. Papa too."

Carrie heard the catch in Peony's voice. And she thoroughly agreed that the girls needed to be taken home. Where was Lainey's home? Suddenly Carrie examined that question. If Lainey was, as she expected, Drew's daughter, then where was her mother? And had Drew pretended to marry her knowing that he already had a wife? Oh, the case against him grew thicker with everything she learned. Carrie turned and climbed the last two steps and entered the bedroom where Beth sat beside the bed into which she had tucked the girl.

"Lainey," said Carrie, approaching the end of the bed, "where are your parents?"

Beth looked anxiously at Lainey and shook her head at Carrie. "Let her sleep tonight Carrie, questions can come tomorrow."

"This is important," Carrie said, as much to Beth as to the girl. "Lainey, is Andrew McGeary your father?"

Lainey sat up. "Do you know him?" she asked eagerly. "Do you know where he is?"

"Yes," Carrie said, sitting down on the bed next to the girl, "I know him, and I think I know where he is. Where is your mother?"

Tears welled up in those green eyes and flowed down her cheeks. "She died."

"When?"

"Just before I came here," Lainey said. Although the tears continued to flow, Lainey only sniffed and did not sob. Carrie handed her a handkerchief. "I came looking for Papa, but the man at the store took me to that awful place. He said Papa would find me, and then he laughed."

The man at the store? Henry? Could Henry do such a thing? Carrie stood and walked towards the door where she motioned Beth outside to speak to her.

"You have to go downstairs and get rid of Bertha Hartson. She has a woman with her who was one of the older women who worked at that place. If you can, slip her a note that I'll write for you. I must talk to her."

Beth nodded and waited while Carrie located a piece of writing paper and a pen. She wrote quickly,

Peony,
I will come to the hotel as soon as I can to talk to you. Please don't reveal me to the others.   Carrie Grey

Chapter Twenty-Seven

Drew sat in Daisy Brighton's private receiving room and chided himself. Once the cargo was sold, he could have left Zach to oversee the unloading. At the very least he could have visited her. He should have visited her. There was no reason he could not have spent every night with her.

"How did she get out?" he asked, his elbows on his knees and his head at rest on his spread palms as he stared at the yellow centers of the daisies on the carpet. It was Sunday afternoon. She'd left on Thursday morning and was probably back home by now.

"I didn't know she was a prisoner," Daisy retorted. "I told you, you should go talk to the priest."

Drew looked up. "What did you think of her, Daisy?"

Daisy leaned forward and put her hand on his knee. "I thought she was a very lucky woman. I was jealous of her from the start."

Drew stood impatiently and began to pace up and down the room. This was insane to let himself be bothered by Carrie Grey. She wasn't even pretty, he had to admit that, but there was something...from the moment he'd seen her standing at the end of the pier, soaking wet, in her undergarments...he'd felt an attraction to her. Damn her!

"Do you think she's still at the Palmer House? I won't go chasing after her. She knew it might be several days before I could come."

"Did she?"

"Well, I told her it would be a day or two."

"Let me see," Daisy said. "She arrived on Tuesday. I entertained her at dinner along with most of the women who are on the committee planning the autumn grand ball."

Drew started to interrupt, but Daisy held up her hand and

continued.

"On Wednesday she joined me for dinner with the ladies from St. James. She was quite a hit with those ladies and persuaded me to donate money to St. James to establish a children's care room.

"Thursday was the thunder storm. It was Vivette's day off and Father Mitchell arrived just before lunch with the note your wife left with him and told me he had put her in his own carriage to be taken uptown. He wanted her trunk sent, but I didn't send it.

"I would have waited for you at least one more day, Drew, but even I would have been gone by noon Friday."

She stopped talking for a moment and watched him. Then she grabbed his arm as he passed her chair and said, "Will you sit and stop pacing up and down. You make my head ache."

Drew stopped in front of Daisy, but remained standing. "Do you believe in love, Daisy?"

Daisy laughed one scoffing ha. "Of course I do. I've been in love with you for years, and what has it gotten me? A chance to teach you a few things maybe, but no solid man at my side. No one I could depend on when I needed him."

Drew sat down in the gentlemen's chair across from Daisy and studied her. "You sound like you mean it," he said.

"Oh course I mean it," she cried. "You are the only decent thing in my life."

"Decent, am I? Then the word has lost a great deal of worth since I last studied it. I brought her down here, faked a marriage for her, and deserted her at a bordello for days on end. Bah!"

He stood again. "Where can I find this priest?"

Chapter Twenty-Eight

Peony sat on one of benches on the long front porch of the Shelton House. She sat in the shadows, away from the light that fell from the dining room window, and waited for Carrie Grey. She watched Carrie walk towards her, struck again by the effect the woman had on her. It was her self-assurance and her obvious independence, Peony thought. Was that also what attracted Drew to her?

When Carrie was close enough, Peony stood and called softly, "Mrs. Grey, I'm over here."

They walked out behind the hotel and sat on limestone boulders at the edge of the slag littered beach and watched the waves roll in. The moon was gibbous and high in the sky, already on its downward arc, having risen in late afternoon. It paved a silver road across the gently rolling water. Neither one of them spoke for a while. They had already shared their stories as if they had known each other for life.

"Do you realize that neither one of us knows what her name is anymore?" Carrie asked. "Am I Carrie Grey, or Carrie McGeary? Are you Peony or Elizabeth Allen?"

"Who do you want to be, Carrie?"

"God help me, I want to be Mrs. McGeary. I still do, but I'm sure I'm not." She waited a moment and then asked, "Did you know the girl was Drew's daughter?"

"The girl who got away? Drew's daughter? Oh, Carrie, it can't be."

"She is," Carrie continued, "and she came here looking for Drew when her mother died. Henry sold her to that man, Stoddy. I'm told they left him for dead on the beach. I wonder where Henry is?"

"Oh, dear god," Peony moaned. "I only saw her from behind the day Henry brought her. I listened outside the door..."

"You'd have known if you had seen her," Carrie said. "She looks so very like him. Did you know Drew was married?"

Peony nodded and looked out across the bay. "You don't know how many times I've sat on the beach watching that moon-paved road across the lake and wished I could follow it. When Drew first brought me here, he was all I had. I was with child from the man who raped me, but one night when Drew was gone Stoddy did it to me, and beat me, and the baby flowed out of my body. That night I waded into the lake and tried to follow the moon. Henry stopped me. He was my friend and Drew was my lover.

"I'm sorry, Carrie, your question about Drew's wife. Her name was Nancy. She lived in Muskegon with their daughter, Elaine. Drew visited them often, because of the child, not her mother. I don't think they were married, but he felt an obligation to her, and he loved the girl. Nancy has been ill for a long time, I'm not surprised she died."

Carrie sighed. "We're always being pushed by the winds of fortune, aren't we? All of us. The question is what do we do now? And shall I call you Peony, or Elizabeth?"

"I think I'm Peony now. I tried on Elizabeth this evening with that preacher's wife. But it doesn't fit, at least not yet."

Carrie stood and helped Peony to her feet. "I intend to go home in the morning and take Lainey with me. I think you should come too. Drew will come, if not for me, for Lainey."

They parted with an embrace and Carrie walked the long way around, following Cedar Lane along the dark back side of Snail Shell Point, setting off the dogs at every house. Her mind went in circles, wrapping back on itself like one continuous wave lapping again and again on the same rocky shore. She didn't know how to do anything but go on. When she came to the house where Eleanor had lived she stopped and stared. It was still empty, as empty as she felt inside.

Edward was sitting at the kitchen table when she returned to the house and she told him everything.

The next morning he went out early and returned to the house to say he had arranged with a schooner bound for Escanaba to drop the three of them off at Cedar Harbor. Henry, he said, was not at the General Store and no one had seen him.

The last two weeks of July and the first week of August passed and the three women settled into a routine at Cedar Harbor. Two days after they had arrived, Lainey was suddenly violently ill, with stomach cramps and vomiting. Peony took care of her and, on the third day, when Lainey felt better, Peony confided to Carrie that she had administered a well known "whore's potion" to the girl to make sure there were no "unwanted effects" of the girl's ordeal.

Lainey spent most of her time on the beach watching for her father's schooner. Peony drew flowers, the quarry, Lainey, and Carrie. She was still trying to capture the elan of Carrie Grey, although it had dimmed noticeably from day to day. She tried to teach Lainey some elementary sketching skills, but Lainey wasn't interested. She sat on the beach, piling the flat limestone, making towers and castles.

Carrie was endlessly busy with small chores. She made two skirts and a blouse for Lainey. One day they caught the stage into Garden where they bought shoes and other things Lainey and Peony needed.

Melanie DeWinter, Carrie's friend at the market there, told them that Henry had returned to Fayette, and as far as she knew, nobody knew about his part in the scandal and she promised Carrie that she wouldn't tell.

She told them that the morning after the brothel was burned and the men of Fayette went to recover Stoddy's body from the beach, he had vanished. Some said the tide had washed the body out into the lake, and others that he wasn't dead after all and had made a clean get-away. He was reported seen in Fairport one day and somebody else swore they'd seen him in Manistique.

There were a great many people searching for the cave where the brothel keeper had supposedly kept a great deal of money. Some swore he had buried it and the area around the burned down establishment was pockmarked with holes. Cottage children and their mothers reportedly spent all day on the Sand Beach, digging while their fathers worked.

"All the women were taken to Escanaba," Melanie said, "except for one, that must be you Miss, that they said ran away as soon as she got her share of the money."

Carrie wanted to ask if anyone had seen Captain McGeary, but wisely avoided giving Melanie an opening to pry into that affair. They walked back to Cedar Harbor, laughing on the way about the gossip Melanie had imparted. Even Lainey's spirits were raised, and after that she began to help out around the house, sweeping every day and doing the dishes after they ate.

It was because of this that Wave Dancer slipped into Cedar Harbor unseen by any of them.

Carrie heard the footsteps on the porch and looked up from her sewing just as whoever it was knocked on the door. She glanced at Peony, and Lainey looked in from the kitchen where she was finishing the dishes from their lunch.

When Carrie opened the door Drew inquired where she would like her trunk. Carrie stared at him. Her first impulse was to throw her arms around his neck, but she held back. Behind her she heard Peony get up and a second later she heard the back door close.

Adopting Drew's nonchalant manner Carrie opened the door wide to a now empty room and said, "You can put it in the bedroom."

Drew turned and called over his shoulder. "Bring it in here." Zach and Delbert appeared, carrying the trunk between them. Peter followed with the other carpetbag in one hand and a hatbox in the other.

"Shall we bring the rest of it?" Zach inquired.

"In a minute," Drew said. "Give me a minute to greet my bride properly."

He closed the door and stood with his back against it, his arms crossed over his chest and looked at Carrie. "Well wife, am I forgiven?"

"Wife?" Carrie stamped her foot. Oh, the arrogance of this man. "Forgiven? You've deceived me from the beginning, Andrew McGeary. Not only did your Captain friend not marry us, but you were already married."

"That is not true," Drew said, "about being already married, I mean."

"And what, pray tell, is Nancy then?"

The color drained out of Drew's face. "Nancy?"

"Yes, Nancy McGeary, from Muskegon. And your daughter, Lainey. How could you do this to me? To them?"

Drew reached into his pocket and retrieved a silver flask. He pulled the cork from it and took one quick swallow. "I'm at a disadvantage here, Carrie. May I sit down?"

"No," Carrie replied sharply. "You stand right there and explain it all away for me."

"How did you find out about them?"

"Never mind. Just tell me about them."

Drew took off his hat and turned it over in his hands several times while he stared at his feet. Finally he looked up at her with such pain in his face Carrie almost yielded at once.

"It's going to be a long story, Carrie," he said. "Please let's sit."

She motioned to a chair and she sat down on the sofa and crossed her arms under her bosom to listen.

"I found Nancy one night in Chicago," he began. "She was a young lass and so unhappy at the life she was living there, her just arrived from Erin and her folks dead on the way over. I took her away with me and settled her in a little house in Muskegon, but I never married her. She didn't ask it of me, knew I was for the Lake and all. Lainey was born that next summer and until I held her I had never known what love was.

I told her mother I'd take care of her and the babe if I could only see the little girl now and then. I went back once or twice a year after that. Nancy was never strong and when Lainey was nine or ten, she became quite ill. The last time I was there, early this spring, just before I met you, she had taken to her bed. I hired a woman to come in and look after her. So help me, that's all."

"And what is Peony's story?" Carrie asked. "I suppose she is not wife either, just a place to sleep when you come by?"

"Peony! My god, woman, do you know my whole life story?"

"No," Carrie said with a sad smile, "but I'm beginning to get the gist of it. What was I to be?"

In one swift movement Drew was kneeling on the floor in front of her. "Carrie, I swear I love you. I came to ask you to meet me in Garden tomorrow. Father Travally is there and has agreed to marry us. Then I'll take you back to Chicago for a real wedding trip."

He seized her hand and then stopped. He looked at her with triumph in his face. "You still have the ring on, Carrie. If you hate me, why didn't you take it off?"

Carrie looked at the small gold band on her left hand and began to cry softly. "I don't hate you, Drew. I love you and I couldn't bear to take it off."

"Then will you meet me tomorrow?" Drew pleaded. "I will walk to Garden tonight and Zach will bring you into Van's Harbor tomorrow on Wave Dancer. Please, Carrie?"

"I think there are more complications than that," Carrie answered. She patted the empty space beside her on the sofa. "My story may be longer than yours."

She told him about the incident at the Hole in The Rock and how the people in Fayette had rescued the girls and burned it to the ground, saving until the last that his daughter, Lainey, had been one of those girls.

"Lainey? How can that be?" Drew rose from the sofa and began to pace back and forth.

"Her mother died and she apparently came to town looking for you. Henry took her to Stoddy, and he, with or without Henry's knowledge, used her badly."

Carrie felt the need to conceal Henry's true part in the affair for now. There was no need to abet murder until Drew had had a chance to see Lainey for himself.

Drew stopped in front of Carrie. Tears ran down his face and he sniffed loudly, drawing the moisture into his nose. "Where is she?"

"Here, with me. I suspect Peony took her out the back door just now when you appeared. I think we'll find them up on the hill or at the garden."

As soon as Lainey saw Carrie and Drew approaching she flew down the hill and launched herself into his open arms.

"Oh, Papa," she began to cry. "Oh, Papa."

"Now, now," Drew said, smoothing her energetic red curls as he held her. "Come, let's you and me go for a ride on Wave Dancer." He looked over her head at Carrie, seeking her approval.

Carrie nodded. "I think that's a grand idea, " she said. "If you've got ten minutes I'll pack a picnic for you."

She looked at Drew, "Or is Bobbie on board?"

"Bobbie's there," Drew replied, "but I'd sooner have a picnic with all of you. Lainey and I are going to go climb aloft and hang out for a while. Then we'll all weigh anchor and have a picnic on Summer Island. What do you say?"

They walked together down to the pier. Carrie held her breath as she watched Drew and Lainey climb the rigging up the mainmast and sit on the small deck half way up. She realized Drew must have been taking his daughter up there since she was a baby. She certainly scrambled up the rigging faster than Carrie had seen Peter do it.

She linked her arm though Peony's. "We better get working on a picnic. I'll fry the chicken and you can go up to the garden and pick some fresh tomatoes and corn."

While they worked Carrie told her about Drew's plans for

them to be married tomorrow in Garden. "What do you think, Peony? Am I asking for more trouble?"

"I think you should do it," Peony said. "And then I should take Lainey to Escanaba for a few days while you two get re-acquainted."

"Drew wants to take me to Chicago again, but I've seen enough of Chicago. I just want to stay right here. Will you be my Maid-of-Honor, Peony?"

That evening, after Drew left to walk to Garden, Carrie unpacked her trunk. At the top she found a white dress of silk and lace with a note from Drew that said, "Will you marry me?" Inside the hat box Peter had carried in was a wide brimmed white hat trimmed in daisies. A little deeper in the truck she found a gift from Vivette, a pair of long white gloves, and from Daisy Brighton, a pearl necklace. Deeper down was a small package wrapped in brown paper. It felt like a book! She opened it to find a leather-bound copy of "Emma" by Jane Austen. It made her remember the books Drew had on board Wave Dancer, and then the story he'd told her about the night of the Chicago fire. Oh, how could she not love such a man?

Her apprehensions about how Lainey would react to the marriage were allayed when Lainey had hugged her and shyly asked if that meant she could call Carrie "Mother" from then on.

"Not until tomorrow," Carrie had told her.

For the first time in a month, Carrie fell asleep as soon as her head touched the pillow.

Chapter Twenty-Nine

During the two weeks Peony and Lainey spent in Escanaba and Zach sailed Wave Dancer to Chicago with another cargo, Drew and Carrie spent making many plans about the future. One of the first things they did was decide to convert the boathouse into a sawmill. It was close to the dock, which Drew decided needed expanding so it would make it easy to load the cut timber unto the decks of Wave Dancer.

"I'm going to leave Delbert here," Drew said. "He's had experience at building and being a lumberjack. I'll make him our sawmill foreman."

"Does that mean you're leaving again?" Carrie asked.

"Ah, my love, I am not a man of leisure, you know. The old boat must continue to dance over the waves or we don't eat."

"You're forgetting about the quarry?" Carrie said.

"The quarry is yours, Carrie. I thought I made it clear that, unlike Henry, I did not seek your hand to obtain your marble quarry. I intend to consult that lawyer in Escanaba and have him draw up papers making the quarry one hundred percent yours."

Carrie was pleased by this and responded by kissing him soundly. Then she asked if he thought it would be possible to have a bathtub, with water and everything like they had in Chicago, in her house. She said it was the only thing she really wanted now that she had him back.

"I don't know much about those things," Drew said. "But I'll find out."

Peony returned to Cedar Harbor with Lainey, but announced that she had bought a little house in Escanaba and would move there as soon as Wave Dancer returned from her next trip to Chicago. She had a list of items she wanted

Drew to obtain for her.

"I'm going to paint," she said. "If I can find some students I'll teach. And I've decided to become Elizabeth Allen after all. My father always called me Liz."

"Shall we call you Liz?" Carrie asked, and got an affirmative.

"I have a wedding present for you," Liz said, handing Carrie a large package wrapped in butcher's paper.

Carrie opened it and saw a painting of her and Drew as they must have looked standing before Father Travally. "Oh, Peony, I mean Liz, it's beautiful. I have no doubt you can support yourself just by painting wedding portraits."

The next morning Carrie sailed with Drew into Fayette. Carrie wanted to visit Louella, but Drew said he had business with Henry and that he'd meet her at the Shelton House for lunch.

Louella welcomed her warmly. "I hear a lot of gossip about you. Now you just tell me how much of it is true."

Carrie laughed. "Probably all of it. Drew came back and Father Travally married us in Garden on the tenth of August. Lainey is doing fine. She calls me mother, Louella."

"Bertha Hartson has it that you are not married, but living in sin out there on that "God-forsaken" harbor. To hear her, Cedar Harbor is the new Hole-in-The-Rock establishment. She says Henry told her that the real owner of that place was none other than Captain McGeary, himself. She even said that you probably had something to do with it too. She claims she saw a, what did she call it? "A portrait in progress" of you in Peony's room."

Carrie was horrified. "Louella. How can she say such things? I don't know anything about a portrait of me. That woman is evil."

"She says that Peony is living with you and all the women who worked at the other place also. What was it she said? 'Not everybody who sails into Cedar Harbor is there for stone.' But I don't think anyone pays much attention to her, Carrie

"I'll pay attention to her if I see her. In fact I am going to seek her out. I can ignore her tongue, but it will reflect on Lainey and I will not see her hurt again."

"Oh, now I'm sorry I told you," Louella said. "Please don't look for trouble, Carrie. Let's go see Beth and see how the kittens are doing. And Beth will want to know that Lainey is fine."

The kittens were tumbling around on the porch of the boarding house. Louella stooped and picked up one of the golden balls of fur.

"This is Goldie," she said. "Can I take her home today, Beth?"

"I think you can take them all," Beth said. She looked at Carrie. "You promised."

"I'll need a basket," Carrie said.

"I'll bring them down to the dock," Beth offered when Carrie told her she and Drew would be leaving on Wave Dancer after they finished their business in town. "And how is Lainey doing?"

"She's just fine now that her father is back. Of course you know that she's my step-daughter now."

"Did you know who she was then?" Beth asked.

"I knew the moment I saw her that she was related somehow to Drew. They look so very much alike, you know. Her mother had died and she came searching for her father, which is how she came to Fayette in the first place."

"But how did she get to the brothel?" Beth asked.

"That is something I don't know," Carrie lied.

Drew entered the general store from the harbor side and stopped at the top of the stairs to look around. There were several women in the store, but he didn't see Henry...just the clerk, Charlie, waiting on customers.

He glanced over at the closed door leading to the second floor. If Henry was working at his desk the door was usually open so he could hear what was going on down below. Drew crossed to the door and opened it anyway. The stairs creaked as he climbed and he heard a chair scrape across the floor. So, he was up there.

Drew paused and waited to see if Henry would get up. He preferred to meet the man on his feet.

"Is that you, Charlie?" Henry called.

"No," Drew answered. "It's your good friend, Andrew McGeary."

"You can't come up here," Henry called. Drew could hear the panic in his voice and the sound of the chair again.

"But I'm here, Henry," Drew said as he reached the top of the stairs.

Henry stood behind the large desk, a pistol in his extended hand. He cocked it.

"Aw, put the gun down, Henry. I thought we were friends."

"You know better than that," Henry. "I'm surprised you have the nerve to even show yourself in town."

Drew kept moving toward Henry, his immediate motive was to get away from the open stairwell. He talked as he moved. "Yes, you and your preacher's wife have put together a pretty good case against me, haven't you? Peony told me what they're saying in Escanaba about me being the real owner of your and Stoddy's establishment. So I've come to collect all the money you owe me for my share."

"I don't owe you any money," Henry said. He waved the pistol, motioning Drew to sit in the chair he was standing next to. "If you leave now maybe you can get out of town before Mike knows you're here."

Drew didn't sit. "Mike Barbarieu? The sheriff of Fayette who has never arrested anyone in his life? Henry, I don't give a damn about money, or Mike, or Fayette. They can all go to bloody hell. I care about one thing, Henry and for that one thing you are going to pay."

Despite the advantage of the pistol in his hand, Henry retreated a step.

"My daughter, Henry."

Quicker than Henry could react, Drew picked up the chair and threw it at Henry. Henry ducked and the chair crashed through the window behind him.

"I didn't know, Drew," Henry whimpered from under the desk. "I swear I didn't know."

"She told you," Drew yelled. He picked up the edge of the desk and tipped it. Henry fired the pistol, but without aiming, the shot went wild. Drew kicked and the pistol flew out of Henry's hand. The second kick was aimed at Henry's head, but he rolled over and was on his feet before the kick landed against the tipped up desk. Henry looked around for another weapon, but just as he reached for the walking stick stuck in the umbrella stand, Drew's fist caught him below his left eye. Henry staggered backward and then lunged at Drew.

Drew was well known up and down the lakes for his fighting prowess. It was said he could beat any two men at once, even when he was drunk. Maybe especially when he was drunk. By the time Charlie had fetched Mike Barbarieu and a crowd of other men, Henry was almost beyond helping.

Mike was a big man, but he couldn't pull Drew off Henry, so he picked up the chair and brought it down on Drew's head. Drew slumped over Henry, both of them unconscious.

"Go get the doc," Mike said to whoever was listening. "Get Sailstad too."

He looked up at the crowd of people in the room and packed into the stairway. "Get out of here," he yelled, "all of you."

Drew was just regaining his senses when Rutherford and Sailstad arrived. Carrie was right behind them. When she saw Henry lying on the floor and Drew struggling to get to his feet she pushed past the doctor and ran to get to Drew.

Rutherford bent over Henry and reached into his bag for a tube of smelling vapors. Henry stirred. "He's alive."

Barbarieu gripped Drew's arm. "Shall I lock him up?" he asked looking at Sailstad.

"Let him go," Jack said.

Henry tried to push himself up.

"Lie still," Rutherford ordered. He wiped the blood away from a cut across Henry's cheek and examined it. "It'll heal," he said.

Then he moved Henry's arms though their entire range of motion and told him to turn his head this way and that. "You're OK. You'll have a headache. Too bad about that, nothing I can do."

Sailstad looked at Drew where he stood with his arm around Carrie. "I think you'd better get out of Fayette, Captain McGeary. Your boat is no longer welcome in this harbor and if you are seen in town again I will have you arrested. I'm sorry Carrie."

"That's not fair," Carrie said. "You don't know what Henry did to his daughter."

Drew pulled Carrie closer and laid his finger across her lips. "Shh. Keep Lainey out of this."

"It's true," Rutherford said. "I've kept quiet in the face of Bertha Hartsons campaign against Captain McGeary, and even Carrie, because Carrie asked me to. But I won't see Carrie hurt anymore.

"The girl who was rescued along the tracks was McGeary's daughter, Jack. And it was Henry who turned her over to Stoddy, knowing full well who she was. Now I don't know what other bad blood lies between McGeary and LaTermaine, but I do know that Henry deserved the beating he just got."

"What do you have to say?" Jack asked Henry. "Is this true?"

Henry had risen and stood leaning against the now upright desk. He looked at Drew and then Carrie before answering. "I knew who she was."

Carrie stepped away from Drew and in front of Henry. "And what about the lie that Drew was the real owner of The Hole in The Rock? According to Peony, it was you Stoddy worked for."

"I sold them the liquor and transported the women," Drew said, "but that was all. The rest of it was you and Stoddy. The young girls— I knew nothing about that. It started as a haven for the women I rescued from the streets of Chicago, women who were running or hiding from men who beat them."

"The stockade girls were Stoddy's idea," Henry said. "When I found out about it, I told him I didn't care as long as you didn't find out about it."

"And he paid you a percentage," Drew sneered. "And you gave him my daughter."

Henry was silent.

"Henry," Jack said, "you collect your pay and be out of town before dark. I'm sorry Carrie, but this is a private town and my ruling about barring McGeary and his ship from the harbor still stands. You, of course, are welcome anytime."

"If my husband is not welcome, then neither am I." Carrie said. "Edward, will you please say good-bye to Louella for me. Tell her I'd still like the kittens if she wants to come and visit me."

Chapter Thirty

It was the third trip into Fayette this week for Delbert. The Cedar Harbor sawmill building was about ready and Drew should be in tomorrow or Saturday with the saw. It would be a wind and steam powered mill, the very latest thing. It was already mid-September and the leaves on the hardwoods in the hills above Carrie's little house were scarlet and gold. Another month at most and they would be dry-docking Wave Dancer and cutting those trees for timber.

Delbert liked being on dry land. Although he'd been raised at Fairport in a family of fishermen, being on the water made him nervous. He'd lost an uncle and a brother in sudden lake storms. Besides, getting off the water for this sawmill project had enhanced his love life. Shirley LeComte had spotted him on his very first trip into Fayette for supplies and she remembered him from the Fourth of July dance. He remembered her too, and the invitation she'd given to meet her behind the icehouse. While he was picking out the correct size nails in the general store she walked by him and whispered. "Meet me behind the icehouse, Big Boy?"

He drove Carrie's wagon pulled by Grant, a big and stubborn ox. Hidden under the drivers box was a comforter Carrie had given him for the bed he had in a small room he'd made for himself inside the mill. When he pulled off the road just past South River, Shirley would be waiting for him again and they'd spread the comforter in the wagon box and make love. She was a crazy lady when he touched her and she made him crazy when she touched him.

He reached their rendezvous point a little early and pulled the wagon off the road and behind a thicket of sumac. The sumac torches were bright red now, as were the leaves of the shrubby plant. A lot of the leaves had already fallen off and the thicket wasn't as much a barrier to other traffic on the road as the lovers were accustomed to so Delbert pulled further off the road then usual. The road was muddy from recent rain but the ox was strong and Delbert didn't worry about it. He jumped down and tied Grant's lead rope to a spindly young birch and then spread the blanket in back of the wagon. He looked around to see if there were any flowers to pick a bouquet for Shirley. She loved flowers.

There was goldenrod everywhere but although it was a pretty color, they didn't smell good. Last time he'd pick them Shirley had laughed and called them weeds. It was because he'd pulled further off the road that he found the catnip with it's bright green leaves and little lavender and white flowers. He picked a bunch, inhaled their invigorating aroma and decided to scatter them over the top of the comfort. That way, he reasoned, when they lay on top of them and crushed the leaves under their warm bodies, they could enjoy the minty smell even more.

An hour passed and Shirley still hadn't come. Finally Delbert rolled up the comfort and put it back under the seat. In that hour however, the wagon wheels had sunk deep into the soft mud of the forest floor and there wasn't enough room for Grant to both pull the wagon loose and turn it around. After half an hour, Delbert unhooked Grant from the front of the wagon and led him to the rear. He had just gotten free of the mud and back by the sumac thicket when he heard horses on the road. It couldn't be Shirley because there was more than one horse. Delbert stood still, hoping they wouldn't see him and the wagon.

"Well, well, well," came a man's voice. "I'll bet this is the spot isn't it?"

Delbert crouched down behind the wagon. He heard the man dismount and the horse stamp the ground nervously. "Looks like this road has been used quite a few times. Doesn't it look that way to you?"

Delbert didn't hear anybody answer and inched up to peer

over the top. Shirley was sitting on a sidesaddle and the man, it was her husband, Frank, held the horses' reins firmly. Frank grabbed her ankle and pulled her down off the horse. She sprawled on the ground and Frank kicked her.

"I said doesn't it look that way to you?" he shouted.

Delbert didn't hear any answer and apparently neither did the husband for he grabbed her by the hair and hauled her up and then slapped her hard across the face.

"You come out of there, or I'll hit her again," Frank yelled looking into the woods where Delbert hid behind the wagon. Delbert slunk down and listened to Shirley yelp when Frank slapped her again.

"You hear me, man?" Frank yelled. Whatever he did to her then caused her to scream.

"Please, Delbert," she cried.

But Delbert crept under the sumac bushes and crawled on his belly until he was over a hump in the road. Then he stood up and ran, crashing though the woods and into the swamp. When he reached the rocky crag along the shore of South River he stopped and looked back. Good, Frank hadn't tried to follow him. Delbert sat and looked out over the shallow reedy bay everybody called South River and tried to decide what to do.

He couldn't go into Fayette now, ever again. Frank must know who he was. He'd made her tell. She told Delbert her husband beat her, and had showed him the welts and bruises on her legs and back. But somehow Delbert thought she liked it, because she always asked him to bite her or pinch her hard and that made her real excited and sexy.

He decided to wait until it was dark and then find his way back and get Grant and the wagon and go back to Cedar Harbor. When Drew came he'd find some way to send Zach into town to get the things he needed, or he could go to Garden. DeWinters should have the things he needed to finish up.

The moon was waning and didn't rise until well past

sundown. When Delbert finally got back to where he'd left the wagon it was gone. The bastard had taken it with him. He walked out to the road and after a moment turned to walk back to Cedar Harbor. That's when he heard the moan from the other side of the road.

Shirley? Delbert moved with caution towards the sound and found her propped against the truck of a maple tree. Delbert knelt beside her. Even in the dim light of the moon he could see the swollen eye and lip. He knelt beside her.

"Can you move?" he whispered.

She groaned again and turned her head to look at him. "Is that you, Delbert?"

"Yes. How come he left you here?"

"He's probably waiting for you," she whispered, and twisted her head the other direction to look around. "I don't think he's gone very far."

Delbert blanched. He could hear a horse moving nearby. Shirley heard it too.

"That's my horse. He said he'd leave it for me and I could come home or not. It was up to me." She grabbed Delbert's sleeve and clung to it. "Will you take me with you, Del? Don't make me go back to him."

"What about your kids? You can't leave them."

She began to cry. "Edna," she whispered. "Poor baby Edna."

Delbert found the saddled horse tied to a tree not far away and helped Shirley up. She insisted that she could ride and that he go back home.

"I'll be all right," she said. "Edna, Frankie. I think I've got one bottle left."

Delbert stood and watched until she was swallowed up by the darkness and then turned around and headed for Cedar Harbor. He found the ox and wagon a half mile from the turn off to Cedar Harbor. Relieved, he climbed up on the wagon box and drove down to the barn where he unhitched Grant. His little room inside the mill felt like heaven after the evening he had just spent. He should have known from the start that Shirley LeComte was trouble.

Frank was waiting for Shirley just up the road, as she knew he would be.

"You gonna be able to ride?" he asked. As usual he was all tender after he beat her, and once again she believed him when he said he'd never do it again.

"I think you really hurt me this time, Frank. It hurts when I breathe."

Frank led her horse slowly and when they reached the house she begged him. "Please take me to Dr. Rutherford, Frank. It hurts so much."

Frank looked at her and realized that he had broken his own rule and hit her in the face. One eye was swollen shut and her face had turned purple. He touched it gently and she winced. "All right, we'll go. But you tell him the horse threw you."

"Sure, Frank," she said. And to herself she thought, *Maybe he'll give me some morphine.*

Chapter Thirty-One

Carrie missed having Lainey around, but they had decided it would be better if Lainey spent the winter in Escanaba with Liz and went to school there. Even before Drew beat Henry up and got barred from Fayette it would have been impossible to send her to school there and Drew said that Garden was too rough for his daughter. It was said that if a young man in Garden didn't drink, fight, and cuss by the time he was eight, he'd never make it. So at the beginning of September Lainey had been bundled off to Escanaba, along with Pearl, the white kitten, to live with Liz.

Drew was away on a lake trip. Carrie hoped he would be home that weekend, but she had learned not to even look for him until he knocked on the front door. He always knocked on the door before he entered even though she told him again and again that it was his home, he didn't have to knock. He said if he always knocked first, her lover would have time to make it out the back door before he could catch him, and then he would laugh and catch her up in a great bear-like hug.

Delbert had been working diligently on the building for the sawmill. This morning he'd hitched Grant up to the wagon and asked her if she wanted anything in Garden.

"I thought you went to Fayette yesterday for the stuff you needed."

"They were out of nails," he said.

"Out of nails? That seems hard to believe."

"I don't think that new manager knows much," Delbert said. "Henry kept the store stocked. This Charlie fellow seems lost."

"Well, he's only a young man who clerked in the store," Carrie said. "I expect they'll have a new manager come in pretty soon."

So Carrie was alone, making applesauce, when she heard the knock at the door. "A moment," she called and then opened and shut the back door in order to play Drew's game with him. "I'm coming."

But when she opened the door there stood Henry LaTermaine.

"Henry? What are you doing here?"

"May I come in, Carrie?" He stood with his hat in his hand. He'd shaved his beard but let his moustache grow with long handlebars, stiffly waxed. His face looked bruised, as if he'd been in another fight.

Carrie stood aside for him to enter and then shut the door behind him. "Will you have a cup of coffee?"

"Thank you. I'd like that," he said.

Henry sat at the dining table and stirred a spoonful of sugar into the steaming cup of coffee. "I came to apologize to you, Carrie."

"Why should you apologize to me?"

When Henry looked at her, Carrie saw how haggard he looked. He hadn't been taking care of himself. There were lines in his face she was sure had not been there before.

He signed heavily. "I need to apologize to someone and you're the only one I can safely talk to."

"Oh, I see. I can't beat you up with one hand tied behind me the way my husband can?"

"You didn't used to be so cruel, Carrie."

"I never knew how low you were then, Henry. Go ahead, apologize."

"Carrie," he started and then stopped. She softened her face and encouraged him to continue.

"Carrie, I did a lot of things wrong. I hid the letter about the quarry from you, hoping you'd marry me before you knew. I was mean to your friend, Eleanor. My god, she was a silly woman."

"Henry," Carrie's voice carried a warning in it.

"Well I certainly didn't want to marry her. But it wasn't

only the marble, Carrie. I always admired you and found you agreeable to talk to. But I messed it up, didn't I? And then I was so angry with McGeary for running off with you that when his daughter showed up looking for him I did the worst thing of all." He looked up and when Carrie nodded he kept on.

"McGeary isn't a saint you know."

"Of course he isn't, but he's not mean."

"It was him started the girls, you know. Stoddy and I just had a gin-house until he brought Peony there, and then another one and another one."

"Henry, all that is immaterial. Have you finished your apology?"

Henry finished his coffee and stood up. "I shouldn't have come. I just thought I could make you understand."

Carrie opened the door for him. "I understand, Henry. Good-bye."

"You'll be sorry, Carrie. Just remember I tried to help you."

Carrie stood on the porch and watched him walk up to where his black horse stood. He mounted and rode away.

"That was strange," Carrie said out loud, slipping into her old habit of talking to herself. "That was really strange." She went back inside and peeled another pan of apples.

Delbert came back from Garden with his nails and the other things he said he needed. He completed the mill and after hanging around the house for a day and a half he asked if Carrie wanted to go up on the bluff and show him which timber she wanted cut. They walked out to the stagecoach road and then back up a faint path that led in a gentle slope to the top of the bluff.

"You'll want your skid road along here," Carrie said. "I think you'd better fence in my garden plot. I don't want it trampled all winter or the ground will be packed down so hard in the spring I won't be able to till it. You'll use Grant to skid the timber out, of course."

They walked, Carrie pointing out various trees she "just really wished they wouldn't cut," because she and Albert had picnicked there (don't tell Drew), or because it had such a pretty shape. Delbert put a large X on these with the timber chalk he carried.

"I don't want the top of the bluff to be bare the way the bluff in Fayette is," she told him. "So use some sense and leave some, especially along the edge where I can see it from the house."

After climbing for some time, the ground suddenly slanted down and the blue water of the lake came into view. They stood in a meadow where only small shrubs grew, mostly the low circular wreaths of yew. Carrie stopped and looked around. She listened to the sounds from the quarry work below and then turned to Delbert.

"This is an Indian burial ground. I've found all manner of things here. Arrow points, a string of beads made from clam shells, and a clay pipe. My late husband, Albert, once dug up a skeleton from its shallow grave and there was a tomahawk buried with him. They buried their dead with their feet to the west, you know, so when the dead man's spirit sat up in his grave he could see the setting sun."

Delbert bent down to search in the grass for a relic. "I don't want this disturbed," Carrie said. "Make a fence around it."

"With all the fences you want, Ma'am, I'll have to go back to Garden in the morning."

"Then I'll go with you," Carrie said. "I've got a basket of eggs for DeWinter's."

"Don't you think the Captain will be back pretty soon?"

"What day is it?"

"I think it's Thursday."

"Well, he won't be here until late afternoon tomorrow, at the very least. I think he'll go to Escanaba and bring Lainey home for the weekend. Maybe Liz will come too. We'll leave for

Garden right after breakfast in the morning."

That evening Carrie sat down and wrote letters to Eleanor and Louella. She really missed both of them and she hadn't been to Fayette since the incident between Drew and Henry. Louella had come out a few days later with the kittens, but since then she had heard only the news Melanie DeWinter shared with her when she went into Garden to shop. It seemed like Drew had been gone an awfully long time this trip. It had been at least two weeks.

Garden had grown even since the last time Carrie had been there. A new saw mill had been built on the shores of Van's Harbor and Delbert insisted that Carrie go look at it.

"Ours won't be near as big, of course," he said.

Carrie smiled at him including himself in the possessive naming of the mill he had built as "ours."

"They got twelve men working there," Delbert informed her, "and more cutting timber for them. We can't compete with that."

"The point isn't to compete," Carrie said, "The point is to cut the timber from our own land and make a profit on it. There will be four of you to work our mill, you, Zach, Peter, and Drew. Drew said Zach and Peter could live on Wave Dancer all winter, although I think it would have been better to build a bunk house. Seems to me like it will be mighty cold sleeping in that boat."

"It'll be warm enough below decks," Delbert said. "I've slept there plenty."

"I'll be doing my shopping first," Carrie said, "and then you can take me for a tour of Van's new sawmill."

They went their separate ways, with Delbert promising to pick her up at DeWinter's in two hours.

It was while she was waiting for Delbert and visiting with Melanie that she overheard Drew's name mentioned. The village men were used to sitting around the table by the window up front and watching people come and go from the post office across the street. Two middle aged men sat puffing on their pipes and generally complaining because their wives were taking too long, when Carrie heard one of them say, "Hear that Captain McGeary got himself in a knock down drag out in Escanaba couple of days ago."

"How's that?" asked the other.

"Stage driver come in this morning. He said McGeary was in the jailhouse. Guess he killed the other fellow."

"What for?"

"Don't know. Arguing about some dame, I guess."

Carrie covered her mouth in disbelief. Melanie looked over at the two men and then confronted them.

"Lee Corbert, that isn't what the stage driver said, and you know it. Mrs. McGeary is standing right over there and you've scared her silly. Now you go tell her the truth. Honestly, the way you men gossip."

Corbert looked around and saw Carrie still standing next to the cash counter behind him. He tipped his hat.

"Honest, ma'am," he said. "It ain't that bad. I don't think the other man was killed, just beat bad. But he is in jail, ma'am, your husband. That's what Jerry, the coach driver, said."

Melanie took Carrie by the arm led her into the back room where the DeWinters lived. She poured Carrie a small glass of brandy, which Carrie drank in one swallow.

"You weren't going to tell me, Melanie?"

Melanie shrugged. "What for? You can't change anything. You can't change him, Carrie. He's been fighting his way up and down the shores of Lake Michigan for years. He was here in Garden the day before the fight in Escanaba. That Henry LaTermaine who used to have the store in Fayette was in Towhey's Saloon and the two of them came to blows. The sheriff locked up LaTermaine and ran Drew out of town. I figured he'd go home to you, but he evidently went back to Escanaba."

"Is there someone with a boat can take me to Escanaba?"

"You wait here," Melanie said. "I'll see what I can find out."

Melanie came back in half an hour and said one of Captain Stephenson's steamers had just docked at the sawmill and would be leaving for Escanaba as soon as she was loaded. "I'll drive you down in my shay."

"Where's Delbert?" Carrie asked. "Did you see him?"

"He's probably down at the mill. If we don't see him I'll tell him where you've gone. Are you sure you want to do this Carrie?"

"He's my husband," Carrie said, "and I don't believe he beat somebody up." But she did believe it. She wondered if it was Henry again.

"Is Henry still in jail here?" Carrie knew he couldn't be. It must have been the day after the fight in Garden that he'd showed up on her doorstep. What was he trying to do?

"Oh, no," Melanie said. "The sheriff let him go as soon as Drew was out of town. Drew swore he'd kill Henry, you know. Everybody heard him say it."

Chapter Thirty-Two

Liz's house in Escanaba was on Wells Avenue, quite a way from the docks, but Carrie went there first. Liz opened the door and didn't seem surprised to find Carrie standing there, but she didn't invite her in.

"I saw Wave Dancer in the harbor," Carrie said. "She's deserted. Do you know where Drew is?"

"Carrie," Liz said. "It's not what you think."

"What is it?" Carrie asked. "Is he here or is he still in jail?"

Liz shrugged and stepped away from the door to let Carrie in. Drew was sitting at the table, a bottle of whiskey in front of him. His hair hadn't been combed and he hadn't shaved. From the smell of him he hadn't washed either. He looked at Carrie and pointed a wavering finger at her. When he spoke, his words were slurred.

"I know you. You're my wife."

"Where is Lainey?" Carrie demanded.

"She's staying with a friend. I sent her there yesterday before I bailed him out."

Carrie sat down facing her husband. He reached for the bottle and she put a hand on his arm to stop him. He made a move to push her hand aside and fell out of the chair. She stood and looked down at him.

"Was it Henry again, Drew, or somebody else this time?"

Drew grinned. "I showed him this time."

"It was Henry," Liz said. "He almost killed him. Funny thing is, when I went to bail him out they said Henry didn't press charges. He told the sheriff he only wanted to apologize."

Carrie nodded. Henry really did want to apologize, she saw that now, that he had been sincere when he had come to the house the other day. What he ought to do, if he had any sense left at all, is get out of the Upper Peninsula.

"Make some coffee," Carrie said. She bent down and tried to lift Drew to his feet but it was like trying to make a bowl of wet noodles stand on end.

"If I were you I'd just let him sleep it off," Liz said.

"Why did you let him get drunk in the first place," Carrie demanded.

"You think I could stop him?" Liz's eyes blazed with an anger Carrie had never seen before. She didn't want to fight with her friend.

"I'm sorry, Liz, of course not. I've never seen anybody like this before. How long will it take?

"He'll sleep a couple hours," Liz said. "Then he'll wake up and want to finish that bottle."

"No he won't," Carrie said and stepped out the door where she emptied the bottle over a yellow mum plant. "He's going to drink coffee. Do you know where I can find Zach and the rest of the crew?"

"They weren't on Wave Dancer?"

"No, I said she was deserted. Why would Zach do that?"

"Drew probably argued with him too, and he quit."

"I thought he was part owner."

Liz shrugged. "I don't know. Look, I think I know where to find him. You stay here in case Drew wakes up. What do you want me to do with Zach if I find him?"

"Have him get aboard and be ready to sail for Cedar Harbor whenever I can get Drew down there. And tell him to make sure there's no liquor on board."

Drew started to stir. He half sat and then lay back down with a groan. Carrie poured a cup of coffee and pulled her chair up to the table. Next time Drew opened his eyes he saw Carrie sitting there, her arms folded across her chest, staring at him.

"Get up, Drew," Carrie said. She spoke in a coaxing voice as if he were a dog under the porch that she wanted to come out. "Do you want some help?"

Drew struggled to his feet and braced himself with one of the chairs. "What are you doing here?"

"I could ask you the same thing," Carrie answered. "Here, have a drink." She offered him the coffee with a warning not to burn his mouth.

Drew sat down and cradled the cup of steaming coffee in his hands. He sipped it slowly, not looking at her. Carrie waited. He emptied the cup and she poured him another one.

"I need some whiskey," he growled, "not coffee."

"Whiskey's all gone," Carrie said. "Drink the coffee."

Drew drank. "You're one tough lady," he said when that cup was empty and she filled it again.

"And what are you Andrew McGeary?"

Drew hung his head. "Stupid?" he muttered.

Carrie ignored that and stood up. "Time for a bath now," she said, nodding at the tub full of water that stood in the middle of the kitchen floor. "It was hot. It's probably just warm now. Get those filthy clothes off."

Drew meekly sat in the tub and let her shampoo his hair and scrub his back. She found a blanket in the bedroom to wrap around him when he got out. They sat at the table again and he tried to explain.

"No matter where I go, Henry shows up. What does he want?"

"He wants to apologize," Carrie said. "If you'd listen to him before you hit him you might find out."

"Apologize?" Drew's voice was incredulous. "Does he think an apology is going to fix things?"

"No, of course he doesn't," Carrie said. "But he needs to say it. He came to the house after you beat him up in Garden and tried to explain it to me. I wouldn't listen either. I didn't understand until I heard he'd followed you here. You don't have to forgive him, Drew. Who could ever forgive such a terrible thing? But listen to him, and then tell him to go away. Tell him you heard him. If you don't, he'll keep haunting us."

He reached his hand out for hers. "And you, Carrie? Are

you still my wife?"

"Of course I am. But I expect you to start acting like a man. What sort of example are you setting for your daughter? And your," she stopped and patted her stomach, "next child?"

Drew's eyes grew big and he gripped her hand hard. "Are you saying we've made a baby, Carrie?"

Carrie nodded. "Yes, I think so. Now are you ready to collect your daughter and go home with me?"

Just then Liz came back. Zach was with her.

"Hello, Captain," Zach said. "I bought you some clothes and thought maybe you'd like for me to give you a shave."

Chapter Thirty-Three

Captain Alphonse was unaware he was sailing the Mary B. into a storm. Peaches assured him that Captain McGeary was a great friend of herself and the four ladies with her. It was obvious to Captain Alphonse what they were, of course, but he was also well aware of Drew McGeary's reputation.

It was just a couple of months ago that Drew had paid him ten dollars and a bottle of good whiskey to perform a fake marriage for him while they waited to enter the Chicago River. She wasn't even a particularly good-looking woman, that one, Alphonse reflected. Maybe Drew's taste in women had changed. This Peaches looked a little past her prime too, but Miss Lola Divine, one of the twits with her was indeed divine.

They had a good time on the three hour cruise across the lake. It was one of those early October, Indian Summer days. There were still enough leaves on the trees along the shore to cast a golden glow over everything. The easy flowing booze didn't hurt either.

Peaches whooped when she saw McGeary walk out to the end of the long pier to watch them approach. Wave Dancer stood at the end of the pier, so that meant his crew was probably there too. There'd be a hot time in the old town tonight! The whore turned her back, bent over and flipped up her dress, exposing her bare backside to Drew.

The other three men, working by the mill, had stopped working to watch. They'd been hard at work for the last week installing the saw and finally had it working.

"Did you see that?" Peter said. "I never saw a lady do that before."

"They ain't ladies, Pete," Zach informed him. "They're trouble with a capital T." He looked around to see if Carrie had seen the display. She was standing on the porch wiping her hands on her apron and evidently had not.

By the time Carrie reached the end of the pier, the women had all piled into the Mary B's long boat with Captain Alphonse and were headed for the shore. "Who are those women?"

Drew looked at Carrie and then at the schooner that had dropped anchor beside Wave Dancer. "I think it's a girl I rescued from Chicago not long ago, and some of her friends. You'll recognize the Captain when you see him. I'm sorry, Carrie, believe me I had nothing to do with this."

"Ahoy, you handsome dog," Peaches hailed Drew as they came along side the pier. She pulled her plump body up with the help of the securing line, and stood unsteadily in the rocking boat. "We've come to call."

Carrie grabbed Drew's arm. "That's the man you had pretend to marry us. What is he doing here?"

"I told you I had nothing to do with it," Drew said. "I'll get rid of them as soon as I can."

By the time Captain Alphonse had unloaded his cargo, Zach, Delbert, and Peter were there to help, and Lainey stood on the shore, watching.

Helena, the tall dark haired girl Drew had left with Stoddy at the same time he left Peaches, threw her arms around Drew's neck and planted her mouth on his. Drew attempted to push her away, but the woman was intent on inserting her tongue into his mouth. Carrie was not so polite. She grabbed Helena by the hair and pulled.

"Yeow!" Helena yelped and turned, ready to take a swing at Carrie. Drew grabbed her arm.

"Here now," he said to Helena. "This won't do. I don't even remember your name, but this woman is my wife and I don't think she took kindly to your actions."

Peaches laughed. "Your wife? Drew McGeary married? And look, there's the young whore that broke out of the stockade and caused us all so much trouble."

They all turned to look at Lainey. Peaches walked towards her. "You remember me, don't you Red? I'm the one that taught you to spread your legs for the nice men with money."

Lainey screamed, then turned, and ran towards the house.

"Get rid of these people," Carrie hissed at Drew, and then she followed Lainey.

Miss Lola Divine sidled up to Delbert. "Well, ain't you tall, dark, and handsome?" she cooed. "Have a drink."

"This is just right," said one of the other women. "Five of us, five of you if we include the old goat what brung us here. You can have him Sadie, I like 'em young."

Peter retreated. "I got work to do," he protested.

"So do I," said the woman as she ran her fingers through Pete's hair. "I'm Kate."

Drew tried to get the situation under control. "Look here, Alphonse. You've got to get these woman out of here."

"Just one drink, McGeary. Have one drink with us and we'll go."

Drew looked doubtful. He looked up towards the house, wondering about his daughter. But he knew Alphonse and knew the only way to get him to leave was to have a drink with him.

The afternoon came and drifted away. One drink led to another and to Carrie's horror the party on the beach went on and on. She finally had to give Lainey a dose of laudanum to quiet her and the girl slept fitfully, tossing and moaning, obviously having nightmares about her days in Stoddy's employ. Laudanum caused nightmares, Carrie thought; nightmares you couldn't wake up from, couldn't run away from. She regretted having given it to Lainey. She'd known women who had been given laudanum so often to calm their nerves that they were addicted to it. It was opium, after all, even if it had been watered down and blended with syrup.

How could Drew sit out there and entertain those people?

Twice she walked out and tried to talk with him. The first time he had told her they'd be gone soon. "Don't worry, I know how to handle these people. One more drink and then I'll put them on the Mary B and they're gone."

Captain Alphonse patted Carrie's shoulder. "I'll take 'em right back, Missus, don't you worry. We'll go soon."

But they had not gone. In fact, the women discovered the bed inside the mill and evidently knew how to put it to good use. Carrie stood on the porch and watched with disgust as every possible pairing of man and woman went in and out of the little building. Only Drew stayed out of the mill. He remained sitting in the cedar grove, talking and laughing with them. Carrie did not understand how he could entertain those people, especially the vile woman called Peaches whose words had caused Lainey to go hysterical, when he had tried again and again to kill Henry. Henry was at least sorry for what he'd done. She had thought Drew would at least come in to see Lainey, but he didn't.

Once Lola Divine wandered up to the porch and tried to talk Carrie into joining the party. She offered Carrie a drink out of the bottle she had. The woman's dress was cut so low in the front that Carrie could see the dark skin where her nipples started. She shuddered, remembering Chicago and the women she had seen sitting in the windows along the street Delbert had called Little Cheyenne.

The second trip Carrie made to the party was with a pitcher of strong hot coffee. She walked around dumping out liquor and refilling mugs with coffee. Nobody paid any attention to her. She came up behind Drew and said, "Drew, I want to talk to you."

He turned quickly. "You know what the problem is with you, Carrie?"

"I didn't know I had a problem."

"You don't know how to have a good time," he said. He yanked the pitcher away from her and dumped the remaining coffee on the ground. "Sit down. Be sociable and have a drink with us."

Carrie shook her head. "Your daughter needs you."

For a moment Carrie thought he would yield. "What's she doing?"

"She's sleeping right now, but..."

"Then leave her be." He grabbed her hand and tried to pull her into his lap.

"Drew, let me go," she said, pulling away.

"Have a drink with me or go to hell," he retorted.

Carrie turned and fled into the house and barred the door behind her. Darkness fell and the moon had risen before Carrie heard the sound of good-byes yelled across the water from the departing schooner. She was tempted to go out and see what kind of condition Drew was in, but resisted even looking out the window.

It was more than an hour before he came to the door. He pounded on it and when it wouldn't open he yelled at her to open the door.

"You go to hell," she screamed at him.

"Carrie," his voice became cajoling, pleading with her to be reasonable.

"Go away," she repeated. "Go sleep on your precious boat."

She blew out all the lights and sat there in the dark listening to him until he finally gave up. After she heard him tromp down the steps she got up and went to check on Lainey. The girl slept more peacefully now with Topaz curled on the pillow next to her fiery red hair. Carrie petted the cat, which began to purr immediately, and briefly caressed the girl's cheek, thinking how deeply the girl had dug her way into Carrie's heart already.

Before the night was over, she hated Drew more thoroughly than she had ever loved him. She was surprised she even fell asleep.

She couldn't tell afterward what woke her up, but she was fully awake in an instant. The pungent smell of burning wood filled her senses and she heard the distinct sound of a pine knot snapping in fire. With no memory of having moved Carrie stood as if her bare feet were rooted to the sand and gravel lane, her hands shielding her face from the horror taking place on the lake in front of her. Black smoke full of live cinders rolled from the top of green tipped orange flames as they rose and fell against the night sky. The new saw mill was fully engulfed in the fire and orange flames flew up the mast of Wave Dancer consuming the sails that Drew had not lowered the night before.

Suddenly Lainey was beside her tugging on Carrie's nightdress. "Where's Papa? Where's Papa?"

The girl's piercing voice unfroze Carrie and she began to run toward the burning schooner moored to her pier. How could it burn so fast? She had to save Drew. She screamed his name as she ran.

The sawmill on shore was almost consumed, but live sparks still flew from the burning side timbers and rose high into the air on the fire created thermals. It must have been one of these that had caught the sails and set the schooner afire. Carrie grabbed an ax from the top of a pile of cord wood nearby and leapt unto the deck of Wave Dancer from the pier and started forward. A lick of flame caught the edge of her nightdress almost immediately. Panicked, she dropped the ax and jumped into the water to extinguish the flames.

She floundered only a moment when her wet clothing began to drag her down but her swimming stroke was strong and she swam towards shore. Her father had insisted she learn to swim. For some reason she had a quick flash of seeing him waiting for her in the shore boat as he beckoned her to keep swimming. "Only a few more feet," he kept encouraging her; "you can make it."

Carrie found her footing and deliberately dunked her head under water to make sure her hair was thoroughly wet. Standing, she ripped off the lower part of her nightdress and wrapped a strip around her head to cover her hair and forehead. She put another under her eyes, over her nose, letting it hang free like a bandits mask.

She gained the deck again and moved forward cautiously, evading the pieces of the burning sail which fell to the deck where oil soaked ropes and dry stacks of cut lumber, loaded two days ago at Manistique for the last trip of the seaon to Chicago, caught fire.

Why had she nailed the forward door shut? Why hadn't Drew come out the galley door? Was he that drunk? Was he already dead? Carrie tried the galley door and it wouldn't budge. She banged her closed fists on the door and called, "Drew? Drew?" No answer. The door seemed to be locked.

Where was the ax? Carrie searched frantically and then remembered that she had dropped it when her dress caught fire. She grabbed the gaff hook that hung on the outside of Drew's cabin. On the third swing of the gaff the door splintered and Carrie shouldered her way inside. He wasn't in the galley. The smoke was dense and Carrie was thankful for the wet mask she'd put across her face. Carrie felt her way towards the cabin calling Drew's name.

Drew lay against the open port window gasping in fresh air. The cabin was filled with smoke. Carrie called to him, but he didn't respond. She used the gaff to break open the forward door and then grabbed Drew under the arms and began to drag him out. The splintered frame ripped at her clothes and scrapped her flesh. Flames were everywhere now; there was no way back to shore along the deck. Probably even the pier was burning. She hauled Drew to the side and with great effort hefted him over the side. She heard the splash of his body hitting the water. The shock of the cold water must have roused him from his stupor for she could hear him thrashing in the water below. He couldn't swim. *Dumb sailor, afraid of the water, he had never even learned to swim.* She gathered her skirt around her waist and jumped over the side of Wave Dancer into the dark water.

The water was warmer than it had been on her first

dunking, perhaps heated by the burning ship. She looked around, but all she could see were bits and pieces from the fallen masts.

"Drew," she screamed, "Drew, for God's sake answer me." From shore she could hear Lainey still screaming over and over, "Papa, Papa."

Carrie treaded water, looking for Drew. She caught a floating piece of an unburned spar and clung to it. Then she thought she saw him, a dark lump, floating near the burning hull of the schooner. She moved closer and grabbed; felt relief that it was him. *Please God,* she heard the voice inside her head as if she'd spoken aloud, *please be alive.*

He was alive and semi-conscious, clinging to a loose board on the side of Wave Dancer. He flinched away from Carrie as she tried to maneuver him to share the floating spar with her. He must be burned or hurt. She could still smell the sweet odor of whiskey on his breath. He was probably still dead drunk. Relentless, she pulled at him again and urged him to hang on.

"Lainey," she shouted. *Dear God, will the girl not stop screaming so she can hear me?* "Lainey, bring the shore boat."

Now Carrie became aware of horses hooves pounding along the lane and could hear men's voices ashore. Who pulled them out of the water, Carrie didn't know. When she became fully aware again, she was in her bed and Dr. Rutherford was standing at the window, his hands clasped together behind him, under his coat tails.

Her hands hurt. Lifting them in front of her she saw they were bandaged. Memory flooded back.

"Drew?" she said, surprised that her voice came only in a whisper. It was enough to cause Dr. Rutherford to turn.

"He's alive, Carrie, go back to sleep." Edward's voice sounded harsh to her, not the kindly tone she was accustomed to hear from her friend.

"Zach? Delbert?" she asked. "Peter."

"Were they aboard?"

Carrie felt sick and struggled to sit before the vomit rising in her throat choked her. The Doctor put a basin in front of her for her to vomit in. She retched twice, emptying her stomach. Dr. Rutherford wiped her mouth clean and then dried her forehead.

"Delbert was in the mill," she said. Her voice sounded to her as if it came from far away. "Zach and the boy usually sleep in the hold."

"We didn't find them."

Dr. Rutherford turned back toward the window for a moment and then once more faced her. He became the physician. "Your hands are raw and your legs are burned. I've put ointment on them and wrapped them. Drink this," he offered a glass of milky fluid.

"What is it?"

"It will dull the pain and put you to sleep again." He pulled her head upright and put the glass to her lips. She drank.

"Where's Drew?"

"In the other room. Sleep," he commanded. "I must go to him now."

"Lainey?" she asked. The drug was already beginning to affect her ability to think and form words.

"Mrs. Brandon took her. She's unhurt."

Carrie fought the stupor creeping into her limbs. She hated laudanum.

She knew when the doctor had returned to her room and sat in a chair next to her. There was daylight showing around the edges of the green window shade and at the bottom where it had been left two inches above the sill. When she stirred the doctor spoke.

"Carrie," he said, "can you tell me what happened?"

Much later Carrie lay in bed listening to horses and the wheels of her quarry wagon grow fainter and fainter until she heard them no more. She had told him about the women and the party, which had been over before she went to bed. But she had made Drew sleep on the boat, she said, because he was drunk and because he hadn't sent them away at once.

"I'll come back tomorrow morning," he'd said "and you can tell me more if you think you need to. I'm taking Drew with me, I can treat him better at my office."

The next time Carrie awoke, Francine, one of Brandon's daughters was sitting next to her.

"Do you want anything?" Francine asked. She had another glass of Rutherford's bitter tasting drink in her hand. Although her hands hurt, Carrie refused the morphine drink; too much of that dream inducing stuff wasn't good for a person. She asked instead for a bottle of Drew's whiskey and had Francine pour her a tall glass. She took a sip and savored the burn of it slipping down her throat. What was it Edward had said to her as he left? "You can tell me more tomorrow if you think you need to." What did that mean, if you think you need to? But she thought she knew.

Chapter Thirty-Four

Hugh Brandon drove the wagon with Drew McGeary and the body of Delbert Julliard in the back. Sheriff Mike Barbarieu and Dr. Rutherford rode along side. The town was just coming alive when they turned down Harbor Street and continued up to Rutherford's house and hospital. A few of the curious started to follow them, but Rutherford waved them away.

The doctor's office, with its convenient walkout at ground level offered easy access for patients and also had the added convenience of letting patients wait outside under the huge maple trees in nice weather. On hot days, the white-washed brick walls kept it cool. In the winter though, he had to keep a fire in the stove night and day. Sometimes, even in mid-summer, a small fire in the morning took the chill out of the room. Although yesterday had been a perfect day, this morning a blustery, and more seasonable, wind began to blow in off the lake as soon as the sun rose. It was the kind of weather the ships on the lake dreaded. It would probably spit snow before the day was out.

Frank LeComte and Bertha Hartson arrived at Dr. Rutherford's office just as the men were attempting to lift McGeary from the wagon. Frank stepped forward and helped lift the fourth corner of the blanket.

McGeary groaned when they lifted him and the blanket sagged beneath his weight.

"Be careful," Rutherford said. "Keep the blanket as taut as you can. He's burned and that right shoulder may be broken."

"What about the other fellow," Frank asked, indicating Delbert.

"He's dead."

They laid Drew on a bed in one of the two rooms that

comprised the hospital. He was awake, but still lethargic from the morphine the Doctor had administered before he was moved, and he growled something in slurred words Rutherford didn't catch.

It was then he noticed the presence of Frank LeComte and Bertha Hartson.

Louella appeared quietly at Rutherford's elbow and he spoke to her.

"Louella, get some weak chamomile tea for our patient, not too hot. And get that woman" he nodded towards Bertha, "out of here." As he began to remove the bandages from the burns on Drew's arms he heard Louella usher Bertha upstairs. The woman was a born trouble-maker.

Drew resisted the doctor's attention and Frank made a move towards him to help Rutherford hold him still.

"That won't be necessary, Frank, I can take care of him."

"I'm going to round up a few men and go back out there to look for Zach Milowski," the sheriff said.

Rutherford looked up from his patient at Mike Barbarieu and out to where Brandon waited by the wagon.

"You lay still," he said to Drew, "you'll only hurt yourself by thrashing around. I'll return in a minute."

Outside the closed hospital room door, Rutherford spoke to Frank.

"Frank, will you go out and help Brandon bring that body in? Put him on my surgery table."

As soon as Frank left the room, Rutherford motioned for Mike to come closer. Taking Mike by the arm, Rutherford spoke quietly to him.

"Mike, I think it would be smarter to wait until tomorrow for that search. If he's drown, the body will wash up. It's more important today that you go out there alone and look around before the scene is disturbed."

Mike, a tall man who had more hair in his handlebar mustache than he did on top of his head, looked puzzled. "What am I going to look for?"

Rutherford knew Mike was inexperienced. After all, the Fayette jail cell had never held a prisoner. Rowdy drunkards from the grog shops outside of town were the only trouble the town had ever had.

"Someone set that fire, Mike. There may be footprints that will give us a clue as to who was on the Grey property that shouldn't have been. You should also be able to find where in the sawmill the fire started."

Mike was clearly still puzzled so Rutherford spelled it out.

"Look, Mike, you need to keep the curious away right now. Send Brandon back and tell him nobody is to come onto the Grey property. He's got three strapping boys who'll help him guard the place. I want to check over the body we have, see if I call tell what he died of."

"Delbert burned," said Mike.

"Maybe he did; but the question is, was he dead before he burned?"

"You can tell that?"

"Sometimes. You just leave the body here with me to examine. Delbert lived down at Fairport, didn't he? Get Frank to send somebody down there to tell his parents. Don't tell anybody else anything about what I just said. I'll saddle up Old Tom and ride out to join you at Cedar Harbor this afternoon to help you look for tracks."

Frank and Brandon entered, the blanket encased corpse hanging between them.

"Where do you want him?" Frank asked.

"On the surgery table."

"Now Frank," Rutherford said, "the sawmill out at Cedar Harbor caught fire, burned to the ground. Also burned McGeary's schooner to hell and gone. The body is Delbert Julliard; he died in the sawmill. His folks live in Fairport. Send somebody to tell them and find out what they want done with the body."

"I'll send someone," Frank said. "Sawmill, you say. I didn't know there was one out there."

"I understand they just finished building it."

"What about Carrie Grey. She all right?"

"Mrs. Brandon is taking care of her and she's sedated. Less said of this the better, Frank. You know how people talk."

Frank nodded. "I'll do what I can, but you're not going to be able to keep people from heading for Cedar Harbor to look for---what did you call him, Zach? It's just human nature."

As soon as Frank left, Rutherford said to Mike. "He's right, you know. You and Brandon get fresh horses from my livery and head out there now. Keep people away as much as you can. Tell Brandon what you're looking for, he's smart, he'll help. The wagon can stay here for now, the quarry won't need it for a day or two. I'll follow as soon as I finish with Delbert here."

Edward Rutherford shook his head as he watched Mike climb up on the wagon seat next to Hugh Brandon. Louella came down the stairs and into the room as he turned, carrying a pot of tea and a cup.

"Go find Jack Sailstad for me, Louella. There has been monkey-business about out at Cedar Harbor."

"Is Carrie all right?" Louella asked.

"Burned a little, but she'll be fine."

"What about the preacher's wife?"

"She's upstairs rolling bandages for me."

"I'd like to stuff one in her mouth," Edward said. Louella agreed and then untied her apron and hung it on one of the pegs next to the door. As soon as she left, Rutherford returned to the room where Drew lay on the bed.

"What the hell is going on?" was Drew's first demand. "How'd I get here and who lit me flesh afire?"

Rutherford calmly picked up Drew's bandage encased arm and little by little began to remove the gauze. He then recoated the burned area, from the shoulder to just below the elbow, with a salve of honey and petroleum jelly.

"I want to check your shoulder," he told Drew, looking at Drew's opposite arm and back where the bruise had turned purple. "Does it hurt here?"

"Like bloody hell," Drew responded, wincing away from the probing. "Ain't broke though."

Rutherford moved the shoulder back and forth and raised the man's arm high over his head. "I agree, but deeply bruised and scraped. You're a lucky man, McGeary. Carrie saved you. I think this bruise is from her trying to push you over the side. You probably bumped the railing pretty hard. You're right, nothing's broken."

"What happened?"

As Dr. Rutherford smeared more of the honey and petroleum jelly salve on the scrapped shoulder he told Drew what he knew of the evenings events. Then it was all he could do to keep McGeary in the bed.

"The sawmill? Me schooner? How'd it start?"

"That we don't know. Carrie discovered it a couple of hours before dawn. Your man Delbert Jouillard is dead and your mate, Zach, hasn't been found. Probably dead too."

Drew cursed aloud but made the sign of the cross across his body at the same time. "If you're finished doctoring me, I'll be up and out there."

"I think you should rest here, at least for the day," Rutherford said in a soothing voice. He handed him the chamomile tea to which he'd added laudanum. "You have this now. Louella, she's my wife, will come in and give you more every now and then. It's important to get fluids when you've been burned."

Drew drank the tea. Just as Rutherford was leaving the room Drew called him back, "What about my wife?"

"She's burned too, her legs and hands. Mrs. Brandon is taking care of her."

The dose of laudanum the doctor had put in the tea had been liberal and Drew lay back on the pillow and slept.

Once back in the surgery, Rutherford turned his attention to the cadaver and began to examine it. Out in the chicken yard, he heard O'Rielly, his Irish Rooster crow.

He did not see Bertha Hartson slip out the door and head straight for Shirley LeComte's. But Frank had not left yet, so after listening at the door for a few minutes, Bertha went into the butcher shop and told Mr. Kitchen everything she knew about the goings on out at Cedar Harbor.

Chapter Thirty Five

Rutherford urged Old Tom into a gallop and let him run for a quarter of a mile before slowing him to a trot and then a walk. His strategy to break the chain of thought in his mind by letting the big black run had worked and he was able to move his focus away from the dead body he'd spent the morning with to those who had survived the fire at Carrie Grey's--he couldn't get used to calling her McGeary, especially now.

First off, where was Zach, the missing First Mate of Wave Dancer? If Mike didn't find a body, did he become a suspect in the murder of Delbert and the setting of the sawmill fire? If they found Zach's body, then who? Carrie Gr... McGeary? Hugh Brandon, or one of his sons? Certainly not Drew McGeary, much as Edward would like to find some reason to take that pirate off the playing board. He'd been dead drunk in his cabin and the door jammed shut, according to Carrie. That bothered Rutherford. But if McGeary was the intended victim, why not just set the schooner on fire? As a diversion? Of course maybe both the schooner and the mill had been set afire. But Rutherford was sure it had started in the mill. Brandon said the mill was almost gone before the fire caught the boat.

In his mind, Rutherford had arranged his suspects and the dead man on a chessboard. Delbert was a pawn, likely just in the wrong place and killed out of expediency. Zach Milowski, where did he fit? Surely in the royal file as a rook or a knight. He put Carrie in the queen's place and McGeary in the king's. He considered Hugh Brandon in relation to the chessboard in his mind. He couldn't find any reason to even put him on the board. He'd only met the man a couple of times, but he knew there was no guile in the man. Maybe one of his sons. He mentally placed three more pawns on the board, just to keep them in mind.

As soon as Old Tom turned onto the lane leading down to Cedar Harbor Rutherford dismounted and led the horse. He walked slowly and stopped often. It was too bad there had been so much traffic on the lane already. The garden spot had been newly fenced in. At the edge of the meadow, Carrie had planted three apple trees. The fragrance of rotting apples under the trees edged agreeably into his senses. Then another scent, one he was so accustomed to he almost missed, drifted in; horse manure. Edward looked around. No horse droppings on the lane. Under one of the apple trees, the furthest one from the lane, Edward thought the grass looked disturbed. He dropped Old Tom's reins and approached the spot on foot and indirectly so as not to disturb anything. In a dried mud puddle was the undisturbed print of a shod horse leading into a small copse of poplar trees. Rutherford proceeded carefully. There, just inside, were the still fragrant day old horse droppings and evidence that someone had sat here on a horse for some time. The horse had scuffed over and over in his own tracks as he periodically shifted while his owner sat on top and watched...who? And why?

Rutherford returned to the single clear hoof print in the dried mud. He drew a small pad and pencil from his vest pocket and sketched it. There was nothing remarkable about the shoe, but maybe the farrier would spot something Rutherford didn't see. The good Doctor added another piece to the chessboard, an unknown horseman. He toyed with the newcomer for a while and finally made him the second knight on the board. In chess the knight was the most maneuverable piece and although his suspect might well have the cunning of a bishop or the single-mindedness of a rook, the man was on horseback, so make him a knight.

Had the man watched from this vantage point until he was sure the fire would do what he wanted, or had he been in the hiding place until dark when he crept in and set the fire and left?

When Rutherford approached the area where he could see the lake and Carrie's house he was stopped by a young man, the same one who had pounded on his door during the night and then apparently rode right back without waiting for him.

"You're Swen Brandon," he said as he reached down to shake hands with the lad. Swen's grip was firm, his hands rough from the quarry work.

Rutherford reached into his pocket for a cigar and offered one to Swen. They bit the ends off and spat them on the ground, then shared a match to light them.

"What did you see and hear last night?" asked Rutherford.

"First I knew was Mam pounding da door yelling dere was fire up at da lady's house. I grabbed my clothes and ran, just like Josef and Stephan. Then Pop said I should ride into town, try to get help."

"Did you see anybody on the road?"

"I rode for Garden, it being closer. Met a bunch coming from dare. Dey seen da fire acrost da bay. Den I turned around and headed for Fayette—ta get you."

"And you saw nobody on that road?"

"Da moon was good, so I could see da road all right. Thought I heard someting onct, but I just kept going, trusting Bess, she's da horse. Was probably just rabbits or someting."

Rutherford thought about this as he struck a match and relit his cigar, offering the same to Swen.

"Do you remember where you heard this something?"

"It were past South River, about acrost from Snake Island."

Rutherford nodded and picked up Old Tom's reins to move on. "Thanks for your information. You don't let anyone else past you now, you hear?"

"Yeah, sure ting," Swen answered. "Sheriff said nobody but you was ta come in."

The sheriff stood at the end of the pier studying the remains of the schooner. Only the forward hull of Wave Dancer remained, tilted away from the pier on her side. Chunks of charred debris floated in the bay, lifted in place by the gentle swell of waves. He turned when Rutherford hailed him and waved. Two men emerged from the water momentarily, drew deep breaths and dove again.

"The other two sons from the quarry," Mike explained. "They're looking for the mate."

"Waste of time," Rutherford said. "What I wish they'd find is the door to the Captain's cabin. I'd like to know why Drew couldn't open it."

"What debris we hauled out so far is piled over there," Barbarieu said.

Rutherford and Barbarieu spent an hour examining the charred parts of Wave Dancer until the doctor found what he was looking for. "Look at this, Mike. Somebody nailed that cabin door shut."

The evidence was indisputable. A single spike had been hammered through the upper left hand corner of the door at an angle that would have held the door into the frame. "If there's one, maybe there was more. McGeary was the target of this thing. What I can't figure is why our man started the fire in the mill instead of the boat."

"Our man or our woman," Barbarieu said. "Didn't you say the Mrs. was angry with him, shut him out of the house after they had an argument?"

"It wasn't Carrie," Rutherford said.

Barbarieu shook his head. "I don't know, Doc, women can do things when they're mad."

"Not this, not Carrie," Rutherford insisted and he told Mike about the hoof print and the hiding place just outside the homestead. He didn't mention what Swen had said about hearing rustling along the trail on his ride into town the night before. He'd check that out on his way home.

"I'm going to look around the house and edge of the woods now, see if I can find any other evidence of someone lurking around. You ought to come with me and see the place first hand, as a witness, so two of us can testify the same"

Rutherford laid out his theory that someone had watched the Harbor from the poplar copse until he was sure the fire would do what he wanted, or had been in the hiding place until dark, then crept in and set the fire.

"That doesn't figure with me," Mike said. "The track is going in but nothing is coming out."

"Right, " Rutherford said. His cigar had gone out and he studied the end of it as if it would re-light with concentration. Finally he took a thin silver cigar box from his pocket. He clipped the end off the used cigar and let it fall to the ground. Then he carefully placed the rest of the cigar inside the holder and returned the box to his pocket. "What we have to do is to find how he got out."

There was plenty of open space behind the hiding place. Rutherford and Sheriff Barbarieu carefully examined the meadow for evidence.

"Here," Mike called. He'd found a set of hoof marks where the horse had dug in to climb an abrupt rise in the ground. They followed and found themselves on the bluff top. Carrie had not allowed cutting of any of her trees and the woods was made up of large white birch, oaks, and maple. Rutherford observed the large X's chalked on several trees. They came to a path, apparently used often, which led to the bluff edge and back towards the main road.

"There's been a lot of traffic on this road lately," Mike said.

Rutherford agreed as they rode toward the edge of the bluff and found the burial ground that Delbert had just finished fencing in a week ago.

"I think they were fixing to cut the timber," Rutherford said, "That's what the X's on the trees are for."

"Makes sense," said Mike, "what with the new saw mill they built."

The view across the lake was spectacular; the Nahma and Stonington peninsulas appeared to float above the blue water. The sun had come out after all and despite the threat of a

storm that morning it was now warm. A tug, probably the Jo
Harris, was pulling three barges of iron ore towards Fayette.
Other boats, some with sails seeking a breeze, moved slowly on
the surface.

"Lake's calm today," Mike remarked.

"Hmmm," Rutherford acknowledged. "Our man went this
way," he pointed towards the main road. "Any idea where it
meets the stage road?"

Mike did not.

"I'll follow it when I leave," Rutherford said. "Let's go back
down to the harbor now and look around. Delbert didn't die in
the fire. His skull was cracked where someone struck him. I
figure there was a fight, the blow came down on the front and
top of his head."

"Then you figure the fire was set to cover up the deed?"

"Probably."

"Zach," Mike said. "They got into a fight and Zach hit him
and then set the fire to cover it up."

"No. Zach's in the lake, I'm sure of it. Carrie said he slept
below decks. He'd been drinking too and was probably as
drunk as McGeary. And he didn't have a horse to sit on up
there and then head off to Fayette."

"So was Delbert the intended victim, or just in the way?"
Barbarieu asked.

Rutherford rubbed his whiskered chin briskly. "Damned if
I know," he said, "what with that cabin door being nailed
shut."

They returned to the pier. Josef and Stephan Brandon
were sitting on the edge wrapped together in a large quilt.

"Dere's nutten down dere," Josef muttered, "cept cold
water." His teeth were chattering and his lips were blue.

"Right," Mike replied. "Thank you both. I'll turn in your
time to the township and you'll get paid. Now go get dressed
and get some hot food in your stomachs."

The men stood, and still sharing the quilt over their

shoulders walked off. Mike called after them.

"You see anything unusual, anything, you let me know."

"Yeah," they said in unison.

After they left Rutherford stood on the shore "Have you searched the shallows along the shore there for Zach?" he asked suddenly and pointed to the reedy inlet beyond the remains of the sawmill where the shore curved and was heavily wooded right down to the edge.

"Not yet," Mike said.

"Those gulls have found something to eat. Let's go see what."

Beyond the sawmill a tiny rivulet ran into the cove from an outcropping of stone. Beyond it the shore was mucky and mostly free of stone. Reeds grew waist high and ducks flew up, flushed by the two men walking where humans didn't usually intrude. Gulls flew screeching overhead.

The walk to the gull's dinner was further than it had seemed and when they arrived all they found was a large dead walleye.

Later Mike and Dr. Rutherford found an oil soaked stain in the ash of the sawmill near where Delbert's body had been found. Two charred lanterns lay on their sides nearby.

"Our man emptied both lanterns unto a pile of dry shavings and lit them on fire," Mike observed.

"I think so," Rutherford said. "You keep poking around and see what else you can find. I'm going to check in on Carrie."

Carrie sat in a rocking chair on the porch. Edward spoke twice to her before she looked up at him. He half reclined against the porch railing. "How do you feel, Carrie?"

She stretched out her legs for him to see. She had on a skirt that was shorter than any Edward Rutherford had ever seen before. It left her burned legs free of the irritation of skirts brushing against them.

"I made them this spring," Carrie blushed as she looked down at her bare limbs. "I noticed that Mrs. Brandon wore her skirts shorter and got about so much easier, so I sewed up a couple for myself on the sewing machine I bought from Henry. I only wear them when no one is apt to see me."

"No need to apologize, Carrie," the Doctor said, "I find them quite sensible and certainly just the thing for you until your legs heal. You can consider it doctor's orders that you continue to wear them. Keep putting the salve on, don't let the skin get dry and crack."

"How is Drew?"

"That scoundrel is fine, Carrie. He's burned, like you, but he'll be all right. Louella is trying to manage him, but I don't expect we'll be able to hold him there for very long.

"May I ask you some questions, my dear?"

Carrie nodded.

"Delbert was murdered," he began, and stopped to watch Carrie's reaction. There was none. Perhaps she already knew. "And we haven't found Zach. One theory is that Zach killed Delbert, set the saw mill ablaze to cover it up and vamoosed."

"Nonsense," Carrie said quickly. "Zach was as drunk as Drew. They all were."

"You don't think he could have been play-acting?" Rutherford persisted. "Was there any hard feeling between Zach and Delbert?"

Carrie glanced up and to her right, clearly trying to remember if there was anything. "No," she said slowly, "I don't think so. Zach was a shy, good-natured fellow. Wouldn't hurt anyone."

"Was there anyone else here, besides the three of them?"

Carrie looked up at that. "What about the boy, Peter?"

"You mean there was another one?"

"Peter... oh no, don't tell me he's missing too?"

"Where was he?"

"I don't know. Maybe in the boat with Zach. I don't remember seeing him after Lola let go of him."

"Lola was one of the women?"

Carrie nodded.

"Are you quite sure all of them left on the boat?"

Carrie nodded and looked closely at Dr. Rutherford and then of a sudden grew pensive and stared out over the lake for so long Edward finally reached out a hand to gently touch her arm. "Is there more, Carrie?"

Carrie turned and looked at him as if startled to see him there. She shivered and hugged her arms around her body, being careful with her sore hands.

"Carrie?" Edward spoke quietly. "Tell me what haunts you."

Carrie lifted a glass from the plank top table beside the chair and after looking at it for a moment, raised it and drained the contents.

"You'd be shocked to know I can drink whiskey like that, Edward. I've come down a long way since that first trip I made to Escanaba with Drew. It was only four months ago, wasn't it, when I sailed on Wave Dancer with him and Mr. Jenny from Chicago? It was the first time Mr. Jenny came about the marble. I was so excited, about both the marble and Drew McGeary. He bewitched me from the first moment I laid eyes on him. I couldn't think of anything else.

"Those three days were a whirl. After Mr. Jenny set the lawyers to drawing up contracts, Drew took me shopping. Just like that," she snapped her fingers, "I bought an evening dress, an afternoon dress, and a walking suit, with shoes and hats and corsets, which I swore I'd never wear, and we were off to meet what I thought was the society set of Escanaba.

"Turns out they were nothing more than the Thomas Street ladies...the same type Drew introduced me to in Chicago. But it was all new and wonderful to me then."

At this she stopped and stared out across the lake again and then began to sob into her handkerchief for several minutes. Rutherford nodded. Thomas Street was the block or two where the madams maintained their brothels in Escanaba.

Finally she got control of herself, blew her nose solidly and continued.

"Then Drew sailed me back home and set me on shore with my packages and sailed away. Would God, I had never seen him again."

Edward decided there was no reason to let her go on distressing herself with that tale, so he asked another question about the fire.

"After the ladies left, did you see anyone else?"

"No. Drew tried to come into the house, but I wouldn't let him. I was angry with Drew and told him to go sleep on the boat. Then I heard Zach and Drew arguing about something. I'd gone to bed already and their noise woke me. They were standing on the deck of Wave Dancer yelling at each other. I was afraid they'd wake the child."

"Did I tell you what they did to her?"

Rutherford said she'd told him the night before. It angered him that McGeary could be so callous about the hurt his daughter had been subjected to. He steered Carrie back to the argument between Zach and Drew.

"Do you know what time that was?"

"No, but then he came into the house."

"He?"

"Drew. I left the door unlocked after I'd looked out and saw them and he must have seen me because, he came back inside.

"He forced me to bed with him," Carrie said. Her voice was matter of fact, hard; a tone Edward had never heard her use. "He said he would prove to me that it was me he wanted and not one of the whores from Chicago. Afterwards he grabbed another bottle and staggered out to Wave Dancer. I lay on my bed and cried for a while, and then I got up, found a hammer and the nails and crept onto the boat. I could hear him snoring in the cabin and I nailed the forward door shut. He could have gotten out through the galley, I suppose. I didn't think of that."

"Why did you do that?" Edward asked, "if he had already done his hurt to you?"

"I had decided that in the morning I would take Lainey in the trap to Fayette and sail away to Chicago with her. I wanted to make sure any attempt to follow me would be delayed."

Rutherford raised his head and looked at her. "Why Chicago?"

"I've got friends there, people who would help me. Mr. Jenny said he would help me buy a house if I ever wanted to come there."

"You have friends in Fayette, too." It was said softly but Carrie raised her chin.

"Suppose you tell me who, besides you? Mrs. Hartson? Shirley LaComte? Jack?" she paused and her voice softened.

"Yes, I suppose Jack, despite everything."

Edward shifted on the chair and tried another tack. "How did you come to discover the fire?"

"I couldn't sleep. I suppose I dozed a few times, but I kept waking. At last I decided I would pack our bags and leave at first light. When I came into the parlor I saw the fire."

"Try hard to think now. Did you see anyone, hear anyone about?"

Carrie shook her head. "No, I don't think so."

"What about Delbert?"

"No. I told you he went into the mill as soon as the boat from Escanaba left."

Rutherford studied Carrie's face. It was partially shaded there on the porch and he thought, of a sudden, she looked years older than she had last time he had seen her. How old was she? No more than thirty, surely. She reached down to scratch her legs and Rutherford yelled, "No, don't do that."

Startled by the sudden sharp tone, Carrie looked sidewise at him. "But they itch so."

"That only means they're healing. But if you scratch you'll open up the new skin and it will putrefy and scar."

Carrie stood and paced up and down the porch. "Then I

think you will have to tie my arms down, for I shan't be able to stop from scratching them."

"Do you have a bathing dress?"

"Why, yes," Carrie answered, "They were all the rage in Chicago."

"Then I suggest you put it on and get into the lake. I believe the cool water will relieve your itching."

While Carrie changed into her navy blue bathing dress she tried to think what she knew about Delbert. He had spent the last month at Cedar Harbor with her, building the saw mill. He was gone a lot, running to Fayette almost every other day to pick up something. Except for the day they'd walked up on the bluff to pick out timber, they'd hardly said ten words to each other. Delbert was at least twenty-eight, she thought. He was slightly built and the first time she saw him she had thought him skinny, but now she knew he was just slim...and well muscled. He was average height, dark-haired and, she suspected, part Indian, although his parents were French. Delbert Julliard, from Fairport. Murdered. On her property. I am living a nightmare, she thought.

Edward was waiting for her and escorted her down to the beach. She waded into the water and found that he was right; the cool water of the lake did relieve the itching.

"I shall have to live here," she called to him on shore.

"Oh, I dare say a dip now and then will suffice. Just keep the bathing dress on so you'll be ready when the need arises. And keep slathering on the salve. Also I suggest a little laudanum before you sleep. I'll be leaving you now, but will surely check on you again tomorrow."

He turned to leave and then turned back in answer to Carrie's call, "Edward?"

"Yes?"

"You won't let Drew back out here, will you?"

"I'm afraid I can't control what he does when I release him, Carrie. Are you afraid of him?"

Carrie hung her head a moment and then raised it, "No. I

just don't want to see him yet."

"Then come into town with me. Louella will be happy to have you for a few days until you feel up to your trip to Chicago."

"Maybe," Carrie replied and waded back into deeper water.

Rutherford found Mike and told him what Carrie had told him about the boat load of trollops who'd been at the Harbor earlier in the day. "I don't think there's any connection there, it doesn't explain anything except why they were all drunk. Oh, and there was another man, young boy about fifteen, Carrie thought. She didn't know where he slept but thought maybe he was in the boat too."

"Then we're looking for two bodies?"

"Probably. I'm going back to Fayette now," Rutherford said. "I'll follow that bluff trail and see what I can learn."

As he rode he thought about Carrie. He was sure she was telling the truth, but yet he couldn't rule out that she had tried to murder her husband and then saved him. Yes, he could— Delbert. She would never had killed him in cold blood just to burn down the sawmill in order to kill Drew. He rested his mind about Carrie, then. The queen was innocent.

Chapter Thirty-Six

Rutherford guided Old Tom back up to the path they'd found earlier and followed it back toward the stage road. Despite the heavy traffic on the road recently, the tracks he was following were clear. The road had been drug, and Edward surmised it was in preparation for use in skidding the timber down when they began to cut. Carrie's ox wagon had traversed the road, probably carrying the wire for the fenced area he'd seen. He'd forgotten to ask Carrie what that was for.

The trail came out just short of the turn off to South River. That coincided with what Swen Brandon had told him. Rutherford paused and then turned Old Bob towards Garden. Swen said a lot of people had come from Garden last night to fight the fire. Maybe someone had seen something.

Rutherford seldom had occasion to travel the road between Garden and Fayette. He spent one day a week there seeing children with colds and old people with creaky bones, but he always made the trip on The Lady Washington. He noticed, as he rode, how sad the land along the road looked, like a beautiful woman who had been shorn of her locks. Even the thinnest of trees had been cut to feed the charcoal kilns. He could smell smoke from the kilns that dotted the countryside floating in the dry still air. Brush piles and scattered branches lay among last season's tall, dry grass. To his left, he caught glimpses of the blue water of Lake Michigan through thickets of cedar trees.

In Garden he learned of the fight between Henry and Drew and of the second fight a few days later in Escanaba. He had thought Henry far away. That certainly added a chessman to the board. He borrowed a sheet of note paper from Fred DeWinter and addressed a letter to Dr. Scholler in Escanaba asking him to inquire discreetly around town to see if Henry LaTermaine was, or had been, there since the incident with Drew McGeary three weeks ago. He addressed a similar letter to the sheriff in Manistique asking him to advise at once if Henry LaTermaine was in that town. Indeed, he advised that Henry be arrested and brought to Fayette for questioning if he was found to be there. He posted both of these with Fred DeWinter to go out by first boat.

Rutherford talked to half a dozen men who had fought the fire. Leon Grafton was able to tell him the exact time he'd seen the flames across the bay. "It was ten of four in the morning," the man said. "I was loading the boat for an early run when I thought I saw a campfire. In minutes it was a roaring blaze. I yelled to Van and we jumped in the boat and headed across. By the time we got there, the mill was about gone and the schooner was aflame."

"Heard all four of 'em died," he said.

"Four?"

"Yeah, somebody said there was four of em, two in the mill and two on the boat. Heard McGeary himself died."

"Who said that?" Rutherford asked.

"Don't know," Grafton said. "Never saw the fellow before."

"It wasn't Henry LaTermaine?"

"Naw, I know him. Ain't seen him around since he and McGeary mixed it up a ways back. This fellow was big. McGeary ain't dead?"

Rutherford assured him that McGeary was not dead. So far, in fact the only body they had belonged to Delbert Julliard from Fairport. The other two were missing.

A big man, someone Grafton didn't know. Stoddy? Did Grafton know Stoddy? No, he said he didn't. Rutherford added another man to the chessboard. As he rode back from Garden he reviewed them all.

First there was Henry. Rutherford thought of him as the most viable suspect. Burning the mill was a cowardly approach and fit Henry's personality. It was likely he had not meant for anyone to be hurt, only to burn the sawmill as a way of getting at McGeary. Not only had he and Henry fought several times but Rutherford had to consider why Henry had turned Drew's daughter over to Stoddy in the first place. He remembered the day Henry had come storming into his house to demand if it was true Carrie had eloped with McGeary. And Carrie said Henry had proposed marriage to her and she'd turned him down, thinking he was only after her marble quarry. Besides the blow to the head that killed Delbert, the only other thing against it being Henry was Grafton seeing a big man he didn't know hanging around Cedar Harbor the night of the fire— someone who thought there were four people dead in the fire; and someone who knew that the young lad had been in the sawmill, not on the boat.

Then where was the boy? There had definitely not been another body in the sawmill. Had he escaped? Where, and most importantly, why? He decided to stop at Cedar Harbor again and look for evidence of the boy.

Then there was Stoddy. He might think he had motive for trying to kill McGeary. Nobody had seen him since he'd been left on the beach for dead the night the mob freed the women and burned the Hole in The Rock to the ground. Some said they should have hung him right off. Now Rutherford would have to send two more missives to Escanaba and Manistique inquiring about Stoddy. He thought of paying a visit to the pretty woman from Stoddy's place, the one Carrie said was her friend. Louella would remember her name. How long could he keep McGeary away from Carrie? Maybe he should have Mike lock him up on suspicion of murdering Zach. Wouldn't hold up in a grand jury hearing, but it would protect Carrie long enough for her to get away, if that's what she wanted to do.

Rutherford kept mulling over everything and felt like there was still a piece missing. Finally he felt like he had to rule out Henry unless he and Stoddy had acted together, which wasn't likely.

He found Carrie and Lainey eating their supper. Mike had gone back to Fayette, leaving Swen Brandon as guard. The doctor examined Lainey and said she needed some rest. He suggested that Carrie send her to her friend in Escanaba, what was her name?

"Elizabeth Allen." She looked at Lainey. "I think she should go, too. She needs to get back to school."

"I want to see Papa," Lainey said.

"Let me take her with me," the doctor said. "She can see her father and then Louella can accompany her to Escanaba on the boat tomorrow."

"Would you like that, Lainey?" Carrie asked.

Lainey nodded yes. "Go pack your things then," Carrie said, "and you can go with Dr. Rutherford."

When she left the room, Rutherford suggested Carrie walk outside with him so he could ask her some things. She listened to his theories.

"No," she said, "I absolutely don't believe Henry did this."

Then she told the doctor about Henry's repeated attempt to apologize to Drew, which had led to him getting beaten twice. "He even came here and tried to talk to me and he said..." Carrie put her hand over her mouth, "Oh dear. As he was leaving he said, 'You'll be sorry, Carrie. Just remember I tried to help you.' What do you think he meant by that, Edward?"

Edward shook his head.

"And did you know he wouldn't press charges against Drew in Escanaba? No, what ever he said, he didn't mean he was going to murder anybody."

"All right. Now what do you think happened to the boy, Peter? I have a man in Garden said he was told Peter went to sleep in the sawmill that night, and if he'd been in there we'd have found a body. Now where could a person hide around here, if he wanted to hide?"

Carrie thought for a minute. "The cave," she said. "Up on the bluff where we found the marble is a cave that the Indians used. Peter knew it was there, at least Delbert did, and he might have told Peter. They spent a lot of time together the last couple of weeks while they were getting the mill running."

"How can I get there?"

"Swen Brandon knows."

An hour later, Swen was back, leading a scared and reluctant Peter by the hand. Carrie sat him in front of a bowl of soup while Dr. Rutherford questioned him.

Peter said he'd gone to sleep in the sawmill long before the girls left. He'd gotten sick from all the liquor and had escaped to the sawmill after the party had got tired of traipsing in and out of bed with each other. The argument between Drew and Zach had awaked him just as it had Carrie. He had gone and sat on the hill behind the house. He'd seen Drew go into the house and back out again. Then he'd seen Carrie come out and heard her hammer the door shut. Then he'd fallen asleep and been awaked this time by a man on a horse passing close by. Then he'd seen the fire and decided the man on the horse must have set it, so he'd followed him.

"You followed him?" It was Lainey. For the first time Carrie realized that Lainey looked at Peter with dreamy eyes.

Peter looked over at where Lainey was lying on the sofa and he suddenly became braver in telling his story. "Yeah, I followed him a ways, and then he gets off the horse and goes back down and helps everybody fighting the fire."

"Who was it, Peter?" Carrie asked.

"Didn't rightly see him," Peter said. "It was dark. Seen his horse good though. I went up and looked good at the horse."

"Why did you hide?"

Peter shrugged. "First I was scared and then I thought that if I came out, everybody would think I did it. I didn't know what to do."

"That's silly," said Lainey. "Why would you do it?"

Peter shrugged again. "Wasn't thinking straight, I guess."

"But you got a good look at the horse," Edward said. "Carrie, now I have a problem. I've got three people to get to

Fayette, and only one horse. What do you suggest?"

Swen Brandon had sat quietly listening to everything. "There's a boat loading down to da quarry," he said. "You want I'll send dem 'round here and dey can take ya to Fayette."

"Who is it?" Carrie asked.

"One of Jenny's marble steamers," Swen said.

"Perfect," Carrie said. "Go and ask them."

"Are you coming, too Carrie?" Rutherford asked.

"No," Carrie said. "I want to stay by the lake for a while. In fact I want to go wading right now."

Chapter Thirty-Seven

D r. Rutherford had the steamer unload them at the dock next to the sawmill. He led Old Tom, with Lainey riding him and Peter walking along beside, around the back and up Cedar Lane where it met Harbor Street and then to his house. In that way they were able to arrive at his office unseen and went up the back stairs and into the kitchen where Louella was peeling apples.

"Louella, this is Peter. He was one of McGeary's crew and I think he can help me finger the man who set fire to the sawmill. I don't want anyone to know he's here."

"And Lainey," Louella said, holding her hands out in welcome. "How are you, dear?"

"Fine," Lainey said, letting Louella enfold her. "Is my father here?"

Edward looked at his wife, "Is he?"

"Still here," Louella said, "but he wants to leave, Edward. I hate to keep giving him that stuff to make him sleep, but if I don't..."

"I'll look in on him," Edward said. "Feed these children, won't you?"

While Louella made sandwiches for Lainey and Peter, Edward went downstairs. He found Drew sitting on the edge of the bed, apparently groggy, but determined to get up. The doctor put on his white coat and pulled a chair up in front of Drew.

"Let me check you over, Mr. McGeary, and if everything is fine you can leave whenever you want to."

With that news, Drew relaxed and let the doctor remove the dressings from his wounds. Edward shook his head. "I don't know. I wish you'd hang around awhile until these are healed. I'm afraid they might putrefy if I can't clean them every day."

He set about cleaning them. Drew winced once or twice, but made no sound. "No more dope," Drew said, when the doctor had finished removing dead skin and applied a fresh coat of his honey and petroleum jelly.

"The dope is for pain," Rutherford said. "If you don't want it, you don't have to take it. You hungry?"

Drew nodded.

"I've got your daughter upstairs, Drew. She wants to see you but I think you should clean up first. I'll have Louella bring down some clean clothes for you. You can wash up out there," he nodded towards his surgery room, "there's warm water from the tap, courtesy of the furnace boilers. You mind if I ask you some questions while you clean up?"

"Go ahead."

"What did you and Zach argue about?"

Drew looked puzzled. "When?"

"The night of the fire, after the girls left."

"Don't remember."

"What do you remember?

Drew scratched his chin with his good arm. Louella had come down with his clothes and a cup of black coffee. He took a swallow and thanked her. As soon as she left, he stood up and asked where that sink was. While he shaved and dressed, he told Drew what he remembered.

"Those girls. I didn't invite them, you know. They just showed up. Carrie didn't treat them very nice and I tried to get them to leave, but they wouldn't. I remember she hollered at me and locked me out of the house. I slept in the boat. Next thing I know she's pushing me into the water and everything is on fire. Then you come and told me Delbert is dead."

He finished shaving and looked at himself in the mirror. "I guess I was damn lucky she found me, wasn't I?"

Rutherford nodded. "You were. I'm only going to say this once, McGeary. Carrie is one of my favorite people and I don't like what you've done to her..." he held his hand up to stop

McGeary's response, "She's not happy you know, about the way you've treated her, and I think she doesn't want to see you anymore. I'm asking you to leave her alone for a while, give her time to sort things out."

Drew shook his head. "I don't understand. What'd I do?"

"You don't remember forcing yourself on her after you and Zach argued?"

"Zach...yeah I remember now. He tried to stop me from going back to the house. I wanted to tell her I was sorry about the ladies. But she wouldn't listen to me."

"So you forced yourself on her," Edward concluded. "That's why she doesn't want to see you now. She's not the kind of woman you're used to, you know."

"But the baby," Drew said. He looked puzzled. "What about the baby?"

"What baby?"

Drew turned around and looked at the doctor. "She's going to have my baby."

"Well, well. Then I suggest you began acting like a father and a husband instead of a philanderer. Will you stay here, in the hospital for a few more days? You know Delbert's dead and probably Zach too, although we haven't found his body yet. I've got young Peter upstairs, and he saw the man who set the fire. I just need you to stay out of the way until we can find him."

"Was it Henry?"

"No, I don't think so. But I think it's somebody here in Fayette." Rutherford turned towards the stairway.

"Rutherford?"

"Yes?"

"Delbert mentioned a girlfriend he had, here in Fayette. He seemed real eager about being able to see her more when I put him ashore to build the sawmill for me."

"You don't know who she was?"

Drew shook his head no.

"I'll see what I can find out," Rutherford said. "I'm going to send Lainey down. You be gentle with her."

After he sent Lainey downstairs Rutherford posed a question to both his wife and Peter. "Seems Delbert had a lady-friend here in town. Know anything about that?"

Peter nodded. "He was telling me what a rambunctious gal she was. Said he never had anything like her," he turned to Louella, "excuse me ma'am. Said she was something else for sleeping with. He never said her name."

"Louella?" her husband asked.

Louella shook her head and said she'd never seen Delbert except at the Fourth of July dance. Wasn't he that young man who had been dancing with Shirley LeComte when Frank attacked him with the club?

"Ah," Edward said. "Indeed. You go upstairs, Peter. Get some rest. I'll come back for you in a bit and we'll go look at horses."

Then he told Louella he was going over to see Jack Sailstad.

"Before you go," Louella said, "I think you should know about something else that's been going on. Bertha Hartson has it all over town that Carrie tried to murder her husband. She's been demanding that Sheriff Barbarieu go out and arrest her."

Edward shook his head in disbelief. "Go see if you can find her and if you can tell her Jack Sailstad wants to see her. I'm going over there."

"What about your patient?"

"He won't cause you any trouble. Leave him alone with Lainey. They need to talk."

Half an hour later Bertha Hartson sailed up to the door of the manager's white house and knocked. The maid answered the door and told her Mr. Sailstad and Dr. Rutherford were waiting for her in the library.

"Please sit down, Mrs. Hartson," Jack invited. "You know Dr. Rutherford?"

Bertha nodded and sat straight backed on the edge of a

chair. Her mouth was drawn up into a tight pucker before she launched into her speech.

"I'm so glad we're going to have a chance to talk, Mr. Sailstad. As you know, I've tried to get that sheriff to do something, but he won't listen. I think it's high time the wicked people in this community were made an example of, and Carrie Grey should at least be questioned about the attempted murder of her so-called husband."

Jack nodded. "That's exactly what we wanted to talk to you about, Mrs. Hartson."

Rutherford cleared his throat. "Mrs. Hartson, since the moment you came into this town you have done nothing but stir up trouble."

Bertha half raised up from her seat, but Rutherford waved her down. "No, you sit and keep your mouth shut for once. To my shame, I let you drive Eleanor Larkin out of town. She was a good woman and a good teacher. I will not let you do the same to Carrie McGeary. I see nothing of Christian charity in you, Mrs. Hartson, and I want you to know that we," he looked over at Jack who nodded, "intend to hold a town meeting in the morning to formally ask you and your husband to take your ministry elsewhere."

"You can't do that," Bertha said.

"I can," Jack said. "This is a private town, Mrs. Hartson, and as General Manager of Fayette, on behalf of the Jackson Iron Company, I can bar anyone I want from entering it. Now I suggest you leave town at once. I will converse with Reverend Hartson after the town meeting tomorrow."

"Well, I never," Bertha exclaimed. She rose and left the room, slamming the door behind her.

"Have a cigar?" Jack offered.

"Don't mind if I do," replied Rutherford. They sat and talked long into the night.

Chapter Thirty-Eight

Josef Brandon rode into Fayette the next morning with the news that Zach's body had washed up among the reeds on the east shore of Cedar Harbor. It was a sad looking procession that left the village an hour later. Edward had persuaded Jack to let a couple of men from the Jackson Iron Company payroll accompany him. Jack sent Frank LeComte and Dave, one of the quarry workers. Frank grumbled as he saddled up his horse, Girlie. Said he'd worked most of the night and needed his sleep.

Edward drove his phaeton with young Peter beside him. Edward thought he would leave his carriage with Carrie in case she wanted to drive into Fayette, or Garden, for that matter. He was hoping to persuade her come in and talk to Drew. The matter of the baby changed everything.

Josef drove Carrie's wagon and Dave rode Old Tom. The wagon carried several canvas tarps, ropes, and spades. Mike Barbarieu and Frank followed. They hadn't gone far out of town when Frank galloped past the rest of the procession, calling out he'd meet them up the road.

"Is that the horse?" Rutherford asked.

"Yes sir," Peter said. "I'm sure it is. I remember those white feet and the white mane."

"Is that the man?"

"I'm not sure, Doc. I seen him from far away and it was just moonlight. He was big like that, though. But that's the horse, that's for sure."

Carrie met the procession and offered them coffee before they began the unpleasant task of recovering the body.

"Where's Frank?"

Carrie shook her head. "I haven't seen anyone," she said.

Rutherford turned to Peter. "Are you sure he never saw you?"

Peter shrugged. "He might have," he said. "Once I thought he looked right at me. That's why I hid in the cave."

Rutherford swore and called Mike over. "I think we've got a problem, Mike." He quickly explained how Peter had identified Frank's horse.

"But why would Frank LeComte want to kill McGeary?"

"McGeary wasn't his target, Delbert was."

"You sure?"

Rutherford said he was sure. "Delbert was meeting Frank's wife and you know how jealous Frank was. Now you take Dave and follow him. Lock him up in Garden if you catch him. Have you got a gun?"

Mike nodded and showed him the gun he carried concealed under his coat. "Well, use it if you have to. Don't kill him; shoot him in the leg or something. Carrie keeps a rifle inside. Dave better take it. Deputize him in case you have to split up."

Edward watched the two men ride off and then sat down to have some coffee with Carrie while Peter and Josef went to get Josef's brothers to help recover Zach's body.

"It will be too wet to get the wagon down to the body," Carrie said. "I think you should take Grant, my ox. You can wrap Zach in the tarp and let Grant pull him out to the wagon."

"Excellent thinking," Edward said. "You sound like your old self."

"How is Drew?"

"He's up and around. He wanted to come with us, but I told him he would have to wait for you to come to him. He said he didn't like it, but he'd do whatever you said. He mumbled something about being an old dog trying real hard to learn some new tricks."

Carrie looked like she wanted to cry. She turned her head

and looked around the house as if she was looking for something. Finally she said, "Is Lainey with him?"

Edward nodded. "He's a good father, you know. I've watched the two of them together."

This time Carrie drew her finger across the corner of one eye before she looked away. Edward decided that was enough for now and told her about Bertha Hartson. First Carrie was indignant that Bertha thought she was capable of murder and then she ended up laughing as Edward did a fine imitation of the way Bertha had pursed her mouth when Edward had told her to sit down and shut up.

Zach's body was in the back of the wagon. Edward was reluctant to leave Cedar Harbor before he knew the outcome of the search for Frank LeComte. His flight put to rest any lingering doubts Edward might have had about his guilt. Finally he urged Carrie to come to Fayette with him.

"If Mike doesn't catch the blackguard, he may come back looking for Peter. I'll feel much better if you're both with me."

Carrie had to admit that she would feel better also. While they had been retrieving poor Zach Carrie had thought about what Edward had told her. He didn't like Drew, she knew that, but he must have seen something in Drew to change his mind. Drew was a good father, he'd said.

Carrie had been angry when Drew hadn't defended Lainey against the cruel remarks Peaches had made about her, but she realized now that anything Drew may have said would only have made things worse for his daughter. You don't argue with a drunk. And his use of her, that had been a drunken act too. Edward said he didn't even remember it.

Lainey certainly doted on him; there was no doubt about that. He was a good father, Edward said. Carrie patted her abdomen. Already she could feel a small mound rising there with their child. She could endure much to have a good father for him— she was sure it was a boy.

And just what, after all did she have to endure? Life was

much harsher for a lot of people than it was for her. A few misunderstandings. They needed a little more time to get used to each other, that was all. Carrie wanted to be with him, to see his smile move from his eyes to a grin, to a belly laugh. She wanted to be in love with him.

So she consented when Edward asked her to accompany him to Fayette. She wasn't afraid of Frank LeComte; she just wanted to be with Andrew McGeary.

THE END.

Appendix I

Contemporary Reference's to the limestone and marble quarry at Gouley's Harbor.

Source The Iron Port, a weekly newspaper published in Escanaba, Michigan.

August 12, 1882

Mrs. Gouley has entered into an agreement which will keep her busy...She has appointed W.L.B. Jenney and L.M. Cobbs, of Chicago, agents for the sale of the products of her quarries.

September 30, 1882:

The court house foundation in Escanaba is of stone from Mrs. Gouley's quarry at Garden Bay, a very fine grained limestone, or clouded marble, capable of receiving a high polish, and is hammer dressed.

October 14, 1882:

We understand from a very reliable source, that Mrs. Gouley, of Garden has just completed a contract with J.F. Farwell of Chicago for marble from her quarry at Garden to be used in an elegant mansion to be built by him and which will cost, when completed, in the neighborhood of $300,000 to $400,000. This quarry is newly opened and is the one from which the stone for our court house was taken and which is supplying material for several other parties here.

January 1, 1883

Mrs. Gouley is working her quarry this winter with the intentions of marketing its product immediately upon opening of navigation, in Milwaukee and Chicago and to supply iron companies with a flux for which she has already acquired contracts.

June 23, 1883

Captain Stephenson is importing stone from Mrs. Gouley's

quarry. We are told Mrs. Gouley of Garden recently refused an offer of $1000 per annum, rental, for her quarry, preferring to work it herself and that she has now contracts with Chicago parties for all the stone she can get out this season. With Farwell for dimension stone, and with Burkhardt for "run of the quarry," three cargoes. She has a fine quarry, in a favorable locality for getting out the shipping of the stone.

March 21, 1885

Mrs. Gouley will commence getting out building stone from her quarries about April 1. What time she can begin delivery here depends somewhat on how many more days of arctic weather we have.

June 6, 1885

Mrs. Gouley's quarry, at Garden, has a vein of first class sandstone, four feet thick, which cannot be excelled for building purposes. It is from this quarry that the Farwells of Chicago get stone for their magnificent buildings.

August 14, 1886

Why not build of good stone instead of poor brick. The basement wall of the courthouse, rough ashlar from Mrs. Gouley's quarry, is the handsomest part of the building.

May 28, 1887

Mrs. Gouley is now ready to fill, from her quarry at Garden, orders of any descriptions and to any amount. A cargo is now ready for delivery. Boats can load direct from the quarry. The quality of this stone is well known. Price moderate.

March 17, 1888

Mrs. Gouley will be prepared to deliver stone for building purposes upon the opening of navigation in any quantity. She also has a quantity of firewood. Address her at Garden, or leave proposals at this office.

July 6, 1888

Mrs. Gouley, by an advertisement in this number of the Iron Port, offers the public building material that won't burn...limestone such as composed the foundation and basement walls of the courthouse, and a gray marble which works and polishes beautifully and would make splendid fronts or fine trimmings for brick at low prices.

Authors Note:

A plat book of Delta County in 1880 showed that Mary Gouley owned the whole of the Garden Bluff and two parcels on South River Bay. While researching this book I interviewed Roy Winters, one of Garden's oldest living residents, and he had no knowledge of the once prolific quarries of Mrs. Gouley.